Critical acclaim for David Baldacci's novels

'A mile-a-minute read that proves once again why David Baldacci has readers the world over flocking for more'
Jane Harper, *New York Times* bestselling author of *The Dry*

'Alternately chilling, poignant, and always heart-poundingly suspenseful'
Scott Turow, *New York Times* bestselling author

'As ever, Baldacci keeps things moving at express-train speed . . . this one will whet appetites for the next appearance of his agent hero'
Daily Express

'A typically twisty plot never flags, and benefits from having the likeably offbeat sleuth (whose gifts include synaesthesia and photographic memory) as its pivot'
Sunday Times

'Already among the world's bestselling writers, Baldacci hardly needs to prove himself but he's created one of the most intriguing, complex anti-heroes . . . Impossible to put down, especially because of Decker, who weaves a powerful spell'
Daily Mail

'David Baldacci is one of the all-time best thriller authors'
Lisa Gardner

'A multi-layered protagonist; a plot as deep and twisty as the setting'
Kathy Reichs

'A plot strong enough to make the bath go cold around you'
Independent on Sunday

'A fast-paced investigation with dark secrets, unexpected twists, well-drawn characters and an intriguing plot'
Candis

'Mystery and suspense surround a fabulous new character in an enticing, engaging thriller that does not disappoint'
Live and Deadly

A Minute to Midnight

David Baldacci is one of the world's bestselling and favourite thriller writers. With over 130 million worldwide sales, his books are published in over 80 territories and 45 languages, and have been adapted for both feature film and television. David is also the co-founder, along with his wife, of the Wish You Well Foundation®, a non-profit organization dedicated to supporting literacy efforts across the US. Still a resident of his native Virginia, he invites you to visit him at DavidBaldacci.com and his foundation at WishYouWellFoundation.org.

Trust him to take you to the action.

By David Baldacci

The Camel Club series

(An eccentric group of social outcasts who seek to unearth corruption at the heart of the US government)

The Camel Club • The Collectors • Stone Cold
Divine Justice • Hell's Corner

King and Maxwell series

(Two disgraced Secret Service agents turn their skills to private investigation)

Split Second • Hour Game • Simple Genius
First Family • The Sixth Man • King and Maxwell

Shaw series

(A mysterious operative hunting down the world's most notorious criminals)

The Whole Truth • Deliver Us From Evil

John Puller series

(A gifted investigator with an unstoppable drive to find out the truth)

Zero Day • The Forgotten • The Escape
No Man's Land

Will Robie series featuring Jessica Reel

(A highly trained CIA assassin and his deadly fellow agent)

The Innocent • The Hit • The Target
The Guilty • End Game

Amos Decker series

(A damaged but brilliant special agent who possesses an extraordinary set of skills)

Memory Man • The Last Mile • The Fix • The Fallen • Redemption • Walk the Wire

Atlee Pine series

(A tenacious female FBI special agent assigned to the wilds of the western US)

Long Road to Mercy • A Minute to Midnight

Vega Jane series

(The bestselling young adult adventure series)

The Finisher • The Keeper • The Width of the World
The Stars Below

Other novels

True Blue • Absolute Power • Total Control
The Winner • The Simple Truth • Saving Faith
Wish You Well • Last Man Standing
The Christmas Train • One Summer
One Good Deed

Short Stories

No Time Left • Bullseye

DAVID BALDACCI

A Minute to Midnight

PAN BOOKS

First published 2019 by Grand Central Publishing, USA

First published in the UK 2019 by Macmillan

This edition published 2020 by Pan Books
an imprint of Pan Macmillan
The Smithson, 6 Briset Street, London EC1M 5NR
Associated companies throughout the world
www.panmacmillan.com

ISBN 978-1-5098-7448-4

1 3 5 7 9 8 6 4 2

A CIP catalogue record for this book is available from the British Library.

Typeset in Bembo by Jouve (UK), Milton Keynes
Printed and bound by CPI Group (UK) Ltd, Croydon, CR0 4YY

To the memory of Bob Schule:
No one could ask for a better friend.
You will always be missed,
You will never be forgotten.

CONFIDENTIAL

FBI SPECIAL AGENT PROFILE

Name: Atlee Pine

Age: Thirty-five

Place of Birth: Andersonville, Georgia

Marital Status: Single

Physical characteristics: At five eleven, Atlee is a tall woman - she got it from her mother. Solid and muscular, which comes from pumping iron religiously. Her features come together in a particularly attractive, almost bewitching, manner. Shoulder-length dark hair and blue eyes. Her body is a canvas of scars. The one on her left temple a reminder of when her skull was cracked when she was six. Bullet wound on the back of her calf. Knife slice on left triceps. Surgery on her lower back from her time as a weightlifter has left its mark. Delt tats: Gemini and Mercury with the words 'No Mercy' on each. You could say the woman wears her heart on her sleeve and her delts.

Relatives: Mercy Pine (twin sister) - abducted from the Pine family home when she was six. The main suspect being the notorious serial killer Daniel James Tor, now behind bars. Atlee believes it was Tor who cracked her skull that night and left her for dead in the sisters' bedroom. It broke the family up, as Atlee's parents divorced shortly after, principally because of what happened that night. Atlee is now estranged from her mother. Her father killed himself, on his daughters' birthday no less.

CONFIDENTIAL

Career: The abduction of her sister has haunted her life. After her parents' divorce her existence seemed aimless until she resolved to live the life her sister never did. Her physical size, natural strength and athleticism led her to be a star sportswoman in high school. She excelled at weightlifting and was on her way to joining the Olympic squad but just missed out on being selected. Instead she joined the FBI and is now a Special Agent, patrolling the rural, remote areas of southwest America.

Notable Abilities: An expert in MMA and kickboxing. Immense physical strength and endurance that have been learned and enhanced with one aim in mind: survival in a profession that is largely a man's world. An excellent criminal profiler and was offered a slot at the Behavioural Analysis Unit at the Bureau, which she declined. She doesn't want to profile monsters, she wants to catch them herself.

Favourite film: *Thelma & Louise*, although she would dearly hope to see a derivation of another popular film that speaks to her and those like her: *A Few Good Women*.

Favourite song: 'Big Girls Don't Cry'(Fergie)

Dislikes: Serial killers and politicians, but she repeats herself

Likes: Cold beer, fast cars and her Beretta Nano backup pistol

A Minute to Midnight

1

Once more she rode into the Valley of Death.

Only this "valley" was in Colorado, at ADX Florence, America's only federal supermax prison. The "death" reference was spot-on, though; the place reeked of it by virtue of the crimes committed by the inmates housed there.

FBI Special Agent Atlee Pine had driven pedal-to-the-metal to get here in her modern-day version of a horse: a turquoise 1967 Mustang with a parchment convertible top. She had spent two years restoring it with the original owner, a veteran FBI agent who had been an informal mentor to her shortly after she'd finished her training at Quantico. When he died, he left it to her. Pine couldn't imagine being without it.

Now, after her swift journey, she sat in the prison parking lot gathering both her nerve and her courage to see one particular monster who resided here among many other human abominations. They were, to a man, the stuff of nightmares. Collectively, they had slaughtered thousands of people, without a smidgen of remorse.

Pine was dressed all in black except for her white blouse. Her shiny FBI shield was clipped to her jacket lapel. It took ten minutes to clear security, where she had to forfeit both her weapons: the Glock 23, her main gun, and an eight-shot Beretta Nano, the backup she kept in an ankle holster. She felt a little naked without the twin pistols, but prisons had rules. And, for obvious reasons, "no guns carried by visitors" was one of the biggies.

She sat on the hard stool in a cubicle in the visitors' room, her long legs curled around the stool's metal supports. Across from her was a thick glass barrier. On the other side of the glass, the man she had come to see would soon appear. A few minutes later, six burly guards escorted a heavily shackled Daniel James Tor into the room and chained him to a bolt in the floor before departing, leaving the law and the lawless sitting across from each other separated by polycarbonate glass that could withstand most bullet strikes.

Tor was an impressive physical specimen, standing six-four and tipping the scales at 280 sculpted pounds. His physique, even now in his fifties, looked NFL ready. She knew that his body was covered in tats, many of them inked on his skin by some of his victims. Tor apparently had such confidence in his control over his prey that he would allow them a sharp instrument with which they could have ended their nightmares. Not a single one had ever attempted it.

He was a freak of nature both physically and emotionally. He was a narcissistic sociopath, or so all the consulted experts had proclaimed. That was arguably the deadliest combination nature could bestow on a human being. It wasn't that he killed with malice; it was actually worse. He could feel no empathy whatsoever toward others. His thirst was solely for self-pleasure. And the only way he could quench that desire was in the absolute destruction of others. He had done this at least thirty times; these were only his known victims. Pine and others in law enforcement suspected the real number might be double or even triple that.

His head was shaved, his chin and jaw the same. His cold, antiseptic eyes flitted over Pine like those of a curious serpent before striking its prey. They were the pupils of a predatory wild animal; the only thought behind them was to kill. Pine also knew that Tor, the consummate con man, could play any role demanded of him in order to lure his victims to their doom, including appearing to be a normal person. And that in itself was terrifying enough.

"You again?" he said, his tone intentionally patronizing.

"Third time's the charm," she replied evenly.

"You're starting to bore me. So make it count."

"I showed you Mercy's picture during the last visit."

"And I said I needed more information." Despite his words about being bored, Pine knew he needed someone to try to dominate. He required attention to justify his very existence. She intended to use that to her advantage.

"I've given you all I have."

"All that you *think* you have. I mentioned that last time. I called it homework. Have you done it? Or are you going to disappoint me?"

Pine was treading a delicate line here. She knew it—and, more important, so did Tor. She wanted to keep him engaged without allowing him to completely overwhelm her. *That* was what bored the man. "Maybe you have some ideas that might help me."

He looked at her moodily. "You said your twin sister was six when she was taken."

"That's right."

"From her bedroom in the middle of the night near Andersonville, Georgia. With you in the room?"

"Yes."

"And you think I struck you but didn't kill you?"

"You actually cracked my skull."

"And I performed a nursery rhyme to decide which one of you to take?"

"Eeny, meeny, miny, moe."

"So whomever the rhyme started on, it would end on the other because of the even number of words."

She leaned forward. "So why did you pick me to start the rhyme with? Because then you knew Mercy would be the loser."

"You're going too fast, Agent Pine. You must slow down if we're to get anywhere."

Pine instinctively decided to punch back. "I don't feel like wasting any more time."

He smiled and rattled his shackles as he responded, "I've got all the time in the world."

"Why did you choose to let me live and not Mercy? Was it just random? A coincidence?"

"Don't let your survivor's guilt run away with you. And I don't have time for whiners." He abruptly smiled and added, "Even with over thirty life sentences to my name." He acted proud of his legal punishment, and she knew he was.

"Okay, but it's important for me to know," she said calmly.

"I cracked your skull, so you said. You could have easily died."

"Could have but didn't. And you always liked to make sure with your victims."

"And you do realize that you're now refuting your own argument that I was the attacker that night?"

"I don't see it that way."

"Let me press the point then. Do you know of any other time when I took a six-year-old from her bedroom and left a witness alive?"

She sat back. "No."

"So why think I did so in your case? Because your hypnotherapist elicited that memory from you? You told me about that the last visit. Curious thing, hypnotherapy. It's wrong as often as it's right, maybe more so. But you would have studied me at the FBI. All of you did because I was required reading," he added casually, though she could detect a glint of pride in his words. "You said you knew I was operating in Georgia around that time. So you know what I think? The hypnosis didn't produce an actual memory, it merely gave you the basis to form a conclusion at which you had already arrived based on extraneous information." He shook his head. "That would never stand up in court. You put me there because you wanted to put me there, and you didn't have the real person to fill in the blanks in your memories. You wanted closure so badly, you're willing to accept an untruth."

She said nothing because the man could be right about that. As she sat mulling this over, he said, "Agent Pine, have I lost you?" He rattled his chains. "Hello, FBI, my interest meter is plummeting by the second."

"You changed your MO over the years. Not all your attacks were alike. They evolved."

"Of course they evolved. Like any occupation, the longer you do it, the better you get at it. I am no exception. I am, in fact, the rule for my . . . particular specialty."

She kept the bile in her stomach from leaching into her throat at this comment. She knew he was waiting to see the revulsion on her face at his comparing murderous activity to an occupation. But she would not give him the satisfaction.

"Granted. But now you're reinforcing *my* conclusion. Just because you hadn't done it before doesn't mean you would never do it. You got better, as you said. Your MO evolved."

"Had you known me to do it since that time?"

Pine was ready for that one. "We don't know all of your victims, do we? So I can't answer that with any certainty."

He sat back and gave her a grudging smile at this slickly played rejoinder. "You want an answer now, don't you? Did I or didn't I, simple as that?"

"Again, it would cost you nothing. They won't execute you for it."

"I could lie and say you're right. Would that be enough for you?"

"I'm an FBI agent."

"Meaning?"

"Meaning I need—"

"You need the body—or skeleton, rather—after all this time, is that right?"

"I need corroboration," she said simply.

He shrugged. "I'm afraid I don't know where all the bodies are buried."

"Then they were wrong about your photographic memory?"

"Not at all. But I've intentionally forgotten some of them."

"Why?"

He leaned forward. "Because they weren't all memorable, Agent Pine. And I don't want to provide closure to every whimpering family member who comes begging to me. That's not exactly my thing, or hadn't you noticed?"

"Do you remember where you buried Mercy?"

"You'll have to come back and have another chat with me. I'm tired now."

"But we just started talking," she replied, a note of urgency in her voice.

"Call me Dan."

She looked at him blankly. She had not been expecting that request. "What?"

"It's our third date. It's time to use real names, Atlee."

"And if I don't want to?"

He clapped his hands silently together. "Then poor, sweet, and probably dead Mercy Pine remains an enigma forever. Poof."

"When do you want to meet again?"

"A month from today . . . Atlee. I'm a busy man. So say it, or we're done. Forever."

"Okay . . . Dan."

Pine walked out, got her guns—and had to force herself to not charge back into the prison and blow *Dan's* fucking head off.

She climbed into her car and headed back to Shattered Rock, Arizona, where she was the sole FBI agent for huge swaths of thinly populated land. An hour into her drive she got an Amber Alert on her phone. A little girl had been abducted. The suspect was driving a gray Nissan pickup very near Pine's current location.

Under the lustrous glow of a hunter's moon, the god of law and order smiled on her that night, because five minutes later the truck flew past Pine going in the opposite direction.

She did a one-eighty, the Mustang's custom rubber smoking and squealing in protest before regaining purchase on the asphalt. Pine hit the blue grille lights she'd installed, laid the fancy chrome gas pedal to the floorboard, and roared off to save a little girl's life.

Pine swore to herself that this time she would not fail.

2

There was a singularly critical rule with Amber Alerts for law enforcement: You got to the victim and the abductor as quickly as possible and walled off any means of escape. After that, you could work the situation any number of ways. Brute force, or talking the suspect out of any violence to the hostage, if that was a possibility.

When the man turned off the main road after seeing the flashing blue lights coming up fast on his butt, Pine knew she would have to read the situation and make that choice soon. At least she knew the terrain. Pine had taken a detour down this very road to let her head clear after her second session with Tor. Thus she knew this was a box canyon, with the road she was on the only way out.

She called in her location to the local police along with her identity and pursuit status. She knew they would deploy a response immediately. But they were in isolated territory here. The cops would not be showing up in a couple of minutes. For now, it was just

Pine, her twin guns, wits, training, and experience—adding up to the best hope the child had to survive.

Dusk was fading to darkness as they wound higher and higher on the switchback road. The lane was growing narrower and the drop-off higher with each passing turn of the wheels.

She tried to see the man and the girl in the truck cab but couldn't make out more than vague silhouettes. But the plate number in the Amber Alert was correct, and the guy was clearly trying to get away. Whether he realized the road was going to run out on him at some point, Pine didn't know. But she *did* know this was going to get complicated. Yet Pine had been rigorously trained in complicated.

A half mile later the point of no return was reached. Pine positioned her Mustang sideways in the middle of the narrow road, blocking the way back out, with the passenger side facing the truck. If he tried to ram her, she would shoot him through the windshield. She took out her trusty Glock and drew a bead through the open passenger window.

The Nissan made a loop and pointed its hood back the way it had come. The man stopped and put the truck in park, the engine idling. Pine could almost see the wheels turning in the guy's head: *Do I try it or not?*

When he turned on his high beams, probably to blind her, she shot them out. Now, Pine figured, she had his full and undivided attention. After she once again reported in their current location to the local cops, Pine sat there with one hand wrapped around her gun grip and the other on the door lever.

For a while, they just sat there. Then, ten minutes later, the driver's-side door of the Nissan opened. The guy had apparently made up his mind.

And the chess match began.

Pine mirrored this move with her door.

Four feet hit the dirt from the Nissan.

Pine swung her long legs out and stood, her boots smacking the asphalt.

As the man and little girl stepped out from behind the cover of the truck door, Pine leveled her pistol at his broad chest.

"FBI. This is the end of the line. Step away from the girl. Lie facedown on the ground, legs spread, fingers interlocked behind your head. Do it now or I will open fire."

The man didn't obey a single one of her commands. Instead he squatted down and placed the girl squarely in front of him.

Okay, she thought, this sack of shit was going to play it the hard way and use a kid as a shield. *Why am I surprised?*

Under the illumination thrown from the truck's interior light, Pine had observed that he looked to be in his early fifties. He was medium height, thick and muscled, with a bald head and a thin line of graying, unkempt hair creeping ivy-like around this dome. His features were weathered, ugly, and demented. He was a walking stereotype of an aging pedophile. He wore a dirty T-shirt that showed off his bulging barbell biceps and dusty corduroy pants with worn boots. The girl was about ten or eleven, tall for her age, with a lean, athletic build. Her twin blond braids dangled on either side of her head. She wore soccer shorts with grass stains on them and a matching jersey. Her knees were dirty, as were the long socks and her Adidas soccer shoes. She looked scared, of course, but there was also a resolute spirit that Pine could see in the girl's eyes.

Pine didn't know if this was a stranger-danger scenario or a family snatch case. He looked too old to be her father, but who knew these days?

"Cops are on the way. Do what I said, and you walk away still breathing."

The man stared at her without answering.

"*Habla ingles*?" she asked.

"I'm American, bitch," he barked. "Do I look like a Mexie to you?"

"Then you have no reason not to follow my instructions."

He pulled a Sig pistol from his waistband and pressed the muzzle against the girl's head.

"*This* is my way out. Throw down your piece or the princess's brains get scrambled."

"You drop your gun, you get a lawyer, and you do your prison time."

"I've been down that road. I didn't much like it."

"What's your name?"

"Don't try that good-cop crap with me."

"I'm sure we can work this out."

"Shit, you think we're doing a deal here?" the man said incredulously.

"Let her go and we can try to solve what's bothering you."

"You believe I'm falling for that mumbo-jumbo?"

They could now hear sirens in the background.

"It's not mumbo-jumbo if it's true."

"I'm not dealing."

"Then how do you see this playing out?"

"With you moving your car and letting me outta here. I got stuff I want to do with this little beauty. And I'm itching to get started." He put his other arm around the girl's windpipe.

Pine's finger moved closer to the trigger of the Glock. Should she chance taking a shot? "And what about the cops coming?"

"You talk to them."

"I've got no jurisdiction over them."

"Look, you dumb bitch, I've got the girl. That means I've got the leverage. You do what I say, not the other way around."

"You're not leaving here with her."

"Then you got one big problem, bitch."

Pine decided to change tactics. She glanced at the girl. "Do you know this guy?"

The girl slowly shook her head.

"What's your name?"

"I'm—"

"Shut up," the man cried out, pushing the gun against the girl's head. "And you shut up too!" he barked at Pine.

"I want all three of us to walk away from this thing."

"You mean two of you. You could give a shit about me."

"I don't want to shoot you, but I will if you force my hand."

"You shoot me, she's dead."

Pine looked at the girl once more, quickly sizing her up. She reminded Pine of herself at that age. Tall, rangy. But she was once more struck by the girl's calm eyes. She ran her gaze over the uniform, the grass-stained shorts and dirty knees. This girl was a scrapper. So maybe, just maybe, this might work. It was risky, but Pine had no options that weren't.

"You play soccer?" Pine asked.

The girl slowly nodded.

The man pulled her back toward the edge. Ten feet more and it was a thousand-foot drop.

"Do not move another inch to that edge," ordered Pine as she moved forward.

The man halted. And so did Pine.

The sirens were growing closer. But if Pine didn't finish this soon, things might escalate when the uniforms did arrive.

"I'm running out of patience here," the man barked.

"I *gave* you an option. The only one I can give. Prison's not great, but it's a lot better than a grave. You don't get released or paroled from six feet under."

The man started toward the edge again, dragging the girl with him.

"Stop!" bellowed Pine, trying to line up her target through the tritium night sight installed on her Glock. Her rear sight ring held twin glowing tritium inserts, while her front post held a tritium insert surrounded by nonluminous white paint. It was very accurate, but she couldn't fire. She might hit the girl. Or the guy's trigger finger might jerk when Pine's round struck him.

The man smiled triumphantly as he read Pine's dilemma in her features. "You won't shoot. Now *that's* leverage, lady."

Pine glanced at the girl. *Okay, it's do-or-die time.* "I played soccer. Only goal I ever scored was on a back kick. Hit it right between the goalie's legs. Bet you're a much better player than I was." Pine held the girl's gaze, communicating with her eyes what she couldn't do with her words.

The man barked: "Shut the hell up about soccer. Now, for the last time, put down—"

The girl's foot kicked backward and up and struck the squatting man right in the crotch. He let her go and doubled over, his face scrunched in pain, and the

Sig fell out of his hand. "Y-you l-little b-bit—" he moaned, his face turning beet red. He dropped to his knees, gasping for air.

Pine raced forward, kicked the man's weapon behind her, grabbed the girl's arm, and pulled her to safety.

That should have been the end of it. Pine had her gun, and he didn't have his. Or his hostage. She was home free. It was over.

But it wasn't over. Because when the man finally stood and straightened, he looked at Pine and spat out, "You think you got me? I got nine lives!" He glanced ferociously at the girl, who was staring back at him with revulsion. "I can't remember how many like her I've done and then cut up and left for the animals. And I'll be out again to do more. You hear me, FBI bitch?"

Pine stared at him for a long moment. In the man's taunting face, she saw someone else.

Pine knew full well she shouldn't take the bait. But she was going to do it anyway.

She looked to the sky, where the moon burned a dull yellow and red.

The *hunter's* moon, she knew, also known as the blood moon.

More accurately the predator's moon, and right now I'm the predator.

She holstered her gun and stepped forward.

In her mind's eye the giant Daniel James Tor stared

back at her. Pine's nemesis, the stuff of nightmares. She was about to make it all go away.

The man grinned in triumph. "You just made a damn big mistake."

"How's that?" But she already knew what his answer would be.

"In case you hadn't noticed, lady, I'm a man." He charged her in a bull rush.

A moment later he staggered backward, dazed, his face bloodied by the devastating blow delivered by the size eleven boot at the end of her long right leg. He bent over, groaning.

"In case *you* hadn't noticed," said Pine. "I'm now going to kick the shit out of you."

She slammed her foot into his chin, lifting him straight up. A palm-out blow delivered directly to the bridge of the nose made the man howl in pain, and he collapsed on his back like he'd been struck with a sledgehammer.

The battle really should have ended there, but Pine jumped astride him and clamped the muscular legs of her nearly six-foot frame around the man's arms, easily pinning them to his sides. Then she proceeded to rain blow after blow down on him, fist, elbow, forearm, open palm, using every technique she had learned from years of MMA and close-quarter battle training.

It was as though nearly thirty years of pent-up anger had just been unleashed. She felt cartilage and bone in his face give way at the same time she heard the FBI angel on her shoulder screaming at her that this was against every rule the Bureau had. And still Pine could not stop what she was doing.

At first the man had struggled against her, but then he had fallen limply into unconsciousness, his face quickly dissolving into a bloody, pulpy mass. She could smell the stink of him rise to her nostrils, mixed with her own sweat. It was both sickening and exhilarating.

Finally, exhausted from the effort, Pine slowly rose off him, her features pale and her limbs shaky. Her mind was suddenly aghast at what she had just done, as the FBI shoulder angel reasserted itself. Pine let out a gush of breath, looked down at her bloody hands and jacket sleeves, and wiped them on her pants. She walked over to the girl, who drew back at her approach. Pine stopped, feeling ashamed at the girl being afraid of her.

"Are you okay? Did he hurt you? Did . . . did he do anything to you?"

She shook her head.

As the sirens grew closer, the little girl looked over at the man.

"Is he . . . is he dead?"

"No. Just . . . unconscious." Pine wasn't actually sure of that. She squatted down on her haunches. "What's your name?"

"Holly."

"Holly, it was so brave what you did. And you understood exactly what I wanted you to do. It was amazing."

"I have three older brothers." Holly smiled weakly. "When they pick on me, I can kick really hard."

Pine put out a hand and squeezed the girl's shoulder. "I'm so glad that you're okay."

"Are you really an FBI agent?"

"I am."

"I didn't know girls could do that. I thought that was like, you know, just on TV."

"Girls can do anything we want. Never doubt that."

Pine stood as the cop cars screeched to a stop a few feet away. She looked over at the bloody man lying motionless on the ground.

Pine took out her creds and headed over to explain what had happened, including the reason why she had nearly beaten a man to death.

This just might be the end of the actually not-so-very-Special Agent Atlee Pine.

3

Pine accessed the secure door of her office in Shattered Rock, Arizona, the closest town to the Grand Canyon. This topographical jewel was the only natural wonder of the world located in America, and Pine had jurisdiction over any federal crimes committed there. Her assistant, Carol Blum, was sitting at her desk in the office's small foyer. Blum was in her sixties and had been at the Bureau for several decades working in various offices and capacities. The mother of six grown children, none of whom lived close by, she came in early and went home late. As she had told Pine, the FBI was now her life, as she didn't really have hobbies for amusement. She was tall and attractive, her hair immaculately styled, her makeup and jewelry understated, and her clothing choices always professional.

"How was your workout?" asked Blum.

Pine normally exercised at the crack of dawn at a gym in the small downtown area of Shattered Rock. The workout facility was beloved by hardcore movers of iron for its minimalist style of fitness. There was no

AC, no fancy machines, no Pelotons and Spandex workout clothes within miles of the place. Only barbells and enormous steel plates and grunting people heaving them into the air with a ferocious intensity.

And lots and lots of sweat.

"I didn't make it this morning. Got back later than I thought from Colorado the other night and decided to sleep in yesterday to catch up. Then I slept badly last night and got up too late this morning to go. Stuff on my mind."

Blum looked at her in concern. "What stuff?"

"Come into my office and I'll fill you in on the 'wonderful' details. Oh, and you might be getting a new boss."

Blum's expression didn't change. Pine loved that the woman was unflappable. In all her years at the Bureau, she had no doubt seen everything.

"Do you want some coffee?"

"Carol, you don't have to make me coffee. That's actually fulfilling a really bad stereotype."

"There's nothing wrong with me *offering* to make you a cup of coffee. Now, if you had demanded a cup, I would have felt differently. I remember a lot of male agents who ran afoul of that rule over the years."

"What did you do when that happened?"

"I just trained them better," said Blum brightly.

She walked over to the Keurig machine on the credenza set against the wall and turned it on, pulling a pod out of a drawer at the same time.

When she walked into Pine's office with the steaming cup of coffee, Pine was seated behind her desk. Blum set the cup down and settled in the chair across from her boss.

The office had been recently renovated, although Pine had told the contractor to leave alone the twin indentations in the wall. The first hole had occurred when a witness Pine had been interviewing decided to take a swing at her. He had missed his target, and his fist had hit the wall instead. The second crack had been caused by Pine's throwing the man headfirst into the drywall. It had been Blum's idea to not repair the wall. As she had said, a picture was worth a thousand words.

"So?" said Blum expectantly. "What happened?"

Pine took a drink of her coffee before answering.

"While I was still in Colorado, I got an Amber Alert. I fortunately ran into the guy. And stopped him from getting away with an adorable little girl named Holly."

"But that's wonderful, Agent Pine. You're to be commended." She paused. "Then I don't see the problem."

"Yeah, well, the thing is, I got a little carried away in subduing him."

"Carried away? How so?"

"He's in the hospital now with a fractured skull among other injuries."

"I'm sure you did what you had to do."

"The fact is, I didn't have to beat him up."

"Why did you do it then?"

"He came at me, tried to attack me, and . . . I took out my frustrations."

"Frustrations?"

"I had just spent time with Tor."

"So . . . so maybe it was Tor you were attacking?"

"I could have stopped. I *should* have stopped."

"But as you said, he attacked you."

Pine shook her head. "After the girl was safe, I decided to escalate things."

"But it would be difficult to judge your actions in the field at that moment."

"The Bureau 'judges' actions in the field all the time, Carol."

"That's true," she admitted.

There was a knock at the outer secure portal. The two women glanced at each other.

"Wolves at the door already?" said Pine.

Blum escorted the man into Pine's office a few moments later.

It was Clint Dobbs, the head of the FBI in Arizona. He was in his fifties, around six feet tall, with broad shoulders, a developing paunch, and graying hair. He was so far above Pine in the pecking order that she saw the man only when there was a catastrophe. She assumed that this situation qualified as such. She was surprised, though, that he was here alone. Dobbs usually traveled with an entourage of agents. She wondered why not this time.

Dobbs sat in the chair across from Pine, who had risen at the sight of her superior. When Blum made to leave, Dobbs put up a hand. "You can stay, Carol. You need to hear this, too."

Blum shot a glance at Pine and then remained standing by the desk.

Dobbs looked back at Pine, his expression unreadable. "Sit down, Pine."

"I suppose this is about what happened the other night," said Pine as she sat back down.

"Not unless you kicked the shit out of somebody else I don't know about," he said gruffly.

"No sir," said Pine quietly. "It was just the one."

Dobbs nodded. "The guy you caught was a registered sex offender, Clifford Rogers. Just got out of prison six months ago. Paroled early after kidnapping and raping a nine-year-old. Only served nineteen years. The prison system was bursting at the seams, apparently, and the dipshit lawyer the scumball got hold of seized on some technicality and ran with it. Rogers was also suspected of murdering an eight-year-old two weeks after he got out. But they couldn't find her body. Had to let him go. In fact, that was the case with four other victims going back about thirty years. Guy was a certified monster, but the law couldn't prove it, except for the rape charge. He snatched the little girl you saved from a soccer match. She'd be dead if you hadn't intervened. Instead, she's back home with her family."

"Has Rogers regained consciousness?"

"He has."

"And?"

"And he said you beat him nearly to death for no reason."

"Did he?"

"And what's your story?"

"I did my job. A bit overzealously, maybe."

"I see."

"Did he say differently?"

"I'm not really sure I care what the guy says," replied Dobbs, which surprised Pine, because the man usually went unfailingly by the book.

"Did he file a complaint against me?"

"He certainly wants to."

Blum said, "Well, minds can be changed."

Dobbs eyed her pointedly. "And what does that mean precisely, Carol?"

"Six years ago, Special Agent Voorhies out of Tucson."

"You have a long memory," noted Dobbs.

"The point is, an understanding was reached. And Agent Voorhies did what he needed to do. He's been a productive agent ever since."

Pine said, "What did he do?"

"Let's just say he crossed the line," said Dobbs. He sat back and his features grew pensive. "How about this: How about I go and have a chat with Mr. Rogers and convince him that filing a formal complaint against you would not be in his best interests?"

"I don't want you taking any heat for what I did, sir," said Pine.

"Which is why I'm offering to do just that. You're a good agent. I don't want this to derail your career."

Blum asked, "Do you think he'll agree to that?"

"Last time he was in prison he got solitary confinement because he begged for it. He goes into gen pop with the rep of a child rapist and killer, he'll last about five minutes. And he knows we can make that happen."

Blum looked at Pine and said, "Okay. That sounds like a plan."

"But surely there will be an internal investigation," noted Pine.

"You didn't discharge your weapon. The guy didn't die. Rogers isn't going to make a complaint. From what I hear from the locals in Colorado, the mayor wants to give you a key to the city."

"Okay," said Pine doubtfully.

Dobbs straightened up. "But I'm not going to beat around the bush, Pine. What you did was way out of bounds. In my book, you get one free card, and you just burned it."

"Does this mean I'll face no disciplinary action?"

"It does. *This* time."

Pine glanced down. "I appreciate that, sir. I . . . I expected far worse."

He stroked his chin. "You haven't taken a vacation in God knows how long, right?"

"A vacation, sir? Well, actually, I was given time off just—"

"That wasn't a real vacation. You know it and I know it. People don't almost die several times during a vacation."

"Okay, it has been a while, yes."

"Me, I go fly-fishing every year. Never catch a damn thing and I love every minute of it."

"And for how long is my vacation to be?"

Dobbs rose, buttoned his suit jacket, and headed to the door. "For as long as you need, Pine." He looked back at her. "How did your visit to ADX Florence go, by the way?"

"It wasn't very productive."

"Well, maybe you can use your vacation to make it more productive." He stopped and looked down at the floor. "This Rogers creep remind you of anyone?"

"Yes, but in only one way."

"Daniel Tor is a few levels above, I would imagine."

"NBA versus a high school team."

"Well, he's locked up for life. You're not. But in a way, I believe you really are, too. What do you think?"

"I . . . have some issues to work through, clearly."

"Good answer."

Blum spoke up. "And I think I should be there to assist her in this."

They both looked at her. Dobbs said slowly, "That's up to Pine."

Pine said, "Carol, you don't have to—"

Blum interjected, "Yes, I do."

Dobbs said, "Well, I'll leave you to figure it out." He nodded to the women and left.

Blum looked at Pine and Pine stared back at her assistant.

"It was a long time ago, Carol. A very long time ago."

"And I've seen you go into every case and come out with a solution. And maybe it's time you took a crack at it."

"I've been to see Tor three times now."

"But there is no guarantee that he had anything to do with your sister's disappearance."

Pine looked down at her hands. "I . . . I don't know if I'm up for this, Carol."

"Well, if you don't mind my saying so, I think you are. At the very least I think you have to be. Like Agent Dobbs said, you just burned your only free card. And you can't leave the Bureau involuntarily or otherwise. You were meant to be an FBI agent."

Pine rose from behind her desk. "But this is not your problem."

"I'm your assistant. I'm going to help you. And that's just the way it's going to be."

Pine smiled at her. "That's very kind of you." Her gaze grew distant. "Well, then we'll need to pack for the trip."

"The trip?"

"Back in time, Carol. Back in time."

4

Blum said, "I know you said we were going back in time, but it looks like we stepped back into the past, literally."

Pine was driving the rental SUV and Blum was riding shotgun. They had flown into Atlanta and then driven a little over two hours pretty much due south to Sumter County, and more particularly to Andersonville, Georgia, population around 250 people. They were now passing through the faded main street of the small town.

"Sometime back in the seventies, the mayor and some others decided to turn the clock back and make Andersonville into a tourist attraction by making it look like it did during the Civil War. We're on Church Street, which is the main drag. The train tracks running perpendicular to it are where the prisoners were brought in on their way to Andersonville Prison. It was the last trip many of them would ever make."

"The prison is close by?"

Pine stopped the car and pointed to the street. "See all those footprints painted on the street? That represents the prisoners walking the quarter mile to the prison. Longest walk of their lives, probably."

Blum shuddered. "How horrible."

"The town put together a seven-acre area called Pioneer Farm, just off here. They have a smithy, a jail, a smokehouse, and a sugar cane mill, among other attractions. You can see the sign overhead from here that says, 'Welcome to Andersonville Civil War Village.'"

Blum read it, nodded, and added, "And an RV park and restaurant."

"About eighty thousand people visit a year, so I guess the mayor's plan paid off. The really big event is coming up shortly."

"What's that?"

"Mock Civil War battles. Reenactments, they call them. There'll be a parade and a marching band coming down this way. Soldiers in blue and gray. More bands playing, line dancing, clogging, lots to eat and drink. Quite the shindig. People selling uniforms and guns and flags and swords and quilts and other stuff. And only four bucks to get in."

"How do you know that?"

"It's on that sign over there."

The pair exchanged a quick smile.

"So all those tourists come here for that?" asked Blum.

"No, they also come because of the infamous Confederate prison that used to be here."

"To visit a prison? That's sort of weird."

"Well, it was the most notorious prison in the Civil War. Around thirteen thousand Union prisoners died there. There's a National Historic Site here and a huge military cemetery. And I read there's some sort of prisoner of war center here too. The commandant of the prison, Henry Wirz, was hanged as a war criminal." She pointed up ahead to a tall obelisk in the center of the street. "That's the Wirz Monument."

"Wait a minute, a war criminal gets a monument?"

"It was erected by the Daughters of the Confederacy. I guess they believed Wirz got a raw deal and was just used as a scapegoat." She paused. "Tor knew about Wirz being hanged. He told me the first time I met him, when I said I was from the Andersonville area."

"So he *was* here then?"

"He was operating in the state when my sister was taken. He committed murders in Macon, Atlanta, Columbus, and Albany. That was why it occurred to me that he might be involved in Mercy's disappearance. But him knowing about Wirz might be because he read up on me before I visited him for the first time. He could have learned about it then."

"You told me on the plane ride that he occurred to you as the abductor in your sister's case after you'd gone to hypnotherapy?"

Pine nodded. "But there's the chicken-and-egg problem. I obviously knew about Tor before I underwent hypnosis. So maybe it was a self-fulfilling prophecy that I think he did it. In fact, he pointed out that possibility to me at our last meeting. But I had already thought of it."

Blum shivered. "I can't imagine being in the same building with someone like that, much less talking to him."

"He definitely has the ability to get under your skin. Turn things around that you say. Appear normal, logical even, though he's a monster."

"Creepy."

Pine thought back to the giant of a man who had so cruelly and violently ended the lives of so many innocent people. "Actually, that term doesn't come close to covering it."

"So is that it for the town? They all work in tourism?"

"No. In the sixties a mine and refinery opened. They ship out thousands of tons of bauxite ore every week from here on the freight trains."

"Bauxite?"

"It's found in the kaolinite clay soil here. Mulcoa is the company that mines it here. It was once used to make aluminum. Now it's used for abrasives and in hydraulic fracturing to get to oil and gas deposits. With all the fracking going on now, the bauxite business is pretty good." She pointed to a storefront as they drove along. "Drummer Boy Civil War Museum. They have uniforms and flags and guns and other artifacts from the war."

"Well, it's nice to see that the Civil War can still be a benefit for some. I really didn't learn much about it growing up where I did."

"It's like a second bible of sorts in the South."

"And where did you live here?"

"I'll show you."

The road leading to her old home was just as Pine remembered it, mostly dirt, potholed, curvy, and isolated.

Blum looked around. They hadn't passed another house for nearly a mile. "What in the world did you and Mercy do for fun? I can see you didn't go on many playdates."

"And our mom didn't have a car. My dad took the only one we had to work at the mine. So we walked or, as we got older, we rode our bikes. Most of the time we just played out in the yard. My mom would take us to Americus on the weekends to do the grocery shopping and other errands. The school bus picked us up right there," she said, pointing out a spot in front of an aged, sprawling oak. "We were only in first grade when Mercy disappeared."

Something caught in Pine's throat and she coughed and slowed the truck, lifted her sunglasses and brushed at her eyes.

Blum looked at her cautiously. "How long since you've been back?"

Pine took a moment to compose herself and lowered her glasses. "We moved really soon after Mercy was taken. I haven't been back here since then."

"Not once?"

Pine shook her head. "There was nothing for me to come back to, Carol."

"I guess I can understand that." Blum put a supportive hand on Pine's shoulder. "And your father committed suicide, you said?"

"On my birthday. He stuck a shotgun in his mouth and pulled the trigger."

"On your birthday? How awful."

"I think it was his bizarre way of letting me know he was thinking of me. You see, my parents blamed themselves for what happened. Then they ended up blaming each other. That was the reason why they split up later. They were both apparently drunk and stoned on weed downstairs when Mercy went missing and I was attacked."

Blum shook her head. "The guilt they must've been feeling."

They navigated a curve and a dilapidated, falling-down, plank-sided house came into sight at the end of a dirt road.

"It looks abandoned," observed Blum.

"No, it's not." Pine pointed to an ancient Ford pickup truck parked partially behind the house. It seemed to have more rust than not. And there was a chunky black Lab with a wide tan collar sleeping on the porch.

"Someone really lives in that? It looks like a good wind would knock it down."

Pine frowned. "And how many broken-down homes do you see in Arizona in the middle of nowhere? People live where they can."

"That's true."

They pulled to a stop in the dirt front yard and climbed out. Pine looked over the only home she had known for the first six years of her life. It was smaller than she remembered, but that was always the case, wasn't it?

The front door stood open, and the porch sagged both from wood rot and gravity's pull. One of the windows was cracked and the planks were warped. The painted surfaces were peeling. Trash was piled in the yard. There was an old fifty-gallon oil drum with smoky ends of debris sticking out. That was evidently the mode used to burn trash here.

The dog stirred, rising slowly to its feet on arthritic legs and letting out a couple of feeble barks. Its muzzle was gray, and it looked unsteady.

"Hey, boy, how you doing?" said Pine in a comforting voice.

She slowly approached the dog, her fist held out. She let him sniff her before she tickled his ears and received a lick in return.

She sat on the porch, looked around, and stroked

the dog's head while Blum stood next to her. "I wonder who lives here now?"

"That would be me."

They turned to see a man who had just come around the side of the house. The shotgun was a Remington twelve-gauge side-by-side, and it was pointed right at them.

5

Pine rose from the porch. "You really live here?" she asked. Her eyes were calm and fixed on the man, even as her right hand slid in the vicinity of her holstered Glock.

The man was tall, lean, and he seemed, despite his white hair and matching beard, to be constructed out of granite. A cigarette dangled from his mouth. A sweat-stained Stetson was on his head, under which the unruly locks of his snowy white hair were visible. His face was sun and wind whipped, and the wrinkles there were pronounced and contained startling depth. Pine gauged him to be well over sixty, a fact belied by his ropy muscles, which were evident because of the short-sleeved shirt he was wearing. His jeans were faded and cut tight to his long legs and slim hips. The pair of crumbling boots he wore looked held together merely by prayer.

"I do, which means you gals are trespassing."

"I used to live in this house," said Pine, glancing over her shoulder.

The man lowered the shotgun, but just a bit. "When?"

"Beginning in the mideighties."

He looked her over. "You must've been a baby then."

"Me and my sister."

He glanced at Blum. "This your ma?"

"No, she's my friend."

"So what are you doing back here? Sightseeing? Ain't much to see. Cemetery and that old Confederate prison."

"I came back to see my old homestead. How long have you lived here?"

"'Bout three years. Who are you?"

"Atlee Pine. That's Carol Blum."

Blum eyed him closely. "And what's your name?"

"Cyrus Tanner. Friends call me Cy."

"Can I call you Cy, even though we're not officially friends?" said Blum. "And could you point that shotgun somewhere else? Because while my nerves and those of my friend are pretty strong, accidents do happen with weapons."

"What? Oh, sorry 'bout that."

He lowered the shotgun and looked at them nervously. "What do you want here then?"

Pine said, "Just to look around. Pure nostalgia. Are you from Andersonville?"

"No, came over from 'Bama. Mississip' before that."

"So you bought the house then?"

He chuckled. "Hell, I don't have the money to buy no house, not even one as run-down as this. I'm, uh, renting." He pointed to the chunky, aged Lab, which had flopped back down. "Me and Roscoe there. Ain't we, boy?"

Roscoe gave a little show of yellowed teeth as he looked happy at hearing his name.

"Me and Roscoe been partners for a long time. Best friend I ever had. Beats people by a long shot on that score."

"Do you mind if I look around?" said Pine.

"Ain't much to see."

"Do you work at the bauxite mine?" asked Blum.

He shot her a swift glance. "The mine? No, I do some odd-job work 'round here. Good with engines and stuff. Anything like that needs tinkering I can most likely fix. Get paid in cash. Don't like to pay no taxes. I get by and cover my bills. Keep a roof over me and Roscoe's head. What do you gals do for a living?"

Pine took out her official creds. "I'm an FBI agent. Carol is my assistant."

Tanner looked wildly at them. "A Fed? Look, I didn't mean that stuff 'bout the taxes—"

"I'm not with the IRS, Mr. Tanner, and I don't care about your philosophy on paying taxes. Or not."

"Well, okay," he muttered, not looking convinced. "What are you really doing here then? It's not on the official Civil War tour," he added with a weak grin.

Pine glanced at Blum before looking back at the

man. "My sister was abducted from this house nearly thirty years ago. The person who took her was never found. And neither was she. So I'm back here now trying to find the truth."

The cigarette nearly fell out of the man's mouth. "Holy shit, you being straight with me?"

"Never been straighter in my life."

He looked back at the house. "I never knew that when I started living here."

"No reason for you *to* know."

"You said they never caught the bastard?"

"Or found my sister."

"So . . . are you here, what, looking for clues and stuff? Been a long time."

"I'm not here to do a forensic scrub, if that's what you mean. But I am here to try to sort some things out. And I thought coming here would be a good first step."

He put the shotgun down on the porch. "You want to take a tour of the place then?"

"That'd be great. You sure you want to leave the gun there?" added Pine.

"Hell, it's not even loaded. I just use it for show. You know, scare folks off."

"You get many trespassers out here?"

"Mostly kids looking for a place to drink and have sex. I got nothing against them doing either one, just not in my house."

He led them into the front room. The wallpaper was hanging down in tatters, and the only items in the room were a large lime green bean bag chair, a scarred side table holding a chunky old TV with rabbit ears on top, and a square of dirty carpet with prominent urine stains.

"Roscoe's got him some kidney problems," noted Tanner in an embarrassed fashion as he gazed at the marks.

"How's the TV reception around here?" said Blum.

"For shit. But I tinker with it here and there. Get some stuff on sometimes. Mostly sports." He grinned. "If the news comes on, I just turn off the sound. Too damn depressing."

Pine took a moment to look around the room. It was hard for her to imagine ever living here. This seemed like foreign soil to her.

"Where did you and your sister sleep?" asked Blum.

Pine pointed to the stairs. "Up there."

Tanner drew back and let her lead the way up the scarred, uncarpeted plywood stairs.

Now, with every step, Pine was drawing closer to that horrible night in 1989. The landing outside the bedroom door found her mind and soul, if not her body, returning to that time in her life. She stared at the closed door for a moment as though it might plausibly be a portal to another universe that would answer all her questions.

Nothing like setting the bar too low.

Tanner said, "You can go on in, ma'am. Ain't nothing in there now. I sleep on the bean bag chair downstairs. Don't have no bed."

Pine gripped the doorknob like it was the only thing tethering her to the earth, turned it, and pushed the door open. When she stepped through, in her mind's eye, the room and she had been fully transported back to the late eighties, to the absolute worst moment of her life.

She saw the bed, the nightstand, the cheap light fixture, the chest of drawers on top of which she and Mercy had kept their dolls. And the square of carpet with the My Little Pony graphic on it. The tiny closet where their few clothes hung. The blue ball that Pine loved to kick and throw, and the little ballerina dress that Mercy, the dancer and more girly of the two, loved. She would wear the garment until it grew so dirty the white had turned brown, forcing her mother to whisk it away in the middle of the night and wash it in the sink, for they had no other means to launder their clothes.

And finally, the one window in the room. Through which Tor, or someone like him, had climbed and clamped gloved hands over the mouths of the little girls. Then had come the nursery rhyme, the thumping of their foreheads. The selection of Mercy to take, the fist smashing into Pine's head, fracturing her skull and leaving her for dead. Her mother tottering in the next morning, nursing a hangover from the comingling of pot and beer. Only to discover one daughter gone and the other near death.

The ambulance ride to the hospital, the anxious faces hovering above her, the stark white ceiling of the ambulance—perhaps an early glimpse of Heaven—the gurney sprint through the hospital. The pinch of a needle, the unconsciousness of anesthesia, the subsequent cut into and repair of her skull, though she was clearly not aware of that, followed by the long, frightening recovery. Frightening because she really had no understanding of what had happened to her.

Then back home, to find Mercy still gone, her parents inconsolable. Unable to talk about their other daughter, unable to let Pine out of their sight, yet reluctant to hold her, or to talk to her about any of it. The thickness of guilt lay heavy over them all, crushing out what little family nucleus was left to them.

"Agent Pine?"

Pine came out of these thoughts like she remembered waking up from her surgery. Instantly alert and curious but still befuddled somehow, as though she had risen too quickly from deep water and there was something potentially deadly floating inside her.

Blum was looking worriedly at her. "Are you all right?"

She nodded. "Just remembering some things."

"Anything helpful?"

Pine crossed the floor, opened the window, and looked down.

"A ladder. The man had to use a ladder to get up here."

"Did they find one?" Tanner asked curiously.

"No. At least not that I know of. I was only six. The police didn't really talk to me. Not after they learned I couldn't really help them."

"Were there ever any suspects?" asked Blum.

"My father was the first suspect, perhaps the only one."

Blum and Tanner exchanged a quick glance.

"You think he did that to his own kids?" asked Tanner, clearly not believing this.

"No. It wasn't my father. I would have recognized him. And why come in through the window? And they were drinking and smoking pot that night. He couldn't have made it up the stairs, much less climbed a ladder. And I saw the man come through the window, though I really couldn't describe him back then."

"But the police didn't believe that?" said Blum. "They still pursued your father as a suspect?"

"It's why we had to move from here. Everyone in town thought he had done it, despite there being no evidence to support that."

"And your daddy?" asked Tanner.

"He's dead now."

"And your ma?"

Pine didn't answer right away. In some ways, the mystery of her mother had overshadowed even Mercy's disappearance, at least to Pine. Blum looked at her curiously, but Pine didn't seem to notice.

"I'd rather not talk about it," replied Pine. She closed the window after searching her memory, going back to that night and trying to confirm that it was indeed Daniel Tor coming through the window. She arrived at what she had expected: no firm conclusion.

They went back outside, where she sat on the porch and stroked Roscoe's head.

"He likes you," said Tanner approvingly. "And Roscoe's a good judge of character. Got to be where if he don't like somebody I bring around, they don't come back around. Yep, old Roscoe keeps me from making dumb decisions. Well, at least fewer than I used to."

"I needed a Roscoe in my life a long time ago," opined Blum.

She and Tanner exchanged a knowing look.

Pine rose and said, "Thanks for letting us look around, Cy."

"You gonna be in town long?"

"As long as it takes."

"Well, I might see you 'round then. Me and Roscoe eat at the little café on the main street most nights. They call it the Clink, after the prison, I guess. Good food and cheap beer."

"We might see you there then," said Blum.

Tanner took off his hat in a gesture of good-bye, fully revealing his thick wavy hair, and tacked on a broad smile.

They got back into the rental and headed out.

Pine said, "I always wondered what happened to the Marlboro Man. Now I know."

"He's a hottie," said Blum, looking in the side mirror and seeing Tanner standing there. "The picture of ruggedly handsome. I bet he has a two-pack, which is like an eight-pack for a twenty-year-old."

"If he really wants to be healthy, he should stop smoking."

"That just adds to the bad-boy mystique."

"Control yourself, Carol."

"I am always in control, Agent Pine. It comes with being a mother of six. Once you keep your sanity with that, there's nothing ever again that can overwhelm you."

"Just checking."

"So you don't want to talk about your mother?"

Pine started to say something and then stopped. She seemed to recalibrate her thoughts and said, "I know what happened to my father. I don't know what happened to my mother."

"Do you mean you don't know how she, what, died?"

"For all I know my mother is alive."

"But you don't know where she is?"

"No."

"Have you tried to find her?"

"Many times. With no luck at all."

"But you're an FBI agent. How can that be?"

"Good question, Carol. Good question."

6

They had a reservation at a bed-and-breakfast located right outside the small downtown area of Andersonville. It was a large, old home renovated to cater to guests and called the Cottage.

Pine was normally a light packer, a one-suitcase sort of girl. But for this trip, she had brought a second small suitcase. She set it on her bed and opened it. She looked down at the oddball assortment of items carefully packed inside.

This represented, along with the photo of her and her sister, the sum total of her possessions from her parents. There was a black bow tie of her father's. A key chain with the bauxite mining company's name and logo engraved on it. A dozen drink coasters that she and Mercy had used as makeshift checker pieces. A lavender hair ribbon of her mother's. A ring and pair of earrings, both costume jewelry, but still precious to her. A small book of poems. A pocketknife of her father's with his initials. A *Wonder Woman* comic book. A cracked teacup.

And . . . She lifted the small doll with the dented

face from inside the suitcase and moved a strand of fake hair away from its bulging right eye. This was her doll, Skeeter from the *Muppet Babies* TV series.

Mercy had had a matching one, only hers was named Sally. Pine had wanted Mercy to name her doll Scooter, because Skeeter was his twin sister. Only Mercy wouldn't hear of it because Scooter was "a boy." Pine smiled at the memory.

She had almost thrown all this in the trash a long time ago. But something had stayed her hand, she wasn't sure what. Pine slowly put them all away and zipped up the suitcase.

She met Blum in the front room, and they headed to dinner at the place Tanner had recommended, the Clink café.

They walked from the Cottage to the main street, which was quaint if somewhat downtrodden. It was a nice crisp evening, and there were numerous people out and about. Many, Pine could tell, were tourists because they would take out their cameras or, more often, their phones and take photos of items in different store windows or interesting pieces of architecture or sculptures or signs in their path.

The Clink had a cheery sign albeit with a silhouette of a man behind bars, and a colorful striped awning out front. The window was engraved with old-fashioned lettering promising: GOOD FARE AT FAIR PRICES, NO IMPRISONMENT REQUIRED.

They went inside and were guided to a table by a

young woman with blond hair tied back in a ponytail and wearing a black hip-length blouse, dark jeans, and flat ballerina shoes. They looked over their menus and made their decisions. It was heavy on red meat and root vegetables. Pine also ordered a beer on tap and Blum a gin and tonic.

"Nice place," said Blum, looking around at the full house. "Seems like pretty much everybody who lives here is at the Clink for dinner."

"I imagine quite a few of the tourists come here, too."

They gave their food orders to a gravelly-voiced waitress with stringy gray hair and a tired expression.

As they sipped their drinks, Blum said, "Do you remember much of the town?"

"Not really. This restaurant wasn't here then. And we didn't come into Andersonville very often. But it hasn't changed all that much, at least from what I do remember. I don't think all this Civil War touristy business was really around then, at least not as prominently."

"Well, a town has to do what a town has to do. Little places just trying to survive."

"Little places made up of *people* trying to survive," Pine amended.

Later, as they were nearly finished eating, Cy Tanner came in and looked around. He had an older woman with him. His gaze fell on them and he hurried over to their table with the woman moving slowly in his wake.

Blum greeted him with a smile. "Hello, Cy. Where's Roscoe?"

He grinned at her and doffed his hat. "Hey, Carol. Old Roscoe's outside chewing on a rubber bone and being the unofficial greeter." Then he turned to the woman with him. "This here is Agnes Ridley." He looked at Pine excitedly. "She remembers your family, Agent Pine."

Pine shot the old woman a curious glance. She was in her late seventies with fine white hair through which her pink scalp could be glimpsed. She was small and round with a kind face and wore a flannel shirt, granny jeans, and white, clunky orthopedic sneakers. Her blue eyes contained flecks of gray, behind thick, horn-rimmed glasses.

"Please, sit down, Mrs. Ridley," she said.

Ridley said apologetically, "I don't want to interrupt your meal, dear."

"You're not. Please. We're pretty much done."

They took their seats while Pine continued to look at her.

Ridley stared back at her with an expression of abject wonder, as though she couldn't believe her own eyes. She finally said, "I imagine you don't remember me. And I see you grew into your feet. Both you and your sister were tall."

"I'm trying to recall you, but—"

"Well, you didn't call me 'Mrs. Ridley.' You called me 'Missy Aggie.'"

A look of comprehension came over Pine's features. "I *do* remember that."

"Well, that's so sweet," responded Ridley, obviously pleased. "We lived a few miles away, but here in Sumter County. I met your mother at church. I had no children of my own and I stayed at home, so I quite often babysat you and your sister."

Pine's eyes widened. "Me and Mercy?"

"Yes, dear. Now Atlee is a name I know well. I had an aunt with that name. Course we called you 'Lee.' But I've never known anyone else named Mercy."

"Folks called me 'Lee' until I went to college."

Her face crinkled. "You two were quite the pair. Inseparable. Never could tell you apart."

Blum looked at Pine. "Identical twins then. I never knew that. You never said." She sounded a little disappointed.

"I . . . I've never been very comfortable talking about it." She paused and her expression softened. "My sister had a freckle here," said Pine, pointing to a spot next to her nose. "I didn't. Mercy said God gave her a kiss because she came out first, and it turned into the freckle."

"Well, that's beyond precious," commented Blum.

Pine turned back to Ridley. "So you remember my parents?"

Ridley's smile vanished. "I knew and liked your

mom very much, Lee." She caught herself. "I mean, Atlee."

"'Lee' is just fine, Mrs. Ridley."

"I was older, of course. But we were good friends, me and your mother. Julia worked some to make ends meet and had to go on errands and appointments, and that's why she needed a babysitter. Your dad, I didn't know as well. But he sure loved his little girls."

"How did my mom get to those places? She didn't have a car that I knew of."

"Oh, I'd let her take my old Dodge pickup truck. That's what I would drive over in. She couldn't pay much, and I rarely asked for any money. My husband had a good paying job. We didn't need anything extra." She paused and her face crinkled even more deeply, like a flower reversing to a bud. "My 'payment' was to spend time with you girls."

Blum said, "I wish you'd lived near me. I had six kids, all under the age of twelve at one point. Most days I felt like I'd been hit by a freight train."

"And you remember what happened then?" asked Pine, her gaze on Ridley.

The old woman nodded slowly. "Yes, I do. It hit the whole town hard. Never had anything like that happen here. And thank God we've never had anything like that again."

"What can you tell me about it?" said Pine. "I was still very young and really have a lot of memory gaps. Plus the adults back then didn't talk to me about it."

"Well, I'm sure they were quite worried about how it affected you. Now, I went to the hospital to help your mother. She pretty much never left your side while you were in there."

"I remember waking up and seeing her."

"She was so broken up. Lost one daughter and nearly lost the other. I don't know if you realize how close you came to dying, Lee."

"No, I guess I don't. What about Mercy's disappearance?"

"Well, as you probably know the police were as puzzled as everyone else."

"Sheriff Dalton from Macon County," said Pine. "I didn't remember his name, of course. I looked him up later."

"Yes, well he's dead now, but one of the deputies who worked on the case is now the sheriff over in Macon."

"Which deputy?"

"Dave Bartles. He was one of the first deputies at the house after your mother called 911. I know because Julia called me, too, and I rushed over there. Now he's getting close to retirement."

Blum said, "But we're in Sumter County, like you said. Why would the Macon County police be involved? And why not the police here in town?"

Pine glanced at Blum. "Andersonville doesn't have its own police force. The law enforcement comes from the Sumter County Sheriff's Office. But we lived right across the line in Macon County, so the Macon County Sheriff's Department did the investigating."

Ridley nodded. "And they called in the state police to look at things. And the FBI, too."

"Because it was a kidnapping," said Pine.

"Yes, I guess that's right. Now, Cy told me about you being with the FBI. I . . . I suppose your becoming an agent maybe had something to do with what happened to your sister."

"It did, yes," said Pine. *Maybe more than I thought.*

Ridley drew a long breath and eyed Pine anxiously. "Well, the long and the short of it was the police believed your daddy had done it."

"And I told them it wasn't him," Pine said firmly.

The old woman said, "I knew your father had nothing to do with it. And the fact was they could never prove anything against Tim, and then y'all moved away."

"I don't think we had a choice," said Pine. "My dad got fired from the mine. We couldn't survive here."

"The thing is, Lee, you and your family disappeared in the middle of the night."

"I remember we moved very quickly one night, but you mean they didn't tell anyone?"

"No, they didn't. You were there one day and gone the next. This was only a few months after you got out of the hospital. I went over to check on everybody and the place was empty. Not that y'all had much. But there was really nothing left. A few sticks of furniture. Your parents must've gotten a U-Haul trailer or something. I couldn't believe my eyes. There was no note or anything. Not a word to anyone. Haven't heard from them since."

Pine slowly took this in. "I don't know why they did it that way."

"Now, Cy told me about your daddy being dead. I'm very sorry. Like I said, I didn't know Tim all that well. But I liked him. Now, is Julia still alive?"

Pine said, "I'm . . . I'm not sure."

Ridley looked taken aback by this. "Have you not been in touch with her lately?"

"It's longer ago than that," said Pine vaguely.

"Oh," said Ridley, looking sad. "Well, I'm sorry about that."

"Did your parents not explain things to you when you left here?" interjected Blum, who could see how uncomfortable Pine was looking. "Or at least told you where they were moving to?"

"I remember the new house and then going to school and finding out I was in South Carolina. About fifty miles outside of Columbia."

"Good Lord," said Ridley.

"I was only six. I guess my parents didn't think it mattered to me where we had moved," Pine said, a little defensively. "And we moved several times after that."

"Until they divorced?" said Blum.

"Yes," said Pine curtly. It was clear she did not relish sharing her personal history with two strangers, or even Blum.

They all fell silent at this as Pine felt her face burn and she looked down at the tabletop.

"I suppose you're back here to try to find out what happened?" Ridley finally said.

"I should have done it a long time ago."

Ridley stared at her for a moment. "Lee, have you ever heard the phrase, 'Let sleeping dogs lie'?" she said quietly, glancing at Tanner nervously.

"I have. But in this case, it doesn't apply."

"Why not?"

"Because my sister could still be alive."

"Do you . . . do you really think so?" said Ridley doubtfully. "After all this time?"

"The odds are clearly against it. But my life has been full of beating the odds."

Ridley looked her over. "I guess I can understand that. I mean, you want to know the truth. Whatever it might be."

"I do."

"And what if the truth is your father *did* do it?"

"Then I'll have to accept that. But we're not there yet."

Tanner spoke up. "How do you plan on tackling this sucker?"

"There are standard protocols for investigating cold cases. It starts with looking at the established records and going from there, hoping for some lead or inconsistency that no one has discovered previously."

"So you'll be talking to this fellow, Dave Bartles?" said Tanner.

"Yes."

Pine looked at Ridley, who said, "Lots of folks already know you're back in town."

"From when we checked in at the Cottage?" said Blum.

"Gladys Graham owns the place and she likes her gossip." Ridley smiled knowingly. "Although she doesn't go by Gladys any more. Don't think she much liked that name." She laughed. "Look at me. How many parents name their kids Agnes anymore?"

"What name does she go by?" asked Pine.

"Lauren."

"Is that her middle name?"

"No, I just think she thought it was classy, you know, like that famous clothes guy with the white hair."

"You mean Ralph Lauren?" said Blum.

"That's the one. She had it legally changed and everything. Anyway, we don't need that social media down here. Gladys is like Facebook and Twitter all rolled into one." Ridley put a small, puffy hand on Pine's arm. "Honey, do you really want to dive back into the past?"

Pine stared back fiercely at the old woman. "I don't think I have a choice, if I want to have a future."

7

Pine and Blum were crossing the front parlor of the Cottage when a voice called out.

"I guess you don't remember me."

They both turned to see the woman walking toward them.

She was in her midforties, slim and pretty, with red hair cut close to her head, and an active spring in her step. She had on dark green slacks that contrasted sharply but attractively with her hair, with a thin black leather belt, a white blouse open at the collar, and black pumps.

"I'm Lauren Graham," said the woman, her hand extended to Pine. "I was in high school when you and your family lived here. Sorry I wasn't around when you checked in."

Pine shook her hand. "I'm afraid I *don't* remember you."

"It's no wonder. You were so little."

The two women stared awkwardly at each other across the small space separating them.

Graham said hesitantly, "I guess it must seem sort of surreal being back here."

"Well, it doesn't appear to have changed much."

"In some ways, yes. In other ways, I think it's changed a lot."

Pine took this in and nodded. "I guess every place changes, whether we want it to or not." Pine cleared her throat and said in a more businesslike tone, "Did you come out to the house when we lived there?"

"I used to help your mother with cleaning and doing some shopping. I didn't see you and your sister all that much. It was sporadic, certainly not every week. But I was glad for the work."

"I just saw Agnes Ridley at dinner."

"Yes, that's right. She babysat for you and Mercy."

It was strange for Pine to hear people talk about her sister as though she was somewhere living her life just like everyone else.

"I was surprised to see you back here. When your family left, I never thought you'd come back. Not after that awful night."

"I understand we sort of moved away in the dead of night?" Pine said expectantly.

Graham stared at her for a moment before answering. "I remember it was the talk of the town for a few days. No sign you even lived there. And nobody ever heard from your parents again."

"Agnes Ridley told us the same thing. That must have been a shock," said Pine.

"Look, I don't blame your mom and dad. The things people were saying. It was disgusting. I would have moved, too. Who needs that crap, especially after suffering such a loss."

"They were saying those things because they thought my father was involved somehow?"

"Either that, or they thought he cared more for his beer and pot than he did his kids. But that's not the way I saw it."

"Why's that?"

"They made one mistake, and someone took advantage of it. You can't watch your kids twenty-four/seven. They loved you and your sister very much. Your mom would have died rather than let something happen to her girls."

Pine seemed taken aback by this statement. "I . . . uh, never really talked about it with her. She didn't want to . . . go there, I suppose."

"I guess I can understand that. But I can also understand that you probably had a million questions you wanted answers to."

Pine now looked at Graham in a different and perhaps more favorable light. "I did. Only I never got those answers."

Graham looked down at the FBI shield on Pine's hip. "FBI agent now. Very impressive."

"You could tell from just glancing at the shield?"

"I googled you after you made the reservation. Recognized the last name."

"It's a job I enjoy doing."

"Where are you living now?"

"Arizona."

Graham looked wistful. "Never been there. Hear it's beautiful."

"It is," interjected Blum when it appeared Pine was not going to respond. "Quite different from here. But this part of the country has its own charm."

Pine looked at her and said apologetically, "I'm sorry, where are my manners? This is Carol Blum, she's my assistant."

"Hello, Carol." Graham smiled. "I've never really been anywhere. I went to college at Georgia Southwestern State University. Worked in Atlanta for a while in the hospitality sector, and then came back here."

"Are you married?"

"I was. But no longer." She looked around at the space. "I bought this place and started my little business. It's mostly tourists coming to see the prison, but it pays the bills and lets me get by. I used to have more ambition, but this seems to fit me okay now. Though I would like to travel a bit. And who knows, I might get married again."

"This is a charming house," said Blum, looking around.

"Thank you. I grew up in it."

"What? This was your family's home?" said Blum.

"Me and my four siblings. My parents died years

ago. My brothers and sister didn't want it. Sort of all clicked. I had saved my money, bought them out and took the plunge." Graham turned to Pine. "They never found out what happened to your sister, did they?"

"No."

"So, are you here trying to change that?"

"What do you remember about what happened?"

Graham glanced at Blum. "Would you both like some coffee? I just made a fresh pot. There's a bit of a chill out there. We can talk out on the side porch, where we serve our complimentary breakfast."

Pine and Blum moved to this room and took a minute to look around.

They finally arrived at a glass display cabinet set against one wall. The cabinet was so large that it rose all the way to the ceiling. Inside was a collection of dolls, some quite large, almost lifelike, and some small, all dressed in old-fashioned clothing.

Blum drew closer to look at them. "These are really nice. Vintage. The largest one isn't really a doll. It's like a mannequin. Cost a pretty penny to put this together, I bet."

"I see you've noticed my little collection."

They turned to see Graham standing in the doorway with a tray of coffees and a plate of sugar cookies. They sat at a table and she passed them out.

Graham glanced at the cabinet. "My mother actually started collecting them. When I was little they were like my fantasy friends. I gave them all names and histories and . . . well, they became very real to me." She looked down, seemingly a bit embarrassed.

"Children have very vivid imaginations," said Blum diplomatically, as Pine looked strangely at Graham.

"Yes, well, I've never had any of my own."

Pine glanced at Blum before refocusing on Graham. She seemed nervous but also excited, thought Pine. She imagined there wasn't much that was thrilling in Graham's life, and recollecting a mystery might liven things up.

"About that day," prompted Pine.

Graham began, "I was at school and it was all anyone was talking about. Police sirens and the ambulance taking you to the hospital. Then the Georgia Bureau of Investigation was called in. And even the FBI," she added, once more looking at Pine's shield. "I went over that night to see if I could help with anything. Your father was there, your mom was with you at the big hospital over in Americus." She looked embarrassed. "There was a crowd of people around just gawking. It wasn't right. But I was there to help," she added quickly.

She paused and took a sip of her coffee, shooting glances at Pine and Blum as though to gauge their reactions to her words.

"Did you see my father?" asked Pine in a strained voice that made Blum look at her.

Pine wasn't sure what she was feeling. She had not

prepared well for what this trip might do to her emotionally, when preparation had been key for everything she had done in her life.

So why did I drop the ball this time?

Graham said quietly, "Your father . . . well, Tim had been drinking some. And who could blame him? I mean, after what had happened?"

"And . . . ?"

"And he got into a fight with one of the men. Somebody broke it up, luckily."

"Why weren't the police there?" said Pine. "It was a crime scene. It should have been secured as such. Even my father shouldn't have been there."

Graham regarded Pine from under hooded eyes. "You mean because he was a suspect?"

"Yes. In fact, he was the *only* suspect."

"I think you're right about that. As far as I know, there was never any other." She broke off and stared uncomfortably at Pine.

"I told the police it *wasn't* my father."

"You were only a child, Lee."

"I go by Atlee now."

"All right, Atlee. And you'd been terribly injured. I believe by the time you could tell them anything at least a week had passed. The person had hit you so hard, your skull had fractured." Tears clustered in the woman's eyes.

"So I guess they didn't believe me that it wasn't my dad."

Pine suddenly felt like she had been swallowed whole by something, and that she was now sinking into a horrible muck of her own making.

Blum glanced at Pine and took up the line of questioning. "What else do you remember, Lauren?"

"The FBI was called in when it became apparent that the local and state police couldn't solve it."

"Meaning they didn't have any evidence against Agent Pine's father even though he was their only suspect?"

"We have crime here now," said Graham. "And we had crime back then. But not kidnapping. And no murders. Today, it's either fights among usually drunk or drugged-up men, or people stealing stuff. Now, Julia Pine swore that her husband was passed out on the floor of the living room drunk as could be and that Tim hadn't moved from that spot when she woke up around six on the couch and went to check on you and your sister. And from the number of empty beer bottles and the remains of smoked joints they found between them, I guess that seemed plausible."

"There was never any forensic evidence tying my father to what happened."

"Well, I imagine his prints and DNA were all over the house," said Blum. "Since he lived there it would be hard to exclude him based on that."

"Plus, I saw a man coming through the window," said Pine. "And he was wearing gloves. There would have been no trace really."

Graham nearly spilled the coffee she had picked back up. "You *saw* a man?"

"Yes, that's why I knew it wasn't my father. Why would he come through the window?"

"And you told the police that?"

Pine hesitated. "I believe that I did. But I was just a kid with a cracked skull. I doubt they cared."

"Have you been out to your old house?"

"I have. A man named Cyrus Tanner lives there now. He said he was renting it."

Blum interjected. "He's quite attractive and interesting."

Graham smiled. "Yes he is. And Cy Tanner says lots of things. It doesn't make them all true."

"So he's not renting it?" asked Blum.

"I don't think anyone even knows who owns that place anymore, so I doubt he's sending in payments to anyone."

"Then he's squatting?"

"He's not the only one. The town has lost nearly thirty percent of its population since 2000, not that we had a lot to begin with. Now, the rest of Sumter County is doing better. Wages are up and so are employment and property values. There's more young people. But there are abandoned places, and your old home is one of them."

"I guess I can see that."

"Do you really think you can solve it all these years later?"

"Lots of cold cases get solved," Blum pointed out.

"But most don't," said Graham.

"How do you know that?" asked Pine.

"I'm actually working on a crime novel," answered Graham. "As I mentioned, this place gives me a living but not much more. I'm hoping to break out of that rut by establishing myself as a writer of historical crime fiction."

"So you have more ambition than you let on?" said Blum.

Graham glanced at her lap. "I guess so."

"Let me guess—your story takes place during Civil War times," said Pine.

"Nice deduction. Good historical fiction reeks of atmosphere. And the war is fully settled into every fiber of this town, for good and bad. For me, I hope it's good. The point is, I've done a lot of research into old crime cases. And most remain unsolved."

Pine rose. "Well, mine won't, not for lack of trying anyway. Now if you'll excuse me, it's been a long day."

Pine walked out of the room, leaving Blum and Graham alone.

Graham looked at Blum. "Do you think she can really do this?"

"If she can't, I'm not sure who can."

8

"All grown up now, I see."

It was the next day, and Pine and Blum were seated across from Dave Bartles at the Macon County Sheriff's Office in Oglethorpe, Georgia.

Bartles was in his fifties with iron-gray hair, a solid, fit physique, sharp-edged features, and the look of a man who had seen his share of depravity over his law-enforcement career.

"All grown up," said Pine, her lips set in a firm line.

"FBI agent, I hear."

"That's right."

"I guess I know why you're here."

"I'm sure it was an easy deduction."

"We didn't solve the case back then, and neither did the GBI, or even your own agency."

"You had a suspect."

"Your father."

"Do you still think he did it?"

"We didn't even have enough to charge him. And we could never find a motive. They were both really young, but from all the people we talked to, they were doting parents." He paused. "When they weren't drunk or stoned."

"So is that what you think? He was intoxicated and did what he did because of that?"

"I *did*. At first. But then what did he do with the body? They only had the one old clunker car, and no one saw him driving it that night. We looked all over the property and the woods around. No freshly dug graves. No body turned up in the water. No body turned up anywhere. It's hard to hide a corpse sober. Much less drunk."

"Daniel James Tor was operating in the area right around that time."

Bartles looked at her thoughtfully. "He killed a little girl from Macon, about an hour from here. The FBI finally got the bastard. You think he took your sister?"

"They did investigate his presence in the area, but my sister's abduction did not fit his geometric pattern of activity."

Bartles frowned. "Geometric? What does that mean?"

"Tor was a math prodigy. And he selected his victims based on their locations adhering to mathematical shapes. That's how he was eventually caught. They predicted his next area of activity and had assets there that deployed swiftly."

"So your home's location didn't fit this 'math' pattern?" He looked skeptical.

"No. Over the course of eighteen months in 1988 and 1989, Tor was suspected of abducting and killing four people in the state of Georgia, one each from Albany, Columbus, Atlanta, and the little girl you mentioned from the city of Macon. That formed a rough geometric shape. I called it a diamond. He corrected me and called it a rhombus."

"*He* corrected you?" Bartles said sharply.

"I've been to see Tor three times now at ADX Florence."

"I didn't even know that monster was still alive. They should have executed his ass."

"He's serving enough life sentences that he'll never see the light of day."

"Hang on, if you went to see him you must've thought he did it, even though it didn't fit his *pattern*."

"I suspected he might have been involved because he was in the area at the time."

"I remember after you got out of the hospital, you told us you saw a man come through your bedroom window. You think it was Tor?"

Blum was watching Pine closely.

"I had some hypnotherapy done recently, to bring out repressed memories."

"Did it work?"

"I don't know. The man I saw could have been Tor. But since I knew all about Tor before, and also knew he was in the area at the time . . ."

"You mean that could have influenced your memory, maybe erroneously," said Bartles.

"Right."

"Well, what did Tor say?"

"He's never going to admit to it. And even if he does, he'll never provide corroborating evidence. He has no incentive to. So that's a dead end."

Bartles spread his hands. "Which explains why you're here."

"Can I look at the file?"

"You can. I just don't know what you expect to find three decades later."

"Neither do I. But I can only give it my best shot."

Bartles slowly nodded. "I'll have the file brought up and copied. Just to warn you, there's not much there. It's not that anything is missing. There just wasn't a lot there to begin with."

"I'm surprised you haven't purged the files after all this time."

"Normally we would have. But the case was never solved, Agent Pine. So we held on to it. You just never know, right?"

"Right."

As he was escorting them from his office, Bartles said, "I never imagined you growing up to be an FBI agent."

"Life can be unpredictable."

"I hear you work out in Arizona."

"Did you hear that from the Lauren Graham information network?"

Bartles chuckled. "We *are* friends. Nice gal. You like it out there?"

"Yes, it's very different from here in some ways. In other ways, it's a lot alike."

"People are people," said Blum. "No matter where they are."

"If you find something out, let me know," said Bartles. "We don't have many unsolved cases around here. And I'd like to close that one, if I could."

"Okay."

Pine and Blum started to head to the lobby.

"What was that Tor fellow like?" he asked abruptly.

Pine turned back around. "Take your worst nightmare and multiply it by a hundred."

"So it's that obvious? You can just tell that by being around him?"

"No, you can't. That's what makes it a nightmare. You won't realize he's a monster until it's too late."

9

"Bartles wasn't kidding when he said there wasn't much here," said Blum.

They had spread out copies of the documents, notes, reports, and evidentiary photos on Pine's bed in her room at the Cottage. It was, under any measure, a sorry collection.

She picked up a photo and held it out to Pine. "You and your sister?"

Pine took the photo and nodded. "Our fifth birthday. I have the same one in my wallet. It's the only picture I have of us. My parents didn't have a camera. My mom borrowed a friend's Polaroid and took three pictures. One for each of us and one for herself. She must've given this one to the police so they could search for Mercy."

"You and your sister really were mirror images of each other."

Pine stared at two little girls from what seemed a thousand years ago. All bright eyes and smiles. "We were inseparable. Mercy and Lee Pine. Two people but really one. Only that was a long time ago," she added wistfully. "I think every day about what it would have been like to have my sister around all this time. We were always each other's best friend. I . . . I would like to believe that we would have always been best friends."

Pine thought about what Mercy would be like now. Would they still be identical in appearance, or would the years have carved differences into them? She just hoped that Mercy wasn't dead. But how realistic was that?

"If none of this had happened, you might not be with the FBI," Blum pointed out.

"I'd take that trade-off in a heartbeat."

"I would, too, if I were you," said Blum. She picked up a hospital record with X-rays attached. "Your injuries really were very serious, Agent Pine. You nearly died."

Pine nodded absently. "I remember opening my eyes in the hospital and seeing my mother hovering over me. At first, I thought I was dead, and she was an angel." She glanced at Blum in embarrassment. "Silly thoughts of a little girl."

"I'm sure seeing your mother was very comforting to you," said Blum firmly.

Pine looked over the items on the bed. "Not even the FBI could really find much. No trace. No leads. No motives. No nothing. A complete dead end."

"No one heard or saw anything?"

"You observed how remote it was. It was the same back then, if not more so."

"What did the police do?"

"Other than thinking my father had done it? Not much."

Blum looked at her watch. "It's dinnertime."

"Okay."

"Same place?" asked Blum.

"I suppose. Why, are you hoping to see Cy Tanner again?"

"Don't make me blush, Agent Pine."

"You know, I'm really not hungry. Why don't you go without me."

"Are you sure? I can wait."

"No, I think it'll be better if I'm by myself for a bit."

"I know this is a lot to deal with."

"I've been dealing with it for a long time now. But if you do the same thing over and over again, how can you expect a different result? Which is why I'm here."

"Call me if you need me."

"I will."

After Blum left, Pine slowly gathered up the pieces of the file and put them back into the box the sheriff's office had provided.

She left her room and headed out onto the main street of Andersonville.

The night air again held an autumnal chill and she was glad of her jacket as she walked along the quiet streets. She had few memories of the place. She had been so young when she had left. And that time in her life had been dominated by the abduction of Mercy.

The town's buildings, though old and not in the best shape, seemed not to have changed much. The water tower on metal stilts emblazoned with the name of the town was still there. She passed rustic shops, all with old A-frame roofs and deep front overhangs, and consignment shops with their wares; she glimpsed through a dimly lit window stacked cases of old empty pop bottles in a place selling "antiques." The town reminded her a little of the movie *To Kill a Mockingbird.* A quaint Southern hamlet on the rocks, unsure of its future but still plugging along somehow, trusting that better times were just around the corner.

Then there were the ubiquitous railroad tracks running through the area, which was really the only reason there was a town. The National Prisoner of War Museum and the prison site and the vast, adjacent cemetery dominated the area, and there were numerous signs proclaiming this as an enticement for visitors to take it all in and spend their tourist dollars. She supposed the town had to make the best of the hand it had been dealt. A notorious prison in its midst was ripe for exploitation to bring in needed revenue. At least it could be an important history lesson in the cruelty that human beings could show other human beings.

She stepped over puddles of a recent rain that had laid bare the hard, nonporous red Georgia clay. Tall, thin scrub pines with their shallow roots thrived here, though storms and accompanying high winds would easily shear them off or even pull them from the earth itself.

She sat on a damp bench and stared out into the darkness.

Her mother had confided in Pine years later that she had been in so much pain during the delivery that when it was over, she had named the first daughter to come out Mercy, since it had been a "mercy" of sorts for her that the ordeal was halfway over.

When her oldest daughter had vanished that night, Julia Pine had not said her name out loud for the longest time. In fact, she had only told Pine the origins of her sister's name when Pine had gone off to college.

And then Pine had come home from college one summer to find her mother gone, with only a brief note left behind that really explained nothing. She thought of the moment she had walked into the apartment she shared with her mother and found only a single piece of paper, leaving her to somehow make sense of another grievous loss. Pine smacked her fist against the arm of the bench and had to fight back the compulsion to scream.

Why did you just leave me like that, Mom? Leave me with nothing? First Mercy, then Dad, then you.

Tor had told her on the first visit to the prison that losing Mercy had meant that Pine had a hole in herself that could not be filled. That she would never be able to trust anyone again. That she could never be close to anyone again. That she would die alone feeling the loss of her twin just as strongly as the day it happened.

And maybe he's right about that. But I can still find out what happened to her. Maybe that will close the hole. If only a little.

But what about the disappearance of her mother? How could she fill that void? Unlike Mercy, Pine's mother had left of her own free will. Pine remembered just sitting on the floor stunned, as she held the paper in her hand. And then going around in a fog for days afterward, before collecting herself and doing her best to get on with her life.

She had called the police but Pine was no longer a child, so there had been no question of abandonment. Over the years, she had searched for her mother. When she had joined the FBI she had continued that search, but there had been no trace of the woman. She had vanished so completely, it was like she had never existed at all.

And if I can't figure out this part of my life, I can't do my job as an agent. And Dobbs will be as good as his word. Another incident like with that creep Cliff Rogers and I'm gone from the Bureau. And then what do I do?

In her anxiety, Pine rose and started walking again, until she heard the screams.

Then she automatically started sprinting toward the sound, her gun drawn.

Her long legs carried her quickly to an ill-lighted and empty part of the main street. Pine saw the old woman first. She had dropped her bag, the contents strewn across the darkened street.

"What is it?" cried out Pine, taking her by the arm.

The old lady pointed with a shaky hand at a space in between two darkened buildings.

Pine could just make out what was lying there.

It can't be, she thought. *Please, it can't be.*

10

A woman in her late twenties, pale skin, slender but shapely, with long, light brown hair and unusually sharp facial features.

Unfortunately, each of these details was rendered in death.

Two deputies from Sumter County were next to Pine staring down at the body. They were standing behind a screen that the men had erected to shield the body. One deputy was tall, thin, and in his twenties. By the sickened look on his face, this was his first homicide. His partner was fortyish and hefty, and he didn't look much better.

"Are you two investigating as well?" Pine asked.

The older man shook his head. "Just securing the scene. The Investigative Division does the processing and the rest. GBI will probably be called in, too," he added, referring to the Georgia Bureau of Investigation.

She had already showed them her shield and credentials. The old woman who had been the first to find the body was sitting on a bench, still showing the effects of the discovery in her sobs and shivers. Pine had tried to comfort her, to little avail.

Some onlookers had gathered, but the two deputies had quickly taped off the area and then erected the screen.

"What's the get-up she's in?" said the younger deputy.

Pine had noticed this the moment she had seen the body. "It's a veil. Looks to be a wedding veil."

"Wedding veil? So what the hell does that mean?" asked the older deputy.

It doesn't mean anything good, thought Pine.

As they stepped from behind the screen, a rattling ancient Crown Vic sedan pulled up and a man in his late fifties climbed out. He was around six feet tall, with a portly frame, thinning gray hair, and weighty jowls. His suit was baggy, his shirt wrinkled and his tie askew, but his gaze was firm and active, and he carried himself with a quiet confidence. He walked over and identified himself as Max Wallis, with the GBI. He nodded at the deputies. "I'll be over to see the body in a minute." He looked at Pine. "Did you find the victim?" he asked.

She pointed at the old woman on the bench. "I was second on the scene."

"I'll still want to talk to you," said Wallis.

"She's FBI, sir," said the older deputy.

Wallis looked like someone had slapped him. "Come again?"

Pine held out her shield and official credentials. "I was in town visiting. I used to live here. I heard screams and came running."

Wallis studied the information on her credential card for a few moments, his eyebrows hiking at certain intervals. "Okay, just don't go anywhere."

He walked over to the old woman and sat down next to her. Pine watched as he conversed with her, giving her some Kleenex when she started to sniffle and holding her hand and patting her shoulder supportively at other times.

That was a good technique, thought Pine. It was reassuring and designed to set the person at ease, with, Pine hoped, a clearer account from the woman about what had happened.

Wallis finally rose, walked back over to the deputies, and ordered one of them to drive the woman home. They had already collected the dropped items from her bag.

The younger deputy departed with her while the other stood guard at the scene.

"Was she any help?" asked Pine.

Wallis flipped through his notebook. "Not really. She saw the body and panicked, dropped her bag. But she didn't see or hear anything. She doesn't know the victim, either."

"A town this small, people pretty much know everybody. So she might not be from here."

"The crime scene techs will be here any minute. She may have ID on her."

"Doubtful."

"Why do you say that?"

"No bag or purse. She's been laid out in a posed position. Thought went into this. I don't think the killer would have left ID behind. But if he or she did, it was because they wanted us to know the vic's identity." She looked at her watch. "It's been forty minutes since I arrived at the scene, the old woman was here maybe a couple minutes before that."

"So whoever put her there is long gone."

"It was dark when I arrived here. And this is the far end of the main street. You have some trees just behind."

"You don't think he carried her here in his arms?"

"Transport in a car is much more likely. The shops here are all closed. That's not the case on the other end of the street. And there's better illumination that way too."

"Which shows familiarity with the area," said Wallis.

"It'll be interesting to see the time of death."

"Why?"

"I don't think she was killed here. When I arrived, I looked around the whole area, listened for sounds, the works. Nothing. I think she was killed off-site and then the murderer placed the body here for someone to find."

"You sound like you've done this before."

"I have."

"And you're here just visiting?"

"More or less."

He thought for a moment. "Look, you want to work with me on this?"

"Can I?"

"GBI has a lot of good people and expertise, but this is rural Georgia and assets are stretched. I'm not too proud to ask for expert help when it so conveniently presents itself."

Pine looked at the screen. "All right. But there's one thing you need to know."

"What's that?"

"You'll see it for yourself, but the killer put a wedding veil on the woman."

"A wedding veil?"

"Yes."

"How do you know she didn't put it on her herself?"

"She's in her late twenties wearing expensive jeans, a cashmere sweater, and a suede jacket with low-rise croc-skin boots. No way she's walking around in that outfit with a veil. And it looks to be vintage, a lot older than she is."

Wallis scratched his stubbly cheek. "So that veil must have some meaning for the killer? Something symbolic?"

"This scene was meticulously laid out. So everything

has meaning. It's almost like a little ceremony put together by the killer. Everything just so."

"Okay, so what's your preliminary observation?"

"I'm pretty sure of one thing."

"What?"

"I don't think this will be the last time we see his work."

11

Pine and Wallis stared down at the body.

The forensic processing team and a member of the Sumter County Sheriff's Investigative Division had shown up in a single black van. A minute later a small, thin man dressed in a dark suit arrived. He was the coroner, called in to officially pronounce a death they all knew had already occurred.

As they began their tasks, Blum showed up after getting a text from Pine and being cleared through the secure perimeter.

Pine introduced Blum to Wallis.

"Sorry to interrupt your visit here," said Wallis, eyeing Blum. "I've taken advantage of your boss being here and roped her into helping."

"I doubt much effort was required for that," replied Blum. She looked down at the body. "A wedding veil," she said, glancing at Pine, who nodded.

"Yes."

"Symbolic?"

"I believe so."

Blum took a closer look. "It's old. My mother's

generation. You can tell by the design and the style. World War II–ish."

Wallis gave her an appraising look. "You got a good eye."

"Well, I certainly try to keep both of them open at all times."

Pine squatted down and ran her gaze over the dead woman. Her eyes were open and bulging. There were marks and bruises around her throat.

"Death by compression of the windpipe," said Pine as Wallis nodded. "Asphyxiation."

The coroner had stooped next to the victim on the other side and begun his examination. This included checking out the deceased's eyes and shining a light down her throat, and feeling around the base of her neck.

He said, "I agree with that. Hyoid bone is crushed."

"Petechial hemorrhaging," added Wallis, pointing to the woman's eyes.

The coroner nodded. "Strangulation puts pressure on the blood vessels servicing the eyes and they burst." He looked at the eyes more closely, hitting them with a pen light. "Pupils have contracted, eye fluid has dried, and the irises have altered. This is not a recent death."

Pine touched one limb. "And she seems to be in full rigor. How far along I don't know."

"Let me see if I can firm that up a bit." The coroner made a small incision in the abdomen, inserted a liver temp probe through it, and checked the reading. "Factoring in the ambient temp and air dampness, the size and age of the deceased and her clothing, I'd say she's been dead over twelve hours. That would coincide with the degree of rigor and the condition of her eyes. They'll know better once they get her back and open her up."

"ID?" Wallis asked one of the techs.

"None on her that we can find."

"There's an engagement ring and wedding band," noted Blum, indicating the woman's left hand. "A fairly expensive ring judging by the stone and setting. If it's real, that is."

"Note the posed look of the body," said Pine.

Wallis nodded. "Yeah. She was carefully placed. Hands over her stomach, like she was in a—"

"—coffin," Blum finished for him.

Wallis looked at her strangely. "Exactly."

The coroner moved off to jot some notes down while Pine checked the victim's fingers.

"I don't see anything under her nails, no blood or tissue or hair." She slid up the woman's jacket and sweater sleeves. "No marks here."

"So no defensive wounds or evidence she fought her attacker," noted Wallis.

Pine said, "It had only been dark for about a half hour when I arrived at the scene." She looked between the buildings and to the tree line behind.

"The body couldn't have been lying here for hours," noted Wallis.

"I doubt it was there too long before the woman saw it. And there would be far more insect infestation if she'd been lying out here for hours."

"So we have a bit of a time window to work with."

"If we can compile some suspects we can check alibis. Not just for the murder, but also for the placing of the body here."

Wallis said, "A lot of strangers come through here every year because of the prison tour and other Civil War stuff. Even my wife and I have done it. Had an ancestor die here."

"Union or Confederate?" asked Pine.

"Union. I'm originally from New York. Joined the Army, trained at Fort Benning. Liked the weather down here better. When I got out, I stayed and joined the police force."

"Well, I'm not sure if the killer is a stranger here."

Wallis nodded absently. "So strangulation, body posed, possibly a local or someone familiar with the layout and goings-on of the town."

"When was the last homicide you had here that was out of the ordinary?" asked Pine.

Wallis closed his notebook, put it away, moved out from behind the screen, and crossed under the police tape. Pine and Blum followed. He lit up a cigarette from a pack he pulled from his jacket pocket. "Didn't want to contaminate the crime scene," he explained.

He took a puff of the cigarette. "We had an abduction about thirty years ago, but no murder, at least that we know officially." He stared at Pine pointedly.

She gave him a knowing look. "I thought you seemed to recognize my last name when I introduced myself, and you studied my creds for a longer time than normal."

"I had just started at the GBI after being in uniform. Wasn't really involved in what happened to your sister, but I read up on it because it remained unsolved. And because of something else."

"Daniel James Tor being active in the area at the same time?" said Pine.

Wallis nodded and blew twin trails of smoke from his nostrils. "Among other things." He looked down at his cigarette. "Tried to quit about a hundred times. Maybe I should try that vaping thing before I drop dead from a heart attack or stroke."

"Vapes have nicotine, too," Blum pointed out. "And in my experience that just makes it harder. And it's hard enough as it is," she added in a sympathetic tone.

"No other murders, though?" interjected Pine. "In all that time?"

"No, there have been. But you said out of the ordinary. What we've had down here, it's almost always one guy shooting or bludgeoning or stabbing another guy. Over drugs, cash, or a gal. We haven't had any posed victims wearing old wedding veils, at least that I'm aware of. The killer was pretty straightforward in those other cases. Not like here." He dropped his smoke and tapped it out with the heel of his shoe. "So, no trace, no prints, and no witnesses other than you and the old woman."

"What happens now?" asked Pine.

"Coroner will report his findings to the medical examiner's office. They'll request a postmortem. Because of the circumstances it'll be granted, of course."

"Where will they do it?"

"There's a regional pathology lab in Macon. The body will go there."

"Let me know when they're going to do the post," said Pine. "I'd like to be there."

He gave her a thoughtful look before glancing over at the forensic team coming and going. "The techs don't seem to be finding much."

"I think this perp was careful and knew what to do and what to avoid doing."

"Meaning?"

"It's not his first rodeo."

"So you're really here just visiting?" Wallis said, looking at her pointedly once more.

"Maybe we can have a talk about it later."

He nodded, started to reach for another smoke, and then looked at Blum. "You think cold turkey is the best?"

She smiled encouragingly. "It can be done. I speak

from experience. The first few days will be rough. Chew gum and keep busy."

He nodded and walked back over to the screen.

Blum looked at Pine. "This is an unexpected development."

"I've come to believe that in my life the unexpected is the norm. How was dinner?"

"Not nearly as exciting as this."

"Was the place crowded?"

"Pretty full, yes. Why?"

Pine didn't answer her.

Later, they watched as the body of the woman was placed in a black, zippered bag and carried away on a gurney to a waiting vehicle.

"An engagement ring and wedding band," said Pine.

"Right."

"So where's the husband? Because nine times out of ten they're the killer."

"Makes me comforted I'm single," replied Blum.

"Me too," agreed Pine.

12

Another postmortem in another morgue.

Pine hated them, yet they were an absolutely essential tool for her line of work. But she was also disturbed that she had grown so desensitized to the carving up of another human being that she could watch it happen without really feeling anything at all except professional curiosity.

I can't let it get personal because then I can't do my job. But how do I remain human in the process?

It was the next day, and the body of the dead woman lay on the metal exam table. The examiner was a woman in her fifties with a no-nonsense look to her. She was big boned and broad shouldered, but with a delicate touch as she had spent the last two hours slicing and dicing the victim, while Pine and Wallis had watched.

The light overhead was powerful and invasive. A microphone was suspended on a cord from the ceiling for the medical examiner to record her findings as she had progressed through the autopsy. Pine had hung on every word.

The organs had been removed, examined, weighed, and measured, and then replaced neatly in the chest cavity. The scalp had been pulled down and the skull Stryker-sawed open; the brain was taken out and the same exam was done to it. The familiar sutured Y-incision in the chest caused the deceased to look like something out of a horror film. And there was horror in all of it, as her life had been violently taken away.

Now Pine stood next to Wallis, who had on a suit that was just as baggy as the one from the night before. But his shirt wasn't as wrinkled, and his tie was straighter.

"Anything jump out?" he asked.

"Death by asphyxiation, clearly," said the ME.

"Any defensive wounds, trace under the nails?" asked Pine. "I did a cursory exam at the crime scene but found none."

The ME shook her head. "I struck out on that, too." She looked down at the body. "I did find some things of interest."

"Like what?" asked Wallis.

"Like she's had at least one child." She pointed to the woman's face. "And she's had work done here and here. Cheeks lifted, nose narrowed, jaw line reconfigured." She pointed to the woman's groin. "Vaginal tearing there."

"Was she raped?" asked Wallis.

"It's not recent. No signs of sexual assault." She

pointed to the woman's large breasts. "She's also had breast implants. Help me turn her."

They did so, and she pointed at the woman's buttocks. "Implants here too. And anal tearing, again healed up like the vagina."

"Conclusion?" asked Wallis.

"Most likely a prostitute," replied Pine.

"Bingo," agreed the ME.

"Unfortunately, they're often the victims of homicide. It's a high-risk business."

Next, Pine pointed to some odd-looking marks on the woman's hamstrings and buttocks.

"Round shapes," observed Pine.

"They could be the impressions of something she was lying on," noted Wallis.

Pine nodded. "Maybe something in a car trunk? When her body was being transported?"

"Maybe."

"Lividity is fixed now, so the marks won't really go away," said the ME.

"We'll need photos of them," said Pine.

"Already done."

They laid her back down.

The ME pointed to tracks on the woman's arms. "She's a regular drug user. I could tell that in several ways, but these are the clearest indicators. I'm pretty sure the blood work will show elements of whatever she was using."

Pine looked at the woman's teeth. "They're stained. Coke, meth, heroin can all do that."

"She's worn her teeth down, too," noted Wallis. "Addicts grind. And drug use reduces saliva in the mouth."

The ME nodded. "And check her septum. It's basically dissolving."

Pine looked at it and said, "Lady snorted coke."

The ME placed the sheet back over the deceased.

Pine said, "So prostitute with a drug addiction gets strangled and placed in a posed position with a wedding veil."

"The veil is circa 1940s," said the ME. "I did some online research."

"Your assistant was spot-on with that one," said Wallis to Pine. "Where is Ms. Blum?"

"Working another angle," said Pine.

"I thought she might be squeamish about the autopsy."

"She's pretty tough. How about the engagement ring?"

Wallis said, "It looked expensive, but wasn't. Cubic zirconia."

"So the killer might have placed it on her finger along with the wedding band," said Pine.

"You think?" replied Wallis.

"Well, there certainly are exceptions, but I don't know many women who would knowingly wear a fake engagement ring."

The ME gave her a knowing smile.

"Any luck identifying her?" asked Pine.

"We're running her DNA and prints through the usual databases. No hits so far."

"How about facial recognition databases?"

"I can do that," the ME said, looking over at Wallis, who nodded.

"She might be in a missing persons bank," noted Pine.

"She might be."

"Any known prostitutes gone missing lately, or brothels around here that are missing somebody?"

Wallis said, "Prostitution is illegal in Georgia."

"Prostitution is illegal in a lot of places, but it still happens," retorted Pine.

"I'll check."

Pine looked more closely at the woman's face. "I know you said she's had work done, but some of her features, they seem more Eastern European to me."

Wallis said, "We'll get her picture out to the public and see if we get any bites."

He and Pine left the room together and walked down the hall.

"If the woman was a prostitute she could have been abducted by a john, killed, and then her body placed where it was found," said Wallis. "It happens."

"She could have been unconscious, maybe from a drug overdose, when she was strangled. That would explain no defensive wounds or trace under her nails."

"Our first priority is identifying her and then tracing her movements."

"Can we get the DMV records of all the men in Andersonville?"

Wallis shot her a glance. "Why? We don't have an eyewitness."

"Carol was at the Clink last night for dinner, probably shortly before the body was placed where it was. She said it was pretty full. If she can ID who was there based on their DMV photos, we can start eliminating possible suspects."

"Come on, you think she'll remember the faces?"

"If it were most people, I wouldn't even bother. But like she said before, she keeps her eyes open. And it's worth a shot unless you have a better idea."

"No, I don't. So you think it might be a local man?"

"I don't know. But if it is I'm betting at least some of them were at the restaurant."

"Okay, I'll get that in the works for her to look at." He paused and slipped a cigarette from a pack and put it unlit into his mouth. Off her look he said, "I'm taking baby steps."

She nodded. "You've been on WebMD, I take it."

"A blessing and a curse. I think I have about six other diseases, all of which are fatal. You said this wasn't the guy's first rodeo?"

"I can't be sure of that, obviously. They all have to start somewhere. But this had an element of sophistication that you don't typically get right from the commencement of a career in serial murder."

Wallis looked askance at her. "Jeez, you make it sound like just another job."

"It's much more than that for the people who commit these types of crimes. They can't stop themselves. It's an obsession. It's the only reason they exist. To satisfy that need."

"I guess Daniel Tor is like that?"

"Yes he is. His brain is different from yours and mine."

"And you said you think the person will strike again?"

"Unless this was a one-off, I think we're going to see his handiwork again. The posing and veil meant something to the killer. I think he has more to say on the subject."

"Any idea as to the future targets?"

"I have some theories, but nothing solid. It's a pretty wide-open space right now."

"I know the vic might not be local, but should we alert people around here?"

"I would say yes. But don't panic them. They can take some pretty basic precautions. Don't go out alone. Avoid areas that are isolated. Keep their doors locked and their eyes open."

Wallis nodded. "What's your next step?"

"We're checking with Quantico to see if they've

ever documented this type of serial murderer signature before. That's actually what Carol is doing."

"Like a bomb signature that terrorists use?"

"Yes, like that. Once they get a method down, bombmakers don't like to deviate because that could get them blown up. With serial murderers, they have their symbolism, but they also don't want to get caught. I'll let you know what I find out."

"Thanks. You heading back?"

"I am. While I agreed to help you on this case, there is another reason I'm here."

"Your sister's case?"

"That's right."

"Well, good luck on that."

"I'm going to need a lot more than luck."

13

"Back again?"

Cy Tanner watched as Pine climbed out of her truck and approached the house. He was dressed similarly as he had been before, though he had on a T-shirt with an image of the Doobie Brothers silk-screened on it.

"I am. Where's Roscoe?"

"Probably in the house peeing. Where's your partner?"

"Running some things down. Do you mind if I look around my old room again?"

"Help yourself. I've got an engine I'm rebuilding in my little workshop out back. Nearly done and that sucker will pay my living expenses for the next four months if I'm frugal, which I am." He looked around at the ramshackle house and chuckled. "But I guess you can see that for yourself."

"I once helped a mentor of mine at the FBI completely rebuild a 1967 Ford Mustang."

Tanner gave a lopsided grin. "Damn, what color?"

"Classic turquoise with the parchment convertible top."

"Now if that ain't my dream car it's damn close to it."

"Rides as pretty as it looks."

"I bet. Well, I'll let you get on with it. Just don't step in Roscoe's little surprises."

He headed to the backyard and Pine went inside. She found Roscoe not peeing, but sound asleep in the bean bag chair. She didn't wake him but just headed up the stairs.

Pine opened the door of her old bedroom, walked over to the window, and looked out. A ladder had been necessary to reach this spot. Too high to climb and no handholds on the plank siding to help someone attempting it. But a ladder was hard to hide or get rid of. And the presence of a ladder should have made marks in the dirt. She knew from the report that the police had looked at that element and found nothing.

So, to take one from Sherlock Holmes, the way I said it is impossible, so in some way I must have said it wrong.

She once more turned her mind to 1989. In her head the bedroom was now full of furniture. She went through the inventory again. Bed, chest of drawers with swivel mirror atop it. A small table and two chairs, with Winnie the Pooh and Tigger painted on them, where she and Mercy would have their imaginary tea parties. An old hat rack and a pine chest at the end of their bed where they kept their toys for the most part.

She walked around the room, pacing the small footprint over and over as time moved on. She finally stopped and rewound the images in her memory.

Something had just occurred to her that never had before.

A chest of drawers topped by a mirror on a swivel.

It had been placed right next to the window.

Right next to the window.

She closed her eyes and willed herself to try to remember that night so long ago.

She and Mercy had been sleeping in the one bed. The bed had been facing the window. It was open that night, she remembered, because it had been so hot that day. The house had no air-conditioning and their mother wanted her girls to catch the night breezes.

A sound had awoken Pine. She was a lighter sleeper than her ten-minute-older sister.

She scrunched her eyes tighter.

Come on, remember. The guy came through the window. You saw him. He took up all the space there. You have to remember.

She superimposed Daniel James Tor into that scene. It was him. It had to be him.

But then her thoughts took a jolt.

Could it possibly be? This had nothing to do with who the intruder was. It was all about *how* he had come into the house.

She looked at the door leading into the room.

Had it not been a man coming through the window, but the *reflection* of the intruder in the mirror right next to the window? Which meant he had actually come into their room through the *door* and not the window. That would explain the absence of any traces of a ladder.

That also meant the person had come through the house, and gone past her parents, who had been downstairs. Or was there another explanation?

She closed her eyes and felt sick to her stomach. *It couldn't have been my father who had done it. It couldn't have been.*

But that meant that the person who had taken Mercy, and nearly killed her, was most likely someone who knew her parents. Maybe someone who was smoking weed and drinking beer with them that night?

She leaned back against the wall as she heard footsteps on the stairs. A moment later Tanner appeared in the doorway.

"Just came to check on Roscoe and thought I'd see if you needed anything." He looked around the empty room. "Figure out anything yet?"

"Yeah, I might have."

"Well, that's good."

"Maybe. The only thing is: What do I do next to follow it up?"

"I guess solving cases like this ain't easy."

"None of it," she said. "Not a damn thing."

"You're not thinking of giving up though, right?"

"If you really knew me, you'd never have to ask that."

However, as Pine left the room, her words seemed surer than she actually felt.

On the short drive back to Andersonville proper, the thoughts were swirling rapidly through Pine's mind. They were filled with both cautious hope and logistical tangles. The basic problem was, how many of the people that her parents had known while they lived here were still in the area? She thought she might have a ready answer for this, though. Agnes Ridley and Lauren Graham were both still here, but she regarded neither as a viable suspect. However, either or both of the women should be able to help her with whoever was still around Andersonville who had known her parents.

She called Blum and told her what she had possibly discovered. She arranged to meet her at the Cottage. Blum was going to find Graham so they could talk to her. After that, they would go to see Ridley.

Pine took a long, hopeful breath. After all these years, she had a possibility. *Which means I have a chance.*

14

"I'd have to think about that," said Graham after Pine had asked her question. They were once more in the breakfast room at the Cottage. Graham was sitting across from Pine and Blum at one of the tables. She had on a light blue skirt, black sweater, and ankle boots. Her hair and makeup were perfect, if overly managed, thought Pine. But then what did she know about such things, really? She used mascara maybe twice a year and lipstick the same.

"I'd appreciate it," said Pine. "I have a vague memory of some visitors and friends. I was going to ask Agnes Ridley as well."

"Can I ask why you want to find these people?"

Blum glanced at Pine, who said, "Just standard protocol in an investigation like this. You never know who might have seen or heard something. It might seem unimportant to them, but it could be significant to my investigation."

Graham nodded but didn't look wholly convinced by this answer. "What about the poor woman who was found dead?"

"What about her?"

"Does anyone know who she is?"

"Not yet. We're working on it."

"*You're* working on it?" said Graham in surprise.

"They asked for my help and I agreed to give it."

"So, no names off the top of your head of people who still live around here who might have known the Pines?" asked Blum.

"There is one," said Graham after a few moments of thought. "Jackson Lineberry."

"Name doesn't ring a bell," said Pine.

"He was more your dad's friend, I believe."

"Where does he live?"

"About an hour from here. Due north towards Atlanta. He has a beautiful home, well, an estate really. Probably the nicest in the area. He's very wealthy. Has his own jet."

"What does he do to make that kind of money?" asked Pine.

"Investments. He moved away for a while and then came back."

They got his address and contact information from her. Pine thanked Graham and asked her to let them know if she thought of anyone else. The woman promised that she would.

They climbed into the rental and headed out after Pine called Lineberry and set up an appointment.

"What did you learn from your search?" Pine asked Blum.

"I accessed the ViCAP database through the secure link like you asked me to," she said, referring to the FBI's Violent Criminal Apprehension Program. "I fed in the details that we know currently. There have been other serial killers that have dressed their victims in particular clothing, but nothing that quite matches what we have."

"Hopefully, we get an ID on the victim soon. That could give us some leads."

Blum looked out the truck window as they drove north toward Lineberry's home.

"So you really think that you actually saw the man's reflection in the mirror and *not* him coming through the window?"

"I can't be certain, but I think it's more likely than not."

"But it was so long ago, and you were so young."

"That memory was seared into me, Carol."

"But for all these years you had thought he had come in through the window," said Blum.

"I know," conceded Pine. "I think it was triggered by my being in the room again. I should have come back here a long time ago. I don't know why I didn't."

"It was terrible what happened here. Most people would not want to revisit it."

"I'm not most people. I'm an FBI agent. I run toward the problem, not away."

"But still."

They drove along in silence for a few moments.

"Why Andersonville?" she asked.

Pine glanced at her. "Why not Andersonville? Serial killers have struck in rural areas before. They're not restricted to urban or suburban locations."

"Well, it's easier to evade capture with lots of people around."

"But there are a lot more law-enforcement resources in the metro areas. If I'm a serial killer, do I want to go up against the NYPD with all it can do and cameras everywhere, or come to a place like this that doesn't have those assets?"

"I see your point, but there's something else that's worrying me."

"What?"

"Was it a coincidence, or cause and effect?"

Pine gave her a sharp look. "What are you talking about?"

"Was it a coincidence that a dead body turned up the day after you arrived in town? Or did it happen *because* you came back to Andersonville?" Blum looked worriedly at Pine.

"You're saying my coming here to investigate my sister's disappearance may have triggered what happened to that woman?"

"I'm only saying it's a possibility. But otherwise, it seems a strange coincidence."

Pine slowly shook her head. "That would require a lot of planning in a very short period of time, including selecting a victim and committing the murder."

"I guess that is unrealistic," conceded Blum, with a sense of relief.

Pine glanced at her again. "And are you also thinking that maybe whoever took my sister killed that woman?"

"Well, I admit it did cross my mind."

Pine shook her head. "No way."

"So you *don't* believe this murder and your sister's disappearance are connected?"

"It's been thirty years. Serial killers almost never operate that long. Most retire in their forties if not before."

"Most, not all. And some take a hiatus before becoming active again."

"Thirty years would be an extraordinarily long hiatus."

"But not impossible."

"Let's listen to what Lineberry has to say before we run off in other directions."

"All right."

After a while, Blum said, "How does it feel being back?"

"So far, it sucks."

15

"She wasn't kidding about this guy being in the money," exclaimed Blum.

"It's like something you might see in Bel Air, or Montecito, California."

The property was gated and made mostly of stone, and it looked to be about the size of a shopping mall but with far greater sophistication in the materials and design.

Pine pulled up to the gate and rolled down the window. There was a video screen there, and she identified herself and held up her creds.

The massive gate opened and they drove on.

Reaching the front of the house, they climbed out and were immediately met by two men in dark suits.

"Are you armed?" one asked. He was tall and lanky and around forty.

"Of course I am," said Pine.

"You'll need to turn over your weapons then."

"That won't be happening."

The other man was physically a carbon copy of the

other, though a few years older. He said, "Then you're not allowed in the house."

"Fine, he can come out here and talk to me."

"Mr. Lineberry doesn't come outside to talk to people," the first man barked.

"Jerry, Tyler, it's okay, they can come in, guns and all. This is an old friend."

They all turned to see the tall, elegant white-haired man standing in the open front doorway. He was dressed in neatly pressed dark slacks, an open-collared white shirt, and ostrich-skin loafers.

The man named Jerry looked at Pine and said, "You heard the man, let's go."

When he reached out to put a hand on her shoulder to hurry her along, Pine stepped away and said, "Don't do that."

"You think you're special?"

"No, I just don't like to be screwed with when it's not necessary."

"Sometimes you don't have a choice," he retorted.

"Well, you're never going to make that choice for me, *Jerry*. Now suck up your hurt feelings and lead the way. Don't worry, I've got your back."

Jerry's face turned red and his expression angry, but he whirled around and marched up to the front door. Blum and Pine followed.

Blum whispered to her, "Have I ever told you how much I admire your style?"

Lineberry greeted them warmly and dismissed

Jerry. He led them down a broad, elegantly outfitted hallway with marble flooring, to a large room laid out as an office that was teeming with luxurious touches. These included an enormous antique partners desk with three computer screens topping it, plush seating, and a theater-sized TV screen on the wall. There was also a bookcase made of solid pine with gilded edges, along with oil paintings and a full bar complete with high-backed stools.

He motioned them to a leather couch and asked if they wanted anything to drink. Both asked for coffee. Lineberry hit some buttons on an electronic screen on the wall, before sitting down across from them.

"It'll be in shortly," he said. He smiled warmly at Pine. "You could have literally knocked me over with a stick when you called. Lee Pine. I never imagined I would see you again. Always knew you would be tall. Julia was about six feet, nearly as tall as me."

"I was told that you knew my parents pretty well."

"Yes, though I knew your father better. Tim and I worked at the mine together."

"*You* worked in the mine?" said Blum. "I somehow can't picture you with a hardhat and pickaxe."

He grinned at her. "You don't go down into the earth for bauxite like you do coal. It's a surface-mined ore. You scrape it off, or sometimes you'll use explosives to get at slightly deeper deposits. Tim drove some of the heavy equipment needed to get it out. I was management, worked in the office. But we became friends. We went to the same church."

Pine said, "I heard you were into investments. Funny transition from bauxite mining."

"I became a day trader to make some extra money, and got so good at it that I started my own investment fund. Now my firm, Jackson Lineberry and Associates, manages billions of dollars of other people's money, along with my own. We've done very well over the years, and that accords me this sort of lifestyle."

"I thought all those investment fund guys were in New York or California," said Pine.

"With available technology, you can work from anywhere these days. I'm less than an hour out of Atlanta. I go there for culture, restaurants, and I keep my jet there, although if need be I have a runway on this property that I can use."

"What kind of jet?" asked Blum.

"Bombardier 7500. It can fly from here to Moscow on a tank of gas."

"Would you ever fly it to Moscow?" asked Pine.

Lineberry grinned. "Can't think of one reason why I would. I'm literally just repeating what the account exec told me about the aircraft."

The door opened, and a woman in a maid's uniform walked in carrying a tray. She set the coffees, spoons, creamer, and sugars out for them on the table in front of the couch and departed.

Pine and Blum took theirs black while Lineberry liberally doctored his with cream and sugar. While he did so, Pine studied the man. He was handsome, with features that one might see on an older actor or fashion model. Yet there was something about the man that seemed familiar. Then again, she had known him all those years ago.

"So, getting back to why you're here," said Lineberry.

"My sister, Mercy."

His expression turned somber. "It was beyond awful. They never found her, did they?"

"No, they didn't. You know they suspected my father?"

Lineberry dismissed this comment with a wave of his hand. "Tim had no more to do with what happened than I did. He was devastated. It ruined his marriage." Lineberry blanched. "I'm sorry. That was uncalled for."

"No, I knew firsthand what it did to their marriage. You feel it was because they both felt guilt over what happened?"

Lineberry appeared uncomfortable with the question. "Yes."

"We moved away from here *before* my parents split up, so how did you know that happened?"

Lineberry took a sip of his coffee and then cradled the cup in his hands. "I kept in touch with your father."

"I was recently told that my parents moved out of Andersonville in the middle of the night. That no one knew where we had gone."

"Yes, well, that was true. We all wondered what had happened. But your father got in touch with me some years later."

"Why?"

"I think he knew I had been looking for him, wondering what had happened."

"I lived with my mother after they split up."

"Tim told me he thought it would be best that way, and, quite frankly, you wanted to live with your mother, Lee."

"So you know what happened to him then?"

"He shot himself on your birthday. You had just turned nineteen."

"How did you know those details?" she said suspiciously.

Lineberry hesitated and then said quietly, "I was the one who discovered his body."

Pine just sat there stunned for a long moment, while Lineberry watched her closely.

"I thought your mother might have told you."

"She didn't."

"Your father was my friend. I'd always thought he'd gotten a raw deal. It wasn't enough that he lost one daughter, but he was also suspected in her disappearance. He blamed himself for being . . . drunk that night."

"My mother was drunk, too."

"But your dad was old-school. It was the man's job to protect his family."

"So you found his body why?"

"After he contacted me, I decided to offer him a job. Your dad was a smart guy. I knew he could do a lot more than drive a bulldozer around. So I offered him a job, and we had arranged to meet to finalize details. He didn't show up for the meeting. I called and got no answer. This was before smart phones and everybody in the world having email. So I went to where he was staying." Lineberry paused and looked down. "And I found him . . . dead."

"In a crummy motel in Louisiana."

Surprisingly, Lineberry shook his head. "No, it was at his apartment in Virginia. He'd moved there to work. Some sales job, he told me."

Pine was so rocked by this that she stood and paced the room while Blum and Lineberry nervously watched. "That's not what my mother told me." She made her hands into fists and looked like she wanted to punch the wall. "She wouldn't let me go with her to see my dad. She went there and then had him cremated."

"You didn't want to see your father like that, Lee. Trust me. I had to preliminarily identify the body and it was . . . difficult. The shotgun had—"

"I don't like being lied to."

"I'm sure your mother thought it was the right thing to do," said Lineberry.

Pine sat down and said brusquely, "Did you see my mother when she came down?"

"No. I must have left town by then." He shook his head sadly. "She had lost so much, and even though they were no longer together, I know that they still cared for each other. And, of course, that would mean that you had lost your father, too."

She said slowly, "He would come to visit from time to time. Nothing regular and he never stayed long . . . but I always wanted to see him. To see him *more*."

"Of course, Lee. Of course you wanted to see him. Families are special."

"Do you have a family?" asked Blum.

"No, I never took the plunge. And before I knew it, I was in my sixties."

"Never too late to say, 'I do,'" said Blum.

"I think it is for me."

"I came back home to find out what happened to my sister," said Pine, drawing both of their attention back to her.

Lineberry nodded slowly and put his cup aside. "I thought it must be something like that." He looked at the shield on her hip. "FBI agent? I guess if I were a psychologist, I could make something out of your decision to go into law enforcement."

"It wouldn't take much expertise to figure that one out," noted Pine.

"How can I help you in your task?"

"You knew my parents. Can you tell me the names of some of their other friends in Andersonville?"

Lineberry sat back. "Can I ask why you want to know?"

"You believed my father had nothing to do with what happened to my sister."

"Correct."

"Well, somebody took her. I want to find out who that was."

Lineberry's jaw slackened. "You . . . you think it might have been someone who knew the family? I always assumed it was some stranger."

"Stranger snatches do happen, but it's far more likely to be someone familiar with the family."

"I can't believe that. I mean, it was such a small community."

Blum said, "The thing is, sometimes you think you know someone, but you really don't."

"Meaning we all have our dark sides?"

"And some people's 'sides' are darker than others."

Lineberry looked at them a bit warily now. "Well, *I* was a friend, so I guess that makes me a suspect."

Pine shook her head. "I'm not saying anyone's a target; this is just one line of inquiry. Even if it was a stranger, someone who was around my parents and the house might remember someone watching the place or some other information that might be helpful."

"Well, have you talked to your mother? She would certainly know those sorts of things."

"I haven't talked to her, nor is it likely that I will."

"Can you tell me why that is?"

"Let's just say that it was because of her choice, not mine."

Lineberry took this in and said, "Okay, that's your business. I won't pry any further."

"Thank you. I appreciate that."

"So, friends. I can't imagine there are many left in the area."

"Just any you can recall. I'll take it from there."

"Leave me your contact information and I'll get back to you."

"Thanks."

As they were leaving, Lineberry said, "What if the truth turns out to be worse than not knowing?"

"I'm not sure that can ever be the case. But if it is, I'll just have to deal with it."

"I don't envy your position."

"Frankly, neither do I."

16

Pine got out of the shower the next morning and stood in front of the bathroom mirror while she dried her hair. On her sculpted delts were tats of Gemini and Mercury. And tatted down both her forearms were the words, "No Mercy."

The forearm tats had double meanings to her, neither so esoteric. She had no Mercy in her life because Mercy had been taken from her. And compared to what had happened to her sister, Pine's life was a breeze. So she couldn't grant herself a break for anything. It was always pedal to the metal, take no prisoners, and don't complain when someone kicked your ass.

No mercy for me.

The delt tats were similarly obvious: Gemini, the god of twins. And the planet Mercury, ascendant for twins.

She put her hands on the sink and stared at her reflection.

I guess I do wear it on my sleeve. And my shoulders. And

I guess I am that obvious. And I guess I don't care what people think at this point.

She fingered the St. Christopher's medal that she wore around her neck. It had been a present from her mother. Her last present from the woman, as it turned out. More than once she had attempted to chuck it into the trash. But something always stayed her hand.

Maybe one day it will bring me good luck. Maybe one day it will lead me to her.

Pine slowly dressed and thought about what she had learned since she'd been here.

It wasn't much. The intruder perhaps coming through the house was by far the biggest breakthrough, but only if it turned out to be true. And all these years later would she ever be able to really conclusively prove that one way or another?

She looked out her front window onto the street. She vaguely recalled her parents taking her and her sister to the cemetery here, where white grave markers seemed to go on and on without end. For her they just meant there were dead people everywhere, and that had scared her and Mercy.

She closed her eyes and leaned back against the wall. She well knew how nearly impossible it would be that Mercy was still alive. The best, the absolute best, she could reasonably hope for was a lead that would take her to her twin's grave. There would only be bones there now, like there were at the prison cemetery. Her twin would just be a skeleton now.

I would take bones. I would take finding her remains. I just want to know . . . what happened.

The small, familiar hand in hers, the face, like a reflection in a mirror, looking back at her. There was comfort, reassurance there. She thought she would have it forever. She had had Mercy in her life for only six years. In a real sense, Pine had been alone ever since. She had never felt that comfort or reassurance again. That sort of connection perhaps came only once in a lifetime.

And maybe that's why I find it so hard to connect with anyone else.

As she was finishing dressing, her phone buzzed. It was a text from Jackson Lineberry. He knew of only two other family friends in the area.

Myron and Britta Pringle. They were in their fifties, around the same age as Pine's parents. She didn't really remember the names, but she hoped visiting them would provide her some lead to go on.

She met Blum for breakfast downstairs in the screened-in porch. Over coffee and croissants, Pine told her about the message from Lineberry.

"And you don't remember these Pringle people?" asked Blum.

Pine shook her head. "Not at the moment." She paused and added a little bitterly, "I don't seem to remember much, do I? It's ridiculous, actually."

Blum put down her cup and placed her hand over Pine's. "Do you realize the trauma that you suffered in this town at the age of six? My God, it's a wonder you can function at all, Agent Pine. You need to stop being so hard on yourself."

Pine would not look at her. Something had gripped her gut and wouldn't let go. "I can't do that, Carol. I don't deserve for things to be easy."

"When have things ever been easy for you? You obviously didn't grow up with a silver spoon in your mouth. You were nearly murdered as a child. Your dad killed himself on your birthday. You're estranged from your mother. And you lost your twin. And fewer than one in four special agents at the Bureau are women. So you sure as hell bucked those odds. And you didn't do it by luck. You worked your butt off."

"Any luck with Jack?" asked Graham as she walked in with plates of eggs, grits, biscuits, and bacon and put them down in front of the women. She had on dark slacks, a white blouse, and a colorful bandanna in her hair. Her makeup was immaculate and her eyes alert. Maybe too alert, thought Pine.

"Good first meeting," said Pine as Blum looked curiously at the grits.

Pine noted this and said, "They're grits, Carol. Sort of like *gritty* porridge but with lots of salt and butter."

"If you say so," replied Blum, focusing her attention on the eggs and bacon.

Graham hovered next to the table. "Jack has done really well for himself."

“For certain,” said Pine, who was only poking at her meal.

“Not hungry?” observed Graham.

“Hungry for answers more than food. Lineberry did contact me with the names of two other people who lived here back then.”

“Who?”

“Myron and Britta Pringle.”

Graham’s face fell. “The Pringles, of course. I hadn’t thought of them.”

“Did you not know them well when they lived here?”

“Not well, no. I had pretty much forgotten about them.”

“Not so memorable?” asked Blum.

“No, it’s not that. In some ways they were very memorable. Especially the husband, Myron. But a lot of years have gone by.”

Pine exchanged a glance with Blum. Pine said, “Lineberry gave me their address. He didn’t have their phone number or email, which seemed odd.”

“Well, I guess you could just drive over there and see what happens.”

“What can you tell me about them when they lived here?”

Graham pulled up a chair and sat down. “The first term that comes to mind is *odd*. Myron Pringle was some sort of, oh, I don’t know, genius. Maybe now you would say he's on the spectrum, if they even use that phrase anymore."

"What did he do for a living?" asked Pine.

"Back then, he worked at the mine. In the office."

"And his wife?"

"Britta wasn't nearly as odd as Myron, as I recall. They had kids, a boy and a girl, but I don't really remember them. I was older. They would be closer to your age. Britta was nice enough, but they didn't come into town much. If she worked, I don't recall where. Most women in Andersonville back then were either stay-at-homes or else they had part-time work."

"If their kids were my age, I suppose we would have played with them. I vaguely recall some kids coming over from time to time."

"Well, it's not surprising you don't really remember. You were so little. But they lived the closest to you. It was that little green-and-white house on the road to your place. Last house you see before you got to where you lived. It was still a hike between the houses. Over a mile or so."

Pine thought back, but there were no firm memories of either the house or the Pringle family.

Blum said, "Well, I guess we'll find out when we see them."

They finished their meal and about a half hour later climbed into the rental and set off.

"Hoping for a big breakthrough with the Pringles?" asked Blum.

"These cases are almost never solved that way. It's baby steps all the way. But if a big breakthrough comes our way, I won't say no to it."

17

"Okay, if I were going to shoot a horror slasher film, I think I just found the perfect location," said Blum.

They had turned down a gravel road that turned and twisted along, the whole path darkened by the overhang of old oaks draped in Spanish moss that created the sensation of being in a tunnel. The sunlight was mostly blocked out. They were back in Macon County, about a forty-five-minute drive from Andersonville.

"I guess this is why Graham didn't know they were back. This is pretty far from town. I doubt they ever come to Andersonville at all."

"You really don't remember anything about them?" asked Blum.

Pine shook her head. "But we're about to find out."

The oak tunnel ended but the sun was still obscured by a grouping of other trees clustered around the house that had been revealed when they passed a final curve.

"Well, I never would have guessed this is what we

would have found back here," said Blum. "I was thinking it would be more like the House of Usher."

The home was large, new, and contemporary in design, with lots of metal and glass.

"Looks like something you'd see a tech mogul build in Palo Alto," commented Pine as she slowed the SUV and then pulled to a stop in front of the house.

They got out and looked around.

"See anyone?" asked Blum.

"No. No cars, either, but the garage might be around back."

"Can I help you?" said a voice.

They turned to look around for the person.

"Can I help you?" said the voice again.

The sound seemed to be coming from the front door.

"They must have one of those video security systems," said Pine. They stepped up to the front door and Pine held up her badge. "I'm FBI Special Agent Atlee Pine. Jack Lineberry gave me your address. I think you knew my parents, Tim and Julia Pine?"

The voice said nothing back. Pine looked at Blum. "Did I say something wrong?"

The front door opened and an attractive woman in her fifties stepped out. She was of medium height with dyed blond hair cut short, accentuating her long neck. She was fit and trim and stylishly dressed in black slacks, shoes with a chunky heel, and a pale blue blouse with a light sweater over it. Even from here they could see the chunk of diamond on her ring finger.

"Lee Pine? Is that really you?"

"It's really me."

"My God, I never would have recognized you," said the woman.

"You're Britta Pringle?"

"Yes, I am. I guess you don't remember me, you were so young."

"This is my assistant, Carol Blum."

They all shook hands.

Blum noted, "Beautiful home you have here. I . . . I wasn't expecting anything like—"

"—like this out in the boonies?" said Britta with a weary smile. "Who would? It's my husband's design. He's Silicon Valley. I'm more of a Cape Cod girl."

Britta looked up into Pine's face and smiled. "I certainly see your mother in there. And just a bit of Tim, too, in the cheekbones."

This threw Pine off her stride. During interviews with potential witnesses, she had her agenda and her protocols and she always stuck to them, adding in the possibility of flexibility with the script depending on the subject and how things went. But she had to remind herself, this was not like any other investigation she'd ever pursued.

This is about my family. Ultimately, this is about me.

"I'm sure," she said curtly.

"So what in the world are you doing out here? And you say you're an FBI agent now?"

"I am. Have been for over a decade."

"How time just flies."

"And I'm here because of my sister."

Britta's features slackened. "Your sister?" She glanced at Blum and then back at Pine. "Did they . . . have they found her?"

Again, this response hit Pine right in the gut, heightening her direct personal connection to this inquiry. She found part of herself wishing she could just focus on the murder of the unknown young woman. She could approach that clinically, professionally, with none of the personal baggage.

"No, that's why I'm here. I'm trying to make sense of what happened back then."

Britta folded her arms over her chest. "After all these years? Well, why not? I guess I would if it were my sister." She seemed to catch herself. "Oh please, come on in."

She opened the front door and motioned them inside.

The foyer soared three levels. Pine looked around the interior, which was all glass and metal and, despite all the trees outside, full of light. The floor plan was an open one, and seating areas were visible throughout along with what looked to be one-of-a-kind light fixtures and customized furniture. Thick and colorful area rugs broke up the large tile flooring that held fossil patterns.

"Wow," said Blum.

"Yes, we usually get that reaction," said Britta. "But you mentioned Jack Lineberry. If you've been to his place, it's three times this size with all the latest gadgets."

Blum said, "We have been there, and it is quite something. You both have done well for yourselves."

"Well, our success is connected to Jack's."

"How so?" asked Pine.

"Would you like some coffee?"

"Sure, thanks."

She led them into a kitchen area with sweeping views of the rear grounds. There was a large pool, and a guesthouse that seemed totally out of place with the main residence. It was constructed of wood cladding painted gray, soaring turrets, a picketed front porch, and what looked to be a widow's walk on top. There was also a detached six-car garage fronted by a paved motor court and a barbeque area with a built-in grill and other stainless-steel accoutrements.

Pine thought that *Architectural Digest* would have a field day here.

As they walked into the room a Hispanic woman dressed in a maid's uniform came through another doorway carrying a mop and a bucket. She appeared startled to see the three women there.

Britta said, "Oh, Kalinda, I'm sorry, we've had some

unexpected company. Can you go work in another part of the house for now? Thank you."

Kalinda, who was in her fifties, thin, and gray haired, nodded dumbly and hurried from the room. Britta watched her go.

"That was Myron's idea. Hiring her. I told him I can take care of this house all by myself."

"But it's a big space, it must be nice to have help," said Blum.

"That's true. And I know she sends money home to Guatemala. She may be illegal for all I know, but those people deserve to make a living too. And she works very hard."

As Britta started filling a Keurig with water, she pointed to the smaller guesthouse and said, "That was my input into all this. I spend a lot of my time out there. This place feels too cold and antiseptic for my tastes."

They carried the finished coffees over to a table overlooking the rear yard and sat down.

"So, Jack Lineberry?" prompted Pine.

"Yes. Well, as he probably told you, he has an investment company, a very successful one. It relies a lot on computerized trading and the rapid purchase and sale of stocks and other investments. I don't presume to understand all of it, but the long and the short of it is, the success is based on moving fast, far faster than an individual stock trader could. And Myron is a world-class computer geek, for want of a better term. He puts together algorithms and other trading programs to help power Jack's investment business. He did some of that in the mining office, though algorithms and all that stuff weren't nearly as important then as they are today. That's how Jack and Myron met."

"Well, it clearly worked," said Blum.

"Where is your husband?"

"Myron is a night owl. Up until all hours and then he sleeps until past lunchtime and then wants his breakfast." She smiled, a bit sadly, Pine thought. "I guess we must allow geniuses their idiosyncrasies," Britta added.

"I guess we must," said Blum.

"Now, how can I help you?" asked Britta.

"I'm surprised that Lineberry didn't tell you that we had met. I got your address from him. But he didn't provide a phone number or email."

"Well, he couldn't because we have neither."

"You have neither?" said Pine slowly.

"Myron won't have them. He says it's too dangerous. Too many ways for people to use that against us. You know, to spy on us."

"Another little idiosyncrasy of his?" asked Pine.

Britta smiled into her coffee. "Yes. It's quite a tally."

Pine took a sip from her cup and sat forward, planting her elbows on the table. "For a number of reasons, I've decided that now is the time to try to make some headway on what happened to my sister."

"Okay," said Britta, all attention now.

"I have long believed that a man came through our window that night and took Mercy."

"A man through a window? I didn't know that."

"Apparently, the police didn't believe me. I had a head injury, too."

"That nearly killed you," Britta said indignantly. "You poor thing. You were in the hospital for a long while. Julia was frantic the whole time."

"She'd already lost one daughter, she didn't want to lose her other one," said Pine as she watched Britta for her reaction.

"Yes, I think that was part of it."

"Only now, I'm not so sure the man came through the window."

Britta gaped. "I . . . I don't understand."

"I think he might have come through our bedroom door, which obviously means he first came through the house."

Britta said, "But your parents? Wouldn't they have—"

"My parents were . . . incapacitated at the time. I thought you knew that."

"It's been a long time, Lee. My memory is good, but it's not that good."

"Of course. I'm sorry."

"But still, even with your parents . . . incapacitated, if a stranger passed right by them?"

"What if it wasn't a stranger?"

"But surely." Britta stopped and stared at her. "Is

that why you're here? Do you believe that one of your parents' friends . . . ?"

"I'm an FBI agent, what I believe doesn't matter. It's what the facts will show. I have to consider every angle, and one angle I have never considered before was whether the person who took Mercy, and nearly killed me, knew our family."

"Well, I hope you're not accusing us. I mean—"

"No, Britta, not at all. You were obviously friends with my parents, with no motive to do something like that. Please understand, I'm just feeling my way."

This seemed to mollify the woman. She nodded and her features softened. "Of course, I can only imagine what you're going through, Lee. How can I help you?"

"Just tell me anything you can remember from back then."

Britta took a sip of her coffee. "Andersonville was a small town all those years ago, and it's still a small town. Everybody knew everyone else."

"And that fact could make my job easier, or harder."

"Many people have moved away over the last thirty years. Or died."

"That's the harder part," noted Pine.

Britta pursed her lips and shook her head stubbornly. "I can't believe that anyone here, especially someone who knew your mom and dad, would have done such a terrible thing. I mean, what would have been the motive?"

"Some people don't need a motive."

Blum interjected. "Agent Pine is referring to serial killers, Mrs. Pringle. Their motive is they are obsessed with doing what they do. They can't stop themselves."

"So that's who you think it was, a serial killer?"

"It's possible."

"But we never had anything like that happen around here back then."

"It could have been the beginning of someone's career. Or the end of it."

"Well, I just don't see it," Britta persisted. "Why would a serial killer come here?"

"Unfortunately, it happens," Pine said, "What do you remember about that time? Anything you can recall."

Britta said nervously, "I remember your mother calling me, panicked. We had a phone back then and lived the closest to your house. She was out of her mind with fear. Your sister was gone. Your father was out with the police looking for Mercy. You had been badly injured and had been taken to the hospital. Your mom rode over with you and then rushed back home to get some other things you needed. Then we drove back over to the hospital together. Your mother never left the place until you did, I don't know if you know that. Your father came and went but Julia never left your side."

"I didn't know that until I got back here. Agnes Ridley told me that."

"God, names from the past. I haven't seen or heard from Agnes since we moved away."

"What else do you remember? Anything my parents may have said?"

Britta took a long drink of her coffee while she thought about this. "I recall that your mother couldn't find your sister's doll. I don't even know why she was looking for it at a time like that. But people do strange things in moments of crisis, I suppose."

"Was your husband with my father looking for Mercy?"

"No, Myron was at work. He went in early to the office. When your mother called me, I didn't have a car. I just half ran the whole way."

"How did you and my mother get to the hospital then?"

"A police officer took us."

"Did you ever notice any strangers in town? Anyone who gave off an odd vibe?"

She shook her head. "Lee, we didn't go to town all that much. Neither did your family. We were all just scraping by back then. Myron hadn't found his calling with the computers yet. We were living paycheck to paycheck, same as your mom and dad. But you girls never wanted for anything. Never went hungry or anything."

"You have children, I understand?" asked Blum.

"I *did*. Joe and Mary." She looked at Pine. "They used to play with you and Mercy."

"You *did* have kids?" said Pine.

"Sadly, neither one is still alive."

"What happened? They were my age, I recall."

"One in an accident. And one, well, there was a substance-abuse issue." Britta looked down into her coffee.

"I'm very sorry about that," said Pine.

"Would you like to see their pictures?"

Pine shot Blum a glance. "Um, sure."

Britta took a framed photo from a shelf. "This was taken about three years ago."

Pine and Blum looked at the photo of Mary, a very lovely young woman with long blond hair and an impish smile. Next to her was Joey, a tall man with his arm around his sister.

"They were very close. They died within a month of each other."

"Oh my God," said Blum. "That is so terrible."

"Yes, yes, it was." She set the photo down on the table.

Pine cleared her throat and let the silence hang for a few seconds. "Lauren Graham told me that my father got into a fight with a gawker at the house later that day. But somebody broke it up. Do you know who that was?"

"That 'somebody' is me."

They all looked over at the doorway, where a man

in his fifties, about six feet five, stood. He had flyaway dark gray hair, wide brown eyes, and gangly limbs. He wore khaki pants and a wrinkled T-shirt, and he was barefoot.

"I'm Myron Pringle."

18

Britta rose, looking surprised, and checked her watch. "Myron, what are you doing up?"

"I was tired of sleeping," he said, not taking his gaze off Pine.

"This is—"

"Yes, I know. Lee Pine. Tim and Julia's surviving daughter."

Pine and Blum glanced at each other over this odd phrasing.

"Myron, please, I mean, really," said Britta in a scolding tone.

Pine rose and put out her hand. "Hello, Mr. Pringle."

He reluctantly shook hands.

"This is my assistant, Carol Blum."

Myron didn't even look at her. "You're back here investigating your sister's disappearance?"

"I am."

"The odds are very much against you."

"Myron," said his wife, reproachfully.

He ignored her, opened the fridge, took out a carton of milk, and drank from it. He wiped his mouth with the back of his hand and said, "I'm just speaking to raw statistics. You *could* succeed, I'm just telling you that the numbers do not favor you."

"Thanks, but I already knew that."

He put the milk back, shut the door, and leaned against the granite-topped kitchen island.

"So you broke up the fight?" she said.

He nodded. "Your father was drunk."

"Myron, please," implored Britta again.

Pine could tell from Britta's weary tone that this was a constant refrain from her.

"Well, he was. But one daughter had vanished. And the other one was badly hurt. I would have been drinking, too," he conceded.

"Who started the fight?" asked Pine.

"A man named Barry Vincent."

"How did it start?"

"Vincent accused your father of attacking you and being involved in your sister's disappearance."

"I don't believe he was alone in thinking that," said Pine.

"Your father would never have done such a thing," said Britta forcefully.

Pine eyed Myron. "What do you think?"

"I think people are capable of anything. But I saw how your father was with you and your sister. He doted on you both. You were his pride and joy. The man worked hard at his job. He provided for his family. That was really all he had. I don't see a man like that destroying it."

"But he was drinking and smoking weed that night," Pine reminded him.

"He drank and smoked weed a lot. I know, because I did it with him. Those things didn't make him violent. They just made him sleepy."

"Which would seem to jibe with him sleeping through everything that night," said Blum.

"So you two weren't with them that night?" said Pine.

Myron said nothing. Pine looked at Britta.

She said, "I think we were out that night, Lee. I remember the next day like it was yesterday. But the night before, no. But we weren't over at your parents', I know that."

Pine looked back at Myron. "Anything to add to that? You seem to have a good memory."

"Nothing to add. What's your next move? You talking to everyone who knew your family and who're still here?"

"Yes. That includes Jack Lineberry. I understand that you two have built a lucrative career together."

"Jack makes most of the money, but we've done okay, too. I'm just a computer guy. He does all the selling and schmoozing. He's good at that. Always has been. Even back in the bauxite mining days."

"So, algorithms?" said Pine.

"More accurately, automated trading programs.

Some of it is just to move large blocks of investments efficiently and for lower cost. Another side of it is to invest via computer programs so you can boost your returns. They call that black box trading. Complicated math formulas and hyperfast computer networks to execute on the strategies flowing therefrom. If it can see the right pattern in the movements of financial markets, just the slightest ripple, it can make a huge difference. That's why pretty much the entire financial market is automated. It's a race to the bottom, really, when you think about it. It has improved market liquidity, but it also contributed to the 'flash crash' in 2010. But computers don't have emotions, so when the market plummets, the computers bring us back faster than if humans were calling the shots. But still, it's a rigged system."

"Meaning the little guys get screwed?" said Pine.

He glanced at her, his furry eyebrows twitching. "In the financial markets, the little guys *always* get screwed. That's how the system is designed, because it's designed by the big boys. And they like to keep the gold away from the rabble, meaning everybody else."

"Do you have to keep changing the algorithms?" asked Pine.

"Absolutely. The spoils do not go to the complacent. They go to the hypervigilant. And since pretty much everyone has the same sort of algorithms firing away, the competition is fierce. Anyone who knows how to do Python code, for example, can execute algorithmic trading. It keeps me and my team jumping. But that's why Britta and I can afford a place like this. People like me are in great demand. But the only reason for that is the system got greedy and decided to go with technology over humans."

"But you're a human," Blum pointed out.

"Right, but, for example, a couple years ago Goldman Sachs fired around six hundred traders and replaced them with a couple hundred computer engineers to oversee the automated trading programs. Lots of other places have followed suit. And it's not just the financial sector, pretty much all sectors are becoming automated. I see people with a lot of free time on their hands in the future. They just won't have any money to do anything. The Silicon Valley billionaires know it's coming. That's why so many of them are calling for a guaranteed national income for everyone. But they're not doing it out of benevolence, at least most of them aren't."

"Why then?" asked Blum.

"They need people to buy the crap they're selling and, more important, they don't want the rabble coming over the walls of their estates and butchering them."

"Really, Myron, I doubt it will come to that," admonished Britta.

"Then you'd be wrong."

"Do you work here or at an office?" asked Blum.

"I have my office here."

"Could we see it?" asked Pine.

"Why?" he asked sharply. "It can't have anything to do with what happened all those years ago."

"You never know."

"I don't let people in there as a rule."

"There are always exceptions to rules. And in an environment where you obviously spend a lot of time, something might occur to you that wouldn't in any other place. I would really appreciate it if you would. Maybe for old times' sake?"

Myron looked put out, glanced at Britta, finally shrugged, turned, and walked out of the room.

Britta chose to stay behind, so Myron led Pine and Blum down a sleek hallway and up a curving set of stairs made of zebra wood with stainless steel hand-rails and stout, smooth wire stretched between them.

They reached a door on the second floor that had a security port next to it containing a red light. Myron said, "Before you go in, you need to power off your phones."

Pine and Blum glanced at each other, looking puzzled, but they both complied with his request.

Myron bent down to the portal and put his eye to it.

"Retina scanner," he said as the heavy portal clicked open.

"I can see that," said Pine.

"No pun intended," quipped Blum.

The space they entered was a good thousand

square feet set out in a rectangle. There were no windows in the room. The flooring was soft and springy underfoot.

"Welcome to the world of cyborg finance with a dash of digital alchemy," said Myron drily.

Pine touched the walls. They seemed to be made of concrete. When she asked Myron about it, he confirmed this and added, "With a layer of copper underneath. To block electronic signals."

"Spies here in Macon County, Georgia?" said Pine.

"Spies everywhere," replied Myron crisply. He pointed to the ceiling. "Satellites ringing the earth."

She noted a sign on one wall. It was a series of odd numbers: 1, 3, 5, 7, 9, 7, 9, 5, 3.

He saw her staring at it and smiled. "I like odd numbers over even, up to a point."

"Okay," she said, looking confused.

On a desk about the size of a large dining table was perched a row of supersized computer monitors. They were all dark at the moment.

He held up a white plastic card. "The system in the room senses the number of people present. If everyone doesn't have a badge like this with the requisite clearances, the system knows there are unauthorized people in the room. So, the screens go black."

"Intel agencies have the same sort of systems," said Pine.

"I know. It's where we got the protocols."

"So you sit in here and work on . . . algorithms?" said Blum.

"Not just that. I also oversee security on the pipelines, go over procedures, that sort of thing. But yes, refining, tweaking, coming up with new platforms is something I spend a lot of time on. It's heavy lifting, and there are long lead times. Coding is not easy. And bugs have to be worked out. And hackers come at us twenty-four/seven. The Russians, the Chinese, groups in India, the Middle East, fourteen-year-olds with a Mac looking to blow up the financial world, hell, everybody."

"But if this place is sealed off from electronic spies getting in, how are you connected to the web then?" asked Pine.

"Proprietary," replied Myron. "But I can tell you it's an amalgam of hardened pipelines, and a standalone cloud-based infrastructure that is not available to the general public or anybody else."

"Are you the only one who does this for Lineberry?"

"No, we have a whole department scattered around the world, but I'm the head one. I run the others, and it's a group that has grown exponentially over time. Our IT is our most precious resource. Without that, we're just a bunch of old farts playing at Monopoly. We communicate around the clock through the secure, encrypted-at-both-ends pipeline that I just alluded to."

"Your wife said you don't use phones or emails."

"And I don't have Alexa or Google assistant or any other spies in my house. And I don't use a credit card. And I never surf the web. Ridiculous. Most people are suckers. They give up privacy for convenience."

"I guess they do," said Pine. "But it seems to work."

"Oh, it *does* work, for the other side. They know everything. They know more about you than you even know about yourself. Why do you think Facebook and Google are so valuable? It's not about posting cat pictures for your friends or being able to look up an answer to any question. It's not about building a 'community,'" he added derisively. "It's not even about selling ads, although that's how many of them make some of their income. It's about the collection of data. Data about all of us. It's the greatest scam ever perpetrated. And even now that we know it is a scam, people won't give it up. They're like drug addicts. You remember way back when people would always light up a cigarette, no matter what they were doing: driving, eating, sitting, drinking. Now what do you see everybody doing? Checking their smartphones. Young, middle-aged, and old. Cradle to grave. The world is hooked. Big Brother is getting fed terabytes of data every millisecond. And they don't pay a damn cent for it."

"That's a scary thought," said Blum.

"Not scary enough, apparently, to persuade most people *not* to do it. Hell, it's already too late. The world is a slave to this. There's no going back. There's too much money to be made and influence to be had."

Pine said, "I understand a computer's mic and camera are always on. They can watch and listen even when we don't know it." She stared at his desktop units.

"They can. You can be talking with your friend out on your deck about dog food. The next thing you know an ad for dog products pops up on your phone. Gee, I wonder how?"

"As you said, Big Brother is alive and well," noted Blum.

"And that's why this gear is customized. No mics and no cameras. No rats on this ship."

"Which is why you asked us to turn off our phones," said Pine.

"Now you're catching on."

Blum pointed to a framed, official-looking certificate on the desk.

"Is that a patent? I recognize the document."

Myron smiled. "It is. You can't patent an algorithm, just like you can't patent a mere idea. But you can patent the *implementation* of an algorithm—software, for example. And I did. Made some decent money off it."

"But wouldn't that belong to Jack Lineberry's company?" said Pine. "I mean, you work for him. Why didn't his company apply for the patent?"

"In this country, only individuals can apply for a

patent, although companies can of course own the application rights of the patent. But to answer your question, I did this on my own time. And the boss had no problems with it. It wasn't in the investment field, so I didn't license it to any of his competitors. It was for a totally different industry and application. Nice six-figure payday."

Blum peered closer at the patent. "So you're listed as the patent holder. But the algorithm is called . . . Stardust?"

Myron's smile deepened. "I used to go to Vegas regularly. I didn't exactly count cards, but I had my own system. Went to the old Stardust Casino a lot when it was still around. Did well. Made quite a lot of money. When the patent opportunity came up, I thought it would be fun, you know, to use that name. Another jackpot, as it were."

He sat down in an ergonomic chair and spun around to face Pine. "Now, why are you really back in town?"

"For the reasons I already told you."

He stared at her long enough that it grew uncomfortable. "I'm not sure I believe that."

"Can you tell me where you were the night my sister was taken?"

"Didn't you already ask that downstairs?"

"I did, but you didn't really answer."

"I said I had nothing to add."

"That's not really an answer. And it could mean more than one thing."

"I forgot that you're now an experienced investigator and not a six-year-old girl."

"And would that impact your answer?"

Myron tapped his fingers absently on the arm of his chair. "I don't know."

"Can you tell me anything?"

"I don't believe anyone who knew your parents could have done this."

"I don't want to believe that, either. But right now I'm just collecting facts."

"I don't think I have any to give. Right now."

Pine handed him a card. "My cell phone's on there. When you figure it out, call me."

"I don't have a phone."

"There's a pay phone at the Clink. And we're staying at the Cottage. If we're not there, leave a message."

"I don't get to town very much. I don't really have any interest, you see."

Pine took a few moments to size him up. It was clear he had not told her all he knew. This was not surprising to her. Rarely in one interview did anyone spill all. Sometimes it was unintentional, or the person simply didn't remember. But her gut told her that was not the case here. Myron Pringle knew exactly what he was doing.

"Well then," she said. "I'll just have to keep coming back until I get what I need."

"You can't force me to talk to you."

"True, but I can be a real pain in the ass."

"You mean to harass me?" he exclaimed, looking at her darkly.

"I mean to find the truth. If you have a problem with that, then you have a problem with me. I'll see you around, Myron."

She turned and left and Blum quickly followed her out, leaving Myron Pringle to stare moodily after them.

19

Max Wallis came by about an hour after they returned to the Cottage. Pine and Blum led him into the breakfast room, where they sat at a table. He laid a three-ring binder notebook down in front of him. His suit and shirt were heavily wrinkled, and his dark eye pouches told of little sleep.

"We got an ID on the victim," he said, yawning.

"Who is she?" said Pine.

Wallis flipped open his notebook. "Hanna Rebane. Your instincts were right. She *is* Eastern European, from Estonia."

"What's her story?"

"She's got a lengthy record, drugs, solicitation, petty thefts. Nothing too serious. Almost no jail time, just fines and some community service. And one led to the other, probably. To pay for her addiction she was engaged in prostitution. It's the old story."

"Or else someone got her hooked on drugs and forced her into turning tricks," said Pine. "That's the new 'old story.'"

"But how did she get here?" Blum asked. "Was she plying her trade?"

Wallis studied his notes. "No, I don't think that's the case. Somebody would have seen her. And her priors were from Atlanta and Charlotte and one over in Asheville. I'm running down her last known address."

"So she headed further south at some point," said Pine. "I wonder why. Or maybe it wasn't her choice."

"Meaning the killer picked her up from one of those areas and brought her here."

Pine nodded. "And if he did he must have kept her somewhere, either alive or dead, before we found the body. Anything else?"

Wallis passed the notebook to Blum. "DMV photos of the men in the area for your friend to look at. Just put an *X* under the ones you remember seeing at the restaurant that night."

"Will do."

Wallis looked at Pine. "How's your 'other' investigation coming?"

"Slowly. Not unexpected, after all these years."

"You need anything from me, just let me know."

"I appreciate that."

"When I get Rebane's last known address, I'll let you know. If you want to tag along?"

"Yes, we do."

After he left, Pine stared absently out the window.

"Can I afford to hear your thoughts on a government salary?" asked Blum.

"I'm not sure they're worth the price."

"Try me?"

"Agnes Ridley, Lauren Graham, Dave Bartles, Jack Lineberry, and the Pringles. All of them lived around here when I did. We've spoken to them all. And we've learned some things that have been helpful, but we have a long way to go."

"Well, it's early days yet. We've really just started. And you did have that epiphany about the reflection in the mirror. And you learned new details about your father's death from Jack Lineberry."

"Yes, I did," said Pine in a bitter tone. "If Lineberry is telling the truth, and I have no reason to doubt him, my mother lied to me."

"She may have had her reasons, Agent Pine. I don't think most mothers would lie to their kids unless they had a very good reason."

"Well, I wish I could ask her what it was."

"You really have no idea where she is?"

Pine shook her head. "I don't even know if she's still alive."

"Surely, if anything had happened to her you would have been contacted."

"Not if she didn't tell anyone about me."

Blum stared over at her boss with a look of trepidation. "Ridley mentioned letting sleeping dogs lie.

Did that spook you? I thought it might have from your expression."

Pine nodded. "Maybe more than I care to admit. Especially after my 'revelation.'"

"Do you want to elaborate on what's really bothering you?"

Pine leaned forward, her hands clasped on the table, her gaze downcast.

"If my father . . ."

". . . had something to do with what happened, you mean? Because now you believe the intruder came from *inside* the house?"

Pine nodded but didn't look up.

"Well, either you want to know what really happened or you don't. We can go home now if it's the latter. But what will that mean for you going forward? Will you be seeing Daniel Tor in every suspect you confront from now on?"

"I don't know, which is reason enough to keep going to find the truth." Pine glanced at the notebook. "Why don't you take that up to your room and go through it."

"And what will you do?"

"I'm going to take another walk down memory lane."

Rain was coming. Pine could feel it in the temperature dropping and the wind picking up. She had on a weatherproof jacket with a hood, so the prospect of inclement weather didn't trouble her. She kept walking along the main strip of Andersonville as the skies darkened.

When it started to sprinkle, Pine made her way back to the spot.

The memory lane she had mentioned was actually quite a recent one.

She stopped and eyed the spot where the body of Hanna Rebane had been placed by her killer. She took in the broken streetlight above and the surrounding cobbled area. The police tape that had been previously strung was flapping in the wind. The screen was gone and there was no officer present to secure the scene. She supposed that they didn't have enough manpower to do that sort of thing. The crime scene apparently got one going-over and that was it.

The public had been duped into thinking that all police departments and all police investigations were conducted just like those on the TV shows. Cool offices, every forensic gadget available, limitless resources, hunky men with awesome firepower, and women in tight clothes showing cleavage.

The idea of limitless resources was a joke, even for the FBI. And the last time Pine had shown cleavage while on the job was . . . never.

She ducked under the tape and headed behind the line of old buildings on the main street. This was the way the killer had to have come. And Pine was careful to keep far to the side of the path. She would have liked to assume that the local police had already covered this area for footprints, other markings, and traces of any kind, but she couldn't safely trust that such had happened. At least not to the level of detail she would want.

She walked the area back and forth for over an hour, reaching all the way to the tree line before concluding that she could find nothing there.

She then took a small Maglite from her pocket and went into the trees just as the rain started to fall harder. Fortunately, there was no thunder and lightning. She followed a worn-down path until she was free of the trees once more. There was a dirt road here that was quickly becoming mud. Any tire tracks that might have been there had long since been obliterated.

She walked back to the main street and ducked under the cover of one of the storefronts. Her hands in her pockets, she thought about what to do next.

The ME had emailed her the photos of the round marks on Rebane's backside and hamstrings. She took out her phone and looked at them, scrolling through them one by one. They could have come from many things, although Pine ideally needed to drill that down to one source to make any progress on the case.

She looked around the small downtown. The rain had scared away most of the pedestrians, although there were a few hardy souls still out and about. The place looked pretty much the same, at least the little that she could recall. She wished at this moment that her memory could be perfect, but that was simply not possible. Eyewitnesses, she knew, were not reliable. The average person really saw little of what was going on around them and remembered even less. Even then, they got the details of what they did remember wrong more than half the time. That had always troubled Pine about eyewitness testimony in a court case. It was often the deciding factor for a jury deciding whether someone was going to lose their liberty, or their life.

She leaned against a support post and watched the rain now pour down, quickly flooding the road. *And while my memory is better than most because of my training, I didn't possess that training at six years old. So on that score, my recall is as bad as everyone else's.*

She had proof of that with her realization that maybe her attacker and Mercy's kidnapper had not come through the window, but rather his image had been reflected in their mirror.

But what if that memory also turns out to be false? What if I really didn't see anyone in the mirror?

Pine was a seasoned detective. But none of her other cases had involved a family member. She felt confused and unorganized, things she could not afford to be if she really was going to get to the truth.

She knew one thing, though: She was going to have to take another crack at Myron Pringle. He had not been entirely truthful with her, and she didn't know why.

"You look pensive."

She gazed over at the black Porsche SUV that had slowed down in front of her. The rear window was down, and Jack Lineberry was peering at her.

"Just thinking some things through."

"Got time for lunch? I know a place over in Americus. I can drop you back at the Cottage."

Pine really wasn't hungry for food, but she was for information. "Okay."

She dashed to the SUV as the rain picked up.

20

Pine noted that Jerry the very nasty security guard was driving, and Tyler was riding shotgun. Jerry gave Pine a once-over glare in the rearview and hit the gas before she could buckle up, throwing her back against the seat with the forward momentum.

Lineberry was dressed in a navy blue blazer and gray woolen slacks and a white open-collared dress shirt, with a pocket square the same color.

"Chilly for this time of year," he said.

"Rain doesn't help," she said back as she snapped her harness, after giving Jerry a WTF look in the rearview.

"I guess you don't get much rain in Arizona."

"It's pretty dry. But when it rains, it pours."

"I guess Andersonville seems pretty backwoods to you now."

"We have places like this in Arizona. Folks just digging in and getting by. Nothing wrong with that. The town where I live is pretty much like that. Working-class, Native Americans, immigrants, transients from other states who want warmer weather. No billionaires in sight." She glanced at him. "No offense."

"None taken."

"Nothing wrong with making money."

He nodded. Then his features turned somber. "I heard about the dead woman they found. Have they identified her yet?"

"They're working on it," said Pine noncommittally.

"Are you working on that case, too?"

"Does it matter if I am or not?"

"No, I guess it doesn't. I was just wondering. I would think the case involving your sister would be a full-time job."

"It might turn out to be. I saw the Pringles this morning."

"You saw Myron, in the *morning*?" He looked surprised.

"So you know of his sleeping habits?"

Lineberry nodded. "An odd bird, but a brilliant one."

"He showed me his office."

"That's odd. He's so security conscious."

"All the computer screens went black because we weren't authorized. And he made us turn off our phones."

Lineberry smiled. "Of course he did. Were he and Britta helpful?"

"Not particularly. What can you tell me about them? Where did they come back from?"

"I believe they moved to North Carolina not that long after you and your parents left here."

"Then how did you hook up with him?"

"Like your father, I knew him from the mining days. I could tell the talent he had with computers. He didn't go to MIT or Stanford or anything, he was just a natural at it. His talents far exceeded the requirements of the job at the bauxite mine. When I was setting up my company, the reality of automated trading was really getting going. I guess I had a notion that it would be important. I felt Myron could be an invaluable asset, and he has been."

"I'm not sure he was straight with me."

Lineberry glanced sharply at her. "How so?"

"He wouldn't tell me where he was on the night my sister disappeared."

"Well, I can hardly believe Myron had anything to do with that."

"Then why wasn't he up front about where he was?"

"Maybe he didn't remember."

"I'm not sure the guy forgets much."

Lineberry was about to say something but then caught himself. "I believe I would agree with that," he said cautiously. "But still."

Neither one said anything else for the rest of the drive.

The restaurant in Americus was across the street from the Windsor Hotel, a Queen Anne architectural-style building.

"You ever been here?" asked Lineberry.

"This restaurant or Americus?"

"Both."

"No on the restaurant. Yes on Americus. They took me to the hospital here when the guy shattered my skull."

Lineberry looked embarrassed. "I should have remembered that."

"No reason for you to. I don't really remember much about it. I was told later."

They ordered and their meals came a few minutes later.

"Dr. Martin Luther King Jr. was jailed here in 1961 for protesting segregation in Albany, did you know that?" asked Lineberry.

Pine shook her head. "But I guess that wasn't unexpected, this being Georgia."

"On the other side of the coin, Habitat for Humanity has its headquarters here."

"I read that somewhere."

He took a sip of his iced tea. "One night I was leaving town after a dinner back in, I think it was 2007. That's when this massive tornado came through town here. Don't know how it missed us. It cut a nearly forty-mile-wide path of destruction through Americus, destroying homes, businesses, churches, and it demolished the regional hospital. They finally had to tear it down. I watched it go through. Scariest thing I've ever seen."

"Looks like they rebuilt okay."

He looked at her over his soup bowl. "I bet you've seen a lot scarier than that in your line of work."

She thought about Daniel James Tor. "I've seen some scary human beings. I don't know how they compare to facing a tornado."

Lineberry nodded and looked down.

Jerry had stayed outside in the Porsche, while Tyler had taken a table near them and was sipping on a cup of coffee. Pine eyed Jerry through the restaurant's broad front window.

"How long has Jerry been with you?" asked Pine as she sipped her iced tea.

"About five years. He's former Secret Service."

"Is that right?"

"Does that surprise you?"

"That you would hire former Secret Service as security? No. They're some of the best in the world."

"What then?"

"He escalated a situation with me back at your house that he didn't need to. I know a lot of Secret Service, both active and retired. They don't do that. They're calm, respectful, and professional. They defuse until that doesn't work anymore. Escalation is never their first move unless someone has a weapon out."

Lineberry glanced toward the street where the Porsche was parked. "Well, he's done a good job for me."

"What about the other guy?"

"Tyler Straub came from a private security firm. A good man."

"Why so much security, Mr. Lineberry?"

"Please, it's Jack. Not to toot my own horn, but I do have great wealth, and unfortunately with that, one becomes a target."

"Any threats?"

"There have been, yes. Some are generic, you know, I'm a capitalistic bastard draining the lifeblood from the world. Others have come from former employees and even one ex-client who went a bit mad and thought we had ripped him off."

"And you didn't?"

Lineberry smiled. "If I made a habit of ripping off clients, I would not be in business long."

"Bernie Madoff did okay for a long time."

"We're independently audited every year and the investments we hold for our clients are in real companies and other securities. We're totally transparent. Their reports come directly from those companies and concerns they've invested in. We do not make up our own statements, other than to show overall investments and performance by our firm, which we are legally required to do."

"So what was this guy's beef?"

"That instead of making him a hundred million dollars in profit in five years, we only managed to make him fifty million. That still represented a doubling of his initial investment, a pretty damn good return over that time frame, when most everyone else was getting half that return."

"And he really had a beef with that?"

"He sued me, then he threatened me. Then he came to my office with what he said was a bomb."

"What happened?"

"He's currently in a secure psychiatric hospital. I think all that money addled him."

"So I guess money really can't buy you happiness."

"No, but it can buy you freedom and convenience."

"I don't mean to be rude, but why the sudden lunch invitation?"

"I was in Andersonville and was coming here anyway. Then I spotted you."

She shook her head. "It's in my DNA to be skeptical. So I'm thinking for a busy man like yourself there has to be another reason."

Lineberry wiped his mouth and laid down his spoon. "Okay, maybe there is."

"I'm listening."

"I'll be blunt. What happened to Julia?"

It suddenly hit Pine that she should have been expecting this query. "Why?"

"She was a friend, a *good* friend. I know what happened to your poor father. I'd just like to know that she's okay now."

Pine eyed him appraisingly. "I guess it depends on how you define *okay*."

He grimaced. "That sounds rather ominous."

"It's been a long time and you've had a whole other life since then. I know you were friends, but . . ."

"We were all young, though I was the oldest in the group. And the friends you're around when you're sort of starting out in life are important ones. And I never had any family of my own, so I guess I sort of adopted everyone else's kids as my own. It tore me to pieces when Britta and Myron lost both of theirs."

"An accident and an overdose."

"Yes."

"What sort of accident?"

"Is that important?"

Though Pine really couldn't remember them she said, "We were kids here. We played together. You don't have a monopoly on that sentiment."

Lineberry looked thoroughly admonished. "Yes, yes, of course. Well, Joe was cleaning his shotgun and it discharged."

"He was cleaning a loaded weapon?"

"I believe he'd been drinking."

"Where did this happen?"

"In North Carolina. He was living there then."

"And Mary? Britta said it was an overdose?"

"Heroin, I think."

"She was a longtime user?"

"No, I don't think so. I believe it was her first time."

"And her last."

"Yes. Mary died first, and Joe about a month later. It really tore them up."

"But they seem to have recovered, to the extent anyone can."

"Myron is Myron. He . . . well, he looks at everything logically. And then he moves on. Britta? I'm not sure she'll ever move on, really."

"She has the Cape Cod place in the backyard. Doesn't like the contemporary stuff."

"I think she spends a lot of time there. Thinking about things."

Pine nodded.

"So, your mother?"

"I'll be candid with you. She's had a lot of challenges."

"What sort of challenges?"

"I'd prefer not to go into that."

He cocked his head. "So, is she in a hospital or something?"

"Or something," Pine said vaguely.

"What's her prognosis?"

"I'm not sure there is one, at least that I know of."

He nodded. "I'm sorry to hear that."

She shrugged. "That's life. You take the good with the bad. Do you remember anyone else other than the Pringles that I could talk to?"

"No, that's it."

"Okay. Then I guess we're done here." She reached for her wallet.

"No, I've got it. I invited you."

"I'll feel better paying my way," said Pine. She handed him a twenty.

A minute later the three of them went back out to the Porsche and got in, and Jerry drove off.

"Next time you see your mother can you tell her I said hello?" asked Lineberry.

"I will." *If I ever see her again*, thought Pine.

They dropped her off back at the Cottage.

"If you think of anything else, give me a call," said Pine.

"I will," promised Lineberry.

As they drove off Pine thought, *Why do I doubt that?*

21

"Understand I can't be a hundred percent sure, but I've marked the men who were at the Clink that night to the best of my recollection," said Blum, handing the notebook over to Pine.

Pine set it down on the bed in her room and flipped through it. "Looks to be about twenty men who weren't there, though half of them look too old and frail to have even picked up the woman, much less carried her any distance."

"Agnes Ridley and Cy were there, too. So I had them go through the photos as well, to check my memory. We came up with basically the same list."

"But no Myron Pringle and no Jack Lineberry."

"I asked around town. Neither frequent the Clink."

"I would suppose not. They don't live that close. Lineberry probably has his own chef, and Pringle would be afraid someone might try to put an ingestible spy chip in his mashed potatoes."

"How did it go on your end?"

Pine told her about finding zip at the crime scene

and her unusual lunch with Lineberry. "It was funny he was asking about my mom like that."

"They *were* friends."

"It was a long time ago. And he kept in touch with my dad, but not my mom?"

"Well, he said he didn't know where she was. So what will you do with my list?"

"Pass it along to Wallis. It might generate a lead."

"The trouble is our killer might have been a tourist and has already left the area."

"There was nothing we could do about that. We couldn't very well shut the whole town down. I wouldn't imagine there are many surveillance cameras around here."

"I doubt there are any in the relevant area, or else you'd think the police or Wallis would have mentioned something like that."

Pine took photos of the men who weren't at the restaurant and emailed them to Wallis. "Let's see what he can run down on that."

"Next steps?" asked Blum.

Pine's phone buzzed. It was Wallis acknowledging receipt of the photos and adding something else.

Pine listened and then clicked off. "He's found out Hanna Rebane's last known address. He's heading over here to pick us up."

"Fort Benning land," said Wallis as he drove Pine and Blum in his dusty and rusty Crown Vic. The interior was littered with fast-food containers, dented soda cans, plastic coffee cups, and the comingled smells of degrading French fries and cigarette smoke.

"Columbus, Georgia," said Pine. "On the border with Alabama."

"Right. You been there?"

"Once, when I was conducting a joint investigation with Army CID."

"I've done some stuff with CID. Who'd you work with?"

"CID Special Agent named John Puller."

Wallis said, "Puller? Wasn't his daddy a war hero or something?"

"Still is. And so is John. Good guy. Taught me a lot about the military. It's a whole other world."

"I damn sure know that from my abbreviated tour of duty," agreed Wallis heartily.

"So what's the scoop on Hanna Rebane?" asked Blum.

"She shared an apartment with another gal."

"Is the roommate Eastern European too?"

"No, her name's Beth Clemmons. That's her real name, not her professional one."

"Professional one?" asked Pine.

"She's a porn actress. Goes by Raven McCoy in the, um, films."

"Was Rebane into porn films as well?" asked Pine. "That would explain some of what we found at her autopsy."

"That's what we're going to find out."

The apartment complex they drove into was within sight of the Chattahoochee River, which formed the boundary line between Georgia and its neighboring state of Alabama.

Pine looked around at the upscale building as they got out of the car.

"It's nicer than I thought it would be," she said.

"I guess her work pays well," noted Blum.

"I phoned ahead; Clemmons is waiting for us," said Wallis.

They checked in with the building concierge. Pine gazed around at the plush interior of the lobby and thought that it was far nicer than where she lived in Arizona.

They rode up on the elevator to the sixth floor, where Wallis knocked on the door of Number 611. It was instantly opened by a petite, busty woman with dyed blond hair and bloodshot eyes. She had on a halter top and black leggings and was barefoot. A clump of tissues was clutched in one hand.

Beth Clemmons looked devastated.

She stepped back to allow them in after Wallis and Pine badged her.

Clemmons led them into a sun-streamed room with sweeping views of the countryside and the Chattahoochee River beyond. To Pine's eye the place was professionally decorated, and the furniture and paint choices were informed and imaginative. She had led a Spartan existence, but during her investigations Pine had seen the homes of a great many people with financial means, and thus she knew the difference between good taste and throwing cash at something to see what stuck.

They sat around a large wooden-and-metal coffee table. Clemmons patted her eyes dry and gazed at them.

"Are you sure it's Hanna?" she asked, her voice hoarse.

Wallis took out a photo. "Her prints matched. But I can show you this."

"Is she . . . ?" said Clemmons fearfully, her eyes wide as quarters.

"Yes. But it just looks like she's sleeping."

He passed it across. Clemmons glanced at it for a second and then handed it back and nodded. "That's her. That's Hanna." She looked like she might be sick.

"I'm sorry," said Wallis. "No one should have to die that way."

Clemmons let out three deep breaths and calmed.

"You said she was strangled and left on the street in, what town again?"

"Andersonville, Georgia."

"Had you or she ever been there?" asked Pine.

Clemmons shook her head. "I've never even heard of it. I don't think Hanna had been there before, but I don't know for sure."

"Exactly how did you know her?" asked Wallis, his notebook and pen ready.

"I won't beat around the bush. We met when we were both employed as . . . escorts." She eyed Wallis nervously.

He caught the look and said quickly, "I'm investigating a murder, Ms. Clemmons. I have no interest in anything else. Nor do I plan on passing along anything you tell us to colleagues who might have jurisdiction over . . . escorts."

She nodded. "But the fact is we were no longer escorts. We were actors in film. I got into it first and then got Hanna involved. She had this incredibly exotic look to her. Different from the other girls. Facial bone structure I would die for. My looks are a dime a dozen, but not Hanna's. She was going places."

"This is the *adult* film industry you're talking about?" noted Blum.

"Yes," said Clemmons, a defiant look in her eyes.

"But you can't shoot porn films in Georgia," said Wallis. "Can you?"

Pine interjected. "The Supreme Court considers it free speech so long as everyone is over eighteen. You put a camera in the equation and pay everyone a wage and it's art, not prostitution. But I don't know specifically about Georgia's laws."

"It doesn't matter because we don't film in Georgia," said Clemmons. "We fly out to South Florida every two months, film for two weeks, and then come back here."

Wallis looked around at the richly appointed room. "How much does it pay?"

"Well, it varies a lot depending on your name recognition, popularity, and experience. We both worked our way up. Hanna was making about three grand per film. And I was pulling in twenty-five hundred even though I started before her. That was the exotic look I was talking about. And we could shoot about a dozen films in two weeks."

"Twelve films in fourteen days?" exclaimed Blum.

Clemmons nodded. "Well, it's not Shakespeare. I mean, nobody's getting an Oscar for this. The story lines are pretty basic and the dialogue, well, people don't watch porn for the dialogue. Hair and makeup can take a couple of hours. But we typically use different rooms in the same house, so we don't have to change locations. They bring the guys in for different segments. The cameraman moves around to get all the angles so we don't have to stop and keep setting up new shots. It happens pretty efficiently."

"So Hanna was making thirty-six grand for a half month's work?" said Wallis.

"Well, I would imagine it's pretty grueling work," said Pine.

"It definitely can be," said Clemmons, giving her an appreciative smile.

"Right, right," Wallis said uncomfortably. He

cleared his throat. "Now when was the last time you saw Ms. Rebane?"

"Four days ago. We were planning to return in a week for more filming. We used to spend more time together here, but we've sort of gone our separate ways of late. I mean, we're still friends and all. And we obviously still lived together."

"How long *have* you lived together?" asked Pine.

"For about two years now. Most of it here. We bought this condo together."

Wallis said, "So you last saw her four days ago? Where was this?"

"We had a late lunch together at a place about a mile from here. After that I went to my boyfriend's place for the night. I got back the next afternoon."

Wallis asked, "Do you know who her other friends were? Did she mention having a boyfriend, someone new in her life?"

"She didn't have a boyfriend, at least that I knew of. She didn't really have many friends."

"But you said just now that the two of you have gone your separate ways, so you may not know about a boyfriend," pointed out Blum.

"That's true."

"And was there a reason for the two of you going your separate ways?" asked Pine.

Clemmons looked uncomfortable and didn't answer.

"Ms. Clemmons, if you know something that could help us . . . ?" prompted Wallis.

"Just call me Beth, please." She sighed and kneaded her thighs with her fists. "Hanna had gotten a little weird as of late."

"Weird how, Beth?" asked Pine.

"She was withdrawn, secretive. She even told me she was thinking of getting out of the business altogether. She actually told me that at our lunch."

"Did she say why, or what she was planning to do instead?" asked Wallis.

"Not really. But, well, it seemed that *someone* was influencing her." She smiled in an embarrassed fashion. "She was beautiful and all, but it wasn't like Hanna was any great thinker or anything. She lived day to day. She was only twenty-seven. She didn't have her whole life mapped out. She was carefree, enjoying what she had." She looked around the spacious, light-filled room. "She loved all of this. She grew up really poor overseas."

"She was from Estonia," said Pine.

"I didn't know that, she never said. Only that she wasn't born here. You could tell that by her accent. It was kind of thick. It was hard to understand her sometimes."

"She had a lengthy criminal record," said Wallis. "Solicitation, drugs."

"That was years ago," she said defensively. "She'd been clean for a long time. And we were making a lot more money from film than we ever did—" She caught herself and fell silent.

"The postmortem showed that she was still using drugs, Beth," Pine said. "Coke, meth, it was pretty obvious. I can't imagine you could live with her and not know this."

Pine glanced at the woman's bare arms. She had already noted they were free of needle tracks. But there was something . . .

"Beth?" prompted Pine.

"We were both in rehab together," she blurted out. "Okay? She was clean. For a while. Then she fell back into bad ways. I was all over her case about it, but I couldn't get through to her. And she could still do the work, but . . ."

"Maybe someone came into her life to convince her to change what she was doing," said Blum quietly, keeping her gaze on Clemmons. "Someone recent. Someone who got her to go down the bad path again?"

"Maybe someone did. But she never mentioned anyone like that to me."

"Had she ever spoken of getting married?" asked Pine.

Clemmons's large eyes widened. "Married? No, nothing like that. Why?"

"Just checking all the boxes. Did she ever show an interest in looking at wedding gowns or veils?"

"No, never."

"Did you know that she had had a child?" asked Wallis.

Beth looked stunned by this statement. "What? Oh my God, are you serious?"

"The postmortem showed that as well."

"She, no, never. I had no idea. Jesus, that is so . . ." Her voice faltered and she started to bite at one of her cuticles.

"Does she have any relations that need to be notified?" asked Wallis.

"Not that she ever said. No family ever visited here. Certainly no child."

"Can we look around her room?" asked Wallis.

"I guess so. It's right down here."

Clemmons led them to Rebane's bedroom, and then walked back down the hall.

The three of them gazed around at the large bedroom with an attached bathroom.

Pine briefly thought of the woman who would never be coming back here and then her focus snapped back to the business at hand.

"Well, let's get to it."

22

An hour later Pine sat on the bed and watched as Blum and Wallis continued their search through the belongings and life of a dead woman named Hanna Rebane.

Wallis came out of the bathroom and shook his head. "Not much here," he said.

Blum closed the last drawer in the walk-in closet and came back out. "She had some designer clothes, shoes, and purses," noted Blum. "The real things, no knockoffs."

"But no phone, although there's a phone charger over there for it," said Pine, pointing at a small desk built into the wall by the bed, where a power cord was plugged into the outlet.

"If she took her phone, why not take the charger?" said Wallis.

"Maybe she didn't think she would be gone long enough to need it," replied Pine. "If she wasn't planning to be gone overnight, she wouldn't take her power cord. There have to be exterior cameras around this place. Let's have them pull the footage and see if it shows her coming and going and when. And more importantly whether anyone was with her."

They walked back into the other room, where Clemmons was drinking a cup of tea.

While Wallis went to check with the building security about any surveillance footage, Pine and Blum sat down across from the visibly distraught woman.

"Did Hanna have a car?" asked Pine.

"No. Neither do I. If we needed to go somewhere we'd use Uber or Lyft, or a Zipcar for anything longer than just one ride. We could walk to everything we needed. That's why we picked this building to live in."

"The way of the millennials," noted Blum. "When I got my license at sixteen the first thing I did was start saving for my own car."

"So if she left here, she would have taken a car ride service?" asked Pine.

"Yes."

"You haven't seen her phone?"

"No. She must have taken it with her."

"Did she have a laptop or an iPad or something like that?"

"No, just her phone. She used that for everything."

"We can still check into her account to find out if she was picked up by a service," said Pine while glancing at Blum. "And we can try to track her by her cell phone signal." She refocused on Clemmons. "Didn't you worry when your friend didn't come home? Did you file a missing persons report?"

"No. I mean, Hanna would go off before. Three, four days, and then she'd come back safe and sound."

"Did she tell you where she was going during these times?"

"No, and I didn't want to pry."

"Was she strung out when she came back?"

Clemmons looked uncomfortable. "I don't know. Maybe."

"Had she been going away the whole time you lived here or was it something recent?"

"It was the last month or so that she started going out and staying somewhere else. Although she was free to bring anybody here. I've brought my boyfriends over to stay before. It was no big deal."

"And she never mentioned a boyfriend? No pictures on her phone?"

"No."

"Social media, Facebook, Twitter, Instagram, any of the others?"

"She used to do that stuff, but not for the last six months or so. Neither one of us do Facebook anymore. She did Instagram, but she hasn't posted anything for a long time."

"Did she give a reason for that?"

"No and I never asked. I mean, some people just get sick of doing it all the time. And it's not like we have a zillion Instagram followers and could make money off it by putting our pictures on there or endorsing some product or other. We're not like the Kardashians or anything."

"Do you have any theories for what might have happened to Hanna?"

Her eyes welled with tears. "No, I wish I did. She was really nice. And I can't understand why anyone would want to hurt her."

Pine said firmly, "Well, it might be a good thing that you can't understand people who would do this sort of thing. Because it's a pretty dark place."

This comment drew a sharp glance from Blum.

"I . . . I guess," said Clemmons, rubbing her eyes.

"So other than her telling you she wanted to leave the adult film business when you two had lunch, did anything seem off about her that you noticed? Was she tense, unfocused? Did she seem scared?"

"No, not really. We just had lunch and that was it. I was surprised that she was giving up such a great gig, but I can understand it. I plan on doing it for maybe two more years and then I'm going to nursing school. There's a shortage."

"Good for you," said Blum. "And a much better way to spend your life."

"I hope you're not judging my decisions," Clemmons said, frowning.

"I could lie and say I'm not, but everyone always judges everyone else's decisions. My mother was the queen of that."

"You sound like *my* mother."

"I could very well *be* your mother. And I'm sure she wants you to be happy *and* safe. And like it or not, a career in nursing is safer and healthier than one in adult films, at least if you look at the statistics."

"But the money is so good."

"Of course it is, Beth. That's the whole point. But would you rather be helping a child get well, or help a male actor get off?"

"You're very blunt."

"I've lived long enough to know when politeness is required and when directness gets me to where I need to go. I do wish you the best of luck."

Pine rose and so did Blum. Pine handed Clemmons a business card and said, "Anything else occurs to you, please let me know."

Clemmons looked down at the card. "And you'll let me know when you catch whoever did this?"

"We will," said Pine. She knelt down to tie her shoelaces, rose, glanced inscrutably at Blum, and then they left.

They met back up with Wallis in the lobby. He looked excited.

"They *do* have exterior cameras here. I got them to pull what they have. They have a little room in back for us to watch it. I asked the concierge if he had ever known of a guy visiting Rebane, but he didn't. The same for the security guard on duty. I asked them to check with their counterparts to see if they ever had. And we'll canvass her neighbors with the same question."

He led them to a room at the rear of the lobby where a uniformed security guard was at a control board. Wallis gave him the date parameters and the man loaded the info onto the system.

They stood behind him and watched the TV monitor on the board come to life.

An hour later Pine saw it first. "There, coming out the front door. Freeze that."

The guard hit a key on the board, and the picture they were looking at stopped right there.

Wallis eyed the time stamp on the side of the frame. "That was probably the night her roommate was staying at her boyfriend's."

"Let it run now," said Pine.

The guard did so, and they all watched Hanna Rebane walk out the front doors of the building and move out of range of the cameras. She encountered no other person on the way.

"She's dressed like she's going on a date," noted Blum, who peered closely at the image. "Designer dress, handbag, and shoes that don't look like knockoffs."

Wallis stared at her. "You can tell all that from the video? That's impressive."

Blum glanced at him. "You just have to know what

to look for, Detective. Plus, she had all those designers in her closet."

They watched the film for a long time.

However, Hanna Rebane never came back.

23

It was quite late as they drove to Andersonville in silence, each of them lost in their own thoughts. Pine stared out the window at countryside she had seen only decades ago as a child. It was beautiful land: open fields intermingled with large stands of pine and oak trees. And yet there was an isolation here, which meant a great deal of criminal activity could flourish without serious challenge.

And it did flourish that night in Andersonville with no challenge at all.

Wallis dropped them off at the Cottage and promised that he would see if there were any other surveillance cameras near the apartment building that might pick up where the visuals around Rebane's residence had left off.

"In addition to canvassing her neighbors, you also need to get a tech team over there to dust for prints and collect other traces," Pine had told him. "Whoever she might have been seeing could have visited her there when Clemmons was away. If he's in the system, it would be a shortcut to find out who he is.

That and checking her cell phone or credit card activity and seeing if their locations can be traced."

"Right."

After Wallis drove off the two women walked into the empty breakfast room and sat down opposite each other.

"Well?" asked Blum.

"Did you believe everything Clemmons told us?"

"Of course not. I never believe anything anyone tells me until it's corroborated. FBI 101. But do you have anything in particular you're thinking about?"

"She lied about the drug use."

"You nailed her on that."

"I meant her *own* drug use."

"Come again?"

"She injects between her toes. When I went down to 'tie' my shoelaces, I noticed it."

"You must have suspected she was a user if you employed that sort of subterfuge."

"Her edginess was natural today, but it struck me as a little over the top, meaning chemically turbo-charged."

"Her eyes weren't dilated. I checked."

"No, they were pinpricks. Which means she was either on an opiate like Oxycodone, or maybe morphine or heroin."

"It's a wonder she was able to function. Those aren't lightweight drugs."

"I would imagine she's built up a tolerance," said

Pine grimly. "She might have taken a quick hit to prepare for meeting us."

"That is very sad."

"I also found a bottle of Narcan under Rebane's pillow."

"You didn't mention that to Detective Wallis. Any particular reason?"

"Just my gut. We're sort of in foreign territory right now, Carol. I'd like to play things close to the vest. Wallis already knows Rebane had relapsed. He didn't need to know about the Narcan to reach that conclusion."

"So what do we do now?"

"We have to wait for Wallis to get some more leads. Hopefully, some of the other people at the apartment building might have seen our mystery man."

"So you definitely think he exists? Clemmons wasn't even certain there was anyone."

"Other things being equal, the change in her, wanting to get out of adult films, being withdrawn and secretive, all point to someone out there influencing her. And Clemmons seemed to think she was susceptible to that. Predators key on people that way."

"But," said Blum.

"But that doesn't mean that person killed her."

"I wonder why the killer picked Andersonville to dump the body."

"That could imply some connection to the place. Killers like familiar surroundings. They want ingress and a way to escape all planned out beforehand. They still get the high they crave, but it takes away some of the risk of being caught."

"Do you believe the person will strike again?"

"Yes. I'm afraid it's just the beginning." Pine paused, her face tensing.

"What?" asked Blum.

"And you might have been right. My presence here might have been the catalyst for the killings to commence."

"I know I raised that possibility, but this is in no way your fault."

"I know that, Carol. But at the end of the day that doesn't matter. People will still die."

"Well, he made a mistake then."

"What's that?"

"He did it while you're in town. My bet is on you to bring him down."

"I appreciate your confidence."

"I don't give it out freely. You earned it."

Blum went to her room to go to bed while Pine stayed in the breakfast room.

"You look lost in thought."

Pine glanced up to see Lauren Graham standing in the doorway.

She had on light blue slacks, a cream-colored sweater, a matching blue headband through her short ginger hair, and shoes that matched her sweater.

Pine thought the woman must plan her wardrobe using a paint color wheel.

"Just chilling."

Graham came over and sat down in the seat Blum had been in. "Why do I think you never 'chill'?"

"I had lunch with Jack Lineberry."

"Where?"

"Americus. At a restaurant across from the Windsor Hotel."

"He's never asked me out to eat," she said with a trace of bitterness.

"He said it was a spur-of-the-moment thing."

"Doesn't sound like Jack."

"I didn't believe him, either," said Pine, drawing a sharp glance from Graham. "He was really interested in what became of my mom."

"Well, that's not so strange. They were friends."

"Thirty years ago. They haven't seen each other since."

"I haven't seen your mother in all that time, and I've wondered what happened to her."

When Pine didn't respond Graham said, "So, is she doing okay?"

"I'll tell you what I told Lineberry—she has her challenges. It hasn't been easy for her."

"I'm sorry to hear that."

"How's the novel coming?"

"Slowly. It's harder than people think."

"I never thought it would be easy to write a book."

"Any progress on the woman who was found dead?"

"Running down some leads."

A few moments of silence passed.

Graham stirred and gave Pine a nervous glance. "Look, I know this is an odd segue, but would you be willing to talk to me about some of your cases? For my novel, I mean."

"I can't talk about specific cases."

"No, I know that. I just mean some general things."

"Let me think about it."

Graham looked put out by this but didn't respond.

Pine rose. "Well, it's been a long day. Think I'll hit the hay."

"What else did you and Jack talk about?" Graham asked in a casual tone, but Pine observed her to be anything but relaxed.

"That was about it."

"Really?"

"Really. If you'll excuse me."

Pine walked off.

24

It was a restless night of scattered dreams with Pine's chasing various iterations of Daniel James Tor and Clifford Rogers around in the darkness until she awoke at around six in the morning.

There were no gym facilities at the B&B, but Pine had a workout app on her phone, with the only necessary equipment being her body and willingness to sweat. Which she did in her room for forty-five intense minutes. As she sat on the floor afterward breathing hard, she had to admit that the release of endorphins was always a good way to start the day.

She showered, dressed, and headed out into an awakening day. There was no one else walking along the pavement and no cars or trucks driving down the road.

She steered her rental across Highway 49 to the Andersonville National Historic Site.

The area mainly consisted of the old prison site, some impressive statuary, the vast cemetery of Union dead, and the National Prisoner of War Museum.

The place didn't open until eight, so Pine parked

and walked along the perimeter of the area. The Prisoner of War Museum hadn't been here when she lived in the Andersonville area. She learned it had opened in the late 1990s.

Pine entered the grounds right when they opened. A National Park Service Ranger greeted her, and since there were no other visitors at the moment he offered to show her around. He introduced himself as Barry Lamb. He was around forty, about six feet tall and muscular, with a clean-shaven face and large green eyes. His Ranger uniform fit him well.

"FBI?" he said, noting the shield on her belt.

Pine nodded. "I'm assigned to the Grand Canyon. Just visiting out here."

"The Grand Canyon?" Lamb said in a wistful tone. "I'd love to have a shot at going out there to work."

"Popular destination for park rangers. But you should give it a try. It's pretty unique. How long have you worked here?"

"Six years. It's interesting for sure. But after a while you know every square inch of it. It's not that big. And the theme is sort of depressing. All those Union soldiers died for really no good reason."

"But they helped end slavery. That *was* momentous."

"You're right about that. Just a damn shame it took a war."

He showed her the old prison site, which was represented by a replica of a portion of the prison's stockade. Lamb pointed out a spot set back from the wooden wall, something he called the "Deadline."

"You passed that line, you got shot dead," said Lamb. "Hence the name. I think some prisoners did so just to end their misery. They were starving to death and disease ridden."

"I could see someone in such a situation doing that," said Pine.

"Until 1864 the Confederates would just carry their prisoners around with them. When that became unmanageable, this prison was constructed as a solution. It was built to hold ten thousand men. Problem was, in the single year it was in operation, it would hold over four times that many."

She looked around at the sheets of cloth strung over wooden stakes in the middle of the stockade. "So where were the prisoners housed?"

"There were no shelters built, no cells, no buildings. They'd have a dozen prisoners under two gum blankets strung over sticks, like that one over there. When a prisoner died, the survivors would fight over his clothes and shoes. When the prison was liberated in 1865 the remaining prisoners looked like something you would have seen in a German concentration camp. Henry Wirz, the commandant, was later executed for war crimes."

"Yeah, I knew about that. He has the big statue in town. Did anyone ever try to escape?"

"Some men escaped in transit or while on work

details. A few others did so by tunnels. There are still remnants of some tunnels around. Like this one over here."

He led her to a spot some distance from the edge of the replica. There were warning signs around it and a steel grate in the earth. "It begins here, which would have been rather in the middle of the prison grounds. It extends out to the west, well under the walls of the original prison and into some very thick woods. Some made it to the Union lines from here."

"Good for them."

"Let me show you what I call the 'mother' of all the prisoners here."

It was a large statue in marble. The engraving on it said it had been erected by the state of Michigan in memoriam for Michigan soldiers and sailors who had been prisoners here. Pine's gaze was riveted by the other part of the monument. It was of a woman with a headpiece and long flowing robes who had her left arm draped over the top of the monument and her gaze downcast, as though in grief. This obviously was the "mother" Lamb had been referring to.

"That's very moving," said Pine in a low voice.

"There's nothing like a mother's love."

"Or a mother's grief," added Pine quietly.

As they walked over to the cemetery he stopped at a spot and pointed out a row of graves. "These are the six leaders of the Raiders. You know about them?"

Pine shook her head.

"They were a group of prisoners who terrorized other prisoners."

"And the guards did nothing?"

"There weren't nearly enough guards to really control the prisoners. This place was like a shanty-town you'd see in a third world country. So the prisoners were pretty much on their own."

"So what happened?"

"This group called the Regulators rose up and took out the Raiders. Then Henry Wirz held a series of trials with the judges and juries being fellow prisoners. Most of the men convicted received light sentences, at least light by the standards back then. Stockade, thumbscrews, having to run a gauntlet where they were beaten with sticks. But the main six leaders, they were called the 'chieftains' who ran their own little gangs, were convicted and executed. And that's where their graves are. They're set off from the others to denote this."

Pine studied the sunken plots of dirt. "It doesn't take much for civilized people to become animals."

"I guess you see a lot of that in your line of work."

"More than I would like."

She left the ranger there and ventured to the museum.

It was a large building that held a library and a film room, and told the story of American POWs from the Revolutionary War up to the present. This theme was filled in with exhibits and information about the capture of POWs, their living conditions, relationships among prisoners and their guards, escape attempts, and liberation of some POW camps. When she walked out of the place later Pine was both overwhelmed by the bravery shown by the POWs and depressed that a "civilized" world allowed such things to actually happen.

She stood outside in the growing heat as the sun rose overhead and the humidity picked up. Pine involuntarily glanced to her left at the rows of graves in the cemetery. The somberness of the place could not be overstated. And it was very likely that Mercy was also in a grave somewhere. Only not in a formal cemetery, but in a shallow hole in the middle of nowhere, which animals would have long since desecrated.

She touched her Glock and wished she could right this very minute shoot and kill whoever had taken Mercy. But that was not going to happen. She had to get there another way.

She got into her SUV and drove back across the road.

She wondered how long they would have to wait for the killer of Hanna Rebane to strike again.

As it turned out, it wouldn't be long at all.

25

Pine was used to getting phone calls at odd hours; that came with being an FBI agent.

When she heard Max Wallis's voice and saw the time was two minutes past five in the morning, she sat straight up in bed and swung her feet to the floor.

"Where?" she said instantly.

He was too much of a veteran cop to ask how she knew.

"The cemetery. Across the road from you."

Pine's jaw slackened. "The National Historic Site? I was just there yesterday morning."

"I'll meet you at the front gate."

It took her five minutes to dress. She didn't wake Blum. There was no reason to do that right now. She could be filled in later. Pine was starting to regret even bringing Blum here. But then again she hadn't anticipated a potential serial killer commencing operations in Andersonville, either.

She was out the front door of the Cottage a minute later, started her SUV, and a couple minutes after that she was at the cemetery. The darkness was total. There was no hint of dawn yet, just inky blackness.

A murder, darkness, and a cemetery. What a combo.

Two county police cars were already there, along with Wallis's Crown Vic.

The detective was standing by the front gate wearing a tattered beige trench coat and holding a cup of coffee. He looked about ten years older than the last time she had seen him.

Pine walked up to him even as she could see lights off in the distance. They started walking in that direction.

"It's a man this time," said Wallis. "Black guy around thirty."

"COD?"

"Prelim is a single gunshot wound to the chest."

"Anything unusual?"

"You'll see for yourself," he replied cryptically.

They reached the cemetery and walked between the rows of graves until they arrived at the bank of work lights that had been set up next to a popup tent, which Pine assumed had been placed over the body.

"Who found it?"

"A ranger coming on duty early. Guy was laid right over a grave."

Pine looked around and suddenly realized where she was. "You mean on a *Raider's* grave."

Wallis looked at her blankly. "Come again? Raider's grave?"

Pine explained the distinction.

"You think that was intentional?" asked Wallis.

"Right now we can't afford to assume that it wasn't. Let's see the body."

They passed by the officer guarding the tent and ducked inside it after putting on booties and latex gloves.

Pine and Wallis stared down at the man lying on top of the grave. There was a light shining on the body so they could see it clearly.

Pine's eyes widened. She said, "He's in a tuxedo. With a top hat on his stomach and a corsage on his jacket."

"It's old-fashioned like the veil." He glanced at her appraisingly. "So what's your take?"

Pine said, "It was a *wedding* veil. She's the bride. And this guy's the groom. It's like they're the toppers on a cake."

"Right, that one I figured out. So what the hell is the perp trying to say? Is he striking out against marriage in general? But Hanna Rebane wasn't married, at least that we know of."

"But she did have a child. Maybe this guy was the father."

"How the hell do we prove that? We don't even know where the kid is."

"We have to ID this guy. If he has a connection to Hanna Rebane, we might have our answer."

"We've taken prints and are running them. Hopefully something will pop."

Pine squatted down and ran her gaze over the man and the ground surrounding the body. She touched his hand. "Cold." She tried to bend the arm. "He's in rigor. Been dead at least twelve hours, probably more."

"Coroner said the same thing. We'll have more after the post, of course."

Pine examined the wound on the man's chest. "He obviously wasn't killed here. His estimated time of death would place that no later than late yesterday afternoon. And there's no blood on the ground. He bled out elsewhere."

"Like the first vic. Killed somewhere else and placed later."

She opened the jacket and looked for a label but didn't see one. She did the same for the hat with the same result. "He might have bought the tux somewhere. Top hats aren't that easy to come by. If he ordered it online that might be a lead. The corsage looks pretty fresh. That's another lead."

"Lots of people order corsages."

"But not top hats. It's something, at least. Although he might have already had them in his possession. The tux and hat look pretty decrepit. Or he could have gotten them at a secondhand shop. Or even inherited them."

She looked at the man's fingernails. "No obvious signs of skin or blood. Any defensive wounds?"

"Not that we could see. But you wouldn't necessarily have them with a shooting."

Pine rose and looked down at the dead man.

"What are you thinking?" said Wallis.

"I wonder if the race of the victim was coincidence or it has meaning."

"You mean white bride and black groom?"

Pine nodded. "Maybe we're looking at some sort of hate crime. Or maybe it's something else altogether. We just don't know enough yet to tell."

"We've got to ID this guy as fast as we can."

"If he doesn't have a criminal record, that might be tough. I can make some calls and have his prints run through other databases."

"I'm not too proud to ask for help, so yeah, make the calls. I can text you the print deck."

"Let me know when the post is."

"Will do."

"Anything on the rest of the security footage from Rebane's apartment building? Or any activity on her phone or credit cards?"

"We looked at all of it yesterday. Nothing on any other surveillance tapes. Struck out on the phone and credit cards, too."

Pine left the tent and gazed around. Wallis came to stand next to her.

"This was a risk, putting the body in so public a place," she said.

"But nobody was around at the hour he probably did so."

"But if he came from town, he had to drive across the highway. I don't see the guy schlepping a body in his arms across the road in the dead of night."

"He could have come from the other way."

"Still had to drive."

"Lot of cars come and go from here. Asphalt parking lot. We found no useful traces."

"Maybe somebody was out late and saw something."

"We'll be checking all of that," promised Wallis.

"We have a serial murderer here, you know."

"It doesn't take a genius."

"No, I mean, you have to make a call."

"To who?"

"The FBI."

"You *are* the FBI."

"I'm here unofficially. You need to officially request their assistance. This is what they do. They have a ton of resources and specialists devoted to this. I used to be one of them."

"You mean profilers and such?"

"Technically, there is no such thing at the Bureau. They're called analysts."

"Do I tell them about your involvement?"

Pine didn't answer right away. "Might as well. They're going to find out at some point."

"What are you going to do now?"

"Catch a couple more hours of sleep. I think I'm going to need it."

26

"Who do you think they'll send?" asked Blum.

They were at the Cottage in Pine's room. It was later in the morning, and Pine had filled Blum in about the recent murder.

"I don't know. I was offered a position at BAU Three while I was stationed in the DC area," said Pine, referring to the Behavioral Analysis Units that were part of the FBI's National Center for the Analysis of Violent Crime. "But that was a long time ago."

"Unit Three deals with crimes against children," said Blum.

Pine nodded. "And Unit Four deals with crimes against adults and includes the ViCAP database that you accessed earlier. I *did* work there for a year."

"Why just a year? Don't most agents stay there for longer than that?"

"Let's just say I had my fill."

"I've read that some people are critical of using psychological profiling."

"It's not perfect, and it's only one tool that we use

among many. But it got results. Now, with a team being called in, they can do a deeper dive and also integrate what we learn with this latest death."

"A groom's outfit," said Blum with a slight shiver. "This is really getting creepy."

"This guy is sophisticated and focused and organized. And he must know the area. Putting a dead black guy on top of a Union soldier's grave? But one of the Raiders, who were really bad guys because they preyed on those who wore the same uniform? I'm not certain there's a message there, but I also have a hard time believing it's a coincidence."

"What do we do now?"

"We have no leads to run down on that case, so I want to focus on why we came here."

"Do we have leads on your sister then?"

"We have a clue. Eeny, meeny, miny, moe. The guy said that rhyme. I know I didn't imagine it. So if it wasn't Tor who did it, who was it? And why use that device?"

"It was a way to decide which of you to take," opined Blum.

"Why was it a choice?"

"He could only take one of you."

"Why? If my parents were stoned downstairs, and he had already come through the house? If he carried Mercy downstairs, why not me, too? We were only six. He probably could have carried us away together.

But he took Mercy and struck me so hard he cracked my skull."

"Maybe he only wanted one of you, for some reason."

"Right. But I'm just wondering what that reason was. And if he really wanted to kill me, why not just do it? He could have suffocated me, broken my neck. But he chose to hit me. He couldn't have known whether I would die or not from my injuries."

Blum sat back in her chair as she considered all this. "It's a puzzler."

"Myron Pringle knows more than he's willing to tell."

"What are you going to do about that?"

"Talk to him again. We'll have to go out there since he doesn't have a phone or email."

"How about I talk to Britta while you speak to Myron? I think she has some secrets of her own. Maybe I can talk to her, mom to mom, to find out what they are."

"Let's go."

Nearly an hour later they pulled into the unsettling quiet drive and drove down to the contemporary dwelling. Before they even reached the front steps the door opened and there stood Britta Pringle. She had on a light gray pleated skirt that showed off tanned, toned calves, a blue sweater vest, and a white long-sleeved shirt and gray canvas shoes.

"I saw you coming up the drive," she explained. "Myron has the whole place under video surveillance."

"I'm sure he does," said Pine as she and Blum walked up the steps. "I don't like just showing up like this. I would have called, but—"

Britta's look turned weary. "But we don't have phones or emails. Yes, I know. It definitely cuts down on friendships," she added—a little unhappily, Pine thought.

"What can I do for you?" Britta asked.

"I wanted to talk to Myron again. I assume he's up."

"Yes, he just finished eating."

"If he could spare some time."

"What is this about?" said Britta.

"Just some follow-up questions."

She led them into the house and said, "I heard on the news that another body was discovered in Andersonville."

"Yes, at the cemetery next to the prison site."

"My God. Does that mean that there's a serial killer in our midst?"

"It could. They'll probably call the FBI in for this."

"But you're already here."

"Yes, but not in my professional capacity. Where's Myron?"

"He's floating in the pool. He likes to do that right after he eats."

"Not a proponent of the thirty-minute-wait rule?" said Blum.

"Oh, he's not swimming. I'm not sure he can. He's just lying on a float. He said it helps him to think. Like being in a womb, he says."

"Can I head out there then?" asked Pine.

"Yes. Certainly."

When Blum didn't move to join her, Britta said, "Are you not going with her?"

"I think Agent Pine wants to do this alone. Maybe you and I can chat?"

Britta brightened at this suggestion. "I can make some coffee. And I just baked some muffins."

"I would love that."

Pine and Blum exchanged a meaningful glance and then headed off in opposite directions.

27

That's a lot of white skin, thought Pine as she approached the edge of the pool.

Myron Pringle was lying on a blue float wearing a pair of dark swim trunks. His calves hung off the end of the float. He had on a pair of sunglasses. He was so pale and still, he looked like a corpse.

Pine bent down and put her hand in the water. It was heated.

Myron was thin but not very fit and he seemed to have an abundance of hair all over. She didn't think she could see a defined muscle on the man. But then again she assumed his brain was of Olympic caliber.

"Mr. Pringle?"

He didn't react to her voice and she thought he might have glimpsed her coming over to the pool but had chosen not to say anything. "Mr. Pringle?"

He finally turned his head slightly.

"Yes?"

"Mind if I ask you a few questions?"

"Yes I do. This is my thinking time."

She slid a wicker lounge chair over to the side of

the pool and sat down in it. "Well, I can give you something to *think* about."

He lifted his glasses to his long, furrowed forehead and stared at her. "Such as?"

"It's not algorithms, just to forewarn you."

"It's about your mother, correct?"

"Care to fill me in on what you didn't tell me the last time?"

"I'm not sure I know what you're referring to."

"Sure you do, you're a smart guy."

He lowered the glasses. "I'm apparently not that smart, so you're going to have to spell it out, Agent Pine."

"Let me start with a lunch I had recently with Jack Lineberry."

"Jack, huh? Did he tell you to call him that?"

"He did."

"Okay."

"Why? What do you call him?"

"Boss."

"Would you like to know why he wanted to have lunch?"

"Not particularly."

"He wanted to know what had happened to my mother."

"Okay."

"Do you find that odd?"

He lifted his glasses again. "Where are you going with this?"

"Did you know that Lineberry found my father dead?"

"I think he might have mentioned it."

"You *think*? Do you get many people telling you they found the bodies of people who had blown their heads off with a shotgun? I thought your memory was better than average."

"Okay, yes, I do remember him telling me that. But it was a long time ago. What does that have to do with him wanting to know about your mother?"

"Maybe nothing."

"What did you tell him about her?"

"So you want to know, too?"

He lifted the glasses a third time. "I was her friend as well."

"But I don't recall either of you trying to contact my mother after we left Andersonville."

"I didn't know where you had moved."

"But Lineberry had kept in touch with my dad. And my dad knew where we were. All Lineberry had to do was ask."

The glasses came down again. "Yes, well, I don't know what to tell you."

"So I guess you weren't as friendly with my father as you said."

"What are your questions?" he asked in a brusque tone.

"What were you doing the night my sister was taken? Britta said she didn't remember."

"Then why would I?"

"Do you?"

"I'd have to think about it."

"So what about the next day? Run me through that."

"I was at work."

"When did you hear what had happened?"

"Britta called me at the office that morning."

"What did you do?"

"I couldn't leave the office right that minute. But I did get away early. Britta had already gone to the hospital with your mother. I went over to your house. Your dad was out looking for your sister. When he got back I saw him. That's when that idiot Barry Vincent accused Tim of having done this awful thing. He went after Vincent and I pulled them apart. Nearly got beaten up in the process. Luckily, I'm a big guy. And I was a lot stronger back then."

Pine looked him over. He *was* a big man. Taller than Daniel Tor. And thirty years ago he probably was more muscular, and stronger, as he had just admitted.

"Why weren't the police at the house to do that?"

"As I said before, I don't know. I can just tell you that there weren't any. It was only a bunch of gawkers."

"Did they try to determine if anyone other than my parents were at the house that night?"

"Again, I don't know. I only know that Britta and I weren't there."

"So where were you?"

"If you really have to know, we were at our house entertaining some friends."

"Why didn't you tell me that the first time around?"

"You were very blunt in your questioning. It turned me off, if you want to know the truth."

"I always prefer the *truth*. Who were these friends?"

"Just friends. We had some drinks, smoked some pot, and that was that."

"Friends have names?"

"They're no longer in the area."

Pine considered this as Myron climbed off the float, came over to the edge of the pool, and rested his arms on the coping. He said, "Now let me ask *you* some questions. What do you know about your parents' backgrounds?"

"Not a lot. High school sweethearts in Kansas. Fell in love, married early, had me and my sister, and then at some point we moved to Georgia."

"Really? Who told you that?"

Pine scrunched up her face. "They did, why?"

"Because your mother was a model starting at age sixteen. Milan, London, Paris. I doubt they went to the same high school and I doubt it was in Kansas. I'm not sure that Julia even finished high school."

Pine couldn't find her voice for a few moments. "Bullshit."

"Come with me."

Myron climbed out of the pool, toweled off, donned a T-shirt, and led Pine inside the house through a rear door and up to the second floor. He entered a room and beckoned her to join him. The room was set up as a small study. Myron tugged open the drawer of a wooden file cabinet, rummaged through it, and pulled out a magazine. He opened it to a certain page and handed it to Pine.

"Your mother treading the catwalk in London."

Pine looked down at the open page and her mind seemed to flutter uncomfortably as her gaze settled on the tall, leggy teenager who looked remarkably like her.

"A surprise, I take it," said Myron, who was watching her closely.

"Where did you get this?" demanded Pine.

"When your mom had been drinking or smoking pot, she opened up more than normal. She mentioned doing some modeling when she was a teenager. I was intrigued by that."

"But that doesn't explain how you came by this magazine."

"This was long after they had moved away from Georgia. In fact, it was only a few years ago. I did some online research on her. There wasn't anything there, but then I had a guy I knew who had access to the fashion world check into it. I gave him what I knew about your mom, including a picture I had taken of her when she did live here. It took him nearly a year, but he sent me that."

"But it doesn't give her name in the caption."

"Do you doubt that's your mother? Nobody I've ever known looked like her."

"It *is* her. Did this guy you hired tell you anything else?"

Myron eyed her closely. "Well, for starters he told me he thought her name wasn't Julia."

"What?"

"He said she had all the tools to be really something in the industry, but she just upped and left after only being on the scene for a few years. No one knew why and no one knew what had become of her. And no one he could find could tell him her last name. But apparently her first name was *Amanda*. Or at least that's the one she used at the time."

"Why would my mother change her name?" demanded Pine.

Myron, in response, spread his long, thin arms. "How should I know? I'm only telling you what the guy told me. And he wasn't some chump off the street. He came highly recommended. A real pro."

"Can I talk to this 'real pro'?"

"Afraid not."

"Why?"

"He dropped dead of a heart attack about a month after he reported back."

Pine felt like she'd been hit by a truck.

"I can see what a shock all this is for you," said Myron sympathetically.

Pine, her suspicion needle now hovering near the

red zone, said, "And why would you go to all that trouble to track down my mother's past?"

"Like I said, I'm a curious guy. And most people like to talk about their pasts. Neither one of your parents ever did. Not while they were sober. It just made me wonder."

"Wonder what?" Although Pine was already wondering herself.

"That maybe they weren't who they said they were. I mean, I told you her name might've been Amanda. But she comes here and it's suddenly Julia Pine."

"And my dad?"

"I don't know. He could very well be who he said he was. I didn't check into him."

"Does Britta know about all this?"

"She doesn't know that I investigated your mom, no. But she *was* there when Julia let slip that she had done some modeling."

Pine slumped down in a chair as she studied the photo of what was undoubtedly her mother walking the stage at a major fashion show in London. She read a bit of the article and said in amazement, "*Karl Lagerfeld*? This was Karl Lagerfeld's fashion show for Chanel? I basically know nothing about the fashion industry but I've heard of him."

"According to my guy, your mom apparently walked the runways of all the major designers' shows around the world back then."

"So how did I not know this?"

"It was long before Google. You couldn't just look it up online. And as I said, she only did that work for a short time. She wasn't like Cindy Crawford or Claudia Schiffer, who made careers out of it and became world famous. Your mother was taller and more gorgeous than any of those supermodels. But she didn't stick with it. So she passed into obscurity. No Wikipedia page or anything."

"Why? What happened to her?"

"I have no idea. They just showed up here one day with two little kids in tow. From the little bit they told us, I thought they had met on a blind date or something and fell in love."

"So they weren't high school sweethearts?"

Myron took back the magazine and looked down at the photo of the long-legged Julia Pine, sauntering down the catwalk in an elaborate Karl Lagerfeld creation with her hair piled high, looking like she owned the world and everyone in it.

"Does she look like she would be enrolled in a high school in Kansas? She couldn't be more than seventeen there." He gave her a hard stare. "And when I just now said your parents showed up here with you and your sister in tow, you didn't seem surprised. And you knew you weren't born here."

"When I was an adult, I found out I was born in New York. It was quite an eye-opener, actually, because up till then I thought I *was* born in Georgia."

Myron nodded but didn't comment on this.

"You said they didn't talk about themselves while sober. Did my dad ever talk about his past when he was drinking?"

Myron set the magazine down and rubbed his chin. "Actually, he did. Your dad wanted to be an actor. At least that's what he said. That's why he was in New York, working on his career. That might be when he met your mom. That's pretty much the only thing he ever told me about himself in the time that they lived here."

Pine let out a sharp breath, feeling filled with incredulity. "My dad wanted to be an actor? My mom was an international model? You're talking about someone else's life. They never told me any of that. Nothing."

"I don't know why they didn't. Maybe they think it didn't matter. Maybe they thought you'd believe they'd made bad choices, or they'd given up their careers for their kids. I'm just speculating, obviously."

"I knew that neither of them had siblings. That their parents were dead. At least that's what they told me. Is that true, or do I have grandparents or aunts and uncles I don't know about? No one has ever tried to contact me."

"I'm afraid I don't know anything about that part of their lives," said Myron.

"But why would she change her name from Amanda to Julia?"

Even though Pine was ostensibly asking this question of herself and not Myron, he replied, "Maybe she just wanted to disappear. And it's not illegal to change your name."

Pine glanced at the magazine. "Can I have that?"

"With my compliments," he said, passing it over to her.

"Did they ever mention to you why they would pick a place like Andersonville to settle in? I mean, if my mom traveled all over the world, this is a little dull by comparison."

"Well, those places aren't for everybody. Britta and I could live anywhere. But we chose here. Maybe your mom was burned out with all those hurly-burly, glitzy locales and just wanted something simpler."

She stared down at the magazine. "You've given me a lot to think about."

"What will you do with that information?"

"I came here to try to discover what happened to my sister. Now, on top of that, I have to try to figure out who my parents really were."

"I guess you weren't counting on having to do that."

"Who would?" she retorted.

28

"What does Lee want to talk to Myron about?" asked Britta as she prepared the coffees in the kitchen. She had glanced out the window to see Pine approaching the pool, where her husband was lying on the float.

"Just some questions about her parents, I would imagine. She's a skilled investigator. She'll know what to ask."

Britta brought the coffees and a plate of warm corn muffins over and set them down on the table before settling in across from Blum.

"You were obviously close to Julia. What did you think of her?"

Britta took a moment to collect her thoughts. "She was a lovely woman. I don't just mean physically. In that way she was a stunner. So tall and lean. Gorgeous hair, her body and facial bone structure were perfect. I can see that Lee has taken after her in that way. But while she's very tall, too, she's far more, well, muscular than her mother."

"In the world she works in, being strong and fit is

more important than looks. And she worked hard to build that physical strength."

"I'm sure. Anyway, Julia was complicated."

"How so?"

"She never really talked about her past. But I could tell she was worldly from comments she made; she had obviously traveled outside the country. Myron told me she had even been a model. That didn't surprise me. She had a model's body and face and height. Although I don't think she did it long. She couldn't have, really."

"What do you mean?"

"She was so young when she had the girls."

"Do you remember when they were born?"

"Oh no, they weren't born here."

Blum remained stoic, though this remark had startled her.

"The girls were around two when Tim and Julia came to Andersonville."

"Okay," said Blum. "I've only seen one picture. It was just of Agent Pine and her sister. None of her parents. Agent Pine said it was the only one she had."

"Just the one photo? That's strange."

"Do you have one of the Pines?"

"Let me look. I'll be back in a minute."

After she left, Blum watched from the window as Myron got out of the pool, toweled off, put on a shirt, and led Pine up a set of exterior stairs to the second level. Her boss looked surprised. Maybe Myron was giving her information similar to what Britta was providing Blum.

"Here."

Blum turned to see Britta coming back and carrying a small snapshot.

She handed it over to Blum.

"I think this was from when the girls turned four."

The Pines were all lined up in a row. Tim on one end, the slightly taller Julia on the other. In between were Pine and her sister Mercy. Blum looked more closely.

"Boy, you really can't tell them apart, except Atlee is wearing pants and Mercy a frilly dress—at least I think that's right."

"It is. Lee was always the tomboy. Mercy was the girly-girl. That was really the only way we could tell them apart. You almost never caught Lee in a dress, and certainly nothing that frilly."

"Her mother is extraordinarily beautiful."

"And Tim was nothing to sneeze at, either. I can tell you that during the summer when he was working outside in shorts and without his shirt on, well, some of the ladies who lived nearby would find excuses to come by just to sigh, myself included."

Blum smiled. "I think I would have been part of that group. Did they ever tell you anything more about their lives before coming to Andersonville?"

"No, like I said, Julia kept things close to the vest, and Tim wasn't much of a talker."

Blum bit into a muffin and took a sip of her coffee. "So how did you and your husband end up here?"

Britta's features softened. "Myron had a friend in the mining industry. He helped get Myron a job with the bauxite operation."

"And a computer guy liked working at a mine?"

"He didn't do the heavy lifting. His job was more scientific. In fact, he helped come up with a couple of uses of bauxite that they didn't even know about back then. He's always been an out-of-the-box thinker."

"How did you two meet?"

"A blind date over in Huntsville, Alabama. I had just graduated from college and Myron had been out a year. He was very tall and nice looking but quiet. I had no idea he was a genius. He just seemed aloof. Most people didn't understand him, but we hit it off. We've been together a long time . . ." Her voice trailed off. "I thought I'd be a grandmother by now. I thought a lot of things would have happened that never will."

Blum put a hand on the other woman's arm. "I'm so very sorry, Britta. I can't imagine how deeply painful that must have been for you."

"Yes, well, as they say, life goes on. And we've made the best lives we can, considering. But there's not a day that goes by that I don't think of my children. And what could have been."

Blum gave her arm another squeeze and then sat back.

Britta finally sighed, took a drink of her coffee, and looked up. "You and Lee seem to get along really well."

Blum, grateful for the change in the conversation, said, "She's a great boss and a better agent."

"I'm sure you're very proud of her."

"She's worked for everything she's got. The Bureau is still largely a man's domain. But she jumped right in and pulled her weight from day one. She doesn't take crap from anybody, and if you want to be a misogynist around her, you do so at your peril. Believe me, I've seen it."

Britta glanced at the window. "I wonder how she and Myron are getting on?"

"I assume he knows all the things you've shared with me."

"Oh, yes. Maybe more."

"Then he's probably already told them to Agent Pine."

"Can't she ask Julia directly about all of this? She's still alive, isn't she?"

"I don't know."

"But surely Lee would know that?"

"I don't know," said Blum vaguely. "I hate to pry."

"Oh, I see."

"Jack Lineberry wanted to know," Blum said suggestively. "He asked Agent Pine about her mother."

"Really?" said Britta.

"Does that surprise you?"

"No, it doesn't. They were very good friends."

How good? Blum wanted to ask, but decided not to go there.

"Do you enjoy working at the FBI?" asked Britta.

"Yes, I do. It's never a dull moment with Agent Pine. Right before she came out here she saved a little girl on an Amber Alert. The creep who snatched her was a convicted pedophile who had raped and probably murdered young girls in the past. Agent Pine took him on solo, and he got the short end of that stick. The guy's going away for good now and thank God for that."

"She sounds very formidable."

"That's a good word choice, actually."

"Her mother must be proud."

Is she? wondered Blum.

29

Pine and Blum were at the Clink having dinner that night.

Earlier, they had filled in each other about their respective conversations with Myron and Britta.

"This must be very distressing for you, Agent Pine."

"What, knowing absolutely nothing about where I came from or who my parents really were? Or the parts that I *was* told just being lies?"

"What *do* you remember about their pasts?"

"Only what they told me, which was very little."

"What about after you left here?"

"As I said before, we moved to a small town in South Carolina. Then years later my parents split up."

"Because of what had happened?"

Pine played with her paper napkin. "I always assumed that was the reason. They argued constantly. It was about a lot of things, but Mercy's name kept coming up."

"What happened after that?"

"I chose to live with my mom. We stayed in South

Carolina and my dad lived nearby. Then that all changed."

"How so?"

"I was just about to start high school when my mother told me we were moving."

"Moving where?"

"She didn't tell me until the movers came. We ended up going to Texas."

"Did she say why?"

"Not really."

"And did you ever learn where you were actually born? Britta was very clear that you were not born here." She paused and added, "I was very surprised by that—but don't worry, I didn't let her see that."

Pine looked at Blum, easily reading her thoughts. "I know where I was born. I'm sorry I didn't tell you that before."

"You have the right to keep your private information private, Agent Pine. But I hope you know that anything you do tell me will be kept in the strictest confidence."

"I know that, Carol." She paused, marshalling her thoughts. "I was born in New York. They didn't tell me that. I only knew because I had to apply for a passport when I was in college. I was into Olympic-style weightlifting and I had to travel overseas for competitions. I remember looking at my birth certificate, which I needed to get a passport. I had asked my mom for it. I just sat there staring at the piece of paper for the longest time. You see, up to that point I'd always thought I'd been born in Georgia. I really had no recollection of living in New York."

"Well, since Britta believed you moved here when you were around two, it's not surprising you have no memory of New York."

"I asked my mom about it. She just sort of blew it off. Said of course I was born there and that we had moved to Georgia later. She said she had told me, but I don't think I would have forgotten that."

"No, I don't think you would have."

"It was tough moving to Texas right before I started high school. I'd made some friends, now I was starting from scratch." She paused. "My dad wasn't around anymore. I rebelled. I started binge drinking. Did some shoplifting. Smoked some weed. The police got called in. I was definitely going down a bad path."

"What happened to turn you around? Your mom?"

"No, it wasn't her. I mean, she tried to talk sense into me, but I wasn't prepared to listen. I was too upset with her for moving and my dad not being around. And I was really missing Mercy. I felt alone, I guess."

"So, what happened then?"

"This is going to sound stupid."

"I've seen a lot of life. So try me."

"There was a little carnival where we lived. It had a fortune-teller. I got my fortune read. I don't know why. Anyway, the lady told me something."

"What was that?"

"She felt my palm and said she sensed two heartbeats in me, not one. And she told me she thought I knew why."

Blum sat back. "Mercy?"

Pine nodded. "It was like a switch got turned on inside me. I hit the books, started playing sports, worked my ass off to—"

"—live your life and live your sister's life for her?"

"Something like that," Pine said in a pained voice. "And in the interest of full disclosure, I came home from college one summer and my mother had gone. There was a note to me saying that she basically had to move on. She left enough money for me to live off and to pay for the rest of my education. I haven't seen her since."

"My God," said a visibly distressed Blum. "She just . . . abandoned you?"

"Well, since I was an adult, legally that wasn't the case. But in every other aspect of the word, yes, she abandoned me. I called the police and filed a missing persons report, but there's no law against an adult going away voluntarily. There was no evidence of any foul play."

"But still, you must have been crushed."

"I was, for a long time. I looked for her, of course. Then when I became an FBI agent, I looked harder, all in my spare time. I still came up with zip. I keep looking periodically, but it's like she vanished off the face of the earth. She might very well be dead." Pine looked down. "It would just be nice to know one way or another."

"Well, it turned out okay. You're an FBI agent."

"Jury's still out on that," Pine said ominously as she took a sip of her beer. "Despite what Dobbs said, he could pull the plug on me at any time. Why risk his own career for me?"

"Well, I know he can be pretty tough, but he might surprise you, Agent Pine. He gave you this chance to get things right. He didn't have to do that."

"You're right. He didn't."

"What did your mother do for work when you both moved to Texas?"

"Why?"

"I'm just trying to put some thoughts together."

"She didn't work, not right away."

"But then how did she support both of you?"

"She said she'd inherited some money from some distant relative." Pine glanced up to see Blum's incredulous look. "I know. I was just a dumb teenager. I believed what she said."

"But she eventually got a job?"

"Yes. But she never really talked about her work other than saying it was just pushing paper around. And I was totally immersed in school and sports. I never focused on what she was doing at her job."

"Did she ever travel during that time? Go outside the country?"

"No, nothing like that."

"And your father? Did he stay in South Carolina?"

"Yes. I was really pissed about that. I mean, he was my dad. Mom explained it by saying she had gotten this job offer in Texas and needed to take it. And that my dad understood. But that didn't make any sense, because, like I said, she didn't start working right away."

"Well, she was your mother. You should be able to trust her. Did your father ever talk about her moving you to Texas and leaving him behind?"

"When I spoke with him on the phone I could tell he was having to struggle keeping a job. He was drinking too much and maybe doing drugs, too. But he never said a bad word against my mom." She looked down. "He always told me he loved me. That . . . that he was so very sorry about Mercy. But that he was glad that I was still in his life."

"And then?"

"And then, when I was in college, my mom got a call. He'd been found dead. A suicide. I was told that it was in Louisiana in some motel, only apparently it wasn't."

"That's right," said Blum. "Jack Lineberry said it was at your dad's apartment in Virginia, which is where I guess he had moved to. But he never mentioned that to you?"

"Never. Anyway, my mom went to handle the

arrangements, or so she told me. I wanted to go, but she wouldn't let me. He was cremated. She said she spread his ashes somewhere that was dear to him."

"Do you know where that was?"

"No, she never said. And now I found out that it was Jack Lineberry who found his body. My mom never told me that, either."

"Maybe she didn't know."

"He had to know she'd come down after my dad killed himself. But she never mentioned seeing him. And Lineberry said he didn't see her then, either."

"And your mother left you shortly after this happened?"

"Yes. Within a couple of months, in fact."

"This is all so strange," observed Blum.

Pine shook her head. "Here I am an investigator, trained to ferret out the truth, to tell when people are lying, to see things when they're off. And now talking about my own life, there were so many red flags, how the hell did I not see them, Carol? I mean, how in the hell?"

"It's just that when this was all happening you were not a trained investigator. And people want to believe in and trust their loved ones, particularly kids with their parents."

"Well, now I have to see the truth when it's staring me in the face."

"Let's go back to the money she left you. Any idea where it came from?"

"No. It was a lot, though, but the bank said it was okay. It was her money."

"Well, she obviously wanted to take care of you when she left."

"But why did she leave? I'd much rather have had my mother than a bank account!"

Neither spoke for a bit until Blum said, "Your mother was very beautiful. When Britta showed me that photo of her. I mean, wow."

"She has a photo of my mother?"

"Yes. I'm sorry, I guess there's no way you could have known that."

"She turned all the men's heads down here. Even as a kid I could see that."

"Do you think any of this might have a bearing on what happened to your sister?"

Pine took a sip of beer. "Meaning did my parents' secretive past play some role in my being attacked and Mercy's disappearing?"

"Yes."

"I've started to think about that possibility. But we're here now and we have to keep plugging. What we learn here may have a bearing on where my mom might have gone."

"Hey, y'all."

They looked up to see Cy Tanner and Agnes Ridley heading to their table.

Tanner had on the same pair of jeans but a freshly laundered denim shirt. His old Stetson was in his hands. His huge belt buckle was engraved with the image of a Budweiser beer can.

Ridley's cotton dress was yellow and long-sleeved, and she had canvas tennis shoes on, showing red, swollen ankles. Her gray hair hung limply around her shoulders.

"Hey back," replied Blum.

"Mind if we join you?" asked Tanner.

"Come on," replied Pine, eyeing Ridley.

The pair sat down at their table. Tanner hooked his hat on a chair back, raised his hand, and ordered a beer.

"Another body," said Ridley. "My Lord."

"Do they know who it is?" asked Tanner.

"Not yet."

"I heard he was dressed up fancy," said Ridley.

"Who told you that?" said Pine sharply.

"You can't keep nothing secret in this place," commented Tanner.

"So are you investigating that too, Lee?" asked Ridley.

"I'm helping out the detective on the case. But with the second murder, they're going to call in reinforcements."

"Like who?" asked Tanner. The waitress delivered his beer, and he took a long drink before wiping his mouth with the back of his hand.

They all looked over as the door to the restaurant opened.

"Like him," said Blum.

Standing there was a six-foot-tall, broad-shouldered man in his late thirties dressed in a dark suit, white shirt, and a striped tie. Over his suit jacket was a dark blue FBI windbreaker.

When Pine's gaze fell on him her jaw went slack and she muttered, "Son of a bitch."

"Do you know him?" asked Blum, who had heard what Pine had said.

"FBI Special Agent Eddie Laredo," said Pine.

"Is he a friend, or what?"

"Or what," replied Pine.

30

Eddie Laredo's pair of sharp light green eyes alighted on Pine and held there like a magnet on metal. The man had a square jaw and a long, slender nose cleaving his face precisely in two. His thick eyebrows were as dark as his hair. His neck was long and descended into a pair of broad shoulders that nicely filled out his jacket. His torso tapered to a narrow waist, and his muscled thighs rode tight against his dress slacks.

But it was the eyes that held one's attention. Calm, but perhaps a bit threatening in their intensity.

He walked across the room and came to stand next to Pine.

"Hello, Eddie," she said, not looking up at him.

"Heard you were in town, Atlee," he said quietly.

Now she did glance at him. "And who did you hear that from?"

"Just around."

"Phoenix?"

"Just around."

He drew an empty chair from another table and slid it next to her and sat down.

He glanced at the others and nodded. "Agent Laredo, FBI."

Blum ran her gaze over him and flicked a glance at Pine, who still sat stonily in her chair, then said, "I'm Agent Pine's assistant at the Bureau, Carol Blum. Did you get called in to work the two murders? I assume so."

Laredo nodded. "Flew into Atlanta, just drove in from there."

"You alone?" asked Pine.

"For now. That could change depending."

"Right."

Ridley said, "So, do you know each other?"

Laredo glanced at Pine before answering. "Long time ago. We worked at the same place. BAU Four. Behavioral Analysis Unit," he added when Ridley gave him a puzzled look.

"It was for a short time," said Pine.

"Short but intense," retorted Laredo.

"Have you spoken with Max Wallis?" asked Pine, ignoring his comment.

"He's supposed to meet me here, in fact." He looked at his watch. "Any minute now."

Pine rose. "Well, I'll leave you to it."

Laredo glanced up in surprise. "I thought you were working the case. Was my info wrong?"

"No. I *was* working the case. But with you here, my help's probably not needed anymore."

She walked across the room and out the door.

Blum watched her go before looking over at Laredo, who was studying his hands.

"I guess you two have a history," she said.

"I take it you work with Pine out in Shattered Rock?"

"So you know that, do you?"

"The Bureau's not that big."

"It's pretty big. We can give you a debrief of what we've uncovered, along with Detective Wallis."

"I'm sure." His gaze traveled over Ridley and Tanner. "And your friends are?"

"Cy Tanner and Agnes Ridley. Cy lives in the house where Agent Pine grew up."

Laredo shot Blum a glance.

"Yes, Agent Laredo, that's why we're here. At least it was the original reason. Then these murders started."

"Okay. You made any progress on . . . the other thing?"

"Some. But still a long road ahead. And right now I better catch up with my boss."

She rose, said good night to Tanner and Ridley, and left.

Blum didn't have far to travel because Pine was sitting on a bench just outside. She rose when Blum came out.

"You all done in there?" said Pine.

"I am. You didn't have to wait for me."

"No problem. I could use the company."

They started to walk back to the Cottage.

"So, Eddie Laredo," began Blum. "You have any desire to get into that?"

"Not really and there's not much to tell."

"You have a tendency to understate things."

"We worked together and then I transferred out."

"He knew you were in Shattered Rock."

Pine didn't comment on that. "He's a good agent. We just didn't see eye to eye on everything." She glanced at her companion. "Anything else I need to know?"

"I introduced Cy and Agnes. Told him that Cy is living in your old house."

"And?"

"And I threw out a line designed to show how much he knew about . . . you."

"And?"

"And it seems to me that he knows why you came here."

Pine nodded slowly.

"Did you confide in him way back when?"

"No, but my personal history isn't a secret, Carol. You just have to google me."

"So he would just put two and two together."

"That's what he's trained to do."

"Did you know he might be coming down when you suggested that Wallis call in the Bureau?"

Pine shook her head. "Unlike Laredo with my career, I didn't keep up with his. I didn't know he was still at Unit Four."

"So he's been there awhile?"

"Unless he transferred out and then back at some point. That happens. I left BAU because it took me out of the trenches. I'll use their expertise, but then I want to nail the bad guys myself."

"Well, now he's here. Are you really going to just turn it all over to him and take a step back? That's not like you."

"I have no say in the matter, Carol. I'm here technically on vacation. And no matter what Detective Wallis says or wants, I haven't been assigned to work this case. And you know the Bureau is a stickler for the rules and agents staying in their lanes."

"But if Laredo asked you to keep working it?"

She shot Blum a glance. "Why? Did he say he was going to?"

"He didn't really say anything about it. I just meant if he does."

Pine shrugged. "I'll cross that bridge if I have to. We've got other things to occupy us."

"Okay, what's next on your sister's case?" asked Blum.

"We have lots of material and leads. The biggest thing for me is I don't think people are being straight with us. Lineberry, the Pringles. Even Lauren Graham seems to be keeping stuff back."

"Then you're maybe talking a conspiracy. If they're all involved in it. Whatever *it* is."

"I just have the belief that people are not being

forthcoming with us. And one of the main reasons to do that is to hide something. But what would they be hiding? Something to do with my sister's disappearance? What would be their motive? They all seemed to genuinely like and care for my parents."

"It *doesn't* make sense. But then we're back to a stranger's having done it. And that person could be long gone now. Or even dead." She looked at Pine. "What if you can't get closure?"

"I always set the bar high for a purpose, Carol. I don't like underperforming."

"But this might not be in your control. In fact, much of it is not."

"Doesn't matter."

They reached the Cottage and went inside.

"I noticed Agent Laredo had no wedding band on," said Blum.

"Why did you notice that particularly?"

"I just do. And I think a lot of other women do, too."

Pine shrugged. "He was married when I knew him. Maybe he got divorced."

"That happens a lot with the Bureau."

"It's an unforgiving occupation. And a lonely one for spouses."

"Is that why you never took the plunge?" asked Blum.

"No, I never found the right guy."

"There *are* some out there."

"Sure there are. They just never came my way."

Pine headed up to her room.

Blum did not follow. She stood there at the bottom of the steps and made an executive decision.

She made a phone call, asked her questions, and set her phone down. Five minutes later it rang. She answered, listened, thanked the woman on the other end, and headed back out.

Score one for the legendary FBI admin staff.

31

Wallis and Laredo were sitting at the same table as Pine and Blum had been. Tanner and Ridley had left.

Blum came in, spotted the pair, and hurried across, taking a seat next to Wallis.

"Carol," said Wallis. "I hear Agent Pine didn't stick around."

"She had some other things to attend to. But she sent me back to stay in the loop."

Laredo shot her a curious look at this remark but didn't comment.

"Well, that's good to hear. As I was telling Agent Laredo and already told your boss, we've run into a brick wall with Hanna Rebane. Nothing after she left her apartment building that day. No phone activity. No credit card purchases or debit card withdrawals. No one saw her or anyone with her. It's like she fell off the face of the earth."

"Well, she landed in Andersonville, Georgia," pointed out Blum.

"Did you dust the apartment for prints?" asked Laredo.

"Yes. We've done elimination prints and there are none unaccounted for. The only set of male prints was from Clemmons's current boyfriend. He was in Miami at all relevant times."

"What about the second victim? Anything on him yet?"

"Yes. We did luck out there. Prints just came back with a hit. He's Layne Gillespie. Thirty-two years old. Last known address was Savannah."

"What do we know about him?" asked Laredo.

"He was in the Army for a few years. Left with a general discharge."

"Not an honorable discharge, but not a DD, either," mused Laredo, referring to a dishonorable discharge.

"And not a bad conduct discharge, either," said Blum. "But was it a general discharge under honorable *conditions* or not?"

They both looked at her quizzically.

"My oldest son is an MP in the Army," she explained. "So I know the lingo. A general discharge *under honorable conditions* means the person performed satisfactorily but didn't reach the conduct level expected of a military member. By contrast, a general discharge *not* under honorable conditions means the person failed to achieve a satisfactory level of performance. It has to be listed in his exit papers. Which was Gillespie?"

"General discharge but *not* under honorable conditions," said Wallis, looking at his notes.

"And the reasons?" asked Blum.

"The only thing it said was that he failed to achieve the conduct levels expected of him, like you said." He paused. "But part of his military record was redacted. At least the part I got was."

Blum and Laredo exchanged a glance. "I wonder why?" said Laredo.

Wallis shrugged. "I made inquiries and got nowhere. After he left the Army Gillespie bounced around, did various jobs, nothing stuck for long."

"What was he doing in Savannah?" asked Laredo.

"Not sure. Need to run that down. It's only a little over a three-hour drive from here. Planned to go over there tomorrow."

"Anything he was involved in that might have gotten him killed here?" asked Laredo.

"Not that we know so far. The post is tomorrow. Agent Pine wanted to be in attendance when they cut Gillespie up." He glanced at Blum. "Does that still hold? Just because I officially called in the Bureau doesn't mean I don't welcome her continued participation." He shot Laredo a look. "If you're okay with that?"

To this Laredo merely gave a curt nod that Blum took neither as an overwhelmingly supportive response nor as a totally dismissive one.

Blum volunteered, "I think she still wants to be involved."

"Good, well, that's it for now." Wallis rose. "I need

to be getting home. I think my wife is close to forgetting my name *and* what I look like."

He nodded to each of them and left.

Blum immediately focused her full attention on Laredo.

"You want to talk about it, Agent Laredo?"

He fiddled with the paper from his straw as he looked at her from under hooded eyes. "I'm not sure what 'it' is, Ms. Blum."

She sat back. "How long have you been with the FBI?"

"Sixteen years. Pretty much right out of college."

"Good for you. I've been at the Bureau for nearly four decades."

His eyes widened slightly at this. "In admin, you mean?"

She sighed. "I hoped for a more informed response than that from you."

"What exactly does that mean?" he said, his tone hostile.

"In my time at the Bureau I think I've personally trained nearly four hundred agents."

Laredo started to smile until her look told him she was being absolutely serious.

She continued. "There are about 11,000 male special agents and around 2,700 female special agents, or over a four-to-one male-to-female ratio. The professional staff, the *admin* you were referring to, number 9,500 male and well over 13,000 females."

"I didn't know the exact breakdown, but thanks for sharing."

"The ratio of agents has really not been getting more equal," she pointed out.

"Tough being an agent. I'm not saying women can't do it. Your boss proves that. But if you want to have kids and all, it's hard. The Bureau isn't great about accommodation in that regard."

"Maybe they should be better at it, since they're obviously pushing a lot of qualified women out of the running."

"I don't know what to tell you, I'm just one grunt in the trenches."

"I've been working with Agent Pine for some time now. She's terrific at her job."

"I have no doubt."

"And I checked you out, Agent Laredo."

He sat up straighter, his expression growing darker. "Excuse me?"

"After I left Agent Pine and before I came back here I made a call to a friend. To an 'admin' friend. She talked to someone else. I got the 411 on you pretty fast. For *admin* folks."

The light green eyes seemed to dance with an electrical charge. "I'm not sure I like that. I'm not sure you had any right to do that," he added with a spark of anger.

"You never did a 411 call on somebody at the Bureau?"

Laredo started to say something but then apparently thought better of it.

"You'll be glad to know that the results of my call were positive. You're well thought of. No issues or problems in your record."

"I could have told you that if you'd just asked."

"Would you have told me?"

"Doubtful, actually. I wouldn't have thought it was any of your concern. The shield I carry should have been enough proof of my character."

"I like corroboration."

"Now you sound like an agent, not an admin."

"You would be surprised how many agent skills an 'admin' like me picks up. But I'm not sure that cuts both ways."

The thick eyebrows rose. "Meaning what?"

"Do you know all the procedural shortcuts to get requisitioned equipment?"

"Uh—"

"Or how to do a conference call with more than five remote attendees, with some of them in international locations?"

"I—"

"Or the adjusted travel per diems on work performed over various holidays? Or which support personnel at Hoover are critical if you want a priority database search dealing with certain levels of classified material? Or something as basic as which department handles coffee flavor requests?"

"I guess that's why we have support personnel."

"Exactly. We're a *team*. Together we get a very big, very hard job done to the best of our collective abilities."

"Where exactly is all this leading?"

"Back to my original question. Do you want to tell me about you and Agent Pine? That was the 'it' to which I was referring before, not that you weren't aware of that."

"I don't think there's much to tell."

She sat back, disappointed. "Did I mention that I also conducted informal training for agents in order for them to detect when people were obfuscating?"

"You mean lying? And agents are thoroughly trained in that already."

"A refresher course never hurts."

"All right. You tell me. You think I'm lying?"

"You looked down and to your right and crossed your arms when you answered that there's 'not much to tell.' Classic evading/cocooning. Also, I raised six kids. You exhibited the pouty/defiant look of my nine-year-old son when he'd done something wrong but refused to admit it. Do you want to load up and tell me again that there's nothing?"

His expression darkened even more. "You're rapidly coming close to a line here, Ms. Blum. I wouldn't want you to do anything that would jeopardize your *long* career at the Bureau."

She looked at him not in fear, or anger, but in sadness. "I'm sorry you feel that way. But I taught my kids when they were pretty much still in diapers that honesty really is the best policy, Agent Laredo. We obviously don't see eye to eye on that one."

She rose.

"Agent Pine is tenacious, smart, adaptable, and physically formidable."

He shrugged. "You're not telling me anything I don't already know about the woman."

"She's also unforgiving. To herself and to others who have not met the standard she sets."

Laredo looked up at her, his features unfriendly. "I have my own set of standards. And they're pretty damn high. As high as hers, in fact."

"Then you and she should have no problem. I'll just assume that's the case and go forward based on that assurance from you. Thanks for that."

She turned and left, leaving Laredo staring moodily after her.

32

Pine had not gone to sleep. She had not even come close to shutting her eyes. She had sat on her bed, fully dressed, until well after midnight. She had heard Blum come in and go to her room. She might have come out then and talked to her friend, but she chose not to. She wasn't exactly sure why.

Coward.

At one in the morning, Pine rose, walked back down the stairs and out the front door into a damp, chilly night in Andersonville. She drew her coat closer around her and headed out to a destination she hadn't really thought about going to until that very minute.

Eschewing her rental SUV, she hustled on foot across the highway to the Andersonville National Historic Site, barely beating a collision with a late-night motorist zipping down the road and not paying much attention. She entered the grounds and soon reached the location of the second victim's body. The police tape was still up, but there was no one guarding the crime scene; apparently all available evidence had already been collected, or perhaps, like the spot where Hanna Rebane had been found, it was a simple lack of manpower. Although with the Bureau now officially involved additional resources had been deployed.

She had never imagined that the additional resources would be Eddie Laredo.

She looked down at the spot where the body had been found. She didn't know yet that he'd been identified as Layne Gillespie, formerly of the U.S. Army with a general discharge for reasons as yet unknown. She didn't know that he had lived last in Savannah. She didn't know why someone had ended his life and then dressed him like a cheap groom.

There was obviously something systematic about the killer's methods and selection of victims along with the presentation of the bodies in the strange garb. But she didn't know enough to truly nail what his goal was.

These guys never make it easy. I guess that's the point.

She ducked under the police tape.

A sharper breeze was starting to blow in from the north. As a child she had never remembered Georgia as being particularly cold, but now it felt downright frigid to her.

Being in a cemetery at night probably doesn't help.

She knelt down and looked at the grave marker. It was the first one on the left.

"Patrick Delaney from Pennsylvania," she read off. The other names left to right were Charles

Curtis, William Collins, John Sarsfield, W. Rickson, with the U.S. Navy, and A. Munn, also with the U.S. Navy.

Was there any significance that the dead man had been placed on Delaney's grave? The victim had been black, that was also something to keep in mind. But these graves contained the remains of *Union* soldiers. Though they had been bad guys as POWs, they had been fighting to free the slaves.

Or maybe I'm overthinking this and it has nothing to do with the history here at all.

But it had been a risk to carry a body out here. Very risky. But then it had been dicey to leave the body of Hanna Rebane in a public area. This guy liked to take chances, that was clear.

This area smelled of death even though the last burial along this short row of graves had taken place more than 150 years ago. But the stench lingered. It would be here forever because all those who had died here would never leave this place. If you believed in God, you would trust that their spirits had long since gone to a better place. But six feet under her boots, Pine knew the human remains of those "spirits" would have an eternal presence in Andersonville.

Pine didn't know if it was the snap of a twig or just her personal antennae that made her reach for her gun. She pivoted on the balls of her feet to take in as much of her surroundings as possible. Maybe it was a squirrel, maybe it was a late-night visitor like her.

Maybe it was the killer coming back for something.

Maybe coming for her.

Another twig snap.

Now she went on the move, not electing to be a sitting duck. Her first tactic was to force whoever was out there to lose a sight line on her, if he had one. She did this by hustling across the graveyard and reaching the office building for the Park Service. It was a two-story structure made of wood and brick painted red with some trimmed hedges and a wrought iron railing that ran along the first level. Behind it was a large outbuilding. She could see wheelbarrows lined up against one wall, and rows of tools hanging from hooks. That must be the storage shed for some of the landscaping operations that would be required here.

Pine parked herself behind one of the hedges and waited to hear footsteps. The damn wind had picked up, making it hard to hear anyone approaching. She sighted along the top rail of her Glock, pivoting around again as she aimed at the direction from which she had just come.

Another snap of a twig. There seemed to be a lot of twigs on the grounds of a well-manicured and -preserved national cemetery. And someone seemed to be hitting them all.

Shit.

She whirled around right as something hit her from behind, launching them both into the hedge she'd taken up position behind. She could feel the sweat and the booze coming from the man. His long, oily hair whipped across her face as they fell.

The breath was knocked out of her when they hit the dirt, his weight landing fully on top of her. He had the advantage right up until she crushed her Glock against the side of his head.

He cried out, gripped his head with one hand, and landed a weakened punch to her shoulder with the other. Pine absorbed the blow with a grimace, then planted her knee in his groin and kept it wedged there while she landed a straight palm strike to her attacker's nose. He responded by slamming all of his weight down on her, ripping the air from her lungs.

He gripped her gun hand with his, and now things were getting perilous.

Until she got her elbow under his throat and cut off his air. When he pulled back to try to draw a breath, as she knew he would, she slammed the crown of her head against his already busted nose. The nose was a sensitive appendage. One blow hurt; a second blow disabled.

He got to his knees, freeing her from his bulk, his body teetering from side to side. She slid out from under him and drove him to the ground by landing a brutal kick to his kidneys. When he fell sideways, she stomped his head, drilling it into the grass. Red blood now colored the green blades.

She added one more stomp for good measure and the man stiffened, then went slack.

Pine had about two seconds to enjoy her triumph when she was knocked off her feet a second time by another man who hit her right at the waist, lifted her off the ground, and pitched her over his head. She could have hit the ground flat on her back or her head, either of which would have left her stunned. But she put out her hand, let it strike the ground first to give her a bit of leverage, and then tucked and rolled, coming to her feet quicker than her attacker probably thought would have been possible. Although there was now a shooting pain in the arm and shoulder she'd used to lessen the impact of her fall. And, even more problematic, she had lost her gun in the process, and with it her main advantage.

The man rose in front of her. He was big, over six-three, nearly twice her weight. She could tell, even in the dim moonlight, that he was pissed off beyond belief. And he was about to take all this fury out on her.

She sat on her haunches as he gathered steam and whatever wits he possessed.

"I'm an FBI agent, in case that makes a difference to you," she said breathlessly.

He didn't seem to comprehend what she was saying. He had on a dirty sweatshirt and a jean jacket over that. Dirtier jeans below that. Muddy boots, a chain around one wrist. A beard that nearly touched his thick chest. He was maybe twenty-five.

"You hurt my buddy bad," he roared, pointing to the lump lying on the ground and not moving. "Deke might be dead."

"Then maybe Deke shouldn't go around attacking people."

"We were just looking for a good time. That's all. Could'a been nice and sweet for everybody." He looked at his fallen buddy once more. "Now I'm gonna mess you up bad, bitch. For Deke."

"And I'm telling you not to do that because you'll regret it like you won't believe."

The man shook his head from side to side, thumped his chest with a hammy fist, spit a lump of something on the ground, screamed out like a bull, and charged her.

She rose and easily sidestepped him, tacking on a roundhouse kick to his ass as he passed by her. That and his momentum caused him to launch over a bush and land face-first in the grass.

He rolled over, screamed a string of profanities, and lurched to his feet.

"Now you're dead," he hollered.

He charged again.

A second later the Beretta Nano Pine pulled from her ankle holster was pointed at the man's crotch. He pulled up so fast the toes of his boots caught in the dirt and he fell forward again, landing at her feet.

He looked up to see the muzzle of her weapon now pointed at his skull.

"You have the right to remain silent," began Pine slowly, the collective pains in her shoulder, head, ribs, and wrist worsening. "And I strongly suggest you fucking use it."

33

Stupid.

That had been the first word that came to Pine's mind as she sat in a chair at the Sumter County Sheriff's Office. Going out alone at that time of night to a secluded place and nobody knew where she was? It was just the sort of insult she would have screamed at anyone, in particular a woman, for doing what she had done.

She had an ice pack on her bruised shoulder and tape around her aching ribs and right wrist. And there was a yellow-and-purple lump on her upper forehead where she'd head-butted the first guy.

"Deke" was in the hospital with a concussion and other assorted injuries but was expected to make a full recovery just in time to go to prison. His buddy was in a holding cell yelling that he wanted a lawyer and, "That bitch started it."

The cops had shown up about ten minutes after she had called them. Deke had still been unconscious, and the other moron was still screaming at her for busting Deke up.

"Just wanted a good time and there she was, what's wrong with that," he kept saying over and over, as though that was perfectly reasonable and should have been enough of an explanation to let him and his buddy go on their way. "I mean, why else would a gal be out there at that time 'a night 'less she wanted some?"

She had told her story to the first cops on the scene after she called them. She had told her story a second time to a detective with a notepad and a tired expression.

"They obviously didn't know you were armed," said the detective.

"Obviously," said Pine. "Not that it would have resulted in a different outcome."

He had looked askance at her comment. "They were two pretty big guys."

"The bigger they are, the easier they fall."

"Right. I'll go do the paperwork. We'll need you to sign your statement when it's ready."

"With pleasure."

And she had sat right there, signed her statement, and was about to leave when she looked up to see a flustered Max Wallis hurrying down the hall toward her. She inwardly groaned as she saw who was trailing him.

Eddie Laredo.

It was six in the morning. She had not phoned Blum yet. But she was thinking about it. She knew she would get the same lecture from the woman that Pine would have delivered to anyone dumb enough to do what she had. That was principally why she hadn't called. She could imagine everything the older woman would say to her. And Blum would be exactly right.

Wallis drew up a chair across from her. Laredo just stood there, arms folded over his chest, something between a smirk and a scowl on his features, at least to Pine's mind. Inwardly seething, Pine thought that the night had been shitty enough without this, too.

"You want to tell us what happened?" said Wallis. He patted his pockets for something, pulled out a single, bent cigarette, and popped it, unlighted, into his mouth.

"I've already told it twice and signed my statement."

"Please. Just a courtesy." He took out his notebook.

"What are you even doing here?"

"Got a call that lifted me out of my bed. Female FBI agent in some sort of trouble. You're the only one in town."

"I'm glad they get so gender specific down here."

"You're an anomaly. They get noticed."

This came from Laredo.

She didn't even look his way.

Pine told her story. It took her all of twenty seconds delivered via five practiced sentences.

"What were you doing out there at that hour?" asked Laredo.

"Following up a hunch."

"And that was?"

"The position of the body over the grave for Patrick Delaney, one of the Raiders."

Laredo glanced at Wallis. "Yeah, I got filled in on that group. So what's the hunch?"

"Why lay him there when he had over ten thousand other choices?" said Pine, who had not once looked Laredo in the eye. She kept her gaze on Wallis and his open notebook.

"You think it symbolized something? You think there's a connection between this Delaney guy and our killer?"

"If there is a connection, it's an attenuated one. Delaney's been dead since 1864."

"So, symbolic then?" interjected Wallis.

"Maybe. This guy doesn't strike me as random in his planning. Quite the opposite."

"Meaning everything he's done up to this point has been meticulous and meaningful," noted Laredo.

"Yes."

"But you could have waited until morning to go out there," observed Laredo. "From what the locals tell me that cemetery can be unsafe in the middle of the night. Hell, any place like that could be unsafe at night."

Pine decided not to let that one go. She looked up

at Laredo, taking in every molecule of him before saying, "Well, it *did* turn out to be unsafe . . . for those two morons."

Laredo shook his head. "You always took risks. Too many for some of us."

She stared him down, until his gaze dropped to the linoleum.

Pine glanced at Wallis. "What else? Or are we done?"

"That's it. These two idiots are known around here. Got a pretty long rap sheet. Mostly petty shit. But they're going away for a while over this one."

"It'll be my word against theirs. They'll say I assaulted them. Just like the guy's been screaming about this whole time from his holding cell."

"I don't think we'll have a problem getting them to cop a plea. Two men against a gal? No way a jury's going to buy that one, least not in Georgia. And I'd be surprised if those dopes would have the balls to try it. I mean, what's a little prison time if the alternative is admitting that a girl kicked your ass? They'd never be able to walk into a bar again."

"Good to know how enlightened it's become down here."

"So what did your little late-night excursion really score us?" asked Laredo. "I'd like to hear how you see it."

Pine gritted her teeth at this thinly veiled barb. "At the very least it got two asshole felons off the street for maybe five to ten years," retorted Pine. "Because the next girl they'd run into wouldn't be me, would she?"

"I don't think there is another you."

Wallis looked between them, his brows arching, and his expression confused. He said, "Okay, I guess we're done here. You probably want to get some shut-eye."

Pine checked her watch. "What I really need is some coffee and breakfast." She shot Laredo a look. "Taking risks and kicking ass makes a girl hungry."

"Good, I'm buying," was Laredo's surprising reply. "Come on, I'll give you a ride."

He turned and walked off before she could respond.

Wallis looked at her sympathetically. "I take it the situation is complicated?"

Pine, whose mouth had widened perhaps more than she had thought, snapped it shut, gave him a curt nod, and followed Laredo out.

34

"Where are you staying?" Pine asked.

She was riding shotgun in the black SUV Laredo was driving.

"Motel about two miles outside of Andersonville. You?"

"Place called the Cottage in town."

He shrugged. "If it's nicer than a dump it's more than the Bureau per diem."

"Tell me something I don't know. This trip is on *my* dime."

"I love all those TV shows where agents fly around on Gulfstreams, wear designer clothes, and stay at the Ritz. And forensics tests are never wrong. And they get 'em back in two seconds, and the perp tearfully cops a plea two more seconds after that because a hair fiber might match him. And then they all go out and celebrate with hundred-dollar bottles of champagne at this really cool cop bar."

"You mean you *hate* all those shows."

He smiled and nodded. "Right. Hate 'em."

"Where are we headed?" asked Pine.

"Diner down the road a bit. Saw it on the way in." He paused, his fingers tapping the steering wheel. "You must be bushed, no sleep last night."

"How much sleep did you get last night?"

"Like a baby."

"Tell me another lie."

They reached the aptly named Hole in the Wall Diner, parked right next to the front door, and climbed out.

"You can tell class by how much plywood they use on the exterior walls," said Pine, eyeing the place.

"Hey, you grew up here. I'm from Queens. Lived in a six-story walkup. I don't know what they used on the walls there. I just knew there was no grass and you were rich if you had an elevator in your building. And you were a billionaire if you had a doorman."

They walked in, were told by the matronly woman at the front entrance to seat themselves, and chose a table in the far back so they could have some privacy. It really didn't matter. At this time of the morning there were very few customers.

They ordered coffee and food from a skinny waitress in her sixties dressed in a shabby, stained uniform that might at some point in its life have been sterling white. Her face bore the searing marks of a hard life that had probably both over- and underwhelmed its owner. But to her credit, she greeted them with a smile and a cheerful, "Mornin', y'all."

She didn't comment on the bruise on Pine's forehead, or the visible stiffness of her limbs. Maybe she saw battered people come in all the time here, thought Pine.

They sipped the coffee while Laredo ran his gaze over Pine.

"How's your head feel?"

"Why are you really here?" she snapped.

"It's my job."

"Bullshit. You saying you're the only agent in BAU Four?"

"It was my turn."

"Bullshit a second time." She leaned forward. "Why do I think when my name floated across the request for assistance in DC, that you pushed yourself up to the front of the line?"

"Don't flatter yourself, Pine."

"Then tell me I'm wrong, Laredo."

He fiddled with his paper napkin, tearing it into neat triangles. She observed this. "Never got over your little rituals?"

"We all have rituals. Maybe you're on one of yours right now."

"I haven't been back to this place since I was a kid."

"Maybe not physically."

"So now you're a shrink? I'm not even lying on a couch. I mean, come on. You can do better than that, can't you, Eddie?"

An uncomfortably long silence passed.

"Maybe you're right. Maybe I did come down here because I saw you were involved."

"Why would it matter to you? We said our piece and our good-byes a long time ago."

He stopped fiddling with the napkin. "*You* did. I never got a chance to."

She pointed at his ring finger. "What happened there?"

He rubbed the spot with his thumb. "Denise divorced me and took the boys. Long time ago."

"Any particular reason?"

"Let's see. I was never home because I was working ungodly hours. Half the time I couldn't tell her where I was or what I was doing. The straw that broke the camel's back was when I pulled an undercover gig and got outed, and some cartel lowlife threatened my family."

"Were you still in DC?"

"No. Before we called it quits I finagled a transfer to New York. Back to my hometown. I thought it would be good for everybody. Fresh start."

"And?"

"And Denise got a part-time job down on Wall Street and fell for a hedge fund manager who makes more money in a day than I'll make in my entire life. They live in London now. And they have another place in the south of France and travel there on a private jet. She is loving life after ditching her FBI spouse."

"I didn't know her all that well, but Denise never struck me as being that shallow."

Laredo balled up the pieces of napkin and set it down next to the salt shaker. "She's not. She would have stayed with me if I was down to my last nickel, if I had an ordinary job that didn't require me to put my neck out. The most dangerous thing her current hubby does is swing a golf club. A lot less worrying for Denise."

"And the kids?"

"I see them a couple times a year when they come over. I get to show my kids the other side of life at my little apartment in Virginia." The strain now showed on Laredo's lean face. "Fact is, well, they see him as more of their father now than me. Nature of the beast, I guess. I'm like the odd uncle who drops in every once in a while for an awkward visit that everyone involved can't wait to be over. Everyone except me," he added quietly.

Pine dropped her gaze and with it her aggressive attitude. "I'm sorry, Eddie. That must be really tough to handle."

He shrugged. "You-make-your-bed thing, you know."

"Just like that?"

"If you'd like I can cry into the beer I'm probably going to order with my dinner tonight. But I prefer the stoic route. It's in the Bureau handbook, after all."

"Your sons should get to know you better. Understand what you do for a living. I don't know this hedge fund guy from Adam. For all I know, he's a saint. But he's not risking his life for his country. He's not sacrificing anything for anybody. Not like when you wear the shield."

"My boys know. At least I think they do. Maybe when they get older we can hang together more."

"It might be too late by then."

He gave her the eye. "How about you? Is it too late for you?"

"In what context?" she said stonily.

"You could have been in the number three spot at WFO by now," said Laredo, referring to the FBI's prestigious Washington Field Office. "Maybe the number two by the time you were forty. You had the talent. And the drive."

"But not the desire."

"I never did get you. You had all that in front of you and now you're in a one-agent RA in Nowhere, Arizona."

"And happy as a clam."

"The happiness of clams is highly overrated."

That comment drew a brief smile from Pine. "So you knew I was here. Why'd you want to come?"

"I think you know why."

"I'd like to hear it from you."

"I was a dick to you. I was all Mister Testosterone, showing you who was the boss and not believing that women belonged at the Bureau. I did everything I could to screw with you. And despite what you just said, I think I drove you away from the place you were meant to be. And . . ."

"And?"

"And I never apologized for any of that. And I came down here to tell you that. And that I do apologize. You didn't deserve it. And there's nobody to point the finger at except me."

"Okay."

"Okay."

She leaned forward. "But I didn't leave WFO because of you, Eddie. Yeah, you were all those things. But you never made a run at me like some other guys did, thinking I'd be thrilled to fall into bed with them."

"I was happily married back then, and even if I weren't I wouldn't have done that to you. I can be an ass, but not that kind."

"I left WFO because I don't like crowds. I don't like vertical living. I like the wide-open spaces. I like to be by myself handling my own cases without some bureaucrat looking over my shoulder every second. I never cared about being in the number three, two, or one spot. I work my cases and catch my bad guys. That's it."

"Fair enough." He hunched over. "Anyway, after the divorce I got some professional help. Made me see things with more clarity. It was through the Bureau.

They offer that service." He gave her a quick glance. "Did you know that?"

"Why do you ask?" she said coolly.

"Because you've been to see Daniel James Tor three times now."

Her expression tightened. "And why do you know that? And what the hell business is it of yours?"

"The Bureau is a small ecosystem."

"That doesn't answer my second question."

"Amber Alert in Colorado? A perp who you nearly killed? You getting time off to come here and clear your past? That's what this is about, right?"

Pine looked away. Her expression now seemed weary. "Word does get around, apparently."

"There's no *apparently* about it. You're here to find out what happened to your sister and salvage your career. I want you to do both, because I don't want the Bureau to lose you."

She sat back and looked at him in amazement. "Whatever professional help you got they need to bottle. Or else you are a world-class bullshitter."

"It took me a while, but I finally got it right. But you still didn't answer *my* question."

Pine didn't respond right away. When she did, her tone was distant, as though she were no longer in the moment. "You're right about why I'm here, on both counts. And what I do know is I've run out of time not to try anymore. If that makes sense."

He nodded. "It actually does."

"I got a second shot. I don't intend to waste it."

"Okay. I'm down here to look into these two murders, but if you want a second pair of eyes on what happened all those years ago, well, I'm here for that, too. I can't promise you're going to get what you came here for. And I'm no genius. Just an agent doing his thing."

"And is this payback for all those years ago? To make yourself feel better? Because if it is, you don't have to. And I don't want you to."

"I'm an agent. You're an agent. We took an oath to serve and protect. That includes everybody, you and me. We carry the same shield. You want to catch whoever hurt you and abducted your sister. That's a federal crime. That's what I do for a living. That's why I'm here. No other reason than that since I delivered my apology."

She studied him with the intensity of a mass spectrometer. "I think you really have changed."

"We all change, Atlee. For better or worse. Right up until the moment we get dropped in a hole six feet down."

35

Blum told Pine she was not going to lecture her about that previous night, and then she proceeded to do just that. When she'd finished venting, Pine said, "Do you feel better?"

"Not really. How about you?"

"Not really."

"How's your head?"

"The bruising is already starting to subside."

They were once more sitting in the breakfast room at the Cottage. Pine had gotten about five hours' worth of deep sleep, showered and changed, and had some lunch that did not sit well in her belly, because it was churning with a lot of stuff.

She had filled Blum in on her trip to the cemetery and her hunches about the positioning of the body over one particular grave.

Blum was drinking a cup of hot tea as she studied her boss.

"What happened after I left you last night?" asked Pine. "I saw Wallis and Laredo at the police station this morning, but we didn't talk about the case."

"I decided to circle back to the Clink. Found out some info from Wallis." She proceeded to tell Pine about Layne Gillespie being identified and his military background.

"Discharged but not under honorable conditions," said Pine thoughtfully. "Any ideas?"

"*I* didn't have any, which is why I called my son, the MP. He had some ideas."

"Such as?"

"Gillespie did something that the brass didn't like, but it was also something they didn't want to make a fuss about. Solution, the general discharge not under honorable conditions. The Army gets to kick him out without any honor, but doesn't do so in a way that will necessarily hurt his ability to move on with his life. Only other military folks would understand the nuance. And I doubt Gillespie was itching to reenlist in another branch."

"I wonder what those conditions could have been?" said Pine.

"Could be quite a few."

"Your son have any ideas?"

"He called me back and said he thought it would be something personal to Gillespie. If it were related to his service record it would be more cut-and-dried."

"I appreciate his doing that. And I appreciate your asking. I . . . uh, you told me you don't have the greatest relationship with your kids."

Blum's smile was tinged with a bit of melancholy. "As time goes on, it's actually getting better. I think they understand now that their dad was not this shining example of a human being and that I did the best that I could with the hand I was dealt." She paused. "But I bear a lot of the responsibility. I *married* him, after all."

Pine smiled. "I always admire how you never dodge the bullet, Carol."

"It's not worth doing. Eventually, it will hit its target anyway."

"Savannah, huh?"

"Yes."

"Wallis wants to go there?"

"That's what he said."

"When?"

"Whenever you're ready."

"I'm ready now."

"I thought you would be, which is why I phoned him and he's on his way over now."

Blum gave Pine a look that gave her pause. "Yes?" she said to her assistant.

"Wallis told me that you and Laredo went to breakfast this morning."

"We did."

"How did that go?"

"It went okay, believe it or not."

"Did the air get cleared?"

"Is that what you think the issue was?"

"I don't know. I'm shooting somewhat blind here."

"Wallis mentioned to me that it seemed complicated, and I didn't disagree with him."

"Okay."

"So it *is* complicated, Carol. That's as far as I'm going."

"And he's here just to work the case?"

"He did say that he would be willing to help me on my sister's case."

"And you're okay with that?"

"He's an experienced criminal investigator. I can use all the help I can get. When will Wallis get here?"

"About ten minutes. Agent Laredo will be with him."

"As he should be. He's the field agent on this."

"And your sister's case? I mean, with Agent Laredo here, you could focus on that. Detective Wallis has the weight of the Bureau behind him now."

"Do you want to stop working this case?"

"It's not up to me. I came here to support you. I just don't want you to fill your plate up so much, you get disappointed one way or another."

"You really know how to push me into an uncomfortable corner."

"Is there a *comfortable* corner? Because I've yet to encounter one in my life."

"We're women, Carol, we can multitask."

"Since I am a woman, I can tell you that's a glib retort but doesn't really answer my question."

Pine stared down at her hands. "When I was a kid, I never thought about working in law enforcement. When I lost Mercy, I just closed up inside. I didn't make any friends. My parents were there, but there was this void, you know?"

"Yes, I can see that."

"I found my calling in sports. I could play any of them and do well. I enjoyed it, but those were all *team* sports. I . . . I had to be part of something and it was hard. Really hard. I found I couldn't connect with people. I was terrified that eventually the conversation would come around to family, and then what would I say? It was like I was carrying around this terrible dark secret. I know it makes no sense, but I felt ashamed."

"I can understand how that would be very difficult for you."

"Then I started the competitive weightlifting. With that, it was just me against everyone else. I didn't have to relate to anyone. I just had to beat them."

"I get that. But it must have been very lonely for you."

Pine let out a long breath and looked up at her friend. "Incredibly so. Especially after my mom left. Then I got out of college, wandered around for a bit, and then something happened to change my life."

"What was that?"

"I was walking down the street one night when this guy suddenly bursts out of an alleyway. He almost knocked me down. I jumped back and saw that he was armed. I panicked. I didn't know what to do. I didn't know what was happening. It was like out of a movie."

"My God," exclaimed Blum.

"A split second later another person came out of that alley. It was a woman. She had a gun, too. By that time, I had planted myself behind a trash can and ducked down. The guy turned and fired at her but missed. Then she was on him like a runaway freight train. She disarmed him so fast I could barely follow her movements. He was down on the ground and being handcuffed before I could even let out a breath. Then some other cops showed up. After that, she came over to me and asked if I was okay. She was super nice. Super calm, especially after what had just happened. I was still shaking."

"Who was she?"

"FBI Special Agent Marilyn Shales. She'd been staking out this guy for about two weeks. He was bad to the bone. Drugs, armed robbery, murder in multiple states. Marilyn probably came up to my chest and weighed maybe a hundred and ten pounds soaking wet. But she was the toughest person I have ever met in my life. I told her how blown away I was by what she'd done. She gave me her card. I called her a week later. We met, and a week after that I filled out my FBI application."

"Did you keep in touch?"

Pine nodded. "She really became a mentor to me as I went through the process. She even came to my graduation from Quantico."

"Do you still see her?"

"I wish I could. She died three years ago. Breast cancer." Pine drew a short, hard breath. "I love being an agent, Carol. I love everything about it. But mostly I love the good I can do with the shield that comes with it. The little girl, Holly? She was surprised that a woman could be a FBI agent. I told her girls can do anything they set their minds to. Because that's basically what Marilyn Shales told me."

"So you were being a mentor of sorts to Holly. Who knows, maybe you'll be attending *her* FBI graduation one day."

Pine smiled at this. "That would be cool," she said quietly. Then she rose and said abruptly, "So off we go to Savannah."

"I hear it's very pretty. I've never been there."

"I have, and it *is* beautiful. Have you read the book *Midnight in the Garden of Good and Evil*?"

"Yes. It was wonderful."

"But it shows that even beautiful places have very dark sides."

36

Layne Gillespie's last known address was in a part of Savannah that was as far from the town's historic Garden District as it was possible to be. Tiny homes with laundry on lines in yards that held more dirt than grass. Boarded-up buildings, folks standing on street corners without much to do.

There were four of them in the vehicle: Wallis and Laredo in front, Pine and Blum in back.

"Don't see any drug activity," noted Wallis.

Pine shrugged. "Why would you? These days you can order your fentanyl cocktail from a phone app and get it delivered to your home faster than you can a pizza."

"Sad state of affairs," replied Wallis.

"Well, whatever he did for a living, it doesn't look like it paid well," noted Laredo as they cruised toward the destination, a seedy apartment building that was two blocks off a main road and looked to be about a hundred years old. They parked in the small cracked asphalt lot in front of a place marked OFFICE and climbed out.

The man inside was black, worn, and thin, around sixty. He looked at the four as though they were an invading army come to clear out the little he had and then some. He had on a brilliantly white T-shirt, jeans faded by time, and a suspicious expression.

He lit a Camel as they faced off across the narrow width of a worn, broad plank that constituted the front desk.

"Help you folks?" he said. Though they weren't in South Carolina, his drawl was all low country. His expression said clearly that help was not what he really had in mind.

Wallis drew out his badge and ID card. "GBI. Detective Wallis. These folks are with the FBI. We want to talk to you about Layne Gillespie."

"Who?"

"Layne Gillespie," said Laredo. "He lives here. Or he did."

The man grinned, showing off pearly whites the width of his mouth.

"Oh, Layne, thought you said *Wayne*. Right. So, what's up with him?"

"When was the last time you saw him?" asked Wallis.

The man hooked the smoke from his mouth and scratched his stubbly chin. "Hard to say. Folks don't check in with me when they come and go. This ain't no day care."

"Think harder," said Laredo. "It's important."

"Might help if you told me what's going on with the dude."

"We'll get into that, but first things first," said Wallis.

"Okay. Saw Layne, oh, maybe a week ago."

"Did you talk to him?" asked Pine.

"Just to say hello."

"How did he seem?"

"Like normal. Cheerful. Happy-go-lucky, you might say. That was Layne."

"You knew him well?" asked Laredo.

The man's eyes shifted to him. They grew smaller, considering, thoughtful, a million chess moves a second. He took a long puff of the Camel and let it go, slow and deliberate. "Not if he's done something so bad the FBI needs to come to town."

"Savannah lets you light up in a public place?" asked Laredo, fanning away the smoke.

The pearly whites appeared again. "This is my home, man, not a public place."

"It's an apartment building catering to the public," retorted Laredo.

"Well, if you say so, man." He kept puffing on his cig.

"What can you tell us about Gillespie?" asked Pine, with a hard look at Laredo.

"Been here about a year or so. Kept to himself, really. Oh, he'd help folks move in and move out, that sort of thing. Handy with tools. Fixed the air-conditioning here a few times. And the washing machine. I like him." The Camel moved to the other side of the mouth via a flick of the tongue. "He okay?"

"Any reason you can think of why he wouldn't be?" asked Wallis.

"I can think of four." He pointed to each of them.

"We need to see his room," said Laredo.

Another puff on the Camel. "Y'all got a warrant?"

"So you know all about warrants, do you?" asked Wallis with hiked eyebrows.

"I watch the *Law and Order* shows, man, just like everybody else. That Mariska Hargitay is one sexy lady." He eyed Pine. "You remind me of her."

Wallis held up the search warrant and let the man read over it.

"Okay, but Layne might not like that."

"Trust us when we tell you Layne won't care," said Laredo.

The manager opened the door and motioned them in.

"I've got stuff to do downstairs," he said. "Let me know when y'all finish up."

"Will do, thanks," said Pine.

The man hesitated at the door. "He's dead, ain't he?"

Pine looked at him. "You have reason to think that other than us being here?"

He shrugged, dropped the cigarette, and tapped it out on the concrete floor outside the apartment with the heel of his shoe. "I'll let you have your look."

"This won't take long," said Wallis as he eyed the small confines of the apartment. "I'll take the bathroom."

"Closet," said Blum, and she opened the door and poked her head in.

Laredo looked at Pine. "Guess that leaves you and me for the bedroom."

Pine gave him a funny stare but didn't reply.

A thorough search took all of about thirty minutes.

Wallis had found nothing unusual in the bathroom, and all the meds in the medicine cabinet were over-the-counter.

Pine and Laredo had tossed the bedroom and found pretty much nothing.

However, Blum had struck gold in the closet and laid out some of her finds on the bed.

"Look at all this," said Wallis as they stared down at the women's clothing, underclothes, shoes, and purses Blum had placed on the bed.

"These look like serious performance outfits to me," said Pine. She held up one outfit and then the shoes that matched it.

"I agree," said Blum. "And this stuff is not cheap. This is first-rate material and workmanship."

"And he lives in this dump?" said Wallis.

"Maybe he spent all his money on clothes," quipped Laredo.

Pine held up a pair of white panties. "Maybe this explains the Army kicking him out."

"I was thinking the same thing," said Blum.

"I thought they had 'don't ask, don't tell' for homosexuals," said Wallis.

Pine said, "That's no longer the law. But even then, just because he has all this stuff doesn't mean he was gay. And let's not get ahead of ourselves. For all we know these clothes belong to someone else. Maybe a woman who stayed here."

Blum added, "Or Gillespie could have been a cross-dresser or a drag queen. If he were a cross-dresser, *that* could be why the Army might have let him leave with a general discharge, or else they could have been facing some legal trouble. But how they handled his discharge may have been their way of telling him what they thought of his lifestyle."

Pine said, "What the hell? I mean, if he could do the job, he could do the job."

Wallis interjected. "He might have been a distraction in his unit. Or maybe he did something else. I'm inclined to give the Army the benefit of the doubt."

Pine said, "Well, Gillespie might have been working at some club around here. If he was gay, there is a strong scene in Savannah."

"How do you know that?" said Wallis.

"I've been here before. And if you know where to look, the vibe is pretty obvious."

"For such a quaint Southern town," added Blum primly. "Who would have thought?"

"I know I'm just an old fart, but I don't understand

any of that stuff," said Wallis. "But live and let live, that's my motto."

"Well, the guy who killed Gillespie obviously didn't get that memo," said Pine. "So let's go talk to the apartment manager again."

"Why?" asked Wallis.

"Because I'm pretty sure he knows all about it."

"No way that old guy is gay," said Wallis confidently.

"I'm not saying he is or he isn't. I'm just saying I think he knows stuff. So let's go see."

37

The manager's name, he told them when they returned, was Clarence Spotter. He was sixty-eight years old, had a male partner, knew the gay community in Savannah well, and also was aware that Gillespie was working as a dancer at a nightclub called the Silver Shell.

He shook his head sadly when he was told of the man's death.

"Damn shame. Layne was a good person."

"Did he have any friends?" asked Pine. "Folks he hung out with who could help us?"

"He never had anybody come by here. You can check at the Shell. You might find somebody who knows something. Andersonville?" He shook his head again.

"He ever mention the place to you?" asked Wallis.

"No. He was in the Army for a spell till they made him get out. He traveled a lot then before coming here, least that's what he told me. Maybe he just wanted to settle down."

"We knew about his leaving the military but just didn't know the circumstances."

"I never really knew, either. But I imagine it had something to do with who he was." He added sardonically, "The Army probably likes its soldiers in pants at all times."

"You know you could have told us all this when we first got here," pointed out Wallis.

Spotter smiled. "Sure I could have. But I decided not to."

"Why not?" asked Laredo.

"'Cause you never told me what happened to Layne, that's why. You want the whole truth from me, you got to be reciprocal, all I'm asking."

"That's fair," replied Blum.

As they were walking back to the car, Wallis shook his head. "Never would have pegged that guy as a homosexual. He just didn't seem the type."

"What type would that be?" asked Blum.

"You know . . ."

"Flamboyant?"

Wallis shrugged. "Yeah, I mean something like that."

Blum said, "My youngest daughter is a lesbian. I didn't know until she came out at twenty-two. Maybe I should have looked for more *flamboyance* in her."

Back in the car, Pine said, "It's nearly six o'clock. We can head over to this club and maybe talk to some of the folks there before it gets too busy. You good with that?" she added, glancing at Wallis.

"I guess."

"Problem?"

"No, no problem."

"The world is big enough for lots of different people," Pine pointed out.

"Hell, I know that. And I've seen my share of, well, different. It's just all this LGB, whatever that acronym is, it gets confusing."

"LGBTQ," said Blum. "With more letters to come, if they want them."

"See, that's what I'm talking about. How's a person to keep all that straight?"

"But *you* don't have to," said Blum. "The people who identify with those groups do. And I think they have no problem with realizing who they are."

When Wallis looked puzzled she added, "Just think of it this way: You're clearly an MH."

"I'm a what?" said a confused Wallis.

Pine said, "Male heterosexual. Think you'd ever forget that?"

Wallis exclaimed, "It's who I am. How can I forget that?"

"Well, then, you must see Carol's point."

Wallis blinked and then nodded. "Yeah . . . Well, I guess I do, now that you mention it."

"So, Silver Shell, here we come," said Blum.

It was a twenty-minute ride from the apartment building to the Silver Shell, which was a two-story brick building on the corner of an area that might generously be considered "in transition."

"Well, I can see why they call it that," said Blum as she looked out the window.

The place had a wall mural out front of an enormous silver clam shell.

"I wonder what the symbolism for that is?" asked Wallis nervously.

"Maybe the owner just likes clams," replied Pine.

They knocked on the side door, and a man dressed in work overalls opened it. Clarence Spotter had phoned ahead, and they were expected. The same man escorted them to a row of dressing rooms and stopped at the one with the title MANAGER stenciled on it. He knocked and received a verbal okay to enter.

He opened the door and the four of them crowded into the small room. The workman closed the door, and Pine could hear his footsteps going back down the corridor.

The room had a couple of chairs and a battered settee upholstered in a zebra pattern. The walls were painted eggplant; the ceiling was dominated by a chandelier that seemed to have about a million pieces of cut crystal. Against the far wall was a dressing table and an attached mirror with large bulbs surrounding the glass perimeter.

The person sitting there had their back to them and was wearing a long red dressing gown with what looked to be faux fur around the neck and cuffs.

They gathered in the middle of the room, and Wallis cleared his throat. "I guess you know why we're here," he said.

Pine noted that the person's broad shoulders trembled a bit.

Then the person spun around in the chair and faced them.

He was in his forties, with sharply angular features and a mound of blond hair that was being managed with a barrage of hair clips so it would lie flat to his head. He was, Pine gauged, about six-two and a slim 160 pounds, though his build was athletic. He had apparently started to apply his makeup because the cheeks held foundation, and the lips were a bright shade of orange. The eyebrows had been plucked and shaped, and the eyes under them were a startling blue.

"Layne," said the man.

"Layne Gillespie. We understand that he worked here, Mr . . . ?"

The man nodded. "I'm sorry, my name is Ted Blakely. I'm the owner here. I'm . . ." He put a hand to his face and started to sob into it.

Blum grabbed some tissues from a box on the dressing table and handed them to Blakely.

He thanked her with a nod and wiped his eyes dry. When he looked up, there were rivulets through the makeup on his cheeks caused by the tears he had shed.

"I'm sorry, this . . . this is all rather overwhelming."

Wallis said quietly, "I'm sure this is a shock, um, Mr. Blakely. If you want to delay this interview?"

"No, no. I'll do anything to help you catch whoever, whatever monster did this." Blakely blew his nose, tossed the tissues into a wastebasket, and looked up at them. "Can you tell me what happened?"

"Mr. Gillespie was found shot to death at a cemetery in Andersonville, Georgia."

"Andersonville, Georgia?"

"You've heard of it?" asked Pine.

"No. And Layne never mentioned it."

"I take it you and he were friends," said Pine.

"Very good friends and professional colleagues. We performed onstage together."

"How long had he worked here?" asked Wallis.

"About a year. But I knew Layne before that. I was the one who asked him to come to Savannah. I knew he'd be a star here."

"So you knew of his . . . professional abilities?" said Laredo.

Blakely gave Laredo a searching look that ended in an enigmatic smile. "Yes, his *professional* abilities."

"When was the last time you saw him?" asked Pine.

"Right here in this room, three nights ago. We had just finished the last act of the night. It was around two in the morning. We had a drink and went our separate ways."

"Weren't you concerned when he didn't show up for work?" asked Pine.

"No, because he wasn't scheduled to. He was taking some time off, a few days. He'd pulled a muscle in his right quad and his ankle was also swollen. It's not easy doing what we do."

"I'm sure it's not. Do you know what he planned to do during his time off?"

"Just take it easy. I mean, I wasn't aware that he was planning to travel anywhere. Certainly not to this—what was the town called again?"

"Andersonville," said Wallis.

"No," said Blakely. "He never mentioned going anywhere."

"Was he seeing anyone?" asked Laredo. "Or was anyone giving him any problems?"

"No and no, at least that I know. I have a firm rule here: no fraternizing. I don't care what people do with their lives or in their private time. But that sort of stuff always spills over into the workplace. So I just cut it off."

"How many performers do you have here?" asked Pine.

"Including me, about a dozen. Two shows a night and a matinee on Saturday. It's good, you should come sometime. Singing, dancing, acting. We do it all. Even comedy skits." He glanced at Laredo. "You know, good, wholesome family entertainment."

"More power to you," replied Laredo.

"I started life as a corporate lawyer," admitted Blakely. "Hated every minute of it. Now this, this is what I was born to do."

"Did Layne Gillespie feel the same way?" asked Pine.

"I think so, yes. He got kicked out of the Army, you know."

"We didn't know exactly why," said Pine.

"He was caught performing in full costume. It was harmless, and it wasn't even on the base or anything. But they gave him the old heave-ho. And from what I heard Layne was a good soldier. He could fight. Strong as a bull, really athletic. He performed this one act where he had to climb these long, flowing fabric ropes and do cartwheels and such. He was the only one here who could do that. I would've broken my neck." Blakely paused and looked down at his lap. "I can't believe he's dead."

"So no problems with anyone? Or someone new in his life?" asked Pine.

"No, no one that I can think of. Everyone really liked Layne."

"No jilted lover or a patron here who wanted more than to see him in an act?" said Laredo.

"We do have some of that here, but nothing specific to Layne."

Pine thought of something. "What was Layne doing before he came here? How did you know him?"

"Oh, well, it was through a friend of mine."

"What friend?"

"He's dead now. Boating accident down in Miami.

But he was in the um, *film* business." Blakely looked nervously at them.

They all looked at one another. Pine said sharply, "Wait a minute. Do you mean the porn film business?"

"Yes, Layne acted in porn films."

"Where did he do this?" asked Pine, her tone betraying her excitement that they might have finally gotten a break in the case.

Blakely wadded up a tissue as he glanced at himself in the mirror. He absently rubbed a spot of wet foundation off his cheek. "He'd . . . he'd go down to Miami or close to there to do it. It paid really well, apparently. I thought about doing it once, but it just wasn't for me. I . . . I couldn't do it, not in front of a camera." He blushed and looked around them. "I'm sorry, I'm rambling. You don't care about that, I know."

Pine said, "Did Layne ever mention a woman named Hanna Rebane or Beth Clemmons?"

"I don't believe so."

"Please think about it, it's really, really important," Pine urged.

Blakely did so but then shook his head. "I'm sorry. Those names don't ring any bells."

Pine looked very disappointed.

Wallis interjected. "We visited one person who acted in porn films. Her apartment was very luxurious, while Mr. Gillespie's, well, wasn't. Do you know why?"

"Layne was also helping to support his mother, grandmother, a sister, and a brother. It didn't leave much for him, but he never really cared about money for himself. I think he did the films so he could send the dollars to his family. But he stopped doing that when he came to work here. At least as far as I know."

Wallis cleared his throat and said, "Well, it was good of him to take care of his family. That makes him okay in my book. No matter, well, no matter how he went about it."

"Just to be clear, did he perform in gay porn or . . . ?" said Pine.

Blakely looked confused. "Oh, I see. No, it was straight porn, not gay. Why, do you think just because someone performs in drag for a living that he has to be exclusively gay?"

Wallis looked at the others. "Well, I'll admit that I thought that."

"I actually don't know what Layne's sexuality was and I never asked. And while a lot of men who do drag *are* gay, they can be of any sexuality, really. But I will tell you that I have seen Layne with young ladies, and they did not seem to me to be just friends. I'll let you arrive at your own conclusions on that."

Pine said, "We're going to have to. Hopefully, sooner rather than later."

38

They stayed over in Savannah that night and drove back to Andersonville the following afternoon. While in Savannah they checked out some leads provided by Blakely and Spotter, none of which amounted to anything. Gillespie was well liked and had no known enemies.

When they got back to Andersonville around five thirty they split up into two teams. Wallis and Laredo would attend the postmortem on Layne Gillespie, while Pine and Blum headed on to Columbus, Georgia, to speak once more to Beth Clemmons.

"So at least we have a connection between the victims: adult films," said Blum as they drove on the short trip to Columbus.

"But let's not put the cart before the horse. We have no idea if Layne Gillespie knew or worked with Hanna Rebane. But even if he didn't, the killer could be someone with a hatred of porn films and actors. That *could* be a solid lead for us."

"And the veil and tuxedo?"

"No clue as yet. Although it could be some sort of

insult to them. Porn stars made to look like old-fashioned toppers on a traditional wedding cake."

"If Rebane worked with Gillespie, he might have also worked with Clemmons."

"That's what I'm hoping, because we can't ask Rebane any questions."

"What do you think is going on, Agent Pine?"

"Something that seems really complicated." She paused and stared out the windshield. "Which of course means it could actually be incredibly simple."

"Simple? You won't catch me describing it that way."

"Never say never, Carol. It'll save you a lot of time."

They arrived in Columbus a little over an hour after leaving Andersonville. It was around seven in the evening. It was warmer here than it had been in Andersonville, but cooler and less humid than Savannah. Pine had phoned Clemmons but gotten no answer. They pulled to a stop in front of the condo building, got out, and walked into the lobby. They checked in with the concierge, and Pine's badge got them into the elevator and up to the sixth floor. They knocked on Clemmons's door but got no answer.

"She could be out, but you'd think the concierge would have told us that," said Pine.

"Or there could be another reason she's not answering," said Blum ominously.

"We have no reason to go into the apartment. I can't break the door down."

Pine knocked harder. No response.

"That's funny," said a voice.

They turned to see a young, bespectacled man standing in his open doorway across the plushly carpeted hall.

"What's funny?" said Pine.

"Well, I'm pretty sure that Beth is home. I was coming up a few hours ago and she was going into her place."

"She could have gone back out," said Blum.

"No, she said she was going to take a hot bath and stay in for the evening. And I've been sitting in my front room all this time reading. I'm pretty sure I would have heard her if she had gone out."

Pine looked at Blum, then at the door. "Think that gives us probable cause to go in?"

"I would think so."

"You guys cops?" said the man.

Pine produced her FBI shield. "Go down and tell the concierge to come up here right now with a key. Go!"

The startled man raced off down the hall. They heard the elevator ding seconds later.

The concierge and the man came back up a minute later. The former was holding a key.

"What's wrong?"

Pine said, "We have it on good authority that Ms. Clemmons is home but she's not answering our knocks. We're concerned for her welfare. We need you to open this door right now."

The concierge paled, hurried forward, and unlocked the door. Pine took out her gun and motioned the three of them to stay right where they were.

She moved into the darkened apartment, her gun and gaze sweeping the areas in front of her. "Ms. Clemmons?" she called out. "Beth? It's Agent Pine with the FBI. Are you in here?"

There was no answer, and Pine could hear no movement. She cleared the front rooms and the kitchen and made her way down the hall to the bedrooms. She went through Clemmons's bedroom.

It was empty.

But there were some clothes on the floor of Clemmons's closet. And her purse with her phone in it was on the nightstand.

She's here, or at least she was.

The door of the attached bathroom stood open; the light was on.

Pine braced herself. She first got down on her knees and checked for a pair of feet showing from underneath the bathroom door. No one was hiding behind it. She quickly moved into the space, her pistol making arcs in the air.

The bathroom was huge, with a clawfoot bathtub set inside the walk-in shower.

From here she could see water right up to the top of the tub.

Shit.

She feared that the woman had overdosed while in the water, and then drowned.

She slowly entered the shower area and looked down.

This was not what she had been expecting. The tub was empty except for the water.

Confused, she stepped back out and checked the large cabinets lining the walls. There was nobody stuffed into any of them. Well, the full tub was perplexing. There was still Hanna Rebane's bedroom left. But she couldn't understand why Clemmons would be in there when the bath was drawn in here.

She approached the door to leave the room and froze as she fixed on the crevice between the door and the wall.

She edged it farther open. Beth Clemmons was hanging from a hook on the back of the bathroom door, a ligature around her neck and a plastic bag over her head.

39

The quiet, upscale residential building was now full of police activity.

A lot of moving parts and absolutely no traction.

Or so this was Pine's take on things.

While the local police were examining the body and searching Clemmons's apartment, Pine and Blum were across the hall talking to the neighbor who had called out to them.

He sat on his costly couch in his fashionably decorated condo looking like he might throw up on his expensive Oriental rug.

"I . . . I might have been the last person to see her alive," said the man, who had identified himself as Gene Martin. He was in his early thirties and obviously did something for a living that paid handsomely.

"Other than the person who killed her," remarked Blum, causing Martin to stare bug-eyed at her.

"What, yes, of course." He looked at the stoic Pine. "Wait, you can't think? I . . . I had nothing to do with what happened." He jumped to his feet. "Jesus, I would never kill anybody. I'm . . . I'm a CPA. The only way I've ever 'hurt' someone is by disallowing a deduction."

"I don't think you killed her, Mr. Martin. I'm much more interested in what you might have seen or heard."

"But I don't know anything."

"Take a moment to calm down, sit back down, clear your head, and think back. Take it one step at a time. You said you were reading. You had earlier seen Clemmons. She was going to take a bath and relax for the evening. She went inside her place and you went inside yours. Take it from there starting with what time that was."

Martin sat back down, took off his glasses, cleaned the lenses with a handkerchief clutched in a shaky hand, and put them back on.

"Okay, I spoke with Beth and then came in here. I remember looking at my watch. It was a couple minutes past four."

"Okay, so you had seen her a few minutes before that?"

"Yes."

"Was that the only time you saw her today?"

"Yes."

"Why were you home at that time of day?" asked Blum.

"I took a few days off to catch up on some things and rest up. I just finished a financial audit on a large public company. Worked four months straight, seven days a week. I was totally burned out."

"Okay, go ahead."

"I made a cup of tea, that took about two minutes. Then I sat down with my book. It's a biography of Churchill." He picked it up from the coffee table. "It's fascinating, but a door stopper as you can see."

Pine glanced at the thick book. "Right. What then?"

"I sat and drank my tea and read my book."

"No sounds out in the hall? Doors opening or closing? Footsteps? Voices?"

"Most people on this floor don't get home that early. Six, seven is the norm."

"But not Clemmons?"

"No, not her. God, it's so awful to think that someone killed her. Right here in this building." His face paled and he again looked like he might be sick.

Pine said in a calming tone, "Take some deep breaths and relax. Just focus your mind and think back. We'll wait. No rush. Just calm down and collect your thoughts. You're an accountant, so you're detail oriented. That's what we want, details."

Martin took some deep, regulated breaths, sat back on the couch, and tapped the arm of it. As his fingers drummed along, they grew slower and more rhythmic.

"You know, I did hear someone out in the hall. It was about thirty minutes later. A little before five."

"Exactly what sounds did you hear?"

"Someone walking away, but before that, I heard . . . well, I heard a door opening and then closing. It was very slight, but I did hear it."

"Did you get up to look?"

"Not because of the sounds, no. I mean, there's nothing sinister about doors opening or people walking in a residential building. But my tea had gotten cold, and I was going to reheat it. Then I decided to just poke my head out and see who it was." He looked embarrassed. "I thought it might be Beth. Spur-of-the-moment thing. I . . . I liked her. I liked talking to her."

"I'm sure," said Blum. "She was a very lovely young woman."

"And *did* you see anyone?" asked Pine.

"Well, I looked toward the direction of the elevators initially. I mean, that's the way someone would be going, right?"

"Right," said Pine. "But?"

"But I didn't see anyone. Then I looked the other way."

"And?" said Pine a bit impatiently, when it appeared he was not going to continue.

"Well, I couldn't swear to it, but I thought I saw the back of a shoe turn the corner. Obviously a shoe someone was wearing."

"What's in that direction?" asked Blum.

"Well, the freight elevators, for one."

"Was it a man's shoe?" asked Pine.

"Yes. I mean, it wasn't a high heel or anything."

"Could you see anything else?"

"No, not really. Wait, I think he might have had gray pants on."

"Gray pants. Like dress slacks?"

"No, not like that. I misspoke. It wasn't pants, at least I don't think so. It was like maybe overalls. And the shoe I saw looked like a work boot."

Pine looked at Blum. "A workman heading to the freight elevators?"

"Could be."

They asked Martin some more questions but got nothing else of use from him.

A minute later Pine headed to the freight elevators with Blum right behind.

They reached a pair of elevators after taking two turns, a right and a left. They were located at the end of the corridor.

Pine hit a button and they rode the car down. It opened into the underground parking lot for the building near the exit.

"Makes sense," said Pine. "If you're moving in or out, you pull your truck in here and use the elevator to bring your stuff in or out." She looked around. "I don't see any cameras in the vicinity. And there's no gate, so anyone can just pull in or out of here."

Pine looked at the door they'd just exited. She tried to tug it open. "But you need a key card to get in the door," she noted, pointing to a card reader port.

"Presumably the workman had one."

"We'll need the local cops to check this out, talk to Martin, and then see if anybody else saw someone on that hall at around that time."

"But Martin said he only heard a door open and close once. Wouldn't he have heard it when the guy went in, and then again when he exited?"

Pine said, "Not if the guy was already in the apartment and waiting for Clemmons to come home. The bath was full. She was obviously going to get in it. She had undressed and was in her bathrobe. He must have attacked her before she got into the tub."

"So he could have been in her apartment for some time before she arrived? But how did he get in?"

"There was no forced entry. And if she wasn't home to let him in, then he had to have a key. I just wonder where he got it." She looked at the card reader on the rear door. "Maybe the same place he got that."

"Are you thinking what I'm thinking?" said Blum.

"If you're thinking the killer used the key and key card he took from Hanna Rebane, then yes, we're on the same page."

"And the motive was to silence her, because she might tell us something damaging to someone?"

"But there's one problem with that. We already talked to her. You'd think the person would have struck *before* we did that."

Blum shook her head. "But now that Layne

Gillespie has been murdered? Maybe that made a difference."

"Meaning she could have had some info about him *and* his connection to Hanna Rebane?"

"Yes. The killer knew we would come back and talk to her about this second murder."

"It's certainly possible. But then again, anything seems to be possible with this case."

"Do you think this makes it more likely that there was a connection between Gillespie and Rebane?"

"Well, it certainly doesn't make it *less* likely," replied Pine.

"With her gone, how will we find that out?"

"She wasn't the only one to work in porn films. There's always someone else to ask."

"Well, let's hope we get to them before this guy does."

40

My whole past is a lie. Well, that's *a lie. Most of my past is a lie.*

It wasn't much consolation.

It was the next day and Pine was sitting on her bed at the Cottage.

She took out the magazine that Myron had given her. She opened it to the page where her mother appeared. Pine sat there and stared at the image for a long time. She ran her finger along the piles of hair on the head of the woman who had brought Pine into the world. She eyed the writing below. London. Karl Lagerfeld. The runway. Amanda something. She looked beautiful, but maybe too made up with makeup and wearing something too revealing, as models on fashion show runways often did.

From London to Andersonville. What a strange journey. She could make neither heads nor tails of it.

Pine laid the magazine aside, opened her spare suitcase, and picked up her old doll, fingering its hair as the rain started up again outside. They had driven back to Columbus in the rain, which had stopped when they got back to Andersonville. However, the clouds were now increasing and the winds were picking up. More inclemency was just about to hit.

On the drive back she had phoned Wallis and told him what had happened to Beth Clemmons. He, in turn, had filled her in on the developments with Layne Gillespie's autopsy. There had been no surprises there. Death by gunshot. No trace. No defensive wounds. The tux, hat, and corsage had led nowhere. The corpse had given no answers; his killer was no closer to being caught.

She had informed the local police in Columbus about Gene Martin's recollection of the workman heading to the freight elevator. They were following that up, but so far there had been nothing to come from it. There had been a camera outside the parking lot entrance, but it had been out of order. They had determined that it *was* Hanna Rebane's key card that had been used to access the building from the garage. The killer undoubtedly had come and gone that way. And Pine was certain that in addition to the key card, he'd had a key to the apartment, and had used that to access the place and lie in wait for Beth Clemmons.

Three people were dead, all of them connected. Rebane to Clemmons, as roommates and friends, and the two women and Layne Gillespie to the adult film world.

She looked down at the other items on her bed as she set the doll aside.

Barry Vincent. Why had this guy gotten into an argument with her father about what had happened? She couldn't even remember a Barry Vincent. But Myron Pringle did. He'd broken up the fight. Pine wondered what had happened to Vincent. No one had mentioned him. There had been nothing on him in the police investigative file.

Well, maybe she could do something about that.

She walked downstairs and knocked on a door near the front hall that was marked OFFICE.

"Yes?"

Pine opened the door and saw Lauren Graham sitting at her desk in front of a laptop.

"If I'm interrupting something I can come back," said Pine.

"No, I'm right in the middle of writer's block anyway."

Pine closed the door behind her. "I was wondering if you could help me with something."

Graham took off her reading glasses and set them down in front of her. "All right, but have you given my request any thought?" Then she noted the bruise on Pine's forehead. "What happened to you?"

"Ran into a wall. Look, I can talk to you generally about some of my cases, yes."

"Excellent. Maybe this evening over dinner?"

"At the Clink?"

"No. In Americus. There's an Italian bistro there I've been dying to try."

Pine hesitated, but only for a second. "Sure."

"Terrific, what's your question?"

Pine sat down across from Graham. "Barry Vincent. Do you remember him?"

"Barry Vincent?"

"He was the man who accused my father of being involved in my sister's disappearance," prompted Pine. "Myron Pringle told me. He broke up a fight between my father and him outside our old house."

Graham thought for a few moments, pursing her lips. "For the life of me I don't remember that name. Are you sure he was from Andersonville?"

"I assumed he was if Pringle said he was outside my house arguing with my dad."

"Agnes Ridley might know."

"Okay, I'll check with her."

"It sounds like you're making some progress," said Graham, giving Pine, at least to her mind, a strange look.

"Some. You know, you don't have to go to dinner with me. I can just talk to you here about some of my cases."

"No, I think it would be a lot more pleasant over some good food and drink." She looked at her watch. "We should leave by six."

"Fine. I'll see you back here at six."

Graham looked at Pine's clothing: jeans, sweater,

boots, and her FBI windbreaker. "Um, do you have a . . . dress and . . . heels? It's sort of business or cocktail attire at this place for dinner."

"I think I can scrounge up something appropriate."

"I don't mean to sound snooty or anything."

Pine made no reply.

Graham gazed at her keenly. "You're quite attractive, Atlee. You take after your mother. Tall, long torso and legs. Pretty much anything would look great on you. If you took the time . . . perhaps?"

"I have other things to do with my time," said Pine bluntly. "When I need to clean up, I usually manage it."

"I'm sure. I meant no offense. Are you going to talk to Agnes now?"

"Yes."

"Do you think this Barry Vincent person is important?"

"He is until he isn't. But that's the way investigations work, at least mine do. It might seem kind of boring for a novel," added Pine, glancing at the laptop on the woman's desk.

"My job is to make it not boring."

"I guess that's where imagination comes in."

"I hope I have enough of it," Graham said, a tad doubtfully.

Pine left and walked down the street to her truck and climbed in. She had gotten Agnes Ridley's address during her first conversation with the woman. It was a few miles outside of town and on the way to Pine's old home.

There was an old Buick in the gravel drive of the woman's house. It had more rust than anything else, and its Georgia plates had expired three years ago. The house looked a bit familiar to Pine, though she couldn't recall ever coming here. Ridley was home and answered Pine's knock after a few moments. She, too, asked about Pine's bruises, and Pine said once more that a wall and her own clumsiness had been the culprit.

She followed Ridley into the front room that was stuffed with pieces of bulky old furniture, and a great many fragile knickknacks perched precariously on every flat surface. A fat tabby reclined on an arm of the tattered sofa. The feline looked up at Pine with disinterest in her wide, luminous eyes.

"That's Boo," said Ridley, pointing to the cat.

"Looks friendly."

Ridley laughed as she sat down. "Only on his terms. Oh, would you like something to drink?"

Pine shook her head and plunged right in. "Do you remember a man named Barry Vincent?"

Ridley sat back and put a finger to her chin. "Barry Vincent?"

"Myron Pringle said that Vincent and my dad got into a fight the day after Mercy disappeared. Vincent apparently claimed that my dad had something to do with it."

"Oh, I did hear about that, yes. Barry Vincent—my goodness, I haven't heard that name in ages. He did live here at one time. Maybe in town. I'm just not sure."

"Did he work at the mine?"

"Not that I ever knew."

"Any idea where he is now?"

"No. Now, don't hold me to this, but I believe he left the area shortly before you and your parents did."

"What was he like? How long did he live here? Where was he from?"

Ridley seemed overwhelmed by the barrage of questions. "I . . . I don't really remember that much about him, Lee. He wasn't here really all that long."

"No wife or kids?"

"Not that I remember. Why all the interest in the man?"

"I'm just trying to run down leads. I was curious as to why he believed so strongly that my dad was involved in my sister's disappearance that he would have fought my father over it."

"Well, other people had their suspicions about that, too."

"But Vincent was apparently the only one who came to blows over it."

"I wouldn't know about that. You may want to ask Myron. If he remembers the fight, he may recall more about Vincent than I have."

"He's next on my list. I thought I'd try you first. It was Lauren Graham's suggestion."

"Well, I'm sorry I couldn't be more helpful. How is the case coming along?"

"Very slowly."

41

Pine made the drive out to the Pringles'. It was Myron who answered the door. Britta was out, he told her. He was dressed in khaki pants and a bright orange polo shirt with canvas boat shoes. He didn't appear inclined to let her in when she told him she had some questions.

"I'm busy," he said.

"It won't take long."

"Why do I think you always say that?"

"It's really important," she said in a pleading tone that made her stomach tighten uncomfortably. As an FBI agent she was used to asking whatever questions she wanted whenever she wanted and getting answers. But this was not that sort of case. Delicacy was required. And she could manage that, with an effort.

Myron backed away and motioned her in. He glanced at her bruise but said nothing.

He closed the door behind him and just stood there looking down at her.

"Well?" he said.

"Barry Vincent?"

He looked at her, puzzled. "Vincent? What about him?"

"What can you tell me about him?"

"Why?"

"Because he fought my dad. I'd like to understand the context of that."

"I'm not sure there is any, other than what I already told you. He thought your father guilty of a terrible thing. He made his thoughts known and then he punched your dad."

"So who was he?"

"A neighbor, I guess."

"Okay. What else?"

Myron sighed, folded his gangly arms over his thin chest, and leaned back against the wall. "He wasn't really all that memorable."

"Wife? Kids?"

Myron shook his head. "Not that I knew of. If he did, they didn't come here with him."

"Where did he work?"

Now he looked a bit interested. "I'm not sure. Not at the mine. He might have done some odd jobs here and there. A lot of people did back then. And still do today."

"You said he was a neighbor. Where did he live?"

"If I recall correctly, at first he lived in town, in a boardinghouse. After that, I don't know. I wasn't an intimate of his. I would just see him around from time to time."

"What was he like? Describe him."

Myron looked at the ceiling, obviously casting his mind back. "In his late thirties. Not too tall, but burly. Tough. He knew how to fight. Your father was younger and taller, but if I hadn't intervened I don't think it would have ended well for Tim."

"When did he come to town?"

Myron thought about this. "Don't hold me to this, but not that long before your sister disappeared. A few months or so. Right around that time anyway."

"And I understand he left shortly before we did?"

"That might be," he said cautiously.

"What exactly did he say to my father that day?"

"Are you sure you want to hear it?"

"I have to, Mr. Pringle. It's why I'm here."

Myron let out a short breath that was more like a grunt. "This is not verbatim, but he said something along the lines of Tim's having killed one daughter and nearly killed the other."

"And how did he come to make that allegation?"

"I don't know. He just did. I mean, everyone in town knew what had happened. They knew Mercy was gone and you were in the hospital severely injured."

"But he said my father had *killed* one daughter."

"I guess he just assumed that Mercy was dead. He wasn't alone in that. When a kid goes missing in the middle of the night and the other twin is nearly dead? It doesn't take a genius to make that leap of logic."

"Were other people making these kinds of allegations against my father?"

"Not that I heard."

"So what was Vincent's beef with my dad?"

"I don't know. As I already said, I didn't know the man very well."

"And you broke up the fight?"

"Yes. I wasn't going to let this guy kick your dad's ass, especially on a terrible day like that. He had enough to deal with without that jerk Vincent doing what he did."

"So you believed my dad had nothing to do with it?"

Myron said curtly, "I told you that before and I haven't changed my opinion."

"So did you remember the names of the friends you had over to your house that night?"

"No. It must've been nothing special or else I would remember. Do you recall who you were with on a certain night thirty years ago?"

"Yeah. I was in bed with my twin sister getting my skull crushed."

Myron looked away.

"Look, if you were doing something, I don't know, illegal, smoking joints or something, it doesn't matter to me. My parents were smoking joints. And the statute of limitations will have long since passed."

Myron shrugged. "I don't know what to tell you. I

just don't recall who it was. Now the next day, yes, I do remember that one."

"Did you ever ask Vincent why he went off on my dad?"

"No, I broke up the fight. I didn't consider it my job to ask him what his motivation was."

"Did my dad have any other interaction with the guy?"

"Not to my knowledge."

"Small town. You'd think they would have run into one another."

"If they did, I never heard about it. After Mercy vanished, your mom and dad had little to do with anyone here. They circled the wagons. Barely left the house. Tim would come to work at the mine, but everyone knew his heart wasn't in it. And then one day you all just vanished."

"So you and Britta didn't see much of them after Mercy was taken?"

"No. But we were supportive. Britta would make meals and bring them over. She even brought our kids over a few times so you'd have someone your own age around. But I don't think you were interested in playing anymore. Or being a kid anymore."

"That's pretty insightful of you."

"I lost both my children years later. It does make you think."

"Anything else you can remember?"

"I'd give Tim a lift to work, bring him home, that

sort of thing. We socialized a little, but your parents had no interest in partying anymore. It was like the light had gone out for them."

Pine nodded and looked down at her boots. "I guess I could see that."

"What do *you* remember from that time?"

"Hospitals, tests, doctors poking at me."

"And your mom and dad?"

"I think when they 'circled the wagons,' they left me on the outside."

"No, I distinctly remember that your mother barely left your side. She would have sat in the classroom at school with you if she could have."

"I'm not talking physically. Physically, she smothered me. Emotionally, there was a wall that would never come down."

"She was terrified of losing you."

Pine looked up at him, holding his gaze for a few seconds before saying, "Well, we ended up losing one another anyway, didn't we?"

42

Pine was going through her little inventory of childhood mementos once more.

Carol Blum sat in a chair and watched her examining them on her bed.

She had filled Blum in on her meetings with Agnes Ridley and Myron Pringle.

"Do you think this Barry Vincent is significant in some way?" asked Blum.

Pine stopped fiddling with the mementos and said, "I don't know. It's just weird that no one can tell me much about him. He came here after my parents did and left town before they did. He was the only one to get into a fight with my father over it. Myron didn't think that my dad even knew the guy that well. So why would he start throwing out all these allegations?"

"Maybe they had a private beef that only they knew about," conjectured Blum.

"But if it was just between them it's going to be really hard to find out what it was."

"Did your mother or father ever mention him afterward?"

"Not that I remember. I didn't even know he existed until I got here, and Myron mentioned his name." She looked down at the items. "There's so much I don't know about my own family, Carol. My dad didn't die where my mom said he did. Jack Lineberry found his body. I have no idea if my mother even went down there to take care of arrangements and scatter his ashes. She just left and then came back and told me basically nothing about it."

"You'd think if Lineberry found the body and she came down there, that they would have gotten together."

"He said they didn't. But there's no way to corroborate that."

Blum looked at the objects on the bed. "So that's all you have left?" she said.

"Not much, is it?"

"Well, it makes each one that much more important," said Blum judiciously.

"I'd prefer them to lead me somehow to the truth."

"Your sister's doll?" said Blum, rising from her chair and picking up Pine's doll.

"What about it?"

"Britta Pringle mentioned that your mother was looking for it the morning after Mercy disappeared."

"She also said that people do odd things in times

of stress, and she's right. Maybe my mom thought if she could find the doll, she could find Mercy, too."

"Maybe."

Blum put the doll down, while Pine picked up one of the bar drink coasters.

"We used these as checker pieces," she said, in answer to Blum's curious look.

"Very creative."

Pine smiled at the memory, and then that fell away as she focused more closely on the drink coaster.

"What is it?"

"These came from my dad. A bar in New York. The Cloak and Dagger."

"Cool name for a bar."

Pine looked at the collection of bar coasters. "But why would my dad have had so many coasters from the same bar?"

"Could he have bartended there? Or been a regular?"

"I'm not sure if he was even old enough to drink back then."

"Depending on the state you can bartend before you can actually drink. Doesn't make a lot of sense. I'm not sure of New York's laws back then."

"Well, he was trying to break into acting, I was told. I guess actors have side jobs to support themselves."

"That's true."

"The Cloak and Dagger Bar. I wonder why they picked that name."

"You mean was it simply catchy or did it have some other meaning?"

Pine went on her phone and performed a search. "There's a Cloak and Dagger Boutique in New York City and a Cloak and Dagger Bar in DC. But neither was around in the eighties. No Cloak and Dagger Bar in New York, at least currently."

"And in the eighties no websites and probably no digital record today of its existence back then."

"The coaster doesn't have an address or phone number on it. Just the name and it being in New York."

"Well, I've seen coasters like that. They don't all have that information on them."

"Maybe I'm grasping at straws."

"Remember your axiom: Everything is important until it's proven not to be."

Pine started to put her phone away and then thought better of it. "There might be a way of checking on it." She consulted her contacts list, selected a number, and punched it in.

"Hello, Stan, it's Atlee Pine. Yeah, I know it's been a long time. How are you? Right, that's good. Yeah, the Bureau works in mysterious ways. No, I'm not in Utah anymore. I'm in Arizona. Near the Grand Canyon. Yeah, it is beautiful. Look, I have a favor. I want you to check up on a bar for me. It was back in the early eighties. The name was the Cloak and Dagger." Pine paused as the man on the other end said something. "Just anything you can tell me about it. Yeah, as soon as you can. Okay, thanks."

She clicked off and looked at Blum. "Stan Cashings works at the New York Field Office. Has for over two decades. If anything can be found out about that place, he'll find it."

"At the very least it might lead you to something about your father's past that you didn't know before."

"It also might explain why a fashion model chucks her career, gets pregnant, marries my dad, and soon thereafter they give up New York City for Andersonville, Georgia, with two toddlers in tow."

"Nothing about it really makes sense."

Pine put her phone away. "No, it *does* makes sense. We just don't know how yet. But now, I've got to get ready."

"For what?"

"I'm having dinner with Lauren Graham at a place in Americus. I need to dress up a little, or so she not so subtly told me."

"Well, you clean up well. I know that."

"We'll see." She looked at herself in the swivel mirror on top of the chest of drawers, focusing on her bruise. "The swelling's all gone, but it's still a little discolored."

"Nothing a little makeup can't cover. I can help you with that if you want."

"Thanks. I'm not the best with that stuff. It's too much to remember."

"But why are you going to dinner with her?"

"It's on the pretense of my talking about how I investigate my cases. But the real reason is, I don't think the lady's been entirely forthcoming with us."

"Well, that seems to be the general theme in this town," replied Blum.

43

"You cleaned up well."

Graham was looking up the stairs at the Cottage as Pine came down them. Graham had on a knee-length dark red skirt that hugged her hips, with a white blouse and a hunter green jacket over that. Her tights and stiletto heels were both black.

Pine had put on the one dress she had brought with her. It was black, of a simple design, and it rode snug on her frame. Around her shoulders was a turquoise wrap that Blum had let her borrow. Her heels were open-toed, lifting her height to a couple inches over six feet. She had done her hair; instead of its being pulled back like she normally wore it, she had let the dark strands fall around her shoulders. Blum had helped her cover up the bruise on her forehead with a liberal layer of foundation.

"Thanks. You look great," said Pine.

"Do you know what came into my head when I saw you just now? Your mother. The spitting image."

"That's very kind. I don't think I'm nearly in her league. Or that glamorous."

"You might have missed your calling," said Graham.

"I think I found it just fine. You ready? I can drive."

On the ride to Americus, Graham said, "So, have you given any thought to what you can share with me?"

"Investigative methods, some details of cases without identifying what cases they were attached to. And I can answer general questions you might have."

"That's very generous. Okay, first thing, what do you think are the most important traits a detective can have?"

Pine collected her thoughts, though she didn't really need to in order to answer this basic question. "Patience and tenacity. They go hand in hand. The cases can either solve themselves quickly because the criminals were so stupid, or else they can take years and a lot of legwork and going over and over old ground. I've been involved in both kinds."

"Any nuances you can share?"

"Small details can matter more than the big ones. Criminals always fail on the little details. Blood spatters, trace fibers, fingerprints, ballistics matching. DNA. They think they can get rid of all blood traces by using bleach. But if you really want a decent shot at destroying DNA you should use an oxygen-based detergent that produces oxygen-rich bubbles. That blocks the oxygen in the DNA from uplifting to the luminol that we would use to reveal the blood stains. Or you can go the other route, by collecting DNA samples from other people who might have ties to the victim and flood the murder scene with them. That could overwhelm an investigation and give a defense lawyer wiggle room."

"That's fascinating."

"It just comes with the territory."

"And are you always armed?"

Pine touched her clutch purse. "Beretta Nano eight-shot. Just in case. It's a girl's best friend in my line of work."

"I may use that line in my novel, if that's okay."

"Go for it."

Twenty minutes and many more questions and answers later, they arrived at the restaurant, an intimate Italian bistro with an upscale wine list and waiters with black bow ties and starched shirts. They were seated at a table by a window.

"Just so you know, my pocketbook does not cover this sort of a place," said Pine after she looked at the prices.

"This is on me," said Graham. "I'm sorry I didn't make that clear."

"You don't have to do that. I was just going to order water and an appetizer."

"No, please, you've already given me some great material. I really appreciate it."

They ordered and were sipping glasses of red wine from Sonoma Valley when a familiar voice called out.

"Ladies, if I knew you were here, you could have joined me."

They both looked up to see Jack Lineberry gazing down at them. He was smartly dressed in pearl-gray slacks, a striped shirt, and a dark blue blazer with tasseled loafers. A pocket square of color fronted the jacket. His skin was lightly tanned, and his hair was neatly trimmed. Perhaps for the first time, Pine realized what a very attractive man he was.

Graham beamed up at him. "Jack, I didn't know you were going to be here."

"Last-minute change of plans. I just finished up. But I don't want to interrupt."

"Please, join us for a glass of wine," said Graham.

When he turned and focused on Pine his features froze.

"Are you okay?" asked Pine.

His face changed color. "I'm . . . I'm sorry," he said, his grin weak and forced. "For a minute there—"

"—you thought it was Julia," Graham finished for him, her exuberant expression fading quickly as she said this.

Lineberry slowly sat down next to Pine and nodded, his gaze averted from her. "Yes," he said quietly. His face was pale and his voice was husky.

"I'm sorry if it gave you a nasty turn," said Pine.

He lifted his gaze to hers. "No, quite the contrary, it was an overwhelmingly positive feeling." His expression turned embarrassed by this admission and he looked at Graham. "Did you mention a glass of wine, Lauren?"

The waiter must have overheard this because he hurried over and poured one out for him.

"Thank you, William," said Lineberry to the waiter.

As the man walked away Pine said, "I take it you're a regular here?"

Lineberry nodded, but Graham added, "Jack bankrolled this place. Otherwise, it would never have happened."

"Good food and wine should not be the exclusive property of big cities," noted Lineberry. He glanced at Pine. "You look quite lovely tonight, Lee. I . . ." He looked away.

"You didn't realize I had any potential beyond pants, attitude, and a gun?" But Pine grinned as she said this, softening the bluntness of her words.

He smiled warmly. "Something like that."

Graham said, "She was giving me some professional information for the novel I'm writing."

"Wonderful. That's very considerate of you, Lee," said Lineberry.

Pine said, "Just keep in mind that if you're writing a *historical* detective novel, DNA and luminol and all the rest won't be appropriate subjects."

"I know. But I plan on writing a second novel set in current times, too, so there's that." Graham rose from the table. "Just going to hit the little girls' room."

Pine thought that Graham maybe wanted to

freshen up her makeup and hair now that Lineberry was here. But this gave her an opportunity with the gossipy Graham out of the picture for the moment.

"While I have you here, Jack, I'd like to ask you some follow-up questions, if that's okay," said Pine.

He looked startled. "Follow-up questions?"

"About my parents."

He nodded slowly. "Okay, I'll tell you what I can."

Pine inwardly frowned at his comment, not quite sure how to interpret it.

"Myron Pringle gave me a magazine showing my teenage mother to be a fashion model, walking the runway in London. And apparently back then her first name was Amanda and her last name was unknown."

Lineberry just gazed at her dully. "Did you not know your mother's maiden name?"

"Astonishingly not. I know it sounds crazy, but she never talked about her family. Not once. Neither did my father. I just assumed they had no family living."

"Okay."

"Did you know that about her? That she was a model?" asked Pine.

He sipped his wine and set it carefully down. "I recall your mother mentioning something like that once."

"And you weren't surprised?"

"That your mother was a model? No, of course not. She was the most beautiful woman I had ever seen. I . . ." He coughed, looked embarrassed, and stared into his wineglass.

"But to go from all that to Andersonville?"

"I can't in all honesty tell you that I didn't find that odd, because I did. But your parents never chose to explain their reasons for coming here and I was not going to pry. I mean, we all have things in our lives we'd rather not talk about."

"You obviously cared for her," said Pine.

Lineberry reached for his wine again, but then withdrew his hand. He cleared his throat and without looking at her said, "I cared for *both* your parents. What happened to them should not have happened. It troubled me back then and it still troubles me to this day."

"You tried to find my mother?"

"I wanted to know that she was okay, yes." He glanced at her. "I hope that the challenges you mentioned her having are not insurmountable."

His features showed the strain that he was under in making the query.

"In all honesty, I don't know."

He nodded. "Life is quite strange, you know."

"How so?" asked Pine.

"You have a vision, a predetermined idea of how things will work out. And then none of it does."

"I think most people would take how your life has turned out a hundred times out of a hundred."

He looked at her with a sadness there that Pine found deeply confusing.

"Well, things are not always how they seem," he said before finishing his wine and bidding her good night.

As she watched him walk off, Graham came back to the table. Pine had been right. Her lipstick was fresh and her hair had been brushed.

"Is Jack coming back?" she said, sounding hopeful.

"No, he's heading out."

Pine had a sudden thought and looked at her. "Did you know he was going to be here tonight?"

"What? Oh, no. I had no idea."

Graham was a lousy liar, thought Pine.

They watched as Lineberry headed out the front entrance. Pine thought she could see Jerry standing outside, waiting.

"He's such a wonderful man, but he feels things so deeply. Maybe too deeply," said Graham.

Pine was pondering something else.

Exactly when did Jack Lineberry fall head over heels in love with my mother?

44

For the second time that night Pine heard the term "Wow" used in her general vicinity.

She had gotten back to the Cottage after dinner in Americus. Graham had already gone off to her room, but Pine had lingered in the foyer thinking about the discussion with Lineberry when a man had come out of the shadows and spoken the word.

She looked at Eddie Laredo.

"What are you doing here?"

He grinned. "I got a bump on the per diem, extenuating circumstances. I checked in here today. They had one room left. Much nicer than where I was staying." He looked her over. "Where have you been dressed up like that? Some international ball or something?"

"Dinner with Lauren Graham."

"You know, I've never seen you in a dress before."

"Why would you? I never wore one to work."

"Right," he said quickly, taking a step back. "So how did dinner go?"

"I didn't have enough to drink."

"What?"

She checked her watch. "It's early yet. You want to hit the Clink?"

He looked taken aback by the offer but quickly nodded. "Sure. You want to change?"

She eyed him sternly. "Do you want me to?"

He looked even more flustered. "What! No . . . That's up to you." He ran his gaze over her. "You . . . you look . . . um, I don't have an opinion—I mean . . ."

She pushed past him and walked over to the door. "Glad we cleared that up."

The Clink was three-quarters full, and Pine drew stares from all as she and Laredo walked in.

Standing beside her, he had to look up at Pine.

"What?" she said, catching his gaze.

"With heels on, you're taller than me."

"If your male pride is wounded I can go barefoot."

"Depending on how many drinks we have, it may come to that."

That just got him a snort in reply.

They found a table at the back near the singer and guitar player holding forth on an improvised stage.

Pine ordered a Budweiser and Laredo a gin and tonic on the rocks with three limes.

"You haven't changed your drinking habits," she noted.

"Neither have you."

"Cocktails were beyond my pay grade."

When the drinks came she tapped her metal can against his glass.

They sipped their drinks and listened to the singer and musician for a minute, their heads swaying to the sounds. Then Laredo said, "What was the dinner about?"

"Payback for Lauren Graham's help. But there was an interesting development."

"What was that?"

She told him about Jack Lineberry.

"So he had a thing for your mother?"

"Unless I'm reading him way wrong. In fact, for a minute there . . ."

"What?"

"Well, even though she's in her fifties now, for a minute there I believed that he really thought I *was* my mother."

Laredo ran his eye over her. "Well, you do look like some supermodel type." He added quickly, "I mean, you know, dressed up like that."

She gave him an incredulous look. "I'm definitely *not* a supermodel type. I can squat nearly five hundred pounds. My thighs are bigger than a typical supermodel's body."

Laredo glanced at her long, muscled bare legs and then he quickly looked up. "I only know you with a gun in one hand and a badge in the other and I'm leaving it at that."

"Lineberry is really rich. Has his jet and this huge

house. And a former Secret Service guy as head of security."

"So?"

"So a guy like that, if he wanted to find someone, couldn't he hire the best PI firm around and let them loose trying to find her? How hard would it be? My mom didn't even change her name from when she lived in Andersonville. And I was making a name for myself with weightlifting. How many Atlee Pines are out there? I have a frigging Wikipedia page somebody put up that talks about my sister's disappearance."

"I know. I saw it."

"I had nothing to do with making that page, Eddie."

"I know that, too."

Laredo took a sip of his cocktail while he thought about this. "So he could have found you and/or her easily enough but he obviously didn't. So the question becomes why."

"So you think it's strange, too?"

"Everything in this place is strange. They've been trying to feed me something called 'grits' with my breakfast ever since I got here."

"I never appreciated your humor before, Eddie."

"I'm being serious, Atlee."

"I can tell."

"So what's the deal with your assistant, Blum?"

"What do you mean?"

"She gave me the third degree when I first met her. Wanted to know what had gone on between us."

"And what did you tell her?"

"That it was none of her business. And then she told me she'd done a 411 on me."

Pine laughed. "Boy, she really did pull out all the stops on you."

"You really think that's funny?"

"Don't you?"

Laredo finally chuckled. "I guess. Anyway, she said I checked out all right."

"Obviously she failed to talk to the right people." But Pine tacked on a smile to show she was joking.

Laredo finished his gin and tonic and held his hand up for a second and Pine ordered another Bud.

"Getting back to Jack Lineberry," he said when the drinks had arrived. "I actually did a 411 on him."

"What? On Lineberry? Why?"

"He's a really rich guy and he's close by here."

"You think he's going around killing people and laying them out in old clothes?"

"I didn't say that."

"So what did your 411 turn up?"

"That he *is* really rich. His investment business is totally legit. He gives a lot to charities. He's well liked."

"When did he come to Andersonville, or was he born here?"

"He wasn't born here, at least the records I looked at don't show that."

"Where then?"

Laredo's expression turned puzzled. "Not entirely clear."

"How can that be, Eddie?"

"I'm not sure, to tell you the truth. But then again, not everybody has a birth certificate, or knows where they're born."

Pine reflected on this. She hadn't known where she was born until she had seen her birth certificate that she needed to get her passport.

"He's in his sixties, so we're looking at him being born sometime in the fifties. If it was in a rural area and he was born at home or with a midwife instead of in a hospital?"

"It's possible. But to the extent we could track his past, the guy's never been in trouble with the police."

"So he came here at some point and started working at the bauxite mine in management."

"Right. That's what I found, too."

"Did it say when he first came here?"

Laredo took out his phone and scrolled through some windows.

"Sometime in the 1980s. I don't have an exact date. We could get one, I suppose."

"Probably doesn't matter."

"You think he had something to do with what happened to your sister?"

"It's possible but not really probable. He seems to genuinely care for my family, particularly my mother. And he was going to offer my father a job in his investment firm. He was on his way to meet with my father when he found his body."

"Damn. That must have been a shock."

"My mother told me it happened in Louisiana. It was Virginia, according to Lineberry. I was nineteen at the time. In fact, he killed himself on my birthday."

"Wow, I'm sorry, Atlee. That must have been rough."

She sipped her beer. "It was . . . not easy. The biggest thing I felt was anger. That I wasn't there to talk him out of it. That maybe he thought I didn't love or care about him. It should never have happened."

"It's hard to get into the head of someone who's contemplating killing themselves. But don't think that you need to shoulder the blame. If someone really wants to kill themselves, they'll find a way. You know that as well as I do."

"Yeah, I know it when the person isn't my father."

Laredo lifted his drink to her. "Point taken."

They had another round and when some of the patrons started to hit the dance floor, Pine said, "You want to?"

He looked confused. "Want to what?"

She answered by gripping his hand and pulling him up.

Before they took to the dance floor, Pine slipped off her heels and put them on her chair.

She looked *up* at Laredo and smiled. "Feel better now?"

He grinned. "Hey, what can I say? You're intimidating at any height."

They danced for a while, apart for most of it, dipping, swirling, and spinning to the tunes that were mostly country.

"You move pretty well for an FBI agent," noted Pine.

"Growing up in Queens, my main ambition was to become a member of a boy band. It seemed the straightest path to money and girls."

"What happened?"

"I can't carry a tune. I was pretty bummed."

"Do I remember something about you doing track in college?"

"Full ride based on how fast I could run. Sweet deal."

The next song was a slow one. They drew closer, hesitantly. His arm encircled her waist, and Pine's went over his delt.

She breathed in his scent and she assumed he was doing the same to her. She started to rest her head against his chest but then thought better of it.

They would glance at each other and then away.

When the song ended Pine said, "It's late. We should get back."

"Right."

They walked to the Cottage. It was warm and humid. Pine carried her shoes in her hand, and the pavement felt cool to her feet. They didn't pass anyone; the street was mostly dark, with only the moon providing illumination.

"They need some more lights out here, if just to stop people from bumping into stuff," said Laredo.

"Small towns aren't big cities."

"No they are not."

When they got back to the Cottage they walked up the stairs.

"Where's your room?" Pine asked.

Laredo pointed to his right. "Just down there."

"I'm the other way. Just down there."

He nodded. So did Pine.

"Well, good night, Eddie. Thanks for a nice evening."

"It was nice, Atlee. Good night."

She looked at him, sensing disappointment in his features, but maybe that was just her take.

They went their separate ways.

She looked back once, but Laredo never did. He went to his room and slipped inside.

When Pine's door closed behind her, another opened.

Carol Blum looked out of her room, first glancing toward the direction of Pine's room and then Laredo's.

Her look was more or less inscrutable, sort of between a smile and a frown.

She closed the door and all became quiet.

Pine slipped off her dress, hung it up, and stood in the middle of her room in her bra and underwear. She looked toward her door and then shook her head.

I didn't have enough to drink to make that stupid a decision.

But Laredo had been sweet and contrite. And maybe he had changed. And he had seemed disappointed that maybe she hadn't invited him to her room, and her bed, or offered to go to his. But that was his problem, not hers. *And you didn't lead him on, Atlee. Not really.*

However, she wasn't sure she entirely believed that.

45

"The workman angle is a dead end," said Wallis.

He, Pine, Laredo, and Blum were sitting in the breakfast room at the Cottage. It was the following morning. Lauren Graham had served them all coffee before departing.

Wallis continued, "We could find no one that saw him. And there's no video footage."

"Same as Hanna Rebane," noted Laredo.

"Looks like our perp knows the gaps in coverage," suggested Pine. "And he had Rebane's condo key and key card so he could come and go at will. What did you find out about the porn company that Rebane and Clemmons worked for?"

Wallis brightened. "We did get lucky there. Turns out that Layne Gillespie also worked as an actor for that same production company."

"Did he appear in films with Rebane and Clemmons?" asked Laredo.

"Both. They sent me a video file of them in a threesome," said Wallis, his face turning pink. "I, uh, I watched enough of it to confirm that it was all three, for sure. Gillespie used the name ZZ Shaft. At least that's what I could gather from the credits."

"Creative," said Pine drily.

Laredo said, "So that puts the production company in the spotlight. That's the only connection we have right now."

"And that production company is turning out to be a little hard to pin down," said Wallis. "It's a shell company organized in Bermuda. All the information I can get so far adds up to a big fat zero. I've made calls and sent emails and texts and I've gotten nothing except silence in return."

"What about the actual people working on the films?" asked Blum.

"The actors, apparently, know nothing. The producer I got on the phone could only give me the name of the company. He's never met an actual person. Money to fund the films and pay the actors comes in through wire transfers from offshore. The distribution of the films is made through a third-party firm that looks legit. The profits go offshore into a black hole. I'm just a local cop. We're not set up to penetrate that sort of shield."

Laredo and Pine looked at each other. Pine said, "It's not so easy for the FBI, either. Everyone thinks the Feds are the eight-hundred-pound gorilla. Go ask the IRS who has more resources, them or some billionaires they're chasing. It's no contest. The rich sweep the field."

"There might be a connection to Andersonville," said Blum. "I mean, that's where two of the bodies were found."

"That is certainly possible," said Pine. "And whoever is behind this has to have some connection to porn films."

Laredo chimed in. "It could be they're antiporn and this is their way of showing their disapproval, by murdering actors in that field."

"But why dress them up in those getups?" asked Wallis. "What would be the point?"

"A veil and a tux," mused Pine. "Bride and groom, obviously. That has to be worked into the scenario somehow. It was important to the killer."

"Which means we're back at square one," said Wallis. He rose, his expression troubled. "I've got to get back to the office and report in to my superiors. Not something I relish doing, since I've basically gotten nowhere. Let me know if anything occurs to you."

After he left, Laredo looked at Pine. "I got a text from Stan Cashings this morning."

Pine's face was inscrutable, while Blum's eyes widened a bit.

"Okay," said Pine.

"Cloak and Dagger?" prompted Laredo.

"How do you know Stan?"

"I've worked with him. Thought you knew that."

"I didn't."

"Why do you want to know about something called Cloak and Dagger?"

"I think it was a bar back in New York, in the eighties. I think my father might have worked there. Why would Stan have contacted you about that?"

"Because he transferred down to DC last year. WFO," he added, referring to the FBI's Washington Field Office.

"Then maybe I called the wrong person. He didn't mention that on the phone."

"No, he was a good source. He knows New York as well as anybody. If this place existed, he'll be able to find out about it."

"Still doesn't explain why he would call you."

"Because I told him where I was going and that you were going to be there."

"He also didn't mention that."

"Stan plays things close to the vest. It's the FBI way. It's not like you and I don't share that attribute." The two stared at each other for an uncomfortably long moment.

Blum cleared her throat and said, "So, getting back to the murders here."

Pine said, "We've got to run down this connection to the porn films. The killer had to know intimate details of the actors, their real identities, where they live."

"So you think they knew him somehow?" said Laredo.

"Rebane had some man in her life, Clemmons told us. We haven't learned the same about Gillespie but it's possible he had some relationship with the killer. He could have brought them here under some pretext, killed them, and laid them out for us to find. Then he gets cold feet for some reason about Clemmons, maybe because she could tell us the connection between Rebane and Gillespie, and that's why she had to die."

"Maybe someone could have seen them together somewhere," said Blum.

"That's an awfully big task for a few people to track down," pointed out Laredo.

"You're not expecting any reinforcements from the Bureau?" said Pine.

"Not at the present, no. The Bureau is stretched thin as it is. Lots of stuff on the burners."

"Three murders aren't chump change," Pine retorted.

"Preaching to the choir, and I'll ask for help. Just don't hold your breath."

They heard the sound of feet rushing down the hall, and Graham burst into the little breakfast room. Her face was pale, and her features held a stark terror that made Pine and Laredo rise at the same time, their hands near their guns.

"What?" barked Pine.

"You've got to . . . come. Hurry! Oh my God. Hurry."

She turned and fled back down the hall, with the three in pursuit.

They quickly hit the main street and hurried after Graham, and soon she stopped in front of one of the buildings.

It was the Drummer Boy Civil War Museum, a gray painted brick structure with black shutters on the windows and a metal roof over the porch overhang. Out front was the Confederate flag, and large wooden cutouts of figures in blue and gray uniforms and smaller versions of drummer boys in uniform. The faces were blank holes, allowing visitors to fill them with their own countenances and have their pictures taken. You could do the same thing with the cutout of a lady in a hoop skirt.

A woman in her forties with wavy brown hair, wearing a navy blue dress with low heels and nylons, was standing outside, looking even more distraught than Graham. She had one hand against the brick, apparently to keep herself upright. Her other hand was pressed against her chest.

"Lily," called out Graham. "I brought the FBI folks."

Laredo and Pine strode past Graham and swiftly moved over to the woman named Lily.

"What happened?" said Laredo, his hand on the butt of his pistol.

In answer, Lily pointed weakly in the direction of the museum.

"It's . . . it's in there," she said breathlessly.

Laredo's and Pine's gazes swiveled to the front of the entrance.

"'It'?" said Pine.

"In the back. In . . . in the uniform. Oh, it's so very awful."

She buried her face in her hands and started to sob.

Pine eyed Blum and motioned her over to stay with Lily.

She and Laredo opened the door to the museum and entered. The space was filled with Civil War and other memorabilia. There were glass display cabinets and weapons hanging from the walls. In the middle was a large-scale model of Andersonville Prison complete with double stockade walls, prison figures, guard towers, tents, and sandy dirt.

Against the walls and behind black railings with framed information plaques were mannequins dressed in military uniforms. Against another wall was a woman dressed all in black with a bonnet-style hat and a black parasol. Next to her was a soldier wearing his hat, gold sash, and sword.

Pine was the first to see it, and even her hardened nerves took a jolt.

Laredo looked where she was staring and let out a hiss. "Damn, is that . . . ?"

They walked over to the spot. Behind another set of black railings there were two adult mannequin soldiers, muskets held at shoulder arms, with Confederate flags on the wall behind. Pine barely looked at any of this. She was riveted on a small figure standing between them. She supposed it was the eponymous drummer boy, dressed in rebel gray with his drum hanging from a white support band over his shoulder and twin drumsticks in his hand. Only unlike the other display figures, this one had once been a living, breathing person.

46

The windows were covered with brown paper to block sight lines into the museum. Police tape had been stretched across the front. A small group of people was milling around outside. Some spoke with the policeman on duty at the door. Everyone looked worried and upset.

Inside, the atmosphere was tense.

Pine and Blum stood next to the body. It still had the uniform on, since the forensic techs were completing their work and taking their pictures.

The victim was around ten, male, and Hispanic.

Pine looked down at the pair of large brown eyes that could no longer see a thing. Perhaps their last captured image had been that of their owner's killer.

"Murder is always upsetting," murmured Blum, looking away. "But when it's a child." She said nothing else, she didn't have to.

Laredo and Detective Wallis were consulting with a couple of uniformed deputies. Lily, the shaken museum attendant, had been allowed to go home after giving a full account.

She said she had come into the museum, just like any other morning. She had put away her purse and made a cup of tea. She had started to work on a display in the back of the main room when something caught her eye.

She had told them, "The mannequin was white. This . . . this one wasn't."

They had figured out how the body had been propped up: A harness was under the uniform jacket and it had been attached to a bolt in the wall.

In Pine's mind's eye she kept seeing the little soccer girl, Holly. Pine had managed to save her life, but not this little boy's. She rubbed at her eyes, trying to clear both them and her brain.

It didn't work.

Laredo walked over to her.

"No forced entry. Lady left last night around six thirty. Perp would have had to have a key."

Pine nodded. "Front entrance has a security camera attached to the porch roof. I noted that on the way in. There's a back entrance. He would have had to come in that way carrying the victim. He would have had plenty of time to arrange . . ." Pine fell silent and looked down at the child.

"Right," said Laredo, following her gaze.

"Any line on the victim?" asked Pine.

"Not so far. Early days yet."

"We're running out of days. This guy isn't going to stop because we can't keep up."

Wallis rejoined them. "This is awful. A kid." He shook his head.

Pine nodded. "I asked Lily if she had seen anyone acting strangely or someone in the museum she didn't recognize. But of course with the Civil War reenactment coming up the place is going to be flooded with out-of-towners. In fact, she told me the museum has been pretty full the last few days."

Laredo said, "Hey, you think maybe his mom or dad is involved in the porn industry?"

Pine said, "If so, you'd think they'd notice their kid missing. I'd circulate his picture all over. Somebody has to come forward."

Laredo said, "First, a lonely spot on the main road, only a few blocks from here. Then the cemetery. Now this place."

"What about Beth Clemmons?" interjected Blum.

"I don't see her as part of the vic pattern," said Pine. "She was a threat. That was why she was killed. She wasn't dressed, or laid out. She was just murdered to keep her quiet."

Laredo shook his head. "But we found out they acted in films together from another source. We didn't need Clemmons for that."

"Which logically means that Clemmons knew something *else* that was important."

"Then she had to die," said Blum. "As soon as Gillespie did. Because the killer would know that, sooner or later, we would come back to question her about it."

"Exactly."

Wallis said, "I'll go see about getting the boy's description circulated along with a sketch of his face." He looked down. "We'll have to use this image of him. We don't have another."

Laredo said, "And we can also have it put through our databases."

"And the National Center for Missing and Exploited Children," added Pine.

Wallis nodded and moved off.

Blum came to stand next to Pine, who said quietly, "The perp is moving off his original theme."

"You mean first a veil and then a tux?"

"But he dressed the boy in a costume from this place, and—" Pine stopped, fixed her gaze on the body, and knelt down next to it.

One of the techs who was taking a photo said loudly, "Hey, I'm trying to get scale photos here, if you don't mind."

Pine gazed up at him with such a look that he quickly stepped back and started nervously fumbling with his camera.

"What is it?" asked Blum, squatting next to Pine as Laredo looked over Pine's shoulder.

Pine had put on a pair of latex gloves and carefully undid the collar of the jacket on the body. She had just noticed the thin line of silver chain around the neck. She slid it out from under the clothing and held it up.

"It's a St. Christopher's medal," observed Blum.

Pine nodded. "Yes it is." She slid her finger around a part of the medal that had been damaged. "Look at this jagged edge. Something hit it hard enough to rip the metal."

"Do we know cause of death on the boy?" asked Blum.

"No, but there are no obvious wounds. And no signs of strangulation. His neck has no ligature marks."

"Poison, then?"

"I don't know." She studied the boy's head. "But his neck is at an odd angle."

"You think it's been broken?" said Laredo.

"Could be."

She called the photographer over and had him take a series of photos of the medal.

Wallis had rejoined them by this time. Pine pointed out the medal to him.

"You think it was part of the original costume here, or did it belong to the kid?" asked Wallis.

"Or did the perp put it on him?" said Pine.

Laredo said, "Lily reported that the uniform was taken from a mannequin on display. It was found in the back."

"But I think she'll confirm that this St. Christopher's medal isn't part of the costume."

"Is that your gut?" said Wallis. "It could belong to the boy."

"No," said Laredo. "She's going by the perp's pattern. He dressed the two adults. And he dressed this one, whether he brought the clothes or not."

Pine said, "But he added this. He didn't add anything to the other two vics, at least that we could find, other than dressing them as bride and groom."

"So he's subtly changing his pattern," noted Blum.

"It looks to be that way."

"Serial murderers don't usually do that midstream," observed Laredo. "You know that."

Pine nodded. "Most don't. But some do. And keep in mind that we don't really know what his pattern or motive is. It may still be evolving. So we could look at this death and this crime scene and say the guy's changed his MO, but, to him, he's right on schedule."

Wallis said, "I can see why you used to do this for a living. You seem to be able to get inside their heads." His face twitched. "Better you than me."

"It's not a place I want to be, either," said Pine. "But I'll go there if it gives us a shot at bringing this guy down."

Laredo looked at her and nodded in understanding.

Wallis said, "I'll check with Lily about the medal. But if it turns out to have been added, what does that mean?"

In answer Pine pulled out the medal she wore around her neck. "St. Christopher was the patron saint of travelers. Legend has it that he carried a child safely across a river only to find out later that that child was Christ. Ever since then he's been known as sort of the protector of people on a journey."

"Well, he failed miserably with this child," said Blum sharply.

"You may be looking at it the wrong way, Carol," said Pine.

Laredo eyed her steadily. "And what would be the right way?"

"If we could find out how this medal got damaged, I might be able to answer your question."

"You really think it's important?" asked Wallis.

"It might be the most important thing we've found so far."

47

"Who, if anyone, gave you your St. Christopher's medal?" asked Blum.

They were walking back to the Cottage.

"My mother," said Pine. "It was the last thing I ever got from her."

"You mean she gave it to you before she disappeared?"

"She obviously knew she was going to leave me," said Pine matter-of-factly. "I guess this was her parting gift. You know, sort of, 'I won't be around to watch over you, so take this hunk of stupid metal instead' sort of thing."

"Why do you wear it then, if you feel that way?" Blum asked.

"Because it's really all I have to remember her by. And . . . and so it's important to me. Sort of a love-hate thing. Part of me touches it, and I feel that she abandoned me. Then I touch it another time and part of me feels warm and safe, as though I was six again and my mother was holding my hand."

Blum nodded thoughtfully. "Mother-daughter

relationships are complicated. Maybe the most complicated of all. At least they were for me. My sons were a breeze by comparison."

The medal found on the body had already been dusted for prints and none were found. In Pine's mind that made it even more important. Someone had taken the time to wipe it clean.

"I'm hoping the forensics people can tell us how that medal was damaged."

"You really think it's important? Like Wallis suggested, it could have belonged to the boy and was damaged while he had it."

"No. If you noticed how it was damaged, a sharp edge of the medal was bent inward. It would poke into the skin. There were no marks like that on the boy's neck. And you're not going to wear something that cuts into you anyway."

"So it *was* probably added by the killer."

"It was personal, Carol, I'm convinced of that. An object like that inherently is. It was worn by someone, someone important in some way to the killer. It's a direct clue, if we can only find out how."

"Lee?"

They looked up to see Agnes Ridley standing in front of the Cottage.

"Is it really true?" said Ridley. "Another murder?"

Pine and Blum walked up to her. "I'm afraid so," Pine replied, nodding. "This time it was a little boy."

"Oh my God," exclaimed Ridley. "A child? That doesn't make any sense, does it?"

"We have no idea what the killer's motivation is," pointed out Pine. "So we have no idea what his target list encompasses."

"Do they know who the child is?" asked Ridley.

"Not yet. They'll be circulating a description and a sketch of him. Are there any kids missing from around here?" she asked.

"Not that I know of. And you'd think if the child was local, the parents would have already alerted police that they were missing."

"Yes, you would."

"Is there anything I can do?" asked Ridley.

"Keep your eyes and ears open. Anything suspicious, call the cops."

They entered the Cottage to find Graham waiting for them in the front foyer.

"Good Lord, what is the town coming to?" she wailed, as soon as she caught sight of them.

"Why did Lily come here first?" asked Pine. "With everything going on, I forgot to ask her that."

"Lily knew you were staying here," Graham replied. "That's the first thing she could think of when she saw what she did in the museum."

"What exactly did she tell you?" asked Blum.

"That a dead boy was dressed up in one of the uniforms and put out on display. She nearly fainted, she said. Then she lit out from the museum and ran all the way here."

"How long have you known Lily?"

"Nearly all my life. She's worked in the museum for a long time. Doubt she'll ever be able to go back now."

"The mannequin that the killer replaced with the boy was found in the back room. That's where we think he got access. But he must've had a key. There was no forced entry. Any idea how he might have done that?"

"Someone could have had a duplicate key made to the back door, I guess," said Graham. "I doubt that Lily watches her purse every second. And she's told me in the past that the back door lock has never been reliable. She was going to get it repaired, but I guess she hadn't gotten around to it."

"She might want to get around to it now," said Pine. "The place also had a security system. We know it was on when Lily came to work, because she told us she had to turn it off. Which means the killer would have had to have the code. Would it be easy to get?"

"I don't know. I do know they've never had anything like this happen before."

"Well, that's no longer the case, is it?" replied Pine.

48

"Look, about last night," began Laredo.

He and Pine were sitting in the breakfast room at the Cottage. Blum had gone to her room.

"Nothing needs to be said," said Pine curtly.

"You don't think so?"

"We had some drinks and we danced. So what?"

He let out a long breath, the contrition clear on his features. "I'm sorry, Atlee. I'm being an idiot." He paused. "It was just . . ."

"Just what?"

"I guess the drinking and the dancing and . . ."

"I didn't mean to lead you on. If you saw it that way, I apologize."

"For what? Dressing up and being absolutely stunning looking. Yeah, let's not have that in life."

"That's not what this is about. Last night was an outlier. We were both too smart to let it escalate into something we would both regret. So let's just leave it there. You cool with that?"

"I don't think I have a choice."

When she saw his face fall, she put a hand on his arm and added, "Look, I was the one who wanted to go drinking. I asked you to dance. Maybe I was flirtier than I realized. And when we came back here . . . I could see how you thought things were going to go. So, that was on me."

"How did *you* think things were going to go?" he asked, glancing up at her with an earnest look.

"Maybe pretty close to what you thought, Eddie."

"And then what happened?"

"And then it occurred to me that we haven't seen each other or had any contact for over a decade. And I'm not that sort of a girl."

"For the record, I never thought you were." He put his hands in his pockets. "It's been a long time since Denise left. Dating is pretty much impossible with my career."

"Tell me about it."

"Oh come on, I'm sure every guy in Stunted Rock—"

She interjected, "*Shattered* Rock, as you well know."

He grinned and so did she.

"Okay, I'm sure that every guy in Shattered Rock has already fallen hard for you. You probably have to pull your gun to keep them away."

"I don't know about all, but maybe one is interested," said Pine as she thought of a park ranger at the

Grand Canyon she had been seeing named Sam Kettler.

"Well, then he's a lucky guy. I hope he's up to the challenge," he added.

"Only time will tell."

"So long as he doesn't treat you as some damsel in distress."

"Nothing to worry about there."

"I'm happy for you, Atlee."

"You really have changed, Eddie. What gives?"

"The way I had been caused me to lose what was most important to me. Now, I could have been an idiot and doubled down on that. But I decided to use my brain and change how I was conducting myself. Because if you keep doing the same thing over and over, how can you expect a different result?"

"There's somebody out there for you. Don't give up trying. I have no idea if this guy back in Arizona will work out. We might always just be friends. But there's nothing wrong with that, either."

"Well, I'm hoping we can be friends."

"I think we're getting there."

A young woman who worked there came into the room and asked them if they needed anything.

"No, we're good," replied Pine.

When she left Laredo hunched forward, his body language back to all business. "So the kid back there?"

"Yeah."

"I've been thinking."

"I'm listening."

"It might sound crazy."

"Your theory can't be any crazier than whatever the truth will turn out to be, so let's have it."

"So far, in the way of victims, we've got a bride, a groom, and now a young kid."

"I know that, Eddie," she said sharply, and then caught herself. "Wait a minute, are you saying . . . ?"

"Yeah," he said. "Exactly."

"Just to be clear, are you talking about this guy building a . . . family? Of corpses?"

"Building or rebuilding."

"Jesus."

"What did they call them in school?"

"The *nuclear* family," said Pine. "A particular social unit, as opposed to a family with only one parent."

"But there's one difference with our case, at least from what I was taught about it."

She nodded. "With a nuclear family there're two parents, like I just implied."

"And at least from what I remember there are usually *two* kids in a traditional nuclear family."

Pine leaned back against the wall. "Meaning we may have at least one more victim to come?"

"So maybe next time it'll be another kid."

"Then we have to make sure there isn't a next time," Pine replied firmly.

"Easier said than done. We really have no line on this guy."

"Is there any pattern at Quantico that fits this?" she asked.

"Not anything that I've seen. And I checked before I left. With this new revelation I'll go back through it again. But I don't think I'm going to find similarities."

"So maybe this guy is a new player on the block."

Laredo shrugged. "Or he's an old player but he's changed his MO. But what's his motivation?"

"If he's compiling a family, maybe he lost his somehow."

"Wife and kids, you mean?"

Pine said, "Yeah. Or wait, it could be all four; this guy could be looking from the outside at the loss of another family maybe close to him."

"Shit, how do we begin to track that down?"

"This is a small town—if the killer is from here it shouldn't be that difficult. There just aren't that many people."

"But if he's not it might well be impossible. You lived here for a while, Atlee."

"I left here when I was a little kid."

"Okay, since you've been back has anyone mentioned a whole family getting wiped out?"

As she thought about this, Pine's features took on a hollow look.

"What?" he said, noting her reaction.

"I guess it depends on your definition of *wiped out*.

If you define it one way I *do* know of that happening to a family of four people from here."

"Who were they?"

She looked up at him, dread in her features. "My family."

49

Pine drove while Laredo was in the back seat and Carol Blum was riding shotgun.

They pulled up in front of Pine's old house.

Old Roscoe was on the porch and struggled up on his weakened hind legs to greet them with a friendly bark and his tail wagging. Cy Tanner's old, rusted pickup was parked in front of the house.

"This is where you lived?" asked Laredo as they climbed out of the vehicle.

"A different universe from Queens," replied Pine.

"No, really, I like the dirt."

Smoke was pouring out of the trash barrel, and they could all hear noises coming from the rear of the house. Pine walked over to Roscoe and scratched the dog's flappy ears. "How you doing, old man? You doing okay?"

Roscoe answered with several licks to her hand.

"Cy?" called out Blum. "You around?"

They got no answer and walked around to the back of the house, following the noise coming from there. There was an old wooden building standing back there. The door was open, and they could hear the noise emanating from inside.

It sounded like a power saw.

They reached the door and Pine rapped on it once and then a second time, louder.

The sounds of the power saw stopped, and Tanner appeared in the doorway, lifting off a pair of safety goggles. He was dressed in a white T-shirt that showed off the corded muscles in his arms, and corduroy pants with his Budweiser belt holding them up over his slim hips.

"Hey, folks," he said, eyeing them all curiously.

Then, to their amazement, a little girl appeared behind him. She, too, had on a pair of safety goggles, which were too big for her. She looked up at them with blinking eyes behind the plastic.

"Who is this?" inquired Blum, looking brightly at the child.

Grinning, Tanner bent down to the little girl. "This here is Jenny, my youngest daughter's girl. She just turned seven a month ago. She's come for a visit, ain't that right, Jenny?"

Jenny, all blond curls and enormous blue eyes, looked shyly at the adults gathered there and tugged on her grandfather's pants leg.

Pine looked at Tanner. "A visit? Is her mom here with her?"

The grin faded from Tanner's mouth. "Uh, no, she's got some . . . things she's dealing with."

Blum looked back at the house. "And she'll be staying here? But don't you have to work?"

"Well, I was hoping that Agnes could come over and stay with her if need be."

"Agnes is a little old to be looking after a little kid," said Pine.

"Was there no one else Jenny could stay with?" persisted Blum.

Tanner suddenly looked upset. "I can take care of things, okay? And I don't remember asking for permission." He looked at Pine. "What do y'all want anyway? I was busy."

Pine said, "I'd like to ask some questions, but maybe not in front of Jenny."

Tanner looked confused, but Blum stepped forward. "Jenny, have you had some breakfast?"

The little girl looked up at her grandfather, who stared down at her. He said haltingly, "I . . . I was gonna get to that real soon."

"What do you have in the house?" asked Blum. "Cereal and milk, maybe some toast?"

"Yeah, I got stuff like that. But check the milk. It, you know, it, uh . . . I was gonna go to the store today. But I don't have no toaster."

Blum got down on her haunches and looked at Jenny. "I have a bunch of granddaughters and two of them look just like you, Jenny. Do you have any brothers or sisters?"

Jenny shook her head.

"Would you like to see pictures of my granddaughters?"

Jenny glanced at Tanner, who nodded. She said in a small voice, "Okay."

Blum rose and put out a hand for Jenny to take. "Now, let's go get some food and maybe we can find something for Roscoe to chew on too, okay?"

"Okay."

The two walked off to the house.

Pine looked after them for a moment and then turned back to Tanner.

"Cy, what the hell is going on? How did she even get here?"

Tanner sighed wearily, stuffed the safety goggles into his pants pocket, and ran a hand through his thick hair.

"My daughter's boyfriend dropped her off just this morning."

"Were you expecting her?"

"Hell no. I didn't even know about the damn boyfriend. When I saw Jenny in the truck with him I ran over and was about to bust him up. I didn't know why he would have Jenny with him. But then he explained who he was, and that Linda needed me to take Jenny for a while."

"For a while? Where does she live?"

"Alabama. Near Tuscaloosa."

"Tuscaloosa!" exclaimed Pine. "That's over four hours from here."

"Yeah, they started out real early."

"But why would the boyfriend bring her here? Why not Linda?"

"Well, the boyfriend—hell, I forgot his name—said Linda's gone back into rehab."

"Drug rehab?" asked Laredo.

Tanner nodded. "She got hooked on meth a long time ago. Thought she'd kicked it. She fell off the wagon when Jenny was two. Then got clean. Thought things were good, until this morning."

"Is the boyfriend the father?"

"No. Hell, I don't think Linda even knows who Jenny's father is."

"How did they even know where you lived?" asked Pine.

"Linda and Jenny have been here to visit a few times. She gave the boyfriend the directions."

"How long are you supposed to keep her?" asked Laredo.

"Well, that wasn't clear."

"And the boyfriend couldn't do it? Or Linda's other friends?"

"He's an idiot who can barely take care of himself. I'm astonished he could even find my place. Linda doesn't have any friends, least that I know of."

"And Linda's mother? Your wife?" asked Pine.

"Dead six years now."

"I'm sorry," said Pine.

"We were long since split up. Mostly my fault. She

was a good lady. Drank too much sometimes, but don't we all."

Pine said, "But what are you going to do? You can't care for a seven-year-old by yourself. She can't sleep in the bean bag with you. Do you have a working toilet? A functioning kitchen? A place to shower? And there's the matter of her going to school, too. Were you going to enroll her locally?"

Tanner scratched his chin. "Yeah, I know there're a lot of details. But, hell, this was just dropped in my lap," he said defensively. He added, "I *did* have her put on safety goggles when she was in the workshop with me."

Pine and Laredo exchanged a worried glance. Pine said, "Let me see what I can do to help. There might be some folks in town who can . . . assist with the situation. Okay?"

Tanner looked relieved. "That would be mighty welcome, yeah." He changed expressions. "So why are you here again? You said you had some questions?"

Pine looked at Laredo. "Tell him your theory about the nuclear family."

Laredo did so, and Tanner looked like he might vomit.

"What the hell kind of world do we got where sick bastards like that are walking around?" he raged.

"I know, Cy. But if it is in some way connected to my family we need to know if you've seen anyone around here. Maybe a car or truck parked nearby, watching the place. Anyone you've seen showing an interest in this house or the property at all?"

Tanner leaned against the doorjamb and thought this over. He finally shook his head. "Only people come by here are you and Agnes. Wait a minute, that Graham lady came by a couple times."

"Lauren Graham? Why?"

He chuckled. "She brought me a blueberry pie and then some biscuits." He grinned. "Now I could be wrong, but she seemed a little sweet on me. But I'm way too old for her." He looked around at his dilapidated property. "Maybe she's after my money." He laughed.

"Anyone else?" asked Laredo. "Anyone at all. Even somebody stopping to ask for directions?"

"Well, come to think, there was a car parked nearby, oh, this was maybe three weeks ago. Got up real early and was looking out the window and saw it."

"What kind of car?" asked Laredo.

"Fancy. So red it hurt your eyes to look at it. Looked like the damn Batmobile. Never seen a ride like that before."

"No name or emblem or anything on the car that you could see?"

"Well, I did sneak through the woods to get a better look at the thing. I mean, this is rural Georgia. Seeing a car like that here was like seeing a damn Rolls-Royce on the moon."

"So what did you see when you got closer?" asked Pine.

"Thing had four exhaust pipes coming out what looked like the trunk."

"Did you see a name on the car?"

Tanner knitted his brows. "Yeah, never heard of it before. Pag something."

"Pag?" said Pine, glancing at Laredo.

"Wait a minute, a Pagani Huayra?" exclaimed Laredo.

"Don't know 'bout that last name, but yeah, Paganny, that was it."

"You know it?" said Pine to Laredo.

He nodded, still looking disbelieving.

"Is it expensive?" asked Pine.

"Depending on the model, about three million bucks."

"The hell you say," barked a stunned-looking Tanner. "For something you go from here to there in?"

"What can I tell you," said Laredo. "It comes from the having-too-much-money syndrome. You have to spend it on something. Not that I'm ever going to have that dilemma."

Pine slowly drew her gaze from Laredo. "Was there anyone in the car, Cy?"

"Not that I could tell. The windows were dark and I was afraid to let the person see me."

"Why?"

Tanner looked sheepish. "Look, I'm just staying here because I don't have no other place. I was maybe thinking this person had a claim on this house and all. I mean, why else would they be here, right? I didn't want to get into no discussion about that."

"Do you remember the license plate by chance?"

"That's the thing. It didn't have no plate, least on the rear."

"Okay, if the car comes back or you remember anything else, let us know, okay?"

"You got it."

They walked back to the front of the house, where Pine glanced at the trash barrel that still had some flames in it.

"Having a fire in that barrel is not a good idea with a little kid running around."

"Damn thing keeps lighting back up. Must be some embers down there. I'll throw some water on it."

"Good idea."

They found Blum in the house feeding both Jenny and Roscoe.

Blum finished up and pulled Pine aside. "That child cannot stay here. She'll be dead in a week from either malnourishment, the stairs falling down on her, or an army of germs."

"Working on it," said Pine as she pulled out her phone and made a call.

After a couple of minutes of conversation she put it away and looked at Blum.

"She's going to call me back."

"Who?"

"Lauren Graham. She thinks she might have a solution."

As it turned out, the woman did. Later, they collected Jenny and her small bag with her few possessions after explaining things to Tanner.

Jenny was going to stay with a family who had two girls around Jenny's age and who lived one block off the main street. The father was a minister at the local church; his wife stayed at home and had the reputation of being a very caring person.

Tanner had at first resisted but then relented after Pine and Blum spoke with him.

Blum said, "The most important thing is Jenny's welfare, Cy. I know you love her, but I also know you're not in a position right now to give her the care and attention she needs. That doesn't make you a bad person. But right now, the priority needs to be Jenny."

Tanner hadn't said anything for a bit but finally nodded. "When I was a kid my grade school teacher told us about the story of Solomon. Well, I'm not cutting up a kid. She needs to go where she'll be okay." He looked over his shoulder at the falling-down house. "I can live okay here, but a little kid can't."

Blum smiled. "Well, you just showed yourself to be a very wise grandpa."

★

"I'll come visit you every day, Jenny," he told his granddaughter through the open window as she sat in the back seat of Pine's SUV.

"Okay, Pop-pop."

"You be good for these folks, all right?"

He leaned through and gave her a kiss on the cheek. She giggled and rubbed her skin where she had kissed him. "You're scratchy, Pop-pop."

"I'll shave real good before I come to see you again. I promise, sweetie."

Blum put a hand on his shoulder. "We'll check on her a lot. She'll be well taken care of."

Tanner turned to her and said in a low voice, "I know. I . . . I just wish it hadn't come to this."

"In life, it almost always comes to something like this. And then you adapt and get through it. But I would check on your daughter and make sure she really is in rehab."

"Yeah, I was thinking about that, too, Carol." The two exchanged a knowing look.

She said, "We never want to think ill of our children, but sometimes it's the prudent thing to do. Sometimes it's the only way to help them."

Tanner stepped back, and Blum climbed into the truck to sit next to Jenny. Pine started up the SUV. Laredo, who was sitting next to her, said, "There can't be many people around here who might own a Pagani."

"I can really think of only one," said Pine. "Jack Lineberry."

50

They dropped Blum and Jenny off at her new, temporary home to get settled in, and then Pine and Laredo drove back to the Cottage.

On the way Laredo made a call and sent some emails. He finally put his phone away and looked dissatisfied. "I can't find a Pagani registered under Jack Lineberry's name, but he could have it registered under a corporate entity."

"He may very well have."

"But why take such a conspicuous car on what might have been a stakeout of your old home?"

"Wish I had an answer for that."

"I assume we're going to check this out?"

"Yes, we will. But we need to lay the groundwork first."

"You used to like flying by the seat of your pants, if I recall."

She glanced over at him. "I like prep as much as the next person. But you don't always have the time for it."

"I imagine you have to think quick on your feet out in Arizona."

"You would imagine right. I'm usually the only FBI agent around."

"And you really like it that way?"

She gave him a sharp glance. "Why wouldn't I?"

"I like having resources. Make a call and you got a team responding in minutes. Or I need some grunt work done and there's an agent or team of admins to do it."

"I don't mind the grunt work if it leads to an arrest."

"Along with doing a 411, your friend Blum read me the riot act the other night."

"How so?"

"She was defending you. Telling me how high you set the bar. Wanted to make sure I wasn't here to do you dirty."

"She's a good partner."

"She also made it clear that as an admin person she's really running the show."

"I wouldn't disagree with that."

"I know Clint Dobbs runs the Phoenix Field Office. Hear he can be a real pain."

Pine said, "But he gave me an opportunity to get things right, and I respect him for that."

"And if you can't get things right?"

"I'll cross that bridge *if* I get to it."

★

They parked in front of the Cottage and got out. Across the street was a small, open, grassy area. A group of kids was playing there with an old kickball.

"No school today?" said Laredo.

"Guess not."

He headed toward the front door of the Cottage but then noted that Pine was standing there watching the kids.

He walked back over to her.

"Thinking about your sister or maybe Jenny?"

"Maybe both."

Laredo watched the two biggest kids face off with the rest of the group. "Sometimes it would be nice if we could stay young and innocent and play kickball forever."

"Do you know how bored we'd be?" replied Pine.

"Seriously, those kids will have a lot of challenges when they grow up, and I don't mean because they come from a small town. The world is changing way too fast."

"But in some ways it stays the same. It still has bad people doing bad things."

"I guess we'll never want for a job."

"Although it would be nice if we became obsolete."

Pine was about to turn to the Cottage when her attention was riveted on the group of kids.

"Eeny, meeny, miny, moe," began the biggest kid, alternating pointing his finger at two smaller kids. He ended the rhyme on the kid on the right, who was all smiles as he was picked for the team. The other child stepped back, looking dejected.

"Shit," muttered Pine.

"What?" said Laredo.

"The kid the nursery rhyme ended on over there was the clear winner. He got picked for the team."

"Well, yeah, I guess that's right."

"But I always assumed whoever the rhyme ended on was the *loser*."

"I guess it can go both ways, depending on who's setting the rules. In the films *Pulp Fiction* and *Natural Born Killers*, they used that rhyme to pick who was going to die. The person who ended up with the last word of the rhyme bit the dust. I would call that a loser."

When she didn't respond, he said, "And this matters to you why?"

She explained about the intruder all those years ago using the same rhyme on her and Mercy.

"He ended the rhyme on Mercy. I distinctly remember that. But I always assumed that meant she was the loser. She was the one taken. I was the one left. I was the winner."

"And what happened to you?"

"The guy fractured my skull. The doctors said it was a miracle that I survived the night. But I did survive. And that's why I always assumed that Mercy got the worst of it. That he had taken her to kill her."

"So you're saying that by ending the rhyme on your sister it means . . . ?"

She looked up at him. "Maybe by picking her, that means that Mercy is still alive."

51

Pine went to her room, stripped off her clothes, climbed into the shower, and let the hot water drill her.

You are an idiot. For thirty effing years you have been an idiot. And that includes thirteen years as an FBI idiot.

She pressed her head against the fiberglass wall of the shower.

She wanted to both cry and cheer. Cry because of her absolute stupidity by never considering another possibility for the purpose of the rhyme. But she also wanted to cheer because if she was supposed to be the loser that night, then Mercy was the winner.

And you didn't kill winners.

Pine knew she was grossly, and perhaps idiotically, speculating here. Her "evidence" was watching one kid pick another kid for a game of kickball. And in the two films Laredo had mentioned the person the rhyme ended on had died. The absurdity of it all made her want to scream.

She licked water off her lips and closed her eyes. In her concentrated recollection she could see the finger thumping first her forehead and then her sister's. The finger had touched her skin and then Mercy's. Next, the fist had come crashing down, perhaps more than once. She couldn't know for sure because she apparently had been knocked unconscious by the first blow.

But I had to be the loser. Mercy was touched last and he wanted to kill me. Probably thought he had killed me. He took Mercy.

But for what purpose?

There had never been a ransom note. It wouldn't have mattered if there had been. Her parents had no money to pay.

Why take Mercy, then, if not to kill her?

It was true that human trafficking had been going on since time immemorial. But in 1989 on the outskirts of Andersonville, Georgia? Was it someone obsessed with twins? Someone who had been watching the family? And intended to kill Pine? Why?

I was six. The man was masked. I couldn't identify him. If he wanted to keep me from crying out, or going to warn my parents, he could have done any number of things to accomplish that short of fracturing my skull.

She got out of the shower, dried off, and sat on her bed in a towel. She picked up her phone because standing under the water—one of her preferred ways to think—had led to a thought. And a possible lead.

She had taken pictures of all the files in the old

police investigation of her sister's disappearance. There was one that now intrigued her.

Six o'clock in the a.m. That was when the police had said her mother had come into her bedroom and found Pine horribly injured and Mercy gone. She was looking at the detective notes that documented this. And this timing had been corroborated by other witnesses.

Yet the thing was her mother had a routine with her daughters. She put them to bed at nine every night. She would then check on them at ten to make sure they were still in bed and not playing. Pine had been caught out so many times over this that she knew that rule well. Then Julia Pine came to rouse her daughters at seven thirty sharp so they could clean up, dress, eat breakfast, and get to the bus stop for school at eight thirty. Even though this had all taken place decades ago, the routine had been a large part of Pine's life, day after day. Because of that it was ingrained in her.

So the question was, why had her mother come in at six in the morning? And now that Pine thought about it, she didn't remember her mother coming in to check on them at ten.

Pine both liked and disliked discrepancies. She disliked them because they could be inexplicable. But she also liked them because they could lead to a breakthrough.

She was hoping this was one of those times.

It could be that her mother awoke after a night of drinking and smoking weed and raced up to check on the kids. Maybe she had been unaware of the time because of her being hungover. Perhaps she had thought she had overslept and that the girls were late for school.

Pine shook her head clear.

At six a.m. at that time of year it would have still been dark. So how could her mother have thought it was hours later?

As Pine got dressed she knew the answer to that: Her mother would not have been confused about that. There had to be another explanation.

Pine walked down to the first floor of the Cottage to find Blum sitting in a chair there.

"Jenny is in good hands. I investigated the place thoroughly before I handed her over."

"I'm sure you did."

"Mrs. Quarles gave me a ride back here and we had a nice chat. She is a very caring, very nurturing woman."

"I'm glad."

"Jenny is a precious little girl. Once she warmed up to me she wouldn't stop talking."

"No doubt."

"So why do I think you just had a revelation of sorts?"

"Is it that obvious on my face?"

"Not obvious to everyone, but obvious to me. So tell me."

Pine sat down across from her and told her about the time discrepancy.

"That does qualify as a revelation, actually. Any theories?"

"Not sure. Could be a number of reasons. Some innocuous, others problematic."

"Let's hear them."

Pine shook her head. "Not yet. I need to think things through."

"Fair enough."

"I am really glad Jenny is all squared away."

"Who knew Cy Tanner could have a granddaughter that cute? Of course he had no idea what to do with her. I think he can barely take care of himself."

"It was nice of the minister and his family to take her in."

"Speaking of children, any ID on the boy?"

"Not that I've heard. But we do have a lead to follow up." Pine told her about the Pagani outside her old home.

"You really think it could be connected to Jack Lineberry?"

"You think Paganis grow on trees down here?"

"But why would he be watching your old house?"

"Even if it was his car, it wasn't necessarily him inside doing the watching."

"That's true. How are you going to handle it?"

"I haven't decided yet. Eddie couldn't track the ownership to Lineberry, but there are a lot of dodges on that score."

Pine's phone buzzed. She looked down at it and flinched.

"It's from Stan Cashings."

"The Cloak and Dagger issue you asked him to look into?"

Pine nodded as she read through the email.

As Blum watched, the expression on Pine's face turned from curiosity to shock and then to disbelief.

"I don't think I've ever seen you look like that," she said, worried.

Pine looked up at her. "Well, I never imagined it could be something like this."

"What is the Cloak and Dagger? A bar, like you thought?"

"Yes and no," was Pine's surprising reply.

"I'm not following. Isn't it either one or the other?"

"Not according to Stan. He did some deep digging and he says in his email that he couldn't get full answers, not just because of how far back it goes and there not being people around who are familiar with it, but *also* that much of it is still *classified*."

Now Blum looked shocked. "Whoa, classified? What kind of bar was this place?"

"It was a sting operation, set in place by the IC,"

said Pine, referring to the American intelligence community.

"A sting operation? At a bar? Who were they looking to ensnare?"

"From the little Stan could find out, he believes it had to do with international spies."

"They named the place Cloak and Dagger? Didn't they think that was a bit obvious?"

"He asked someone with knowledge of it, and they said it was supposed to be tongue-in-cheek. There were other bars sprouting up around that time with catchy names and themes. You know, like old speakeasies where you enter through a hidden door after using a secret code or go into an old phone booth and call a certain number you've been given that opens some portal. The Cold War was still going on back then, though it was drawing to a close and the Berlin Wall would come down at the end of the decade."

"Did they catch anybody?"

"Apparently so. Without naming names, Stan was able to determine that it was very successful."

"But how does this tie in to your parents? And why did your dad have those coasters?"

"Stan couldn't find that out. No one would tell him the names of anyone who worked on it."

"So . . . ?"

Pine's face turned ashen. "So I think it either

comes down to my dad worked there and maybe helped the good guys bring down the bad guys."

"Or?" said Blum nervously.

Pine stared despondently down at her hands. "Or my dad was a bad guy and went on the run and that's how we all ended up here."

52

The morgue.

Again.

Pine's stomach was churning like it never had before when confronted with a dead body. The reason for this was obvious.

The dead person was a child.

She, Wallis, and Laredo were standing over the metal table where the boy's remains lay.

The ME, the same woman as before, was on the other side holding an iPad in one hand and glancing down at the screen.

Blum had respectfully declined to accompany them today, for which Pine was grateful. A mother of six with over a dozen grandkids should not have to see this.

Hell, no one should have to see this.

"Cause of death?" asked Wallis, who looked downright nauseated.

"If you want the common name, it's a Hangman's Fracture," said the ME.

"That would account for the odd angle of the neck," noted Laredo.

"He died by hanging?" said Wallis. "So, asphyxiation?"

"No. The Hangman's Fracture *can* lead to death by asphyxiation, but this boy wasn't hung. The technical name for it is a fracture of both *partes interarticulares* of the axis vertebrae. But it's really simply a catastrophic hyperextension of the spine emanating from under the chin. The result was his spinal cord was crushed between the C1 and C2 posterior elements. Death would have been instantaneous, or as close to that as it ever gets."

"But how was it done?" asked Pine.

"You see these sorts of injuries in car accidents, skydiving, even contact sports. You run into or hit something with your chin, but with the chin pointed up and the head arched back against the upper spine. If whatever you hit is unyielding enough and you hit it with enough force, it can snap your spine."

"How do you think it was done here?" asked Pine.

"I can't be certain but it's more than a guess because of other bruising on the body. You see the chin is bruised and discolored. The jawbone there is actually cracked, and that's not all that easy to do. It's the strongest bone in the face."

"Wait a minute," said Laredo. "Could he have died in a car crash?"

The ME shook her head. "I don't think so. You'd

see some other indicators if that were the case. And with the sorts of restraints they have these days, you'd have to have your seat belt unbuckled. And if that had happened here, you'd be seeing a whole host of other injuries. But I can tell you this, whoever did it knew what they were doing. It was a clean break."

"Maybe some military training?" ventured Wallis. "Gillespie was in the military. Maybe somebody who knew him back then and held a grudge."

"Still no ID on the boy?" asked Pine, glancing at Wallis.

"Nothing yet. We've circulated his description and a drawing of him to the public and the media and asked for their help."

"No hits on him at the Center for Missing and Exploited Children either," said Laredo.

"It's like he doesn't even exist," said Pine. She looked down at the body. "But he did. He had a life to live. And somebody robbed him of that. And they're going to pay."

On the drive back to Andersonville, Laredo glanced over at Pine, who was driving.

"You okay?" he asked.

"Yeah, I'm just fine, Eddie. Didn't feel a thing back there. How about you? Let's go get some lunch, maybe a beer. Have some fun."

"You know that's not what I meant."

She didn't answer.

"I want to blow the guy's head off too, Atlee. So what? We can't. Our job is to catch the son of a bitch, not execute him."

"I'm not a rookie, so I don't need the lesson in police ethics, thanks very much. I'm just venting. Is that a crime?"

"No. It's actually healthy. So go for it."

"We can't allow another person to die, Eddie. Not another kid."

"You think he picked this kid because it was easy? Maybe no family, nobody to look out for him?"

"Why do it the hard way when you don't have to? But how sick do you have to be to do that to a kid?"

"We usually only deal with sick people, Atlee. By default." He tapped his fingers on the seat's armrest. "You thinking about the little girl you saved on the Amber Alert?"

When she didn't answer, he continued, "You can't make it personal. You know that as well as I do. In fact, if you remember, you lectured me on that back in DC."

"The McAllister case," said Pine automatically.

"Guy raped and imprisoned little girls and had babies with them over fifteen years. And when they hit eighteen he killed them. Doesn't get any sicker than that. I wanted to put a bullet in his head when we finally got him. And you talked me out of it."

"I know, Eddie," said Pine slowly. "I know everything you're telling me is spot-on. And I accept that.

And I'll do nothing to screw it up when we get to this guy."

"I never had any doubts about that," said Laredo firmly.

She glanced at him in surprise. "Really, even after the Amber Alert guy?"

"Hey, everybody gets to vent at least once."

Pine's expression softened. "I like Eddie 2.0 a lot better than the previous version."

"Yeah, even my ex told me that. Denise said it was lousy timing on my part."

"Well, in life, it's really all about timing."

Laredo's phone rang. He answered it and listened. When he clicked off and didn't say anything Pine looked at him worriedly.

"Please don't tell me . . ."

"No. That was Wallis. It's good news. They got a lead on the boy. With an address."

"Where?" she asked.

"You get to go back to Columbus, Georgia."

Pine hit a U-turn and punched the gas pedal flat to the floor.

53

Francisco Gomez.

He went by Frankie, Wallis, Pine, and Laredo were told, probably so he could fit in better in his new life.

They were sitting in the front room of a small house far away from the luxurious condo that Hanna Rebane and Beth Clemmons had recently lived in and where Clemmons had died. It was in a neighborhood that had seen better days, and nights. It was working-class, it was hurting, it was a slice of left-behind America.

The woman sitting in a chair across from them was in her forties, with mousy brown hair and wearing a cotton print dress and flat-soled black shoes. Her name was Genie Duncan, and there were plump tears in her eyes.

"Frankie was a good boy," she said, dabbing her eyes with a handkerchief.

From upstairs Pine could hear kids shouting and laughing, and the tumble and grind of youthful feet threatened the floor joists.

"When did you take him in?" asked Wallis, his official notebook open and ready to go.

"About six months ago. He came from Texas, I believe. Actually, they weren't very clear on that. We take in kids. We have three with us now." She stifled a sob. "Not counting Frankie."

"We?" said Pine. "So, you and your husband?"

"Yes. Roger is at work now. He has a job at a local car dealership."

"Salesman?" asked Laredo.

"No. He's a mechanic. Salesmen are paid on commission. We needed something more steady. He's good at his job and makes okay money. But what they charge per hour for his services, he should make a lot more," she added brusquely. "We barely make ends meet."

"Do you have kids of your own?" asked Laredo.

She shook her head. "We never could. My fault. That's why we became foster parents. These kids need adults in their lives, helping to guide them."

"Yes they do," said Wallis. "That was very good of you."

"We do it through our church. They get children in from other parts of the country. We had to go through all sorts of, I guess they call it vetting. But that makes sense because children are precious. And they pay us, of course. Most of the money goes for the child's expenses and the like, but there's some left over. It's a lot of work."

"I'm sure it is," Wallis said. He slipped something from his pocket. "Now, ma'am, we need a positive ID on Frankie. I, uh, I have a photo here."

Duncan stiffened. "I saw the sketch on the news. That's why I called the number. Do I . . . do I have to look . . . ?"

Wallis said gently, "If you would, ma'am. Just to be sure."

Wallis passed across the photo.

Duncan glanced at it, cringed, changed color, and hurriedly handed it back.

She nodded. "That's . . . Frankie."

Wallis put the photo away and said, "We're very sorry for your loss."

The noise upstairs intensified. Duncan said, "The other kids don't know. They're so young, I was thinking of not telling them what . . . what happened. I thought I might just tell them that Frankie went to another family."

"Whatever you think best, Ms. Duncan," replied Wallis.

Pine said, "When was the last time you saw Frankie?"

Duncan sat back in a chair that had half its stuffing missing and was covered with a frayed throw rug.

"Three days ago. He went to school and then when he didn't come back home, I called around to see if anyone had seen him. He'd already made friends in the neighborhood. I thought maybe he'd gone over to one of their homes."

"How did he get back and forth from school?"

"On the bus. I would usually walk him to the bus stop in the mornings. But in the afternoons he would walk home. There're lots of kids around. And parents."

"But did you walk him to the bus stop that morning?" asked Wallis.

She shook her head, her eyes filling with fresh tears. "No. He . . . he said he knew the way and wanted to walk there by himself. I think . . . I think he was embarrassed to have me with him. You see, most of the other kids just walked there by themselves. They might have made fun of him, for all I know."

"Was it confirmed that he was actually at school that day?"

"Yes, he didn't miss any classes."

"And he was on the bus home?"

"Yes."

"And he got off at his regular stop?"

Now Duncan looked uncertain. "The thing is, the kids and parents I talked to weren't sure that he did. And the police talked to the bus driver, but he lets off so many kids at so many stops, he's not always paying attention who gets off where. And . . . and there are a lot of little boys who look like Frankie."

"Meaning Hispanic?" said Pine.

"Yes."

"So it was not confirmed that he got off at his regular stop?"

"No, it wasn't. But why would he get off somewhere else? He knew the right stop."

"He might have if someone had asked him to."

"But who would do that? And if they did, Frankie wouldn't have done it. I told him never to talk to strangers."

"Well, it might not have been a stranger," pointed out Pine.

"I can't believe that anyone who knew us would have done this to Frankie," she said stubbornly.

"Would he walk home with some of your other kids?"

"No, they're in kindergarten. They have different hours. Frankie was in fourth grade. I never had a second thought about him using the bus. His English was pretty good. He said his mother taught him."

"And where are his parents?" asked Laredo.

"I don't know. No one ever told me. Frankie didn't have any pictures of them. I believe Frankie was born here."

Laredo glanced at Pine. She said, "So what did you do when you couldn't find him?"

"I started phoning around to everyone I could think of, including the school. After that, I called the police."

"And they came and took a report?" said Wallis.

"Yes. And that was the last I heard from them.

Until I . . . until I saw that sketch and the description on the news. I knew right away it was Frankie." She pursed her lips. "Can I . . . can you tell me what happened to him?"

Wallis glanced at the two FBI agents before saying, "His death was not from natural causes, I'm sorry to say."

Her eyes welled with tears. "Someone . . . hurt him?"

"I'm afraid so."

Pine sat forward. "That's why it's so important to tell us anything you can remember. His friends. Anyone he might have mentioned. Someone you might have seen lurking around here?"

"I don't remember anything like that. Frankie hasn't really been here all that long."

"What was he wearing that day?"

"Jeans, a red pullover, and sneakers. Was . . . was he found in them?"

"Not exactly, no. What about your husband? Could he know something useful?"

"Roger didn't spend a lot of time with Frankie. I mean, he's good with the kids and all. He's as committed as I am to them. But he works long hours."

"Did he ever take Frankie to work with him?" asked Laredo. "Little boys love cars."

"Well, now that you mention it, he did. Once or twice. On the weekends."

"What sort of cars does the dealership sell?" asked Pine, giving Laredo a sideways glance.

"Mercedes-Benz." She smiled. "It's funny."

"What is?" asked Pine.

"Roger drives a ten-year-old GMC pickup truck, and I have a third-hand Kia." She looked up at them and smiled brightly through the sheen of tears. "But if you need a fancy car to make you happy, well, something's wrong."

"Makes me think of the Janis Joplin song about God buying her a Mercedes-Benz," said Laredo. "But unlike Janis, my friends don't drive Porsches, either," he added.

"You said your husband is at work now?" asked Pine.

"Yes. He was really upset about Frankie. He and some other fathers from the neighborhood went looking for him and asking people if they'd seen him. But nobody had."

"We'll need to talk to him."

"I can give you the address. It's on the other side of town."

"Thank you. By chance, do you know anyone named Hanna Rebane or Beth Clemmons?"

Pine watched the woman closely for her reaction. She seemed sincerely befuddled.

"No, who are they?"

"Just some other people who might have a connection to the case. Do you have a photo of Frankie?"

"Yes, I took one on my phone when he got here.

I had it printed out and framed. We do that for all the kids. To make them feel part of the family."

"That's very nice. Do you mind if we borrow it?" asked Wallis. "We'll be sure to get it back to you."

She fetched the photo for them, handed it to Wallis, and led them to the door.

"I can call Roger and tell him you're on the way."

"No need to do that," said Pine quickly. "It'll be fine. We probably won't need to talk to him long."

"Okay," said Duncan, looking confused.

Wallis said, "One last thing." He took the St. Christopher's medal from his pocket and held it up. "Do you recognize this? Did Frankie wear it?"

"No, he never wore anything like that."

"Well, thank you."

They walked back to their car.

Wallis said, "Well, either Frankie picked up the medal somewhere or the killer put it on him. I'm opting for the latter explanation."

"Why didn't you want Ms. Duncan to phone her husband?" Laredo asked Pine.

"Just a gut thing. I wonder how many dealerships in Georgia sell Paganis?"

"Pagani?" exclaimed Wallis. "What the hell is that?"

"An Italian-made car that costs about three mill," replied Laredo.

Wallis looked at the FBI agent in disbelief. "Three million dollars! For a car."

"There are people who will pay it."

"In *Georgia*?" said a disbelieving Wallis.

"You never know."

"But Duncan's husband works at a Mercedes dealership, not, not this Pagani thing," pointed out Wallis.

"Right," said Pine absently. Her mind was obviously racing ahead.

"And what's a Pagani got to do with anything?" persisted Wallis.

"One was spotted watching Atlee's old house," said Laredo.

Wallis shook his head. "A three-million-dollar car in Andersonville? Now that's something I thought I'd never see."

"Well, I'd like to *see* that Pagani *and* whoever was driving it," said Pine. "But for now, let's stick to Mercedes-Benz. And Roger Duncan." She glanced at Laredo. "My friends don't drive Porsches, either."

"Well, instead of buying us a Mercedes, maybe God can give us a lead on this case."

"Can I get an amen to that?" said Wallis.

"Amen," said Pine and Laredo together.

54

Roger Duncan slowly wiped his hands off on a greasy rag and motioned for them to follow him to a small room off the work bay where he had been laboring on a Mercedes sedan with a matte-gray finish.

He was tall and lanky with thick, muscled forearms.

They had explained why they were there. He leaned back against the wall, rubbed a shock of blond hair out of his face, folded his arms over his chest, and sighed.

"Shit. He's really dead? Little Frankie? What the hell?"

"I'm afraid so," said Wallis. "Your wife said he sometimes came to the dealership with you?"

"A couple of times. They have strict rules about that stuff, for safety reasons. But it was on a weekend and I let him in the work bay with me and explained some of the things I did. I even let him sit in some of the cars. He thought it was really cool. I never told him how much they cost. He'd probably never be able to afford one, same as me."

"Did you introduce him to anyone here when you brought him in?" asked Laredo.

"Yeah, a couple of the other mechanics. Don, who works in the business office. He and Frankie talked for a bit while I was dealing with something. And one of the sales gals. Why?"

"We're just trying to figure out how he ended up dead in Andersonville, Georgia, so we have to track down all interactions with other people."

"Well, I can't believe anyone here would hurt him. Why would they? They've all worked here a long time, same as me."

"When was the last time you saw Frankie?" asked Pine.

Duncan thought for a moment. "I was out the door to go to work before he left for school that day. We had supper together the night before. He went to bed. Then he went to school the next day." He added defensively, "Genie is a great mom. She watches those kids like a hawk. But they have to go to school."

"And your wife got worried when he didn't come home from school?"

"Hell, yeah. Genie was frantic. The bus stop is only a few blocks over. Lots of kids get off there, so we never worried. She called me at work. Then she called the agency where we got Frankie, but they weren't too much help, according to Genie. Then she was calling around to everybody she could think of. Nobody had seen him after he left school. So she called the cops. I left work early and went looking for him, too, with some other dads from the neighborhood."

"Your wife told us about that," said Wallis.

"How the hell did he end up in this other place? How far is it from here?"

"About an hour and a half by car," said Wallis.

"This is crazy. Do you think some pervert snatched him? Hey, whoever took him didn't . . . you know?"

"He was *not* sexually abused, if that's what you mean," replied Wallis.

"The things you hear about these days," said Duncan in a disgusted tone. "I mean, how can you call folks human who do that kind of crap?"

"Do you have any theory about what might have happened?" said Pine. "Did you see a strange car passing through the neighborhood? A strange person hanging around?"

"No, nothing like that. Our neighborhood is a tight little community. We watch out for each other. Anything like that, someone would have mentioned it." He paused and looked down. "I guess we . . . we need to take care of his . . . remains."

"Right. We'll let you know when we can release the body, Mr. Duncan," said Wallis. "It probably won't be too long now."

"Okay. Damn. I mean, who wants to hurt a kid?"

"The answer to that might surprise you," said Pine, watching him closely. "Do you only work on Mercedeses here?"

"About ninety percent of the time, yeah."

"And the other ten percent?"

"What they call exotic cars."

"Like what exactly?"

"Aston Martin. Rolls-Royce. Even worked on a Lamborghini Veneno once. That was cool." He grinned sheepishly. "That one car costs way more than I'll ever make in my whole life."

"How about a Pagani?" asked Pine.

"A Pagani," he snorted. "Ain't no Paganis around here."

"So you know the brand?" asked Laredo.

"Hell, just seen 'em in magazines. Damn beautiful cars. Love to work on one."

"Who was the person in the business office you mentioned again?"

"Don, Don Bigelow. He's worked here forever."

"Thanks."

Pine led the two men to the business office, where they found Bigelow, a large-boned man with a big belly, in his early sixties, simultaneously pushing paper on his desk and clicking keys on his computer.

"What can I do for you?" he asked, a pair of rimmed specs tilted up on his forehead. "You folks buy a car or need financing? They usually bring in the paperwork first."

Pine held out her badge, as did Laredo and Wallis.

"We're not looking to buy, we're here for some information," she said.

Bigelow looked nervously at them. "FBI? Please don't tell me some folks here have been embezzling or something. Look, you can check all my records. I'm clean as a whistle."

"No, that's not why we're here. We understand that Roger Duncan brought one of his foster kids in recently."

Bigelow looked blankly at them for a moment. "Oh, you mean the little Mexican boy?"

"Yes."

"Yeah, he did. Nice kid. He likes cars. Hell, who wouldn't like a Mercedes in the driveway?" He stopped and looked suspiciously at them. "Why are you asking about the boy? Nothing happened to him, did it?"

"You haven't heard?" said Pine.

"What?"

"Something did happen to him," said Wallis.

"What?"

"Someone murdered him."

A visibly distraught Bigelow slowly rose from behind his desk. "Holy Lord. Sweet Jesus. That cute little boy? Who the hell?"

"That's what we're trying to find out," said Pine. "Did you talk to him when he was here?"

"Yeah, Roger brought him in to see me. I've got six grandkids and we babysit all the time. He was a nice boy. Spoke English real good. You could tell that he and Roger had developed a nice relationship, kidding around and stuff."

"Was he here long?"

"I saw him for about ten minutes. Roger had to step out to deal with something. I sort of described what my job was here, but he wasn't interested in that." He grinned resignedly. "Too boring to hold a kid's attention. He was more interested in sitting in the cars and pretend driving 'em than hearing about how you buy them. Who can blame him? I'd rather be doing that, too. I did give him a little metal replica of a Mercedes race car. We get them for promotion purposes. Had one in my drawer. You'd think I gave the kid a million bucks."

"Roger mentioned that the dealership works on cars other than Mercedes?" said Pine.

"We do, usually for Mercedes customers who have other cars."

"Like exotic cars?"

"Yeah. Exactly. Hard to find qualified folks to work on them around here. Have to go to Atlanta. So we save them a trip. Our mechanics are top-notch. Certified on lots of different types of makes and models."

"Roger said he had worked on a Lamborghini Veneno?" said Laredo.

"Yeah. That would be Mr. Driscoll. He has one. Only man I know who does around here. He made a ton of money in commercial real estate development. And he has some business with the folks at Fort Benning, too."

"Any Pagani owners?" asked Laredo.

He shook his head. "No, we've never had a Pagani in here. I've never even seen one for real."

"Know of any place that sells them around here?" asked Pine.

"There's a dealership in Atlanta that sells Ferraris and Maseratis. They might sell Paganis. They're all Italian cars after all."

Pine said, "Did you ever sell a car to a Jack Lineberry? Or did he ever have any vehicle serviced here?"

Wallis shot Pine a look but remained silent.

Laredo just watched her.

"Lineberry? Don't ring no bells, either. But let me check. I can't remember everybody."

He sat down at his desk and started clicking on his computer. "Nope. Never sold a car to anybody by that name."

"How about service on a car?"

Bigelow hit some more keys and then shook his head. "No, nothing."

"Okay, thank you."

"Who do you think killed the boy?" asked Bigelow.

"That's what we're trying to find out."

"Hope you catch the bastard."

"So do we," replied Pine.

Wallis's phone buzzed. He answered it and moved over to a corner of the room while he spoke.

When he was done he came back over to them.

"We got a lead."

"What?" asked Pine.

"Some kid saw a man talking to Frankie on the way to the bus stop the day he disappeared. And the kid thinks the man might have slipped Frankie a note in an envelope along with some cash."

55

Sarah Toomey was around ten and looked terrified sitting next to her grim parents. She was all dark pigtails, freckles, big eyes, and gapped teeth, and she wore a pair of faded denim overalls with a white T-shirt underneath, and pink Crocs.

Pine, Laredo, and Wallis were perched in chairs across from them.

"Sarah, we just want you to tell us as much as you can remember about seeing Frankie with the man the other day, okay, sweetie?" said Pine.

She had leaned forward in her chair in the small living room so that she was eye to eye with the child.

In a small, shaky voice Sarah said, "Okay, I'll try really hard."

"I know you will. Now, did you know Frankie well?"

"Pretty well. I liked him. We were in some of the same classes. And we had the same homeroom. He was funny. He liked to joke around. And he could speak Spanish. He was teaching me some."

"I bet. Sounds like you two really hit it off."

"I liked him," she said simply. "He was nice."

"I'm sure. From all we've learned he was a really nice boy. Now can you tell us what you saw and heard that day?"

Sarah looked up at her mother, who nodded and said, "You tell them everything you can remember, Sarah. Go ahead, you can do this, honey."

She nodded and put her hands together in her lap. "Frankie was ahead of me on the street that morning. We were walking to the bus stop. It was only another block before we got there. I was going to catch up to Frankie and say something to him in Spanish to surprise him when this man comes out of nowhere and walks up to Frankie."

Pine interjected, "Can you describe him, Sarah? Any detail you can remember. Take your time. There's no rush at all."

"He was tall, taller than you or your friends. A big guy."

"Could you tell if he was white, black . . . ?"

"Oh, he was definitely white."

"Age?"

"Older. He had white hair. It was kind of long and thick. It hung out from under his hat."

"His hat? What kind of hat was it?" asked Pine, shooting Wallis and Laredo a look.

"Like a cowboy hat, you know. Like you see on TV."

"What about the rest of his clothes?"

"Jeans and a shirt. A dark shirt, I think."

"Shoes?"

"I don't remember."

"Okay. What did he do when he reached Frankie?"

"He said something to him and then handed him an envelope."

"Could you tell what was in it?"

"No, but it was like a regular white envelope."

"Okay, what else?"

"Then he handed Frankie some money. Some bills. I don't know what they were. I mean, how much it was. I couldn't see."

"And what did Frankie do?"

"He said something to the man, and the guy patted him on the shoulder and said something back. Frankie smiled. I remember that."

"What happened after that?"

"Then the guy walked off. I watched him for a bit. I was worried at first. I mean, I'm not supposed to talk to strangers and I'm pretty sure Frankie's not, either. But then the man just walked off, so I didn't know what was going on. I thought maybe Frankie knew him."

"What did Frankie do with the envelope and money?"

"He put the money in his pocket. Then he opened the envelope and pulled out a slip of paper. He seemed to be reading it as he was walking along. I was too far away to see what was on it. Then he put it in his pocket."

"Did you ask him later what the man wanted? Why he had given him the money and what was in the envelope?"

Sarah's mouth drooped. "I was going to, but then the bus passed us on the way to the stop. We were going to miss it. We all started running. Frankie was faster than me. When I got there, he was way ahead of me and was already in line to get on. He got on with some other kids and ended up sitting with them. I had to go sit in the back. I was going to ask him about it later when we got to school, but . . . things got busy and I never did."

"Did you go home on the bus that day?" asked Wallis.

Sarah's mother answered. "Sarah had a doctor's appointment that day. I went to the school and got her about an hour before classes let out. We came home directly from the doctor's, so she wouldn't have seen Frankie again."

Sarah looked at them with a trembling look and tears filling her eyes. "If . . . if I had asked Frankie about what that man wanted, he might not be . . ."

Pine put a hand on her quivering shoulder. "None of this was your fault, Sarah. You didn't do anything wrong. This was all someone else's doing. And you've been a big help and told us a lot of things we didn't know that will help us find that person. We really appreciate your help, Sarah. Okay?"

"Okay," said Sarah before she buried her face in her mother's shoulder and started to cry.

On the way back to the car, Laredo said, "Okay, guy gives the kid a note and some money. What do you want to bet that the note said, get off at a different stop and someone will be waiting to take you to . . . I don't know, home, or the car dealership to maybe take a ride in one of the Mercedeses?"

Pine said, "Or they could have told him he would be met by his parents."

"You think he *was* met by them?" asked Wallis.

"Genie Duncan seemed sincerely upset. Her husband didn't strike me as being involved in this. But the guy could have used their names to gain Frankie's trust."

"And he could have gotten that information any number of ways," said Wallis.

"Tall, older guy wearing a cowboy hat," said Pine darkly.

"I know," said Laredo. "Could be a lot of people, but it also sounds an awful lot like your friend, Cy Tanner. Didn't see that one coming."

"Neither did I," muttered Pine.

56

"How do you want to handle this?" said Wallis.

They were in his car outside of Cy Tanner's house. His truck was in front and Roscoe was asleep on the porch.

"We need to get his picture and show it to Sarah," said Pine. "But I don't want him to know what we're doing."

"Okay," said Wallis. "But Carol said this Tanner fellow was at the Clink when Rebane's body was found."

"She couldn't be certain of the timing. He could have dropped the body off and gone right there to establish an alibi. It would take him all of two minutes to walk from where the body was dumped to the Clink. There's no way Carol could know to the minute when he got there, no more than we could know the exact minute the body was placed where it was found."

"Right, good point," said Wallis.

"I can pretend to be taking pics of the house with my phone and get him in one," said Laredo.

"Sounds like a plan," said Pine absently.

"You don't think he's good for it?" said Laredo.

"I have no idea. We need to know a lot more than we do now, that's for sure. But if he is the guy, we don't want to spook him."

They all climbed out of the car. A moment later they heard the sounds.

"He's in his workshop in back," said Pine. "That's the sound of a saw."

"I wonder what he's cutting up?" said Wallis nervously.

Pine walked over to Roscoe and scratched the dog's ears. "Hey, Roscoe, how're you doing?"

"I think old Roscoe might be on his last legs," said Laredo. "His breathing doesn't sound too good."

Pine wandered over to Tanner's truck.

"Don't even think about performing an illegal search," warned Laredo.

"Don't worry, I'm not going to taint any evidence." She looked in the back of the truck and froze.

Laredo, who had noted this, said, "What is it?"

"Take a look at this."

The men hustled over and looked inside the truck.

"What are we looking for? There's nothing there," said Wallis.

"Look at the bolt heads in the floor liner."

Laredo and Wallis leaned in closer. Laredo got it first.

"The marks on Hanna Rebane's back and legs. I

looked at the autopsy photos when I got to town. They match the pattern we're looking at now."

"Yes, they do."

Laredo glanced over at the old barrel that Tanner used to burn things. Some smoke was still coming out of it. He hustled over and, using a long stick he picked up from the ground, started poking around in it.

Pine and Wallis joined him.

"You think . . . ?" said Pine.

"I didn't until about five seconds ago."

He started pulling things out with the point of the stick and setting them on the ground.

"Don't you need a search warrant for this?" said Wallis anxiously.

"The bolt pattern in the truck coupled with Sarah's description establishes enough probable cause," said Pine. "Plus, he had given me permission to look around before, including in the house. I think we can chance it."

Wallis didn't look convinced, but he also didn't argue the point as soon as the next object Laredo speared emerged from the barrel.

Pine snagged it and dropped it on the ground, tamping out some embers with the sole of her boot. She bent down and picked it up.

"That look like a red Nike pullover to you?"

"What's left of it," said Wallis.

"Hey, what are y'all doing here?"

They turned to see Tanner standing at the corner

of his house, a pair of safety goggles flipped up on his forehead.

Pine put the remnants of the pullover behind her back. “Hey, Cy, what’s up?”

He walked toward them. “Carol came by before. She said Jenny got squared away with those folks real good. I’m going over there later.”

“That sounds great.”

“You mind if we go inside?” she asked. “I wanted to take some pictures of the place. It might jog my memory.”

“Sure.” Then he glanced at the debris that Laredo had pulled out of the trash barrel. “What’s going on here?”

“Like I told you before,” said Pine. “The things in there caught fire again. Laredo here was stamping them out.”

“Oh, okay, thanks there, pardner.”

“You’re welcome.” Laredo whipped out his phone. “Hey, let me take a picture of you two together, to make sure I have everything adjusted right.”

He snapped a picture of Tanner and Pine and then they headed inside, with Tanner leading the way. Pine handed off the pullover to Wallis, who stuck it under his trench coat.

They wandered around inside, and Laredo took pictures along the way with his phone.

“You make any headway on the bastard that killed

all them people?" asked Tanner as they trooped back down from the upstairs.

"Working on it. We identified the boy. Went to talk to his foster parents."

"I'll bet they're all broke up."

Pine shot Laredo a glance. "Someone might have seen the guy."

"Really? Who?" blurted out Tanner.

"A witness in Columbus who saw the guy with the little boy we found dead."

"Well, hell, that's great. You could nail the sucker then."

"We're going to try. You heading over to see Jenny now?"

"Yeah, just gonna clean up some. Look, I made her this. What do you think?"

He lifted a doll off the giant bean bag chair and handed it to Pine.

She looked at it. "You made this? From what?"

"Scraps I found here and there."

"It's really good, Cy."

"Hope she likes it."

"Yeah, I'm sure she will." Pine handed it back and he replaced it on the bean bag chair. "We'll wait for you, how about that? And then head over with you."

"Okay, be down in a jiffy. Can't take no regular shower or anything. Just gonna wash off in the sink."

"Why not?"

"No hot water."

He headed up the stairs.

Pine looked at Laredo and Wallis. "Well?"

In a low voice Wallis said, "If he is the killer, he's the coolest cucumber I've ever met. I mean, he kills three people and he's making his granddaughter a doll? For Chrissakes."

She looked at Laredo. "And you?"

"Jury's still out. We need to show this photo to the girl."

"Agreed. But until we get a positive ID, we don't let him out of our sight."

57

The Quarleses were a very nice family. That was Pine's initial impression.

Their house was big and sprawling and old and rickety with lots of yard to run in and lots of kids with whom to run. There were also two floppy-eared dogs, three cats—at least those were the ones Pine could see—a pig named Oinks, and a parakeet in a cage in the front room.

Ted Quarles and his wife, Emma, had greeted them at the door and invited them in. Pine had seen her rental in the driveway and knew that meant Blum was also here. Tanner had ridden over with them in Wallis's Crown Vic, at Pine's suggestion.

When Tanner got down on his knees and gave Jenny the doll he'd made, Pine was watching Blum. The older woman looked like she might cry. That was when Pine sidled over to her and started whispering in her ear, telling Blum the eyewitness account and what they had found at Tanner's.

To her credit, Blum's features barely changed. She glanced at Pine and then over at Laredo, and then her gaze returned to Tanner, to whom Jenny was now giving a hug.

"Do you mind if I try something?" Blum asked Pine.

"Like what?"

"Do you trust me?"

"Yes."

"Okay."

After some chitchat and Jenny running off to show the other kids her doll, Blum walked over to Tanner, who had accepted a glass of lemonade from Emma Quarles.

"Jenny seems really happy," Blum said to him.

He nodded though he looked a little sad. "Thing is, I'm her grandpop, I should be able to look after my family."

"It's not like you won't see her, Cy. You can come by here as often as you want. I'm sure the Quarleses won't mind."

"Yeah, I guess. But I want to pay 'em. Or at least fix up some stuff for them as barter. I don't want no handout."

"I'm sure that can be arranged."

"Well, okay, then," he said awkwardly.

"But it's a good thing you do have them looking after Jenny."

"What do you mean?"

"I would imagine you'll want to visit your daughter in rehab."

"Oh, yeah, I do. I plan on going next week, in fact. I want to let Linda get settled in and all. She's gonna be there about two months. That's what the boyfriend said."

"You going to drive your truck over?"

"Well, yeah, I can't walk to Tuscaloosa. It's not the most reliable thing, but it's all I got."

"You drove it into town that night at the Clink, right? When I was there, and you and Agnes came in. The night they found the woman's body."

Tanner shook his head. "Matter of fact, I didn't."

"Why not? Don't tell me you walked. That's quite a hike."

Pine was a few feet behind them listening intently to this exchange.

"Well, the damn thing wouldn't start."

"Wouldn't start? You have trouble like that before with it?"

"No. I mean, the durn thing's got problems, all right, but not starting wasn't one of them. Till that night, anyways."

"How'd you get to town then?"

"Walked over to Agnes's and I drove her car in with her. She don't drive it much. In fact, I don't think she drives it at all. Clean as a whistle. It belonged to her husband. It's a Buick. Right nice machine. Although the tags expired a long time ago, but hey."

Blum surreptitiously glanced at Pine. "So that's why you two came in together? I remember that."

"Yep. Though it was the darnedest thing."

"What was?"

"The truck. I went out the next morning figuring I'd have to check it all out and fix stuff, but I turned the key, and she started right up."

Blum once more glanced at Pine. "Will miracles never cease."

"Got to have a vehicle out here. Only way I can get to my work. Customers want me to come there most times. Or haul what needs fixing back to my workshop."

"When did you get back from the restaurant that night?"

"What? Oh, I took Agnes home and we talked a bit. She made me some coffee. Then I walked back. Probably around eleven or so. That durn Roscoe was dead asleep on the bean bag, so I slept on the floor. Didn't do my old back any good, I can tell you that."

Blum's face crinkled into a smile. "You do have a soft spot for that dog."

Tanner's eyes became watery. "He was all I had, till Jenny come to town."

Blum patted his shoulder. "Well, now you have both of them to look after."

She walked back over to Pine.

"That was some nice work, Carol."

"I think someone is working awfully hard to frame Cy Tanner for something he didn't do."

Pine blew air out of her cheeks. "I think you might be right. He would make a prime fall guy. They might have sabotaged his truck that night so they could use it. Then dress up like him and meet up with Frankie Gomez, counting on the fact that someone might see him."

"Which means the real killer is out there watching and manipulating things."

Pine said, "The guy in the Pagani? You think that was why he was watching Cy's house?"

"Learning his routine and such, you mean? It's certainly plausible."

"We still have to show Cy's photo to our witness."

"I know you do. And I know you also know that eyewitness testimony is wrong more often than it's right."

"Still have to do it. And then there's the other evidence we found."

"Do you really think he has the wherewithal to come up with a veil and a tux and a corsage? And after seeing how he is with his granddaughter, do you really think he has it in him to kill a little boy?"

"I'm not saying you're not making good points, because you are. But I can't exclude him as a suspect just because of how I might feel about him. I have to look at the hard evidence."

"But what will you do if your witness does ID him?"

Pine looked over at Tanner, who was now patting one of the Quarleses' dogs affectionately on the head.

She said miserably, "I don't know, Carol. I really don't know."

58

"Sarah couldn't be sure," said Laredo. He was on the phone with Pine. It was the next day and he had gone back to Columbus to show Tanner's photo to Sarah. "She said she only saw him from the back."

"Okay," said Pine, who was sitting in her rental SUV outside her old house. "So where does that leave us?"

"In no-man's-land, apparently," said Laredo. "But we do have to check the pullover we found for DNA and take a cast of those bolts in the truck bed to compare against the marks on Hanna Rebane."

"We'll need a search warrant for that."

"That won't be a problem. Wallis is already on it. We have more than enough probable cause."

Pine said nothing.

"What?" he said in a prompting tone.

"I don't think he's good for it. I've been outside his house all morning. I checked on him a couple of times. He's dead asleep in the bean bag chair with Roscoe on top of him and five beer cans lying all around him. And the portable radio plugged into the wall is playing Charlie Daniels nonstop. So you're telling me that's the guy who successfully killed four people, dressed them up, and is making it hard for us to track him down? But then he conveniently burns evidence in his trash barrel and doesn't bother to wrap the body in something so the bolt heads in his truck bed don't get transferred to the victim?"

Laredo sighed. "Well, when you put it that way."

"And there's something else."

"What?"

"Roscoe."

"Who?"

"Tanner's dog. How many serial killers are you aware of who had a pet that they doted on?"

Laredo didn't answer right away. "Well, I can't think of any right now."

"Serial killers usually start off their careers by torturing and killing animals, not befriending them."

"Well, that's true, although there are exceptions to every rule."

"Going with the odds, though, I don't see our killer being a dog person. Especially one with a kidney problem who pees all over the place. So I say we put the search warrant on hold, we keep eyes on Cy, but we need to follow up some other leads."

"Like what leads?"

"I'll let you know when I come up with some."

She clicked off, put her truck in gear, and drove off,

leaving Tanner to his sleep and his Charlie Daniels tunes.

Well, the devil has *come down to Georgia. I just have to find him. And I'm pretty damn sure he's not dead asleep in that house.*

On impulse she drove over to Jack Lineberry's. The gate was open for some reason, and she drove through and up to the main house. As soon as she stepped out of her SUV, a man approached.

It was Jerry, the not-so-friendly security man. He was dressed in a dark suit, white shirt, and tie, and a comm piece was inserted in his right ear.

"What do you want?" he asked briskly.

"I just wanted to see Jack."

"Did you make an appointment with *Mr. Lineberry*?"

"No, I'm just paying a friendly call. Is he in?"

"You have no reason to know that or not."

Pine took a step back and appraised him. "What's your last name?"

"Why?"

"Does everything have to have a reason?"

"With me it does."

"Where were you stationed with the Secret Service?"

"None of your business."

"Ever on the presidential detail?"

"Same answer."

Pine nodded and gave him an amused look. "Okay, Jerry. Hang on a sec."

She pulled out her phone and punched in a number. "Hey, Jack, it's Atlee. Yeah, I'm right outside. But Jerry needs a reason for me to talk to you. What? Oh, sure. With pleasure."

She handed the phone to Jerry. "He wants to talk to you."

Jerry looked at the phone like it was a cobra about to strike.

He snatched it from her, cleared his throat, and said, "Yes sir?" He listened and nodded. "Yes sir," he said again and handed the phone back to Pine.

"Well?" she said.

"This way."

He turned and marched toward the house with Pine following him and doing nothing to hide her gleeful look.

Lineberry met her at the front door and took Pine back to his office.

He had on blue slacks, a white button-down shirt open at the collar, and tasseled loafers. Pine noted once more what a handsome man he was. But there was something underneath the strong features; she couldn't be sure, but it seemed akin to a penetrating sadness.

He said, "Sorry about Jerry, he's overzealous at times."

"What's his last name?"

"Jerry's? It's Danvers. Jerry Danvers."

"You said Secret Service?"

"Yes. So, to what do I owe this visit?"

She looked at the stacks of paper on his desk. "You look like you're busy."

"Nothing that can't wait. Please sit down. Would you like something to drink?"

"No, I'm good, thanks."

They took their seats and he looked at her expectantly.

"Do you own a Pagani?" she asked.

He looked puzzled. "A Pagani? What's that?"

"A car. A really expensive car. Runs about three million."

"No, I don't own a Pagani."

"Not to be too personal, but could you afford one?"

"Yes, but that's a lot of money for an asset that will depreciate as soon as you drive it off the lot."

"Okay."

"For the record, I usually drive a Jag. Hunter green."

"Is that the only car you own?"

"No, I have the Porsche SUV you rode in the other day. And I have a silver Aston Martin convertible. Why?"

"Just wondering."

He looked at her appraisingly. "Why do I doubt that?"

"Did you ever know a man who used to live here named Barry Vincent? He apparently knew my parents."

Lineberry's expression hardened just a jot, Pine observed, and he sat back in his chair.

"Barry Vincent? I seem to remember that name from somewhere."

Pine told him about Myron Pringle breaking up a fight between Vincent and her father.

"Yes, yes, I remember something like that, too. I think Myron might have mentioned it back then. But to answer your question, I didn't know this Vincent person. I'm not sure, but I don't think he was in town long."

"But why would he come here in the first place? Where did he come from?"

"I have no idea on either count."

"He seemed to have it in for my father. For a guy who didn't live here long, and who didn't work at the mine, what would his beef be with my father?"

"I guess you'd have to ask Vincent."

"I would, if I knew where he was. It's been nearly thirty years."

"Well, that is a puzzle."

He fell silent and they spent a few beats staring at one another.

"You know, you really do look remarkably like your mother."

"I'll take that as a compliment."

"It was clearly meant as one."

An awkward moment passed.

He said suddenly, "Would you like to go out to dinner tonight? In Atlanta?"

"It's a one-hour drive from your place. Long way to go to eat."

"It's a nice day and the evening forecast is for clear skies. The Aston Martin hasn't been out in a while. We could head out at six, then home by eleven or midnight. I can pick you up at your place."

She considered this. "Okay. But I'll come over here. It's on the way. And in the interest of full disclosure, I might have some more questions for you."

"And hopefully I'll have more answers for you than I did just now."

Pine left and passed Jerry at the front door. The other guard had also turned up and was watching her closely.

"Mr. *Danvers*, nice to see you again."

Jerry bristled at her remark. "Right."

Pine looked at the other man. "And you're Tyler, right?"

He grinned and put out his hand. "Tyler Straub. Nice to formally meet you, Agent Pine."

Pine shook his hand and said, "Well, it's nice to know one of you has manners."

"You're leaving?" Danvers said, scowling.

"For now. But I'll be back tonight. I'm going to dinner with your boss in Atlanta."

He looked over her clothes. "I hope you have

something else to wear. Mr. Lineberry only goes to the best places."

"Hey, Jer," said Straub, frowning. "Let's dial it back. No reason to go down that road. She's cool. And she's friends with the boss. So don't rock the boat."

Pine looked at Straub. "Good advice. I'm not the enemy here."

Straub slowly nodded. "Mr. Lineberry thinks very highly of you."

"Well, it's reciprocated."

"Just remember to dress up," said Danvers. "Mr. Lineberry will be."

"Don't worry, Jerry, I'll knock your socks off tonight."

He looked at her as though that would be absolutely impossible.

"And it never hurts to smile," Pine added as she walked to her truck.

On the way out she could hear Danvers giving Straub grief for standing up to him.

Jack Lineberry had an interesting household, she thought.

59

On the way back to Andersonville, Pine called Max Wallis.

"I need to get a line on a guy named Barry Vincent who lived here back in the eighties. And I was wondering if you could help."

"Okay. What does this pertain to? Could he have something to do with the killings?"

"No," replied Pine. "It has to do with my sister's disappearance. I . . . I was hoping that you could do me a favor."

"Well, considering you've been helping me, how can I refuse," he said good-naturedly.

"I really appreciate this, Max."

"Sure thing. What do you want to know about him?"

"I want anything you can find out about him, including his picture."

"I'll see what I can do. I should be able to run something down on him."

"That would be great."

"One other thing. Laredo called me and said you want to put a pin in Cy Tanner?"

"Look, that's my opinion, Max, but this is your show. If you want to execute the search warrant and haul him in, I can't stop you."

"But you think it'd be the wrong move?"

"I think it would be the wrong move right now. That may change."

"Okay," he said doubtfully. "What are you up to today?"

"I'm going to dinner with Jack Lineberry in Atlanta. We're driving over in his Aston Martin to some place fabulous, I'm sure."

"Well, ain't you high and mighty," said Wallis in a joking manner.

"But aside from the nice car and food, I want to find out what I can about that night back in 1989."

"You think he's been holding out on you?"

"I think this whole town has been holding out on me. And I'm getting tired of it."

Blum sat in Pine's room that night as her boss got ready to go to dinner.

"That black dress you wore before should do the trick."

"Well, it'll have to since it's the only 'trick' I brought. But I have to tell you, high heels are highly overrated."

"Well, with your height, why bother?"

"I like looking down on men," said Pine with a smile as she slipped into the dress. When Blum raised her eyebrows at this remark, Pine added, "I'm just kidding."

She looked at herself in the mirror hanging from the wall. "Not that I care, but Lineberry's already seen me in this."

"When?"

"When I had dinner in Americus with Lauren Graham. He was there and came over and joined us for a drink."

"And you still had it on when you went out with Eddie Laredo later that same night."

"How did you know that?"

"Heard you two coming back in." She added in a hesitant tone, "I don't know where you went after that."

"We went to our *separate* rooms and stayed there," said Pine firmly. Although at the same time she was thinking it could have turned out differently, if she'd had a few more drinks and was not wrapped up in investigating serious crimes.

"Never doubted it."

Pine glanced at her. "You'd fail a polygraph on that one."

Blum smiled. "I have a different wrap from the one I gave you before. That will make the outfit look fresh to Mr. Lineberry."

"I'm not trying to sell myself to the guy, Carol."

"No, but you do want information. And within the bounds of reason and good taste you're entitled to use every tool in your arsenal to get it."

Pine shot her another glance. "Why do I think you want to use the term *feminine wiles*?"

"I didn't think I had to. And there's nothing wrong with using what you have to your advantage."

She glanced at Pine's earlobes. "Do you have earrings other than those diamond studs? Turquoise would look great with the wrap I'm thinking about."

"No. I only got my ears pierced when I was fourteen, way after all my friends. I guess I wasn't into it. I just have the ones I'm wearing."

Blum rose, left, and came back a minute later with a pair of hoop earrings with turquoise stones set in them. "These will look great and will accentuate your long neck."

Pine thanked her, and when she struggled to get them on properly, Blum assisted her.

Pine said embarrassedly, "My . . . my mom never really did . . . stuff like this with me."

"Maybe after her modeling days she had grown weary of playing dress-up," said Blum. "Besides, weren't you the tomboy?"

"Yeah, but, well, it would have been nice . . . sometimes."

Blum ran her fingers through Pine's thick hair, smoothing out some areas. "I'm sure it would have, Agent Pine. I'm sure it would have."

Pine started applying her makeup and lipstick. She said abruptly, "Jack Lineberry was in love with my mother."

"How do you know that?"

"It doesn't take a genius. I guess lots of men were in love with her."

"Like mother like daughter."

Pine shot her a glance. "Carol, where is this coming from? I am nothing like my mother. She never picked up a weight in her life. And she would have no idea what MMA even was. And if you told her I was an FBI agent . . ."

"What, what would she say?"

Pine finished with her makeup and put her compact and lipstick in her small clutch purse. "I don't know," she said offhandedly. "What does it matter?"

"It clearly matters to you, as it should."

"I really don't want to get into this."

"You may get into it tonight."

Pine glanced sharply at her. "What do you mean by that?"

"Lineberry was in love with your mother. Now he's asked you out to dinner."

"So?"

"So as great an investigator as you are, you're obviously a bit underwhelming in your instincts when it comes to men."

As Pine brushed her hair, she said, "I'm not getting this."

"Exactly my point. You're not getting it."

"You think Jack Lineberry is infatuated with me?"

"And you don't?"

Pine put the brush down and looked over at Blum. "There was an awkward moment at his house when . . ."

"When what?"

"When maybe it seemed like he was seeing my mother sitting there instead of me. You know, like that time before."

Blum silently clapped her hands together. "And there you are."

"It *was* a little odd."

"Which means you have to tread cautiously."

"Carol, you of all people should know I can handle myself."

"If it involves subduing men much larger than you, or finding a clue from pretty much nothing, or taking a tense situation and de-escalating it, you have my full confidence. But this is not that."

Pine sat on the bed to put on her heels and looked at her friend. "So, what then? What do I do if it seems clear that—?"

"—that he's attracted to you? You do nothing. He's a grown man. Whatever his feelings are, don't feel like you're obligated in any way to be responsible for placating him or playing along. When I mentioned using all the tools in your arsenal, I never meant for you to string him along or anything like that to get what you want. Just be yourself. And if he does or says something to make you uncomfortable, let him know it. If he doesn't get the message, then leave." She paused and smiled. "Just please don't beat him up."

Pine snorted.

Blum continued. "I know you know all of that, but sometimes a refresher course doesn't hurt. So you need to draw clear lines. Let him know your interest is only professional. But don't come down too hard on him if he says something that annoys you."

"Why?"

"Because you still need him for information. We're here to solve a mystery, Agent Pine. Don't forget that."

Pine smiled and reached over and patted Blum's hand. "What would I do without you?"

"Well, let's hope we don't have to find out for a very long time."

60

"Is that too much air?" asked Lineberry.

They were sailing along on their way to Atlanta in the top-down Aston Martin.

"No, it actually feels good. This is the Georgia I remember. Warm and humid."

He grinned.

He was dressed in a dark brown blazer, tan slacks, and a patterned shirt. A pocket square completed the look.

"So, life's good for you?" said Pine.

"No complaints." He glanced at her. "What about you? You have some issues I've never had to face."

She moved a few strands of hair out of her face and studied the straight road ahead. "Issues have solutions. I just have to find them."

"That's the proper attitude," he said admiringly. "Are you further along in your investigation of all these awful murders?"

"Further along than we were. But a long way to go. The last victim was a little boy."

"I heard about that," he said grimly. "What I can't

understand is why all this now. And why here? This would be the last place in the world you'd think something like this would happen."

"Murder can happen anywhere because killers can come from anywhere. And go anywhere."

"I suppose," he said doubtfully.

"Where are we eating in Atlanta?"

"A little place I discovered about a year ago. The menu isn't immense, but there's not a weak dish in the lineup. And the wine list is a veritable treasure trove."

"I'm afraid I'm more into beer."

"You know your mother told me that very same thing when I had them over for dinner once."

"Did she?" said Pine without enthusiasm as she continued to stare down the road.

"But she opened up to wine. First white and then red. She was an apt student. Her taste became quite refined. I look forward to doing the same with you."

Pine's pulse quickened a bit at this as Blum's earlier words and warning came back to her. "How did you get into wine? Not from your work at the bauxite mine?"

"Um, no," he replied, like a man who had said too much. "Just from traveling around here and there."

Right, thought Pine. She then recalled that Laredo had never been able to find out where Jack Lineberry had come from before he had turned up in Andersonville.

"I guess that's the good thing about traveling, you

learn things," said Pine cryptically. "I try to do the same."

He gave her an inquisitive glance at this remark but said nothing.

The restaurant was intimate, but every table was occupied by what looked to be well-heeled clientele. The owner evidently knew Lineberry because he greeted him enthusiastically by name and guided him back to a private table set in a book-lined alcove at the back of the room with drawn curtains.

"The reserve wine list," said the man, handing him a black iPad.

"Thanks, Ben."

After the man walked off, a waitress, young and pretty and clearly intimidated by Lineberry, hurried over to fill their glasses with bottled still water.

"Hello, Mr. Lineberry. Good to see you again."

"Good to see you too, Wendy. Thank you. This is my friend, Ms. Pine."

"Ms. Pine," said Wendy, looking in awe of Pine as well.

She hurried off, and Lineberry slowly went through the screens on the iPad with the aid of a pair of reading specs pulled from his jacket pocket. "Do you have a preference? Italian, French, Spanish, Argentinian, perhaps Napa or Sonoma?"

"So long as it's wet, I'm good to go."

Lineberry chuckled and made his selection, inputting it on the electronic device.

He put away his glasses and sat back as Wendy came over and handed them their menus.

"Your wine will be up shortly. Would you like it decanted?"

"For this one, yes. It needs to breathe a bit."

"Yes sir."

She brought two stemmed wineglasses and some warm fresh bread and dipping oils, and then rushed off again.

"She seems a little nervous around you," noted Pine.

He shrugged. "I don't know why. It's not like I'm some high-maintenance ass who thinks way too much of himself."

"I wouldn't have accepted your invitation if you were."

"I treat people like I want to be treated. With respect."

"I'm sure my parents appreciated that."

He took a bit of bread and dipped it into the oil. "I would like to think they did," he said thoughtfully.

"This is a beautiful little private space. Do you usually eat in this alcove?"

"I like the privacy," he said simply.

"Do the curtains close?" Pine said, and then wondered why she had asked.

"I don't know. I've never had occasion to find out."

"What was it like finding my dad's body?"

This so caught the man off guard that he choked a bit on his bread. He swallowed some water and cleared his throat.

Pine said, "Okay, sorry, that was the worst segue ever."

"No . . . it's fine. It's perfectly understandable for you to be curious."

He sat back and wiped his fingers with his napkin. "It was horrible, Lee, if you want to know the truth. I'd never seen a dead body before. Not like that. And I hope to God I never do again."

"I'm sure."

"I guess in your line of work you see many . . . deceased people."

"I do, yes, unfortunately."

"Does it ever get any easier?"

Pine thought back to the body of Frankie Gomez. "Not necessarily, no."

"Well, that might actually be a good thing. I mean, if you get desensitized to something like that, well, I don't think that's a good development personally."

"I would agree with that."

He looked at her keenly. "I didn't mention this before, but you look quite lovely. I mean, very beautiful."

"Thank you."

He looked away, obviously uncomfortable with his comments. "I . . . hesitate sometimes to say that anymore to a woman. I mean, there are so many men who push the bounds . . . Well, I'm sure you see that a lot in your work. Isn't the FBI still very much a male world?"

"Yes. But things are slowly changing for the better. And we should never get to the point where a person can't respectfully compliment another person."

"Agreed," he said, his smile returning.

"Which is why I'll tell you that you look very distinguished."

He smiled resignedly. "That's a good word, *distinguished*. It must be my white hair."

"Men get distinguished. Women just get older."

"Another unfairness in life."

When the wine came and was poured out, they clinked glasses. Pine took a tentative sip.

"Wow, that has a pop." She looked embarrassed. "I'm not sure that's a correct wine term."

"It *is* correct if that's how you perceive it. And just so you know, I've used that description before myself."

"What wine is it?"

"An Amarone, from Verona in Italy. The process for this grape entails special harvesting and drying methods. That brings the tannins and flavor intensity to the finished wine." He smiled self-consciously. "And that concludes my little lecture on wine."

"No, it's fascinating. I wish I knew more about it."

"Just wait a bit as this wine oxygenates and opens more. You'll get an even bigger pop!"

They ordered, and their courses were delivered in

an unhurried manner. The owner came to check on them twice, and no bill was presented at the end.

Pine said, "So do you get free meals here or what?"

"I have an account. It just streamlines things."

"Okay."

"If you're ever in Atlanta and need somewhere to crash, I have a little place here, in Buckhead. Please feel free to stay there."

"That's very generous of you," Pine said, averting her gaze from his.

"I'm not just saying that. I would be honored."

Pine didn't say anything for a few seconds as she composed the question she had wanted to ask all evening.

"When was the last time you saw my mother?"

He took a drink of his wine and wiped his lips with his napkin. He positioned the salt and pepper shakers just so in front of him before answering.

"The day before the three of you left town."

"They didn't tell you where they were going?"

"No," he said tersely. "I have to admit I was . . . hurt."

"But you finally reconnected with my dad?"

"Yes."

"But not my mother. I wonder why? He knew where we were."

"Well, he decided to keep that to himself, I guess."

"But you were friends."

"This was after your parents had divorced. Maybe

Tim didn't want me to see her again. I don't know why."

"You seemed like you were very close to her."

"I was very close to *both* of them," he said firmly. "Like I said, I had offered your father a job in my firm."

"And then he killed himself."

"Yes, yes he did. Awful. Terrible. I . . . I could barely believe it."

"And then my mother came to town to arrange things. And you didn't see her then?"

"She never contacted me."

"And you didn't stay around to see her when she came in?"

He shrugged and wouldn't meet her eye. "I was still in the middle of building my business. Traveling the globe getting clients and expanding my staff and resources. It was a whirlwind for nearly two decades. I was never in one place more than a week or so back then. Thankfully, my pace has slowed." He grinned to himself more than to her. "After all, I'm not as young as I used to be."

"None of us are. Those of us who are still living anyway."

"Yes, right, of course. I should be grateful for all I have." His heart did not seem to be in the statement.

When the Aston Martin pulled up to the valet stand, Lineberry said, "Care for a nightcap?"

"Where?"

"My home is near here."

Pine hesitated. "Shouldn't we be starting back?"

"Well, if we get tired, we can always stay over. I have a guest room."

She stared rigidly at him. "I didn't bring anything for an overnight stay."

"I have things you can use."

Pine looked away, clearly uncomfortable with all this.

He said, "You could ask me some more questions, if you'd like. And I'll do my best to answer them."

Pine turned back to him. "Then let's go."

61

Lineberry's "little place" in Buckhead turned out to be a two-story penthouse suite in a nearly brand-new skyscraper. It had its own private, secure elevator that opened into the vestibule of the apartment.

"Okay, this is another wow," said Pine as he escorted her into the living room that had sweeping views of Georgia's capital city. She walked over to the wall of windows and looked out.

"But no drapes or anything? That can't be too private."

"It's specially treated glass. I can see out, but no one can see in."

"Oh, well, that makes sense. But I doubt it was less expensive than drapes."

"You would be correct," he said with a smile. He had taken his jacket and draped it over one of the armchairs. "What would you like to drink? I have a full bar."

"Actually, do you have any more of that Amarone?"

"I do indeed. I could tell you liked it back at the restaurant. Come on, I can show you the wine cellar."

He led her down a long, wood-paneled hall and then turned right. Confronting them was a wall of stone with two immense wooden, glassed arched doors built into the middle of it.

He hit a switch on the wall and the lights behind the doors came on. He opened one of the doors and motioned her in. He followed and closed the door behind them.

Pine shivered a bit.

"About fifty-eight degrees and a constant level of humidity," he explained. "I have some rare bottles in here, and it wouldn't do to let them go bad by having the wrong climate."

Pine could see that both the bricks overhead and the ones making up the floor looked reclaimed, the wood beams dark and aged. The built-in cabinetry had evidently been done by master craftsmen, with every cut, joint, and curve perfect.

"This is gorgeous. I feel like I'm back in medieval times."

"That's remarkably close to the effect I told the company who did this to go for."

He slid open a rack of wine and looked over the bottles laid there.

"I think this one will do." He pulled it out and held it up. "It's not the same vineyard as the one we had at the restaurant, but I believe this bottle will have even more pop!"

"I trust you."

"Do you?" he asked.

"Is there a reason why I shouldn't?"

"No, but from the moment I met you when you came back to Andersonville, I detected a level of uncertainty."

"Don't take it personally. I'm that way with everyone."

They drank the wine on one of the outdoor terraces that covered three sides of the apartment. They sat in a pair of upholstered wicker chairs around a glass table. The breeze was warm and lightly lifted Pine's loose tresses. Large potted plants abounded around the terrace, and there was even a small putting green. Overhead they watched a line of planes heading to or from Atlanta Hartsfield, the aircraft lights winking in the distance like a string of airborne Christmas lights.

"This is really quite something, Jack. You've done well." She held up her glass. "Here's to being really rich and successful, and also a nice guy." Her face crinkled with a smile. "I'm sure you know that's not always the case."

"I do indeed. But all of this means nothing if you have no one to share it with."

"So you never found the right person?"

Lineberry refilled his glass and topped off hers. "No, I did."

Pine slowly put her wine down. "Who are we talking about?"

"I think you already know that, Lee."

She settled back in her chair. "How long were you in love with my mother?"

"Just take today's date and subtract it from the first moment I met her."

"But she was married, with two kids," said Pine.

"You're assuming that I first met her in Andersonville."

"That's what you told me."

"No, I never said we met there," he responded, shaking his head.

"So where did you meet my parents?"

"I met your mother first. I met Tim later, when he came on the scene."

"Wait a minute. Are you saying you knew my mother before she met my father?"

"Yes."

"Where? How?"

"I can't tell you."

"Bullshit," she snapped angrily. "You can't start to go down that road and then stop."

"If it were my call, I would continue to go down that road, but it's not."

"Whose call is it?"

"I can't tell you that."

"Then why the hell did you even start this conversation?"

"Because you asked how long I had been in love with your mother. And I thought now was a good time to answer that question. In fact, that's why I suggested we come here after dinner."

"But why?"

"Because I might not get another chance to explain."

"I don't understand any of this. Wait a minute—if you knew my mother before she came to Andersonville, that means you followed her down here."

"I did."

"Why?"

"It was my responsibility."

"What was? How does responsibility figure into this?"

"What did your mother tell you about her past?"

"It doesn't matter, since it's all a lie."

"How do you know that?"

"Because I'm an investigator. I find out things."

Pine opened her purse and took out something. It was one of the bar coasters that her father had given her. She laid it on the table so he could see it.

Lineberry showed no visible reaction to it. He merely sipped his wine and looked out over the city.

"So are you clamming up now?" she said. "You said you brought me here to explain things."

"No, I'm not clamming up, just thinking before I speak. I like to do that. It prevents me from making a fool of myself."

Pine's expression softened and so did her tone. "Why would you be at risk of doing that?"

"Every person is at risk of doing precisely that at some point in their lives. I'm no exception to that."

Pine set her wine down. "Are you being cryptic on purpose or what?"

"Your mother could have told you everything," he said suddenly, the tone of his words tighter and harder than before. "The fact that she chose not to do so precludes me from betraying any confidences. I respect her far too much to do that. I hope you can understand that, Lee. And if you can't . . . well, then, you're not the person I thought you were."

Pine looked taken aback by this for a few moments. She picked up her wineglass.

"Okay, I guess I *can* understand that." She glanced at the coaster. "I had a buddy of mine dig into the Cloak and Dagger Bar."

"Did you? And?"

"And it wasn't really a bar. It was a counterintelligence operation."

"No, not exactly."

She sat back and looked at him in amazement. "Then you *were* involved? So what was it?"

"Lee . . ."

"Please, Jack, I really need to understand this. It's my family. I have a right to know the truth. It's been thirty years. It's time, don't you see that?"

He considered this and finally nodded. "As you said, you're a trained investigator. So, let's harken back to

New York City in the early to mid-1980s. What could come to mind in the way of a *sting* operation?"

Pine sat back and thought about this. "Cold War was starting to wind down by then. And counterintelligence ops were more likely to take place overseas or in DC." She looked intently at him. "Can only be one answer. The eighties? The Big Apple? Organized crime."

"In 1985 the leaders of all five Mafia families operating in New York were convicted under the RICO statute and sentenced to over a century each in prison. It broke them down almost entirely. Later prosecutions and the testimony of Sammy 'the Bull' Gravano, who became the first foot soldier to turn rat, helped bring down John Gotti in 1992. But what got the ball really rolling was 1985 *and what happened before then*."

"And why do you know about all this?" she asked.

"I read. I'm a student of history."

She looked at him skeptically. "Right. And my father helped with that somehow? I was told he was trying to break into acting. How did he end up at the Cloak and Dagger?"

"Who said this had anything to do with Tim?"

Pine looked stunned. "What are you trying to tell me?"

He rose and walked over to the terrace's glass wall, carrying his wine.

She quickly followed. "Jack?" she said expectantly.

He wouldn't look at her. He set his glass on top of the wall and rested his elbows there.

She gripped his arm and turned him toward her. "What are you saying?"

He looked at her for an uncomfortably long moment. In his gaze was a fleet of emotions, but the one that finally caught and held was tenderness, imbued with what seemed a sense of relief or resignation; Pine wasn't exactly sure which, perhaps a mixture of both.

"Your mother was a model who traveled the globe as a young woman. During that time, she met some interesting people. People who took a liking to her. People who wanted to be around her."

"What sort of people are we talking about?" said Pine slowly, though she feared she knew the answer already.

"People who had a lot of money and also dubious backgrounds. But she eventually did the right thing, Lee, at great personal risk to herself."

"Are you saying she was a girlfriend to mobsters? Is that what you're telling me?"

"She wasn't even old enough to vote yet. How all-knowing were you at that age?"

"I would know enough not to get caught up with mobsters."

"Well, you can't know that for certain. What they had could be intoxicating. And it's not like any of them personally murdered anyone. They had foot soldiers for that. She never saw that side. In fact, she didn't know they were criminals at first. It's not like they hold out a sign that says, 'Mobsters.'"

"So why did she 'do the right thing' as you just said?"

"There came a time when she was made to see their dark side. And when she did, she was repulsed."

"And who made her see the light? You? Why? How? What was your involvement? And don't lie and say you read about it in a book as a 'student of history.'"

"I didn't always work at a bauxite mine. Or manage other people's money."

"Were you a cop? Were you a spy for our side?"

"I was an . . . asset. I'll leave it at that."

"And you recruited my mother to do what?"

"She never testified, if that's what you wanted to know. But she was our mole. She wore wires. She told us things that she had heard or seen. Things that helped us prevent many deaths and stop a lot of other bad things from happening in many different places."

"But the bad guys found out? And she had to disappear?"

"You see, while the major trials started in 1985, the case was years in the making, before you and your sister were even born. The Cloak and Dagger subterfuge was a great way to get what we needed on top of the other lines of investigation going on. And your mother exploited that venue to the fullest. She'd already gained the trust of some high-up people in several of the families."

"And my father?"

"She met Tim at the Cloak and Dagger. That was near the end of the sting operation. The trials would be starting soon. He wasn't part of any of this. He was just a busboy in between acting auditions. They . . . they fell in love."

"And then what?"

"Your mother confided to him what was going on. What she had to do. She only told me she had done so later because I would have objected. He was supportive. He married her. I'll give him the credit for that. And then they 'vanished.'"

"But you knew where they were. You came here to watch over them."

"Yes, we helped them 'vanish.' Again, it was my job."

"And was it also because you still loved my mother?"

He looked out over the cityscape. "Something like that," he said. "But I did my best to protect them. After a few years passed, it seemed they were in the clear. The Mafia was significantly weakened. The bosses were in prison. The new bosses were not dwelling on the past, they were trying to secure their own futures."

"And then?"

"And then your sister disappeared and you were nearly killed."

"Do you know who did it?"

"No."

"If you're lying to me—"

"I'm telling you the truth, Lee. I *don't* know," he added sharply.

"But you suspected it had something to do with my mother's past."

"Of course I did. And I communicated that conclusion up the line. Efforts were put in place to figure out what had happened. To try to find your sister."

"But you never told the police? You never told the FBI? That would have opened up lines of investigation. The odds of getting Mercy back would have been a lot better." Pine's face was flushed, and her adrenaline had spiked. "You withheld vital information that might have cost my sister her life."

"It was not my call."

"And my parents said nothing, either? This is bullshit!"

"It could have put all of you in danger."

"We were already in danger," she retorted. "I nearly died."

"I know," he said somberly. "I know, Lee."

She drew a calming breath and said, "And when you sent it up the line, was anything found out about my sister?"

"It was a black hole. No one could figure it out."

"Well, it seems pretty obvious to me. Did you bother looking at the damn Mafia?"

"They were all in prison. At least the ones involved with the Cloak and Dagger. There had been no activity at all for several years regarding your parents. I don't think it came from there."

"Then who?" snapped Pine. She grabbed Lineberry's arm. "Who?"

Lineberry's eyes glittered with tears. "I'm sorry. I wish I had an answer for you. But I don't."

He looked at her sympathetically, which angered her. "I know this must be very difficult for you."

"You don't know shit," snapped Pine.

He swallowed the rest of his wine. "Perhaps I don't."

"What was my mother's real name?"

"Why?"

"Why? Because I'm her daughter and I have the right to know."

"No, you don't. You may think you have the right, but you don't."

Pine looked like she might slug him.

"I'm not saying that in anger, Lee."

"My name is *Atlee*," she snapped.

"Okay, Atlee. I'm saying it because it was your mother who risked everything she had—including her life—to do the right thing, at an age when most people can't even get out of bed on time. I told her I would take her secret to the grave. I already broke that promise by telling you what I have. I will go no further."

This was all said with such a level of sincerity and loyalty that gave Pine, furious as she was, pause. She stepped back and looked out over Atlanta.

"I can see how all this would have been difficult for you," she said more calmly.

"I appreciate that sentiment, but my difficulty is nothing as compared to what you and your mother have had to endure." He looked down at his empty glass. "So you really have no idea where she is?"

"No. And even with my skills and resources as an FBI agent, I haven't been able to find her."

"I take blame for that."

"Why?"

"I taught her how to fool people, how to hide. I did it to keep her safe because the forces coming after her would be as clever as they would be ruthless. But she became paranoid about it, especially with her two daughters."

"Why not just put her in Witness Protection?" said Pine. "Those guys are good."

"What makes you think we didn't try that?" was his surprising reply.

"What . . . what happened?"

"You and your family were almost killed. Twice. I think you girls were maybe a year old."

"What?" said Pine, stunned. "It's . . . it's like you're talking about somebody else's life. Not mine."

"I can certainly understand your absolute astonishment. So, that's when others, when the 'element' I was aligned with, stepped in and made a plan."

"And my parents ended up coming to Andersonville with Mercy and me?"

"Yes. It seemed to be far enough away and not a place that anyone would think a former globe-trotting model would escape to. The other good thing was it would be easy to spot any strangers in town."

He went back over and sat down. Pine joined him.

He looked across the table at her. "I'm sorry for all this."

"I guess you had to do what you had to do. Just like my mother."

"And now what will you do?"

"I will do what I have to do," said Pine firmly. "Will you take me back now? I've got a lot to think about and I can't do it here."

When they went back down to the garage, Pine said, "You mind if I drive?"

"No, but why?"

"I feel like I need to be in control of *something* right now. Otherwise . . ."

He passed her the keys. "I understand."

On the drive back to Andersonville, the two didn't say a word.

Until the shots rang out.

62

Pine's first instinct was to pull her Beretta Nano from her clutch purse. Her second instinct was to keep hold of the steering wheel and start taking evasive maneuvers.

"Jack, are you okay? Jack!"

She turned to see him slumped back against his seat, his face ashen. He turned to the side and vomited, his breathing accelerating. She saw the spread of red across his shirt.

Shit.

She steered the Aston Martin well off the road, opened his shirt, and used her wrap to stanch the blood from the gunshot wound. It was in his upper torso on the right side. Lot of stuff to mess up in there, she knew, but at least the shot hadn't hit him directly in the heart or the head.

She leaned him a bit forward and felt along his back. There was no exit wound.

Surveying the area for where the shots had come from, she got on the phone and called Laredo. He answered on the second ring and she told him everything he needed to know.

His only response was, "On it."

They weren't that far outside of Andersonville. She hoped it was close enough.

She looked over at Lineberry, who had grown still. "Jack! Come on, Jack, hang in there." She felt for his pulse. It was weak but still there.

"Jack, hang with me. Help's on the way. Just hang—"

The shots sailed no more than an inch above her head. She ducked down and pulled Lineberry with her.

Pine was about to pull her gun and fire back, but then she decided not to.

She heard a car engine start up.

Okay, that was interesting and told her a lot.

She could smell Lineberry's vomit commingled with the sweet humid Georgia air and her own adrenaline-fueled sweat.

She opened the driver's-side door, slipped off her heels, and dropped to her knees, using the car as a shield.

The headlights appeared about a hundred yards from her position. She couldn't tell what type of car it was. And she couldn't see the driver.

She slipped the Nano from her purse. She had eight shots; she hoped they were enough.

She used the side of the Aston Martin as a fulcrum

point and aimed her gun at the oncoming vehicle. They didn't know she had a weapon. For all they knew, both she and Lineberry were incapacitated. The shots fired her way might have been a way of trying to ferret that out.

That was why she hadn't fired back earlier. She would have had nothing to aim at. Now she did.

The vehicle was gathering speed.

Hold your fire, Pine. Hold it . . . She moved a strand of hair away from her right eye. She exhaled a breath, grew still, physiologically perfect to hit what she was aiming at, just as she had been taught.

The driver apparently decided to just go for it, because he accelerated and what she could now see was a large SUV barreling down on them, ready to finish the job, apparently.

Pine waited until the truck was less than twenty yards away.

Her first shot hit the windshield right in front of the driver. The second shot blew an even bigger hole in the windshield at the same spot. She moved the barrel of her Nano just a bit and fired twice into the passenger side. Then she shot a hole through the front grille and then took out the right front tire. She had two shots left and she aimed to keep them in reserve.

With the first shots, the SUV had swerved to the right and then the left before stopping dead about ten yards from her.

She waited. They apparently waited.

Her Nano was aimed right at the truck. Anyone stepping from it, she would shoot down.

Minutes ticked by.

When she heard the sirens Pine almost screamed in relief.

The people in the SUV must've heard them, too. The truck backed up, its rear wheels spinning to gain traction and then it reached the asphalt and barreled off down the road, heading back the way Pine and Lineberry had come.

She ran out into the road, leveled her pistol, and fired her last two rounds at the wobbly truck, the steam coming out of the engine compartment because of the shot-through radiator.

There was no way that truck could keep going long.

She ran back to the car and checked on Lineberry. He was still breathing, and his eyes even fluttered open.

"Help's almost here, Jack. Hang on."

"L-Lee."

"I'm right here."

His eyes remained open and fixed on her. He put a hand out and gently touched Pine's face. "A-Aman-da."

Amanda?

His eyes closed as she looked up to see a cop cruiser followed by an ambulance flying toward them.

Pine ran toward them, flagging them down.

The cop car swerved toward her and stopped. She didn't even wait for them to get out. She ran to them, flashing her badge, and leaned in the open window to face the two startled deputies sitting inside.

"Shooter's in an SUV and headed that way. I shot out the windshield and a tire and the radiator. He's armed. Go get 'em and call in reinforcements to block their exit. I'll deal with the EMTs."

"Yes, ma'am."

The squad car peeled away, and Pine pointed the ambulance toward the Aston Martin as she sprinted that way.

They got there at the same moment.

"GSW," she cried out to the EMTs as they jumped from the truck. "Upper right torso. He's bled out a lot. He's unconscious. Hurry."

They grabbed their gear from the truck and raced to the car.

They started working on him right there in the seat. Pine marveled at how the EMTs, both young and female, performed their tasks quickly and efficiently. They checked his vitals and then started fluids and plasma while also working away at the wound and subduing the exterior bleeding.

Pine looked up as Laredo pulled up in his rental, along with Blum.

They ran over and joined her next to the Aston Martin.

"Is he . . . ?" began Blum.

One of the EMTs looked up. "He's stable, critical but stable. We got the bleeding stopped and his vitals have leveled out. We need to get him to Americus, stat."

One of them slid a gurney from the back of the ambulance and all of them helped lift Lineberry onto it. As they were about to close the rear doors, Pine said, "I'll ride with him."

As she climbed into the back Laredo said, "The shooter?"

"The cops are after them. I might have hit the driver, and I messed up the truck."

"I'll find out what I can," promised Laredo. "We can follow you to the hospital." He glanced at her arm. "Shit, Pine, you've been hit too."

Pine glanced down at her bloodied and blackened bare arm.

"Bullet didn't really hit me, just grazed. I'll get a Band-Aid."

"You'll get more than a Band-Aid," said Blum firmly. She looked at the EMT in the rear, who had overheard all this. She nodded at Blum. "Done, ma'am."

The doors closed, and shortly they were moving with the siren blaring.

Pine sat next to Lineberry while the EMT monitored his vitals and kept a watchful eye on her patient. Then she cleaned and gauzed Pine's wound.

"Do you think he's going to make it?" asked Pine quietly.

"He's got a decent chance. They'll know more

when they x-ray him. I've emailed what we know about his condition to the hospital in Americus so they'll be prepared when we get there. They'll have to operate right away. Depends on whether the bullet did any really bad internal damage and if he's got a bleeder going on inside. But for now his BP is steady. That's a good sign."

Pine gripped Lineberry's hand. "I need you to make it, Jack, for a lot of reasons."

She pushed her hair out of her face, leaned down farther, and gave him a kiss on the forehead. As she rose back up, it surprised her. A tear was rolling down her cheek. She couldn't remember the last time that had happened. She hadn't had a real, certifiable cry since losing her sister. Back then she had wept for what seemed like months.

She didn't brush the tear away. She let it continue its slide down her face until it reached her lips.

Pine let out a long breath, continued to squeeze Lineberry's hand, and tried to hold it all together as they raced on.

63

The beeps of the monitors were drilling into Pine's head like buckshot as she sat in a chair in the critical care unit of the hospital.

Lineberry had gone through emergency surgery. He was now lying unconscious with tubes and lines covering him. Pine found her gaze constantly drawn to the monitor, checking the man's blood pressure, respiration, and pulse, waiting for the alarms to ring, which they had already done twice, causing nurses and doctors to rush in and do what needed to be done to quell the noise.

She rose and nervously looked down at Lineberry. She'd had several brief conversations with the surgeon and the attending physician. The bullet had done damage inside, cracking bone and severing blood vessels. They had removed the bullet and repaired the damage. They were cautiously optimistic that Lineberry would make a pretty full recovery if he regained consciousness and no other complications arose.

Blum, Wallis, and Laredo had come and gone.

The SUV that Pine had shot up had been discovered, abandoned miles down the road. There was no sign of anyone, but there had been traces of blood in the front seat. It was now being processed.

"The SUV was reported stolen outside of Atlanta about three hours before it showed up near Andersonville," Laredo had told her.

"They were waiting for us," Pine had told him. "They weren't chasing after us, they were ahead of us on the road."

"So they knew you were coming back from Atlanta?" said Laredo. "But how?"

Pine had no answer to give him.

Jerry Danvers was standing guard outside the door along with a police officer from Sumter County.

Danvers had been very upset when he reached the hospital, blaming himself for not having driven them to Atlanta.

"That's my job," he kept telling Pine over and over.

"And he's your boss and he wanted to drive himself," she pointed out, to no avail.

She rose from her chair when Lineberry moved around, moaning slightly. Her eyes darted to the monitor but all the numbers there remained steady.

She leaned down and looked at him. It was nearly inconceivable to her that not that much earlier, they had been in his fabulous penthouse sipping expensive wine and looking out over the Atlanta skyline.

And that was where she was told that her mother had been involved with the mob.

Her head swirled with this revelation. It was like someone had just tossed her off a boat into the middle of the ocean. Pine didn't know whether she was coming or going. But she had Lineberry. He knew all of it. And she couldn't lose him.

"Jack, can you hear me? You're out of surgery. They patched you up. You're going to be okay." She put a hand on his good shoulder and squeezed gently.

Pine was surprised when his eyes fluttered open and he looked wildly around the room.

"Jack?" she said. "You're okay. You're in the hospital. You're out of danger. You're going to be okay."

His gaze finally found her. He looked up at her and his lips parted, his jaw moved, and she realized he was trying to say something.

She leaned down closer. "Jack, what is it?"

"A-Aman-d? I . . . Aman-da?"

Pine didn't know what to do or say. His look was so desperately pleading that she took his hand in hers and nodded. "I'm . . . I'm Amanda, Jack. I'm here for you."

She felt his fingers tighten around hers. He nodded and said, "L-love you."

He searched her features for an answer.

"I . . . I love you too," she said.

He managed a weak smile, his eyes fluttered once more, and then he returned to unconsciousness.

Pine slowly let go of his hand and sat back down.

She involuntarily shivered at what had just happened.

I just played the role of my mother to comfort him.

It was the only thing she could think to do under the difficult circumstances. And yet she had not felt good about it. It was just another act of deception—for good reasons or not, it didn't matter—and Pine was growing sick of the lies she had discovered since coming here.

She left the room and confronted Danvers out in the hall. He was dressed in a suit and tie, but it was wrinkled, and he looked uncharacteristically disheveled.

"Got time for some coffee?" she asked him.

At that moment Tyler Straub came around the corner. He looked neat and dapper and did not seem nearly as emotional about what had happened as Danvers.

"Hey, Jerry, I'm here to relieve you. How's he doing?"

"Mr. Lineberry *will* recover," said Danvers firmly, his features twisted in anger.

Straub gave Pine a wary look. "O-kay. Hey, well, that's great. We get to keep working then."

Danvers barked, "That comment is way out of line."

Straub put up his hands in mock surrender. "Hey, I'm just trying to lighten things up here. And just so you know, I already talked to the nurse. She gave me the good news. I like the guy, okay?"

Danvers calmed down, turned to Pine, and said, "What do you want to talk about?"

"Last night."

"I have nothing more to say. And I'm not leaving my post."

Pine eyed Straub. "Okay, do *you* have time for some coffee?"

Straub again looked in concern at Danvers, who avoided his gaze. "Sure. You okay with that, Jerry?"

Danvers just gave a curt nod.

Pine led Straub to a small kitchen that had a table and chairs and a coffeepot and some coffee cups. They poured themselves some coffee and sat at the table.

Pine ran her eye over Straub. He was a little older than she, maybe late thirties or so. He was around six-three and lean, but the breadth of his shoulders promised great strength. A bulge under his jacket indicated the location of his pistol. His hair was light blond, thick, and wavy. His features were ruggedly attractive, and Pine figured he could have his pick of the local ladies.

"So what's the deal with Jerry?" asked Pine.

Straub shrugged and looked uncomfortable. "Look, he's fiercely loyal to Lineberry. Nothing wrong with that."

"Well, some might say he's over the top. He was Secret Service, I understand."

"*Uniformed* Secret Service," amended Straub.

Pine sat back. "Really? I didn't know that."

"I can tell by your look."

"What happened then? Why did he leave there? He's too young to have pulled his years for a pension."

"I don't like telling tales out of school."

"Make an exception here. It could be important."

"Well, the scuttlebutt was that Jerry was on track to become a full-fledged Secret Service agent. But it got derailed, and he didn't make the cut."

"How?"

"No idea. You're a fed. One little thing is off, you don't get moved up. But hey, it worked out for him. He makes a lot more money doing this than he would protecting the president or running down counterfeiters."

"What do you think of him?"

"He can be excitable. You saw that. And he is very protective of Lineberry. I'm a professional too, but I look at it as a job. Jerry looks at it as his . . ."

". . . life's work?"

Straub took a sip of coffee before answering. "Something like that," he said quietly.

"Talk to me about your security plan."

"Sometimes both of us are on duty depending on the situation, like when you came by the house that day. At night we have electronic surveillance around the whole perimeter and it's wired with alerts to our cell phones. So it's not like we have to be up all night patrolling or watching a security monitor. I mean, the guy's rich but it's not like he's a celebrity or anything."

"Do you sleep on the premises?"

"Yeah, only a few hundred yards from the main place."

"And last night?"

"Mr. Lineberry told us he was driving with you to Atlanta and did not require our services."

"How did Jerry take that?"

"He was never a big fan of Mr. Lineberry's going out alone."

"Does he have anyone who oversees his penthouse in Atlanta?"

"Yeah, full-time housekeeper–property manager and a maid. They have sleeping quarters on premises."

"I was there last night with him and saw nobody."

Straub sat back. "Huh. You went to the penthouse?"

"It was at his suggestion."

"He might have given the help the night off. I don't know." He eyed her curiously. "Maybe he wanted to be alone with you."

"What did you and Jerry do last night?"

"I went to sleep. Like I said, we have quarters behind the main house. Two cottages. Well, *cottage* doesn't do it justice. They're nicer than any house I ever lived in."

"And Jerry?"

Straub shook his head wearily. "He said he was going to track Mr. Lineberry on the app."

"The *app*?"

"Yeah. It's no big deal. But all the cars have a transponder and the app uses a sat tracker to show the location of the Aston Martin."

"So Jerry would know when we were coming back?"

"Well, that's the whole point of an app like that."

"When did you find out what had happened?"

"When Jerry called me last night. Well, I guess it was early morning by then. He said Mr. Lineberry had been shot and was being taken to Americus. That's why he's so upset. He thinks he should have been there for Mr. Lineberry. Dude would take a bullet for the man, I can tell you that. In that regard, he would've made an excellent Secret Service agent."

Pine didn't answer him. She just sat there thinking that with an app like that, Jerry could have been waiting for them at the spot in the road and opened fire.

But why try to kill the man he was devoted to? And, as Straub had pointed out, with Lineberry alive they had jobs. With him dead, they were unemployed.

So Jerry had the opportunity and the means. But what would his motive be?

"Agent Pine?"

She looked up to see Straub staring worriedly at her.

"You okay?" he asked.

"I'm not sure," said Pine. "I'm really not sure. But I want you to do something for me."

"Okay."

"Anything seems off, give me a call." She handed him one of her cards.

"Off how?"

"Use your gut, your instincts. It's important."

"Okay."

Pine walked out, her mind going a million miles an hour.

64

Pine and Blum were sitting in the breakfast room at the Cottage having coffee. She had just finished filling in Blum on all that Lineberry had told her about her parents.

Blum sat there speechless for quite a long time. Finally, she leaned in and said, "Well, that is quite extraordinary and actually explains a lot."

Pine sipped her coffee and set the cup down carefully, though her fingers trembled a bit. "Well, I for one feel like I just got run over by a train."

Blum poured Pine some more coffee and then patted her hand. "And is there any wonder in that? You were told last night that your mother was a plant, or informant or call it what you will, against the mob. That they had to flee for their lives because the four of you were nearly killed while in Witness Protection. On top of that you were nearly killed last night, and you *were* wounded. I mean, that's more stunners than most people get in a lifetime."

"It had to be the reason Mercy was taken and I was nearly killed all those years ago. But as I said before,

I think Mercy was the winner on the nursery rhyme. She had to be. Otherwise, why wouldn't he have tried to kill both of us? Why bother taking her?"

"I don't know, Agent Pine. But what you say makes sense," she added slowly.

"But you don't believe it," said Pine warily.

"As you advised before, I don't want us to get ahead of ourselves."

"You're right. I *am* getting ahead of myself."

"But I guess one thing is clear."

"What's that?" asked Pine.

"Daniel Tor was not involved in this."

Pine grimaced. "He was stringing me along the whole time. I can't believe I wasted all that time with the bastard."

"But you had to go down that road because it was a viable lead. Only it didn't pan out, like most leads."

"But looking back, it didn't fit his MO. He told me himself he had never taken a child in that way. And what we knew about his crimes supported that. But I was trying to pound a square peg into a round hole. Because I wanted a boogeyman to point the finger at."

"I understand that. But there *is* a positive."

Pine recalled her last meeting with Tor, where he had demanded that she call him Dan. "I'm never going to have to see that asshole again." She tacked on a grim smile to this.

"Exactly."

"Okay, we need to follow this up, but in a logical way." She set her coffee aside and sat forward. "If what happened to me and my sister is connected to what my mother was involved in back in New York, that means someone from that world found them down here."

"But in such a small town wouldn't a mobster from New York have been noticed?"

"Well, it's not like all mobsters look like Al Pacino or Marlon Brando and talk like they're on an episode of *The Sopranos*."

"But how could someone have gotten past your parents, even if they were drunk? They wouldn't let a stranger just waltz past them and go upstairs unless they were completely unconscious. That's never made sense to me."

"I have a theory about that."

"What is it?"

"My mother's routine was abnormal that night. Remember I told you that."

"Yes. I assume you've been thinking about it. Have you reached any conclusions?"

"I have." Pine paused to marshal her thoughts. "She put us to bed at the regular time but didn't check on us and she came into our room at six a.m., far earlier than usual. That was in the police file."

"What does that tell you?"

Pine glanced up. "That she and my father *weren't* at the house that night. They were somewhere else."

"Somewhere else? Where?"

"At the Pringles', drinking and getting stoned. They all must have passed out. Then my mother wakes up, realizes what happened, and rushes home to check on us. And finds me nearly dead and Mercy gone."

"But surely the Pringles would have remembered that."

"They lied," said Pine simply. "Myron said he was at work when his wife called with the news after she heard from my mom. But I think he was at home still drunk. He might have gone in to work later, but who would remember that now. No, they lied because they felt shame for what had happened. And they didn't want to be linked to it. That's why neither one could recall what they were doing that night, until Myron finally admitted that they had friends over. He just didn't tell us those *friends* were my parents."

"So she finds you nearly dead and your sister missing. Then they go into panic mode."

"A little too late for that," said Pine, letting out a long breath as she said the words. "The damage was already done."

"And why the nursery rhyme as a way to choose?"

"I don't know. Maybe it was the only thing the kidnapper could think of. Maybe he conjured it from his childhood when he was picking or being picked for teams."

"What are you going to do now?"

"I need information on Barry Vincent and any connection to folks in New York. If there is one, I can start making some traction. If not, I'm back at square one."

Lauren Graham came in at that moment, looking pale and disconsolate.

"Are you okay?" asked Pine.

"I'm just so worried about Jack."

"When I left the hospital he was doing fine. The surgeon was in to check on him and the latest set of pictures they took showed they got all the damage corrected. It'll be a long rehab but he's no longer in danger. And he can afford the best care. I think he's going to be okay."

"Did . . . he ask about me?"

Pine glanced at Blum before answering. "Um, he was unconscious, Lauren. He couldn't ask about anyone." She was not going to tell the woman about Lineberry referring to her as Amanda, *twice*.

"Is he able to have any visitors?"

"He's in protective custody right now because of what happened, but you should check with Detective Wallis. He might have more information."

Graham thanked her and left.

"She's got it bad for him," said Blum.

"Yes, she does. But he's handsome, insanely rich, and nice. I would imagine lots of women would like to be part of his world."

"It is an attractive package," noted Blum.

Pine thought about her time with Lineberry the night before. How he had looked at her. "Maybe Graham has a shot. Because he does seem to like them younger."

Blum was about to respond when Pine's phone buzzed.

"Hello?" she said.

It was Don Bigelow from the business office at the Mercedes-Benz dealership.

"Agent Pine, I just found something that might be helpful to you," he said.

"What's that?" Pine said, sitting up straighter in anticipation.

"I ran that name, Jack Lineberry, through some other files and I got a hit."

"You got a hit? So Lineberry *did* buy something from the dealership?"

"No, not him. Another guy who bought an AMG S63. Sweet car. Fully loaded, it can run you over two hundred grand. Now, that's no Pagani, but still a nice ride."

"What does that have to do with Lineberry?"

"Well, the guy paid cash for the ride, but we still collect information from the customer for sending them stuff and warranty applications and the like. He listed his employer as Jackson Lineberry and Associates. Figure that might be the same Jack Lineberry you were asking me about earlier."

"It is. So what's the name of the guy who bought the AMG?"

Pine thought she knew: Jerry Danvers. But Bigelow's answer was about to stun her.

"His name is Myron Pringle."

65

"Myron Pringle, really?"

Eddie Laredo was sitting in the front passenger seat of Pine's rental.

"That's what the guy from the dealership said."

"How much does Lineberry pay this guy that he can afford a two-hundred-thousand-dollar car?"

"Well, he said he sold an algorithm at some point for a six-figure payday. Maybe that was how."

"But still. I'd like to know how much this guy makes."

"I'm trying to find that out. I can't ask Jack for obvious reasons. But I've put in a call to his firm."

"So what's our plan?"

"We go out there and talk to him. But we don't spook him."

"It's not illegal to buy a car."

"He has a connection to a dealership where Frankie Gomez was."

"You think he's our killer?"

"He's a little taller than Cy Tanner, but he could

probably pass for him with a disguise on, at least to someone who didn't really know Tanner."

"And his motive?"

"That's why we investigate."

She punched the gas and they sped off.

Along the way her phone rang. She answered it and listened for a few moments. "I really appreciate that, thanks."

She clicked off and looked at Laredo. "That was someone with Lineberry's firm. It's fortunate that Jack apparently had told some folks there about me. I didn't ask for Myron's salary, but I did ask if he made enough to pay cash for a two-hundred-thousand-dollar car."

"And?"

"And he can."

"Damn. I'm in the wrong line of work."

"You just figured that out now? I thought you were a fast learner."

They reached the Pringles' house and Pine slowed her truck. When they passed the curve and saw the house ahead, Laredo said, "Wow, I'm really in the wrong business."

"You should see Jack Lineberry's place. It would make this look like a guesthouse."

"Right, kick me when I'm down."

No one answered their rings or knocks.

"Nobody here?" said Laredo, looking up at the front of the house.

"Let's try around back. There's a big garage. We might be able to see if there are any cars in there."

They walked around the left side of the house and reached a courtyard, where there was a six-car garage with large wooden doors, but there were glass windows set in the wood about eight feet off the ground.

"Give me a hand up," said Pine.

Laredo made a stirrup with his hands and boosted Pine up so she could see in one of the windows.

"Holy shit!"

Her hip bumped against his head in her agitation.

"What? Do you see the Mercedes?"

He let her back down and eyeballed her.

"What? Talk to me."

"I can't be sure, but I think I just found the Pagani."

"What?"

She made a stirrup with her hands. "Take a look."

"You sure you can lift—"

She cut him off with an incredulous look.

"Oh, never mind," he said.

She easily boosted him up and he peered through the glass.

"That's a Pagani all right," he said.

She lowered him down to the ground and they both studied the garage.

"What do you think?" said Laredo.

"I think I want to get into that garage, and the house."

"We don't have a search warrant."

"Probable cause?"

"Of what?" he retorted.

They turned when they heard the car approaching. It was the Mercedes AMG. Britta Pringle rolled her window down. "Agent Pine? I thought I recognized the truck out front. What's going on?"

"Is Myron home?"

"No, he's traveling."

"Traveling? Where?"

"On business. He doesn't tell me much, I'm afraid."

"Did you hear about Jack Lineberry?"

"No, what?"

"He was shot last night."

"Oh, dear God." Britta looked like she might faint. "Is he . . . ?"

"He's alive and it looks like he'll make it."

Britta started taking deep breaths. "How? Who? Was it at his house? But he has security people."

"It was while he was driving. I was with him."

"Are you hurt?"

"Just a scratch. When will Myron be back?"

"I'm not sure. He didn't say."

"Is that his Pagani in the garage?" asked Laredo. "We had a peek in the window."

Britta looked suitably disgusted. "Can you imagine paying that much for a car? I feel guilty enough driving around in this one. We just bought it last year and Myron is already talking about trading it in. But where is Jack?"

"He's at the hospital over in Americus."

"Did they catch whoever did this?"

"The police are working on it. Um, can we go into the house?"

"Certainly, let me park the car."

"And I'd like to take a look at the Pagani," added Laredo. "I'm a car guy."

"Okay," said Britta, looking a bit confused.

She opened the garage door and drove in. They walked in behind her and Laredo immediately headed to the Pagani.

"Wow," he exclaimed. "This is a Pagani BC," he said, kneeling down behind the car. "Named after this guy, Benny Caiola."

Pine joined him. "Why does he get that distinction?"

"He's a big-time car collector and good friend of Horacio Pagani, who builds these suckers. It's a V-12 with about 800 horsepower, seven-speed transmission, and weighs under three thousand pounds because it's built mainly out of carbon fiber."

"You really do know your cars."

"Had the disease since I was a kid. I go to the car auctions just to gawk, since I can't afford to buy anything."

"Well, Cy Tanner was remarkably accurate in his description. This does look like the Batmobile."

"Cy Tanner?"

They turned to see Britta approaching them with a shopping bag in hand.

"Yeah, he lives in my old house. He saw the Pagani outside his house early one morning."

"No, he couldn't have."

"Why not?" asked Pine.

"Well, Myron is the only one who drives it, and he almost never does. And if he did take it out, why would he drive it over to your old house?"

"Well, that's one question I want to ask him. And here's one for you. I understand this car retails for about three million. Now, I'm sure that Jack pays Myron well, but I'm not even sure he would lay out three million for a car."

"Well, Myron has always been very clever, especially about making money."

"He told me about gambling and having his systems in Vegas."

"Yes, that was years ago, but he would go out there and come back with very large sums, until they told him not to come back anymore."

"And now, any other sources of income outside of his job?" asked Laredo.

"Not that I know of."

"Do you mind if we have a look at his office?"

"I can't."

"Why not?"

"I have no way to get in."

"You mean, he's the only one set up on the retinal

scanner?" said Pine, drawing a sharp glance from Laredo.

"Yes. I mean, I never had any reason to go in there. I'm not technologically savvy. I have a hard enough time making the TV work."

"What about his little study? He showed me into that before. And there was no security on it."

"Why do you want to look in there?" she said, her features showing suspicion.

"I like to be thorough."

"I'm not sure, Lee. I mean, it's Myron's space. I don't think I have any right—"

Pine interjected. "It's important, Britta. Otherwise, I wouldn't be asking. It might be that something has happened to Myron."

Britta paled and put a hand to her throat. "What? Myron might be in trouble?"

"I don't know for certain. But I might discover something in there that could help me find him. And he might need that help."

Britta looked uncertain for a moment but then nodded her head. "All right."

They headed into the house.

66

Britta led them up to her husband's study and left them there.

The pair stood in the middle of the room and looked around.

"What exactly are we looking for?" asked Laredo.

"Know it when I see it. I hope," she added.

She walked around the room while Laredo looked at the computer on the desk.

"So this guy is some sort of tech genius?" he said, sitting down in front of the desktop and hitting some keys.

"Apparently so."

"Any idea what his password is?"

"Not a—"

Pine stopped pacing and strode over to stand behind him.

"What?" he asked.

"Try . . . one, three, five, seven, nine, nine, seven, five, three, one."

"Where'd you pull that out of?"

"Sometimes geniuses think they're too smart to make mistakes."

He typed it in. "Well, it didn't work, *genius*. Got another one?"

Thinking quickly, she said, "Try what I just said, but instead of the one at the end, put in a zero."

Laredo did as she said and the screen opened up.

"Whoa, how'd you manage that."

"Something Myron told me. He likes odd numbers, up to a point. Get it?"

"A point that's represented by the number zero?"

"Exactly."

Laredo hit some keys and scrolled through some screens. "I'm looking at his search history. Take a gander at some of the stuff he's been streaming."

A number of titles with provocative pictures filled the screen.

"It's all porn," said Pine.

"What was your first clue: *A Few Thick Men*, *Good and Horny*, or *Teacher's Wet Dreams*?"

"So Myron is a porn addict."

"A lot of guys are." When she gave him a funny look, he added quickly, "Present company definitely excluded."

Pine looked over at a cabinet set into one wall. She walked over and tried to open it.

"Locked."

"Well, the owner of the house gave us access, so . . ."

Pine took out her Swiss knife, drew out a blade, and pushed back the lock bolt.

"Well, look what we have here."

She stepped back so Laredo could see the exposed shelves bulging with DVDs.

She started pulling some out. "Porn, porn, porn." She looked on the back of the boxes. "Hold on."

"What?"

She started pulling more boxes out. "These all say Stardust Productions."

"Okay, so?"

"Stardust is the name of a software program that Myron had patented. He named it that because he would go to the Stardust Casino in Vegas and gamble." She looked up at him. "And speaking of gambling, what do you want to bet that Stardust Productions was the money behind the films that Rebane, Clemmons, and Gillespie acted in?"

"But I don't remember that name coming up when we were digging into it."

"There was a *shell* company that we couldn't penetrate to find out what was behind it. Why do I think we just did?"

"So are you telling me that Myron Pringle is the money source behind the porn films?"

"I'm thinking he is, yeah."

"Damn."

"And maybe it's more lucrative than we thought."

"What do you mean?"

"The guy has a Pagani in his garage."

Laredo looked dumbstruck. "There's *that* much money in porn?"

"They were paying Hanna Rebane and Beth Clemmons big bucks. Why do I think their boss was making a helluva lot more than that? And they were only two actresses working for him. He probably had dozens."

"Hold on, then what's your theory? That he was killing his own actors?"

"Frankie Gomez sure as hell wasn't one of his actors," replied Pine.

"That's true, but Rebane, Clemmons, and Gillespie were."

"And you think Clemmons was probably killed not because she was a porn actress but because she could tell us something about the connection between Rebane and Gillespie. But why kill Rebane and Gillespie?"

"Well, the most obvious answer is that Rebane and Gillespie had some sort of dirt on Myron and were threatening him with it."

"So are you saying he killed them and dressed them up for some reason? And grabbed Frankie and did the same?"

"He might have done it to make it look like a serial killer was at work to throw us off," replied Pine. "And he has the connection to that dealership. He could have met or at least seen Frankie there."

"Come on, that's pretty damn warped," said Laredo doubtfully.

"The guy's a genius. He doesn't think like the rest of us. And if that's not the reason, then the truth has to be just as off the wall."

"Well, that's for sure."

"So the big question is, where is Myron? Is he off on a trip killing someone else? Is he down in South Florida overseeing his porn empire?"

"Do you think his wife knows about the porn thing?"

"She doesn't strike me as the type to be into that. And maybe he was being blackmailed with it. Pay us or we tell your wife the whole story."

"We've got to find this guy, fast."

Pine was looking absently at the ceiling.

"What?"

"Someone shot Jack Lineberry."

"Don't tell me that you believe Lineberry is into porn, too. I told you I checked him out. The guy doesn't have to sell porn. He makes plenty off his legit business."

"That's not what I was thinking."

"What then?" said Laredo in exasperation.

"What if I was the one who was supposed to get shot last night and not Jack?"

"You?"

"The person who shot at us knew our route. Knew our plans. We were coming back from Atlanta. Tyler

Straub, Jack's other security guy, told me that Jerry Danvers has an app on his phone that tracks his boss's movements."

"So he would have known where you were."

"And the shooter wasn't following us. He was waiting for us. I only heard the truck start up *after* he had shot at us."

"But why would Danvers want to kill you?"

"One, he's an asshole who doesn't like me. Two, maybe he has this weird thing about his boss. Anyone who gets too close? And he was in the uniformed division of the Secret Service but couldn't make the cut to become a Secret Service agent."

"So you think he's got a chip on his shoulder?"

"Maybe. But could he also be working with Myron and they wanted to get rid of me because I was asking too many questions."

"Now, that's a leap of logic with lots of gaps to fill."

"I know, Eddie," barked Pine. "I'm just thinking out loud."

They went back downstairs and found Britta in the kitchen.

"Did you find what you were looking for?" she asked, rising from her chair. "Did you find something to help Myron?"

"Maybe," said Pine.

"I want you to tell me what's going on, Lee."

"I would, if I could. But I don't really have a lot of answers."

"I can't even call Myron," said Britta, in evident distress. "He doesn't even have a phone!" She looked like she might start crying.

Pine hesitated. She was torn between going full-bore after Myron before he possibly struck again and asking Britta a question that was burning a hole in her gut. Finally, the latter won out.

"Britta, can I ask you something?"

"What?" said Britta cautiously.

"The night my sister disappeared."

"Yes?" Britta looked surprised at this abrupt change in subject.

"My parents were at your house, weren't they?"

Britta looked down at her feet. "I . . ."

Pine walked over to her. "You see, I thought about it and things didn't add up, on both ends. Our bed-time routine was off. Your recollection was shaky. Myron admitted having friends over that night but couldn't remember who they were."

Britta looked up at her, eyes filled with tears. "They never imagined anything like that would happen, Lee. Never in a million years. None of us did."

"They left us alone, two little kids."

Britta looked down. "When she woke up, she rushed out of the house. She ran all the way there to check on you both. And . . . when she got there . . ."

"She found Mercy gone and me nearly dead. So much for never imagining."

Britta looked up, her eyes were dry now, her features set hard. This surprised Pine.

"Your mother loved you. She loved you both. That's what mothers do, you know, they love their children. They try their best to protect them."

"Well, she failed," said Pine bluntly. "And she had warning beforehand."

Now Britta looked confused. "What do you mean? Nothing like that had ever happened here before."

"Well, we didn't always live here, did we?" replied Pine. Changing the subject quickly again, she said, "Please have Myron contact us as soon as you hear from him. And if you find out where he is, please let us know."

"But you said he might be in trouble."

"I don't know for sure. I'm just trying to get to the truth." She paused. "Who brought the used joints and empty beer bottles to our house?"

Britta looked at her blankly. "Someone had to, to make it look like my parents were there that night. Otherwise the story wouldn't hold."

Britta said in a hollow tone, "That was Myron's idea. He was afraid he might get into trouble. I don't believe your parents even noticed."

As a disgusted Pine was about to walk out, Laredo turned to Britta. "Does your husband have any hobbies?"

Pine stopped and turned back around, awaiting the woman's answer.

"He likes cars, but you saw that. Spends way too much on them, in my opinion. But it's his money."

"Was he into movies?" asked Pine.

"Movies? No, not really."

"Does he travel to South Florida?" asked Laredo.

"South Florida? I . . . Not that he's mentioned."

"Is that where he might be now?"

"He didn't say anything about taking a flight."

"But did he take an overnight bag with him?"

"He might have. I wasn't up when he left."

"But you heard him leave?"

"We . . . sleep in separate bedrooms." She added quickly, "As you know, he's a night owl, and I like to go to bed early."

"And what car was he driving? Obviously not the Pagani."

Britta looked confused. "I'm not sure. I . . . I didn't see any other cars missing from the garage." Britta put a hand on Pine's arm. "What is going on here?"

"I wish I knew."

67

As they were driving back to town, they got hung up in traffic heading into Andersonville. There were RVs and pickups and cars and SUVs and even a Hummer with the faces of the Confederate leaders depicted on Stone Mountain painted on one side.

"What the hell's going on?" said Laredo. "I never expected a rush hour in Andersonville."

"The Civil War reenactment is coming up tomorrow," replied Pine. "The 'armies' are marching in."

"Didn't know it was that big a deal."

"You're in the South now. The Civil War will always be a big deal. And it gives overgrown boys an excuse to play soldier."

"Okay."

"There'll be a parade on the main street, and then mock battles on Saturday and Sunday afternoon on the Civil War Village grounds."

When they got back to the Cottage they found Blum in the breakfast area tapping keys on her laptop. She looked up and said, "And what did you find with Myron Pringle?"

They sat down and took turns filling her in.

"Never took him for a porn producer," said a visibly surprised Blum.

"I doubt Britta knew, but she did confirm that my parents were at their house the night Mercy was kidnapped. My mom woke up the next morning and ran back to the house."

"I'm sure that was quite a shock for her," noted Blum.

"Well, she brought it on herself."

"That's a little cold," said Laredo, shooting her a glance.

Pine shot him a glance right back. "No, what's cold is that she never owned up to it. All those years she could have told me the truth and she didn't. And they lied to the police, too. They obstructed the investigation. They messed with the crime scene. The police always assumed the guy came from outside because my parents were downstairs. Only they weren't."

Blum said quietly, "I'm sure your mother never imagined anything would happen to you."

"Yeah, that's what Britta said. She defended her, too."

"I'm sure that Britta feels incredible guilt for what happened to her children. There was apparently not much she could have done, but a mother always feels that guilt when something happens to her kids. The second guessing, the what-ifs. It can consume you."

Pine looked at Blum, her expression becoming

contrite. "I didn't even think about Britta's situation while I was talking to her."

"Well, you were focused on your situation. Most of us do that."

Pine said, "I wonder if they were at the Pringles' just to party, or whether there was another reason."

"Well, both couples had young children. Maybe they visited back and forth after the kids were asleep. And that night it was just when they went to the Pringles'."

"Nice, thoughtless routine," said Pine bitterly because she was feeling bitter. "Go party and leave your kids home alone."

"They probably thought Andersonville was the least likely place for something like that to happen," said Laredo.

"It was just . . . a disaster from A to Z," snapped Pine.

"But do you really think it was a coincidence?" asked Blum suddenly.

"What?"

"That the night your parents decide to party at a neighbor's house after putting their girls to bed, someone just happens to come to your house, nearly kills you, and takes Mercy?"

Pine let out a long, tortured breath. "He could've been watching the house."

"I believe he was definitely watching the house."

Blum sounded so certain that Pine looked at her

funny and glanced at the open laptop. "What did you find out?"

Blum slid her computer around. "After we spoke earlier, I started doing some digging into the mob world in New York in the eighties. See this guy here?"

They both bent down to study the picture of a tough-looking man in a dark suit. He was on the steps of a federal courthouse in New York City.

"Who is he?" asked Laredo.

"Bruno Vincenzo."

"Bruno Vincenzo? How does he figure into the equation?"

Laredo scrolled down to some writing beneath the photo. "Vincenzo was a big-time foot soldier for the Castellano crime family. He was convicted, ratted some people out, went to prison, and within two months got a shiv in his carotid for his betrayal. He bled out before they could get him help."

Pine looked up at Blum blankly. "Am I being obtuse, or are you?"

"Barry Vincent? Bruno Vincenzo? You don't see the similarities?"

Pine scanned some of the article. "I do, but Vincent couldn't be Vincenzo. This says he died in prison in 1987. What happened to Mercy and me took place two years later."

"But Bruno had a younger brother, Ito. I found a picture of him too."

She went to another screen on her laptop.

"The brothers don't look alike," said Pine.

"Well, here's a likeness you'll find interesting."

She opened an email. "I know you had asked Max Wallis to look into Barry Vincent. When I found what I did about the Vincenzo brothers I called him to talk. He had pulled the DMV records and gotten a hit on Barry Vincent. He sent me what he found. It's a photocopy of a driver's license issued by the state of Georgia back in early 1989. This is Barry Vincent. The guy who had a fight with your dad. Look familiar?"

Pine took the photocopy and compared it to the photo of Ito Vincenzo.

"Oh my God. Ito Vincenzo is Barry Vincent." She looked up at Laredo. "Why in the hell did no one see this before?"

"Don't look at me. I was in third grade."

Blum said, "Ito was enough of a degree of separation, I guess. And he wasn't here long. And he so kept to himself that almost no one remembered him, other than Myron Pringle."

"He came down here all those years ago to avenge his brother," said Pine.

Blum nodded. "Apparently so."

"But how did he find them? How did he even know my mother was involved in all of it? Lineberry told me that she never testified. She just acted as an undercover agent and wore a wire."

"What?" exclaimed Laredo.

"I forgot. I didn't fill you in on my conversation with Jack Lineberry."

She spent the next few minutes doing just that.

"I doubt there's any way for us to find out for sure that he discovered your parents were here. Unless we can find this Ito guy and ask him, and then he has to tell us the truth."

"But why not just kill us? The mob had apparently tried to do that before."

Blum said, "Maybe Ito Vincenzo didn't have it in him to kill. I couldn't find anything that showed he had mob connections. I think he did what he did for his brother. He obviously blamed your mother for what happened to Bruno."

"What happened to Bruno falls squarely on Bruno," said Pine sharply. "But if his brother didn't intend to kill me, just knock me out, maybe . . . maybe he didn't have it in him to hurt Mercy."

"That's possible," said Blum. "But we can't know for sure."

"You can have hopes, Atlee," said Laredo. "But don't get them up too high."

"Because it's a long way down. Yeah, I know. I've been there."

Blum said, "We need to find Ito Vincenzo. I can start searching databases and making phone calls and sending emails."

"I can work on that too," volunteered Laredo, but Pine put her hand up.

"You're on the clock, Eddie. I'm not letting you get in trouble on my account. So, let's let Carol do her thing while we run some things down based on what we learned today."

"Namely, where the hell is Myron Pringle," said Laredo.

But Pine didn't hear him. Since it now seemed clear that Barry Vincent/Ito Vincenzo had taken Mercy and nearly killed her, the man's words, as recounted by Myron Pringle, came back to her.

He said my dad had killed one daughter and nearly killed the other. So had he killed Mercy?

Pine just sat there, her whole body feeling numb.

68

Pine awoke the next morning after a mostly sleepless night. She had just finished showering when her phone buzzed.

It was the ME with an answer to one of her questions.

She sat on her bed and quickly read through the brief but detailed email.

The damage to the St. Christopher's medal had been caused, in the ME's opinion, by a gunshot. She had found powder burns and the partial indentation of what looked to be a shotgun pellet. And she had, on a hunch, hit the medal with luminol, which would show blood traces. And she had found them. And they didn't match Freddie Gomez's blood type.

She could make no sense of that.

Pine called the hospital to check on Jack Lineberry. His condition hadn't changed, which she was told was a good thing. They expected him to grow stronger each day.

She put her phone away, got dressed, and contemplated what to do next.

They had to find Myron, and fast. She was fearful that he had sensed trouble coming his way and had maybe gone on the run. With his money he could already be in another country courtesy of a private jet. But the last time she had spoken to him, the man had not seemed nervous or threatened. If anything, he had seemed concerned about *Pine* and all the information she was finding out about her family, in particular her mother.

So maybe his going away had nothing to do with his feeling the walls were closing in on him. But if he was their killer, he might be out there right now planning his next crime.

She wandered to the window and looked out on the main street. She could see men in Civil War uniforms moving up and down the pavement. Some carried muskets, others had rolled-up sleeping bags, and still others sported what looked to be unfurled battle flags. People were gathering along the sides of the street. The parade was to take place that morning.

She had read that many reenactors were fastidious about their uniforms and equipment, even down to the details of their uniforms' buttons and materials. She had never gotten the appeal of refighting these battles, but if it brought in much-needed tourist dollars, there was nothing wrong with that. Towns needed to do what they had to in order to survive.

And so do people.

She lay back on her bed and looked up at the ceiling.

All those years that her mother knew the truth. Even if Julia or Amanda, or whatever the hell her real name was, didn't know who Barry Vincent was or why he was there, she well knew of her own past. She knew they were all targets. Apparently not even the U.S. Marshal's Service could protect them. And yet she had gone off to party with a neighbor and left her young daughters defenseless all night.

Pine suddenly sat straight up as though someone had hit her with a cattle prod. She'd had no revelation or epiphany; she was just angry. Furious, white-hot, beyond anything she had felt before. And it was all directed at her mother.

Slowly, far too slowly for her personal comfort, Pine calmed. Still, she felt weak, and sick. She snatched a complimentary bottle of spring water off the nightstand and drank it down so fast, some of it missed her mouth and dribbled down her front. She wiped the droplets off her with her hand and set the bottle down.

Get a grip. This is not productive. You're no longer a helpless little girl. You're an FBI agent—start acting like it.

Her phone buzzed. She didn't recognize the number but answered anyway.

"Agent Pine?" It was a man. The voice was familiar, but in her current frame of mind, she couldn't place it.

"Who is this?"

"Tyler Straub. I work for Mr. Lineberry. We talked before?"

"He's not—"

"No, he's fine. He's awake now and the doctors are in there checking him out."

"So why are you calling?"

"You told me to give you a ring if anything seemed off."

"And something does?"

"Well, I can't find Jerry."

"What do you mean? He was at the hospital yesterday. I didn't think he ever left."

"Operative word being *was*. No one's seen him for a while."

"You checked Jack's place?"

"Checked everywhere I could think of."

"When was the last time you saw him?"

"Not that long after you left. The thing is, I've been on duty all this time and I'd like to get some relief. But I have no one to hand off to."

"The cops are guarding Jack's room, too."

"Yeah, but the guy is my responsibility. He pays my salary. So . . ."

"Maybe Jerry's gone back to the house for some reason."

"Maybe. But I can't reach him. And I can't leave here to check."

"I'll go over there and see what I can find out."

"That would be great. Just let me know as soon as

you find out anything. His cottage is the blue one. It's about three hundred yards directly behind the main house and right next to mine."

Pine clicked off and hustled down to her SUV.

She drove straight out of Andersonville and headed north.

Then she stopped when she got to the scene of the shooting.

There was police tape up at various spots around the area. The Aston Martin was still there, though it was cordoned off with more police tape wound around orange cones. Two forensic techs were going over the car, and there was a county cop standing guard next to his cruiser.

She parked and got out of her SUV, flashing her FBI creds and badge at the trooper on duty.

"I'm working the case with Detective Wallis from GBI," she noted.

He nodded at her before leaning back against his vehicle.

She walked under the police tape to where the techs were working on the car.

"Anything?" she said.

"Pulled a round from out of the dashboard," said one, a young woman.

"What was the type?"

"Five point five six."

"That's a NATO round," said Pine. "Very reliable

killing at long distance." Lineberry was even luckier than she had thought.

"Lot of blood, too," said the other tech, a man in his forties.

"Yes, there was," replied Pine.

"Is the guy okay?" said the woman.

"He'll make it."

She got back into her SUV and drove on, coming to the spot where the shot-up truck was being hoisted onto a flatbed wrecker service. After she showed her creds to the cop stationed there, he told her the truck was being taken back to a police facility to be thoroughly checked for trace including more blood, DNA, and prints.

She eyed the bullet holes in the windshield, in the grille, and the shredded tire.

The cop noted this and said, "Whoever did all that was a damn good shot."

"Thanks."

The startled deputy said nothing but looked at her suspiciously.

Pine drove on, arriving at Lineberry's about an hour later. The massive estate was unsettlingly quiet. Lineberry was not here, of course. Tyler Straub was at the hospital. Jerry Danvers was the wild card.

The gate was closed, and no one answered her call on the video screen. She drove past the main house and to the rear of the property. This was all fenced in as well, but she managed to clamber over a section of wall and dropped inside the grounds. She stood and looked around. There was a lot of land back here, outbuildings, impeccable landscaping, hardscapes, formal and informal gardens. Lineberry had spared no expense in making his home an exceptional place.

She walked along a pea-gravel path and was surprised not to encounter anyone. She assumed that Lineberry employed people to take care of the grounds, too, and there was the house staff as well. But she was all alone right now.

That did not make her feel any better.

She saw the twin cottages, one blue and one green.

Straub had been right. They weren't your typical "cottage." They looked to be about thirty-five hundred square feet each.

She walked around the blue cottage and looked in the windows. They all had shades pulled down, so that was terrifically unhelpful. She knocked on the door, no answer. She knocked again and heard nothing from inside.

She went around to the back, put her elbow through a pane of glass in the back door, reached through, undid the lock, and opened the door. She expected to perhaps hear the beep of an alarm system about to start shrieking, but there was only silence.

She closed the door behind her and looked around. This was obviously the kitchen. It was scrupulously neat and clean, with everything stacked and placed just so. In addition to maybe being a serial killer, Danvers could possibly be OCD, she thought.

She cleared the rooms downstairs and then headed up the steps to the second floor.

There were three bedrooms up here, and the last one was set up as a home office.

The bedrooms held nothing of interest.

The office was different. In a file cabinet there was a treasure trove. An old Stetson hat, and a stringy white wig. And even more incriminating, photos of Frankie Gomez, Hanna Rebane, Beth Clemmons, and Layne Gillespie.

Pine sat down at the wooden desk set against one wall and stared down at the pictures of the dead people.

She ran her gaze around the room wondering if she was looking at the living quarters of a serial killer who had killed at least four people and perhaps more.

Her gaze found and held on the edge of a wire that was snaking under the bed. It was almost invisible, but the light was coming in at just the right angle to reveal it. She bent down to look at where it was going. She saw the red light.

The next moment she leapt up, pulled the mattress off the bed, ran for the bathroom while dragging the mattress behind her, slammed the door, and threw herself into the bathtub with the mattress covering her.

An instant later the bomb she had seen under the bed detonated.

69

"Lee, Lee, come in here right now. Get off that tree. You'll fall and hurt yourself."

"Momma, don't be mad at her. She's just being Lee. She likes to climb things. She'll figure out how to get down."

Pine looked first at her mother and then her sister. Both stood on the saggy porch of their house. Julia Pine looked mad at her tomboy daughter, while Mercy Pine looked pleased that her sister was, well, just being herself.

That was the way it had always been with them: Lee doing what she loved and often getting into trouble because of it, and her sister defending her to the last.

The swirls of mist in front of her eyes deepened as the two most important people in her life vanished.

The next moment Pine sat up, a rush of air coming out of her compressed chest with such force that she thought she had also expelled both her lungs in the process. It was like she had just surfaced from a long dive. She pushed the mattress off her and coughed and spit up vile things from her mouth. The bathroom was in shambles, the mattress covered with debris.

But I'm still alive.

Yet she could smell smoke and the fire that was causing it, so she wasn't out of the woods yet. She rolled out of the bathtub and rose on unsteady legs, her ears still ringing with the sound of the explosion. The bathroom door had been blown off its hinges and all she could see outside was a wall of fire.

She turned to the only escape route she had: a single window over the tub. She didn't have to break the glass because it had already been shattered by the explosion. She cleaned out the remaining shards using a towel, climbed through the opening and out onto the roof.

She slid down to the end of the shingles, swung her legs over the side while holding on to the edge of the gutter, and hung there for a few moments while looking down and judging the distance she was going to fall.

She let go, hit the dirt, rolled, and came up running.

The fire must have hit a gas line somewhere in the house because the next thing she knew there was a second, far larger explosion, and a concussive wave hit her from behind and propelled her through the air for a good ten feet. She tumbled another dozen feet before coming to a stop, breathing hard and groaning from the punishment she had just endured.

She slowly stood, holding her lower back, her left arm dangling uselessly because it had been popped out of joint.

Son of a bitch.

This had happened to her once before, at a weight-lifting competition gone horribly wrong when one of the collars on a barbell load with weight plates she'd been attempting to lift failed. The weights had tumbled off one side, and she was thrown in the direction of the unbalanced weight on the other side. She had slammed into the floor and her shoulder had been wrenched out of place. And she had had it popped back into place by a doctor in attendance. It was the most searing pain she had ever felt. But it had been only for a second. What she was feeling right now was nearly as bad and would not be going away anytime soon unless she did what she knew she had to do, because the doctor had showed her how, just in case it ever happened to her again.

Pine found a tree, placed her shoulder against it at a precise angle, closed her eyes, took three rapid breaths, and pushed the injured side of her body hard into the solid wood.

She screamed in pain. And fury.

And then it was over. The relief was immediate, though she was still sore. She shook out her arm, turned, and looked back at what had been Jerry Danvers's "little" cottage. There was barely anything left. She used her phone to call the police and fire department and then turned to look at the main house. No one had come rushing out at the sounds of the explosions, and she wondered where the hell the staff was.

She hobbled slowly back to her truck. She couldn't clamber over the wall as yet. She was still too banged up to manage it. But she was able to open the front gate from the inside.

She got into her truck and sat there for a few moments, trying to take everything in.

Her mind kept going back to the vision of her mother and sister, watching her climbing a tree.

"Momma, don't be mad at her. She's just being Lee. She likes to climb things. She'll figure out how to get down."

That's what I'm good at: figuring things out.

Her sister had always believed in her. Pine hoped she was up to the praise.

She called Tyler Straub and told him what had happened.

"Jesus, are you okay?" he exclaimed.

"Barely. Where is Jerry?"

"He wasn't out there?"

"No."

"Then I have no idea. The guy's gone AWOL."

Pine clicked off. Going against all standard FBI protocols, she decided not to wait for the fire truck, but she left the gate open for the emergency vehicles.

As she drove back toward Andersonville, she drew

several long breaths and willed herself to calm down and to think.

Lee will figure it out, Momma, she always does.

She decided to get back to basics to "figure it out."

They had one definitive connection: Myron Pringle and the dead porn stars.

They had another somewhat attenuated connection: Myron Pringle and Frankie Gomez through the Mercedes-Benz car dealership.

She pulled off the road and scrolled through her recent calls. She found the one she wanted and made the call.

"Don Bigelow," said the voice.

"Don, it's Agent Pine with the FBI."

"Hey, Agent Pine. I hope you found whoever hurt that kid."

"We're getting closer. Look, I know that Myron Pringle bought the AMG from you last year, but has he brought it in for service this year, within the last six months or so? It's really important."

"Let me check with that department. Just hold on."

She heard good, old-fashioned Muzak for about a minute before he came back on.

"The car *was* brought in a month ago." He told her the date.

"Okay, now my next question is, was it on one of the days that Frankie Gomez was at the dealership?"

"Hang on again, I'll have to check with Roger

Duncan. I don't know off the top of my head, but he probably would."

"Why don't you just transfer me to him, so you don't have to play intermediary?"

"Oh, good idea. Hold on."

About thirty seconds later Roger Duncan came on the line.

"Don said you were asking when Frankie was here?"

"Yes? Do you remember?"

"It was two different times. I remember because those were the only two Saturdays I worked in the last couple months." He told her the dates. The more recent one coincided with the date of service for Pringle's Mercedes.

"That's great, Roger, I really appreciate it."

"What does this have to do with Frankie?"

"I'm trying to get a connection between him and a guy who had an AMG serviced that day."

"An AMG S63?"

"Yes, you remember it."

"We don't sell many AMGs here. They're pretty expensive. It's basically the same model and wheelbase as the S560, but with a lot more power and torque under the hood."

"Do you remember the man, Myron Pringle? In his fifties, really tall?"

"No, I don't remember anyone like that. But she

was really nice to Frankie. Even bought him a candy bar from the vending machine."

"'She'?"

"The lady who brought the car in. She saw Frankie and asked about him. I told her about us taking him in. She was nice to him, bought him the candy bar and all, like I said."

"Wait a minute, you're telling me a *woman* and not a man brought in the S63 for service?"

"Yeah."

The image of Lauren Graham flashed through her mind. "Describe her."

When he was done, Pine thanked him and pulled back onto the road and sped off to a new destination.

It wasn't Lauren Graham. The description he had given her fit Britta Pringle exactly.

70

On the way Pine phoned Laredo and told him what she had learned and also about being nearly blown up.

"I didn't wait for the first responders. I know that's not how we do things, but there was no way around it."

"I think you did the right thing," replied Laredo. He promised to meet her at the Pringles' and also to loop in Wallis.

She drove fast down the tree-shrouded lane and soon reached the fantastically modern house. She stopped, got out, and surveyed the property, her mind going a mile a minute.

Britta had taken the car in. Britta had met Frankie Gomez and even bought him a candy bar. Why would she have done that? Were both Myron and Britta involved in this? Or was it just her? If so, where the hell was Myron? She was about to head up to the front door but then changed her mind.

She went around back and stared, not at the rear of the main house, but at Britta's Cape Cod. She looked around but neither saw nor heard anyone about.

She pulled her gun, skirted by the side of the pool, hustled up the steps to the Cape Cod, and peered through the window into the room overlooking the pool.

She tried the door adjacent to the window and it opened. She moved through and closed it behind her. The only illumination was from the sun coming through the glass.

She swiftly made a search of the house. It was decorated beautifully and looked totally unlived in, which surprised her. This supposedly was Britta's thinking place. She wondered where Britta really did her thinking.

On the top floor and in a room at the back of the house facing away from the pool, she found it. She knew that because it was the only door in the place that had been locked.

She shot the lock off with her Glock.

When Pine stepped into the room, she noted that all the shades were drawn, casting the room into near total darkness.

She found and turned on a light. It was a sterile environment. Plainly furnished, with not a trace of warmth in the place. And then she noticed the bureau. She opened it. Inside was what could only be described as a shrine to her dead children.

Along with numerous mementos from their childhood and lives as young adults, there were multiple pictures of Mary and Joey Pringle. Pine recognized them from the photos Britta had shown them earlier.

One showed them sitting next to the pool. Mary was wearing a bikini and Joey was shirtless and in jeans. Pine peered closer at Joey. She picked up the photo and took it over to the window, where she drew back the drapes to let the light in.

The next moment Pine confirmed what she thought she had seen.

Joey had a St. Christopher's medal around his neck.

He'd died by gunshot. An accident, Britta had said. The St. Christopher's medal found on Frankie Gomez had been damaged by a gunshot. Blood and remnants of a buckshot found there by the ME.

Now Pine was certain the medal had belonged to Joey. He'd been wearing it when he'd died from a gunshot wound, apparently a shotgun. Now the question was: Had it been an accident, as Britta had said? Or had he been murdered or committed suicide? And if so, why?

There was a TV housed in the cabinet. And in a drawer underneath the TV was a DVD. Written on the case in pen was "Dorothy and the Ruby Red Nipples."

She slipped it out of the case and put it in a DVD player that was attached to the TV.

She took up the remote and fast-forwarded through the credits and into the opening scenes. She hit the

Play button and the film slowed to normal speed. It took about three minutes before she saw her.

Mary Pringle stepped in front of the camera. She was dressed in the same sort of outfit that Judy Garland had worn in *The Wizard of Oz*, complete with ruby red slippers, although it was far more revealing than Garland's. The doorbell rang. She opened it and there were three men there dressed as the Scarecrow, the Tin Man, and the Cowardly Lion. Within two minutes, and after limited stilted dialogue, they had no clothes on and were going at it full-bore right there on the couch, three on one. Mary was groaning and moaning on cue, but Pine doubted the woman had really enjoyed a minute of it. The act looked painful and debasing.

Pine hit the Reverse button and went back to the opening credits. Dorothy was played by Desiree Debauchery, obviously Mary's stage name.

She turned the film off and put down the remote.

In the same drawer with the DVD was a faded news clipping from a paper in Florida.

She picked it up, unfolded it, and read the headline.

"Porn Actress Overdoses."

The news article was brief, but it did say that the person who had discovered the body was Joey Pringle.

And then Joey Pringle died from a gunshot wound shortly thereafter.

Suicide?

Pine took pictures of everything with her phone, including some of the film footage.

She was putting the things away when she heard it.

A splash.

She pocketed the DVD and news article, closed up the bureau, and hurried down the stairs. She walked quickly across the room and looked out the window facing the pool.

There was a red hand truck perched next to the pool. The surface of the water was rippling.

She pulled her pistol and stepped outside.

She looked around but saw no one. She slipped over to the side of the pool and looked down into its depths. As the water stopped moving and cleared, she saw something.

It was Myron Pringle staring back up at her. He was barechested and in his swim trunks. A yellow float was nudging one side of the pool.

Pine laid her gun down, took out her phone, the DVD, and the news article, and put them on a lounge chair, then dove into the water. She quickly reached the bottom, gripped Myron under the shoulders, and kicked off the bottom. She struggled to bring him to the surface, but finally managed to break the top of the water. She drew in a long breath before going under again. She kicked her feet and started moving to the side of the pool. She finally managed it and reached the steps. She tugged Myron up them and onto the side of the pool.

She checked his pulse and found none. His eyes were closed, his chest still.

She started performing CPR, pushing down on his chest, silently counting as she did so.

Come on, come on. Don't die on me.

She kept pounding away, willing his heart to start breathing and his lungs to fill with air and push out the water there.

Finally, with a long gasp and his body lurching upward, he started breathing again.

She turned him on his side and manipulated his diaphragm until he vomited up the water he'd swallowed. Pine laid him back down and checked his pulse. It was weak, but his heart was still beating. If the splash had been him going into the water, she thought she might have pulled him out in time to avoid any brain damage.

Now she had to get him to a hospital as fast as possible. She turned to reach for her phone.

And that was the last thing she remembered as the stunning blow landed against her head.

71

Pine slowly came to and looked around. She had a searing pain in her head and her wet clothes felt as if they weighed a thousand pounds.

She discovered she was back inside the Cape Cod.

Pine focused on the woman sitting across from her and pointing her own Glock at her.

Britta looked remarkably composed. Her hair was perfectly styled, and her cream slacks held not a single wrinkle. Her light blue blouse and white sweater over it were immaculate. She could have been heading out to a garden party or a lunch at a nice restaurant.

"Where's Myron?" said Pine.

"Back where he is supposed to be," she said calmly.

"In the pool?"

"Where he's supposed to be."

"Then he's dead?"

"I certainly hope so. A terrible accident. It happens when nonswimmers fall off their float when no one is around, especially when they've been drinking. When they test him at the autopsy, he will be found to have a very high blood alcohol level. You panic, your lungs fill with water, and it's over very quickly."

Pine looked at the woman somewhat in awe. This was a very different person from the seemingly frightened and out-of-her-depth wife that she and Laredo had recently interviewed.

"You really put on a show for us at your house," said Pine. "You had me convinced you knew nothing and were genuinely worried about Myron."

"I was worried, only not about Myron."

"You wanted us to find the porn videos," observed Pine.

When Britta didn't respond, she said, "Is this all about revenge? I saw the video of Mary. And your son's *accident* was really a suicide, right?"

Britta looked down at the gun in her hand as though she had just noticed it.

She started speaking slowly and quietly. "Can you imagine a man who had a daughter who got into porn because some bastards convinced her it would be wonderful, and these same bastards got her hooked on drugs, and then he decides that producing porn films is obviously so lucrative that he jumps into the business? And this after his only surviving child discovers his sister's body and blows his head off. Does that man even deserve to live? My answer to that was no."

Pine sat up a bit. Britta had not bothered to bind her. Pine hoped that might turn out to be a big mistake for Britta and a way out for her.

"I get your anger at Myron. But why the other murders?"

"I was a mother, Lee. I had two beautiful children. I thought I had a wonderful husband. A bit quirky, a bit less empathetic than I wanted, but a brilliant man who provided a wonderful life."

"Until you decided that wasn't a good enough trade-off?"

Britta leaned forward. "Until he started to make the same trash and work with the same people who killed my beautiful daughter and caused my son to take his own life."

"Frankie Gomez wasn't part of that world. He was just a kid."

Britta sat back, her lips pursed. She didn't answer right away. "As soon as I saw that boy, I knew what kind of life he would have. He was probably an illegal. He'd grow up in poverty and die before he was out of high school in some gang-related thing. I just saved him a world of trouble."

"And who gave you the right to decide that for him?"

"I'm not going to argue with you."

"And the veil and old tux and dressing Frankie up like that? Was that your doing or your accomplice's?"

"Accomplice?"

"There's no way you could have carried Layne Gillespie that far. And you weren't the one impersonating Cy Tanner when he was seen talking to Frankie."

"It's of no importance."

"So why did you pick the porn actors to kill?"

"Layne Gillespie met Mary at a bar. He apparently liked how she looked. He told her what he did for a living. How much money she could make. He targeted her and recruited her for this foulness." Britta's mouth curled in disgust.

"And Hanna Rebane?"

"She 'starred' in movies with my lovely, innocent daughter. They had sex together. And then they introduced her to the world of drugs. And my daughter became unrecognizable. They stole her from me."

"And Beth Clemmons?"

Britta waved this off. "Again, not important."

"How do you know all this?" asked Pine.

"My children died. So I made it my business to know," she said fiercely. In a quieter tone she added, "This has been very hard for me."

"It hasn't been nearly as hard for you as it was for the people who died."

"I thought you would be more sympathetic. You lost your sister."

Pine barked, "Don't you dare try to equate what happened to my sister with the murder spree you've engaged in. And if you'd told the police the truth back then maybe they would have been able to find my sister."

Britta rubbed her forehead. "Well, I can see I'll get no understanding from you."

Pine thought quickly. "You had a son and daughter. Only the 'son' has been killed. The daughter? Who is it?"

Britta said quietly, "Very soon it will all be over. The nightmare will finally be over."

Pine's voice shook slightly as she said, "It doesn't have to be this way, Britta. You can end this now."

"No, I can't. I have to finish it."

"Your beef was with Myron. You took care of him. He's done. So give me the gun and we'll call it a day. It's the right thing to do, you know it is."

"I loved my children so much. I wanted the best for them. And . . . and then just like that they were both gone. So I do have to finish this. For them."

"I know you're working with Jerry Danvers. Please call him and tell him not to kill anyone else. Please."

She shook her head. "There's so much you don't know."

Pine said in frustration, "Then tell me. Like what's your endgame? Do you walk away with a big life insurance payoff or whatever wealth Myron's built up?"

Britta's expression turned ugly. "I want nothing to do with his blood money." She looked down for a moment. "After this, I have nothing else to live for."

"And me?"

"I'm so sorry. I really am. I never thought I would see you again. I liked your parents very much. And you and Mercy were very sweet. You played with my children, you know. Maybe if things had been different, you four would have grown up together and everything would have turned out okay. But I guess it wasn't meant to be."

"Who's the fourth victim, Britta? Please tell me."

"There's nothing you can do about it."

"If you're going to kill me, the least you can do is tell me that."

"No, I'll take that to my grave."

"Do you really want it to end like this?"

"I'm afraid it has to."

"Atlee!"

The voice was coming from outside.

It was Eddie Laredo.

"Agent Pine!"

That was Detective Max Wallis.

Distracted by this, Britta glanced at the window.

That was the opportunity that Pine had been waiting for.

She pulled her Nano, but instead of firing it, she threw it at Britta.

The gun had gotten wet when she had dived into the pool. It probably would not have fired accurately because of that. She couldn't have risked finding out whether it would or not. But it worked just fine as a flying projectile because the gun hit Britta in the face; she cried out in pain.

Pine jumped over the back of the couch, landing at the same instant as Britta firing the Glock at her.

The rounds zipped through the couch and embedded in the wall behind Pine.

Pine slid along the back of the couch as she heard Laredo and Wallis shouting from outside and feet running their way.

When Pine reached the end of the couch, she gripped a lamp there and hurled it in Britta's direction.

When there was no response from Britta, Pine poked her head quickly over the top of the couch, scanning the room in front of her.

Britta wasn't there, but Pine's Glock was lying on the floor. She raced over and picked it up. Next, she ran to the door leading to the pool. She kicked it open and found herself face-to-face with Laredo and Wallis, whose guns were drawn.

"At—" began Laredo. She raced right past him and looked into the pool.

Myron was once more at the bottom and this time he wasn't coming back. He was clearly dead, his eyes open and still.

"Shit!" she screamed.

Laredo looked over her shoulder and saw the body. "Is that Pringle?"

She nodded. "I saved him once, but not twice."

"We heard a shot."

The next instant they heard a car start up. But it wasn't any ordinary car.

"That's the Pagani!" exclaimed Laredo.

"The what?" shouted Wallis.

Pine sprinted toward the garage area with Laredo right behind her and Wallis puffing along at the rear. They reached the courtyard fronting the garage area when the Pagani shot out of one of the bays and accelerated so fast, it seemed like a plane about to take off.

Pine changed direction and raced toward her SUV. She and Laredo reached it at the same time; she jumped into the driver's seat and he into the passenger seat. She fired up the engine and they roared after the Pagani while Wallis was still twenty yards behind.

"You're never going to catch her in this thing," warned Laredo.

"We'll see about that."

All they could see in front of them was a swirl of dust thrown up by the Pagani. It was like driving into a tornado.

"Hang on," said Pine.

She cut the wheel to the right, went off the road, tore between two huge oaks, punched the gas, ripped right through a hedge, and cut the wheel to the right.

The Pagani was twenty feet to the right of them, but they were almost even with it now instead of eating the car's dust.

Pine said, "See if you can shoot out a tire."

"Of a Pagani?"

"Yes, of a fucking Pagani. But just make sure you

don't hit her. We need her to tell us who the last victim is."

Laredo pulled his gun and reluctantly took aim.

Right before he could fire though, the Pagani accelerated at a blistering rate.

"Jesus," said Pine, who had her gas pedal to the floor.

The Pagani hit the asphalt and accelerated so fast it was nearly out of sight by the time Pine reached the pavement.

"We'll never catch her."

Laredo pulled out his phone. "We can set up road-blocks. And the Pagani has one weakness. It gets lousy gas mileage. She can't run the thing at that speed for very long before she sucks the tank dry."

But, as it turned out, they didn't have to worry about that.

As they rounded a bend and the Pagani came into sight they saw a deer bounding across the road right in front of the Pagani.

"Oh, shit!" exclaimed Pine.

The Pagani cut hard to the right, then back to the left. But it was too late. The rear wheels started to fishtail.

"She's lost it," exclaimed Laredo.

A moment later the entire rear of the car lifted off the road. The front wheels turned right and left, and then they rose off the asphalt as well.

The airborne Pagani missed the deer, which had

frozen in the middle of the street, and it sailed past the animal. The deer was gone in a blink onto the other side of the road and disappeared into the thick wood line.

The Pagani slammed sideways into a thick stand of oaks fronting the shoulder of the road. The punctured gas tank ignited, and the flame ball was so fierce that Pine had to slam on her brakes, shift into reverse, and floor it so as not to be engulfed by the fire and concussive force.

They sat in the truck, staring at the smoke pouring into the sky.

"It's gone. The whole damn car is gone." Laredo looked like he might be sick.

"And *she's* gone," said Pine. "And that means the last victim is dead." She beat her fists against the steering wheel.

72

After calling the police and fire department to come to the scene of the car crash, they drove back to Britta's place and met up with Max Wallis. They explained to him what had happened. When the police and forensic crew arrived a few minutes later, they hauled Myron's body out of the pool and laid it on the deck.

They gathered around him and looked down.

Pine had explained to Laredo and Wallis what she had found out about Mary and Joey Pringle and also what Britta had told her.

"He was really financing porn films?" said Wallis.

"Yes," said Pine.

"After what happened to his daughter?" said Laredo. "And his son? What a bastard."

"He was too logical," said Pine. "Too interested in making money. To the point where he lost his heart. I'm sure it was very hard for Britta to live with that."

"But it doesn't excuse what she did," said Wallis.

"Nothing could excuse that," replied Pine.

Her phone buzzed and she answered it.

Carol Blum was on the line and her normally calm demeanor was frayed.

"Cy Tanner was just here."

"What's wrong?"

"It's Jenny, his granddaughter."

"What about her?"

"She's disappeared."

Pine made it back to town in record time. Blum was waiting in front of the Cottage.

She, Laredo, and Wallis jumped out of the SUV and ran up to her.

"Where's Cy?" asked Pine.

"Out looking for Jenny."

"How did she disappear?" Laredo wanted to know.

"She was out in the backyard playing. When Mrs. Quarles went to check on her, she was gone. They looked everywhere, then called the police."

"How long ago was this?"

"About two hours," said Blum.

Laredo glanced at Pine. "She could still be alive. Rebane, Gillespie, and Gomez were taken long before their deaths."

Pine looked around at the empty streets. Then she heard gunfire.

"What the hell?" she exclaimed.

Blum said sharply, "No, it's only the reenactment. They're just starting. The parade was this morning. Everyone's over at the Civil War Village."

"Civil War reenactment," said Pine, almost to herself.

"What?" asked Laredo, noting her strange look.

"Rebane in an old veil laid out on the main street. Gillespie in an old tux with his body on top of a Civil War grave. Frankie in the drummer boy's uniform in a museum on the main street. And now the reenactment?"

"But there are too many people around to try something," countered Wallis.

"That's a fair point," said Laredo.

"But this guy likes to take risks," said Pine.

"Do you know who it is?" asked Blum.

"I think so," said Pine, who'd had a sudden idea.

She punched in a number on her phone, but no one answered, which surprised her.

She next called the hospital in Americus and was put through to Jack Lineberry's room.

When the person answered the phone, Pine could scarcely believe it.

"Jerry?"

"Hello, who is this?"

"Atlee Pine."

"What do you want?"

"I was told you were AWOL."

"Who told you that? I've been here since early this morning."

"Then why did your partner call me and ask where you were?"

"Straub? He hasn't been here all day. I'm beyond pissed off. I could use some help here."

Pine's jaw dropped. "What! Have you spoken to him?"

"He called early this morning and wanted me to go back to the estate. He said I should be on guard at the place. He wanted me to go to my cottage and monitor things from there."

"But you didn't go?"

"No, I decided not to at the last minute. I felt my place was here, with Mr. Lineberry."

Pine thought about the bomb. "You were one lucky guy. Did you let Straub know that?"

"No, I didn't, why?"

"Never mind. Just stay with Jack and make sure he's safe."

"What are you going to do?"

"Whatever I have to."

Pine clicked off and looked at Laredo. "It's not Jerry Danvers. It's the other security guard, Tyler Straub."

"What, he's the one working with Britta?" exclaimed Laredo.

"Do you think he took Jenny?" asked Blum.

"I don't know. But Britta could have found out about Jenny being at the Quarleses' any number of ways. And I think it was Straub in the Pagani watching Cy's house to make it look like Myron was doing it."

"You think they were also trying to blame all the murders on him?" asked Wallis.

"I would think so, yes. But that's beside the point. We have to find Jenny."

At that moment Lauren Graham rushed out of the Cottage.

"You have to see this!" she exclaimed.

They quickly followed her inside. She ran over to the cabinet containing her doll collection and opened one of the doors.

Pine came to a stop next to her. "What is it?"

Graham pointed to one of the figures inside. It was the largest one that was more a mannequin than a doll. It had no clothes on.

Graham said, "Someone took its clothes."

"Its clothes?" Pine stared hard at the doll. "When did it happen?"

Graham looked frantic. "I don't know. I just noticed it."

"Do you know a man named Tyler Straub?" asked Pine.

"Tyler?"

"So you *do* know him?"

"We've gone out a few times. Why are you asking about him?"

"When was the last time you saw or spoke to him?"

"A couple of days ago. Why?"

"Do you have any idea where he is now?"

"No. I can try to call him."

Pine shook her head. "No, I already did that. He didn't answer."

"But why did you try to call him?"

"Is everyone at the reenactment?" she asked Graham.

The woman looked bewildered by the query. "Of course. Where else would they be? It's the biggest event of the year here. You can't find a place to park anywhere. The parade route was packed this morning, and now everyone's watching the mock battles. You can hear the gunfire."

Everyone's watching the mock battles.

"Is the historic site still open?" she asked.

"Well, technically, yes. But I doubt anyone is there. Even most of the employees and rangers over there come to see the reenactment. Some of them are suited up and fighting in it, in fact."

Laredo looked at Pine and said, "Everyone is here."

"And no one's over there," said Pine. "Talk about your perfect storm of distraction."

They ran for the truck.

73

The parking lot at the historic site was packed, but they quickly realized that was overflow parking for all those attending the reenactment.

The grounds looked empty.

They held a brief meeting in the parking lot and decided to split up to cover more of the area.

Wallis said, "I've called in reinforcements, but they won't be here for about a half hour." He eyed Pine. "But if you're wrong about this, that little girl could end up dead."

"This is the only shot we have," retorted Pine. She glanced over his shoulder and cried out, "And I think I *am* right."

She sprinted to a spot near the parking lot where the rear bumper of a vehicle was partially exposed behind some bushes.

She got there, breathless, and looked over the Porsche SUV.

When the others reached her, she explained, "This is Jack Lineberry's Porsche. I rode in it to lunch with him. Danvers was driving and Straub was in the passenger seat."

"So he *is* here," said Wallis, trying the driver's-side door. Only it was locked.

Blum called out, "Look at this."

She was staring through the rear glass. They gathered there and she pointed out some flower petals that were on the interior carpet in the cargo area.

"I recognize them. The Quarleses have those flowers in their backyard."

"They must have been stuck on Jenny's shoes when Straub snatched her," said Laredo.

Pine broke up the grounds into three sections and assigned the two men one each. "Carol will go with me. See anything, call. Okay, let's move out."

They all headed out in separate directions.

As Pine and Blum headed into the grounds, Blum looked around. "Why would he bring her here, in broad daylight?"

"I don't know, Carol. But he *is* here. I'm sure of that. And from the petals you saw in the Porsche, so is Jenny."

The stockade replica was empty, as was the POW Museum. There was one employee on duty, but she had seen nothing and seemed put out that she was missing the reenactment.

They left there and started hurrying along the rows of graves.

"My God," exclaimed Blum. "I have one son in the

Army. And if we get into another war? I'm not sure I could bear the thought of losing him." She looked around. "But every one of these young men had a mother who had to suffer that loss, that grief."

A change came over Pine at her friend's words. Her gaze darted around. "Mother!"

"What?"

"Mother!" She started sprinting away.

"Agent Pine," Blum called after her. "Where are you going?"

Pine didn't answer. She ran as though a life depended on her. And it clearly did.

When Pine reached the statue erected by the state of Michigan in honor of its fallen soldiers and sailors, she stared up at the grieving woman the park ranger had told her was informally known as "mother." She had feared she would see Jenny's body in her doll costume lying across the marble at the woman's feet, but there was nothing like that there.

How would Straub get the body here without anyone seeing him? He couldn't exactly carry the girl in his arms. Even as Pine looked around, she glimpsed a couple of park visitors well off in the distance.

Placing a body in a public area in broad daylight was incredibly risky. She wondered how Straub was planning to manage it.

What would I do?

An answer struck her:

You would blend into the background, but also make it seem that you belonged here. So that if anyone did see you, they wouldn't think it unusual.

She saw the building in the distance. The Park Service office building. She sprinted in that direction. As she ran, Pine pulled out her phone and called Laredo, telling him where she was going and why. He said he was on the way and would phone Wallis and tell him. Wallis was already in that section.

As she drew closer to the building, she saw a man dressed in khakis and a light-colored shirt with a straw hat on come around the side of the building pushing a wheelbarrow. There was a blanket over whatever was in the wheelbarrow.

The next moment, Max Wallis hustled around another corner of the building. This put him within a few feet of the man with the wheelbarrow. Wallis was breathing hard and looked like he might keel over.

"Hey, you!" cried out Wallis to the man. "Stop right there."

Pine saw it before Wallis did.

She aimed her pistol but the man in the hat had already fired at Wallis. The round thudded into the detective's chest and he dropped where he stood.

"Straub!" screamed Pine.

Before she could fire, he stooped down behind the wheelbarrow, lifted the blanket, and pulled something out.

The something was Jenny. She was limp.

With his free hand, Straub held the gun that had just shot Wallis.

"Straub, put her down and throw your gun away," called out Pine.

His answer was to fire at her.

She ducked down but didn't return fire because he was holding Jenny in front of him. Pine didn't know if she was alive or dead, but she couldn't take the chance.

Straub ran to his left and disappeared around the corner of the outbuilding, with Jenny over his shoulder.

Pine rushed forward and knelt down next to Wallis. She felt his neck for a pulse and found none. She rolled him over and saw the wound in the center of his chest. His eyes were open and fixed. Pine reached down and closed them. "Damn. I'm . . . sorry, Max."

"Pine!"

She looked back to see Laredo running up to her. She got to her feet. "Wallis is dead. Straub shot him. He's got Jenny. Come on!"

They raced after Straub.

74

Despite running through a cemetery with wide, open spaces, Straub had managed to completely disappear somehow.

With Jenny.

Pine and Laredo raced around the corner of the outbuilding and quickly scanned the surrounding area. They saw no one.

"Do you think Jenny is still alive?"

"Yes."

"How can you be sure?"

"He took her with him. He wouldn't do that if she was dead."

"That makes sense."

"You go right, I'll go left," barked Pine.

Laredo nodded and sprinted off to the right.

Pine raced ahead for about fifty yards and stopped. How could he have just vanished?

Then the answer hit her. He had an escape plan in place. Just in case.

But what plan would that be?

She looked down at her feet, suddenly remembering something she had been told about this place.

Escape tunnels dug by Union soldiers.

She ran to the spot that the park ranger had shown her on her first visit here.

The steel grate had been forced open. She looked around for Laredo but didn't see him. She called him on her phone and told him what she was about to do. He was clear on the other side of the park. She would have to do this alone.

Pine clipped a Maglite on the rail of her Glock and climbed down into the hole.

She landed on her feet and stumbled a bit. The tunnel was a good six feet under the surface. It was about twenty degrees cooler down here. Righting herself she moved forward, her hearing acutely tuned to anything up ahead of her. She headed down the tunnel, slowly at first, but then picked up her pace when she heard the sounds of a girl cry out.

Jenny. She had regained consciousness.

Pine chugged along, her light making slashing moves in the darkness. She didn't know if Straub would be waiting to ambush her. She eventually saw the proverbial light at the end of the tunnel. Pine was cautiously approaching the exit when she heard a voice.

"Let me go!"

That was Jenny.

She rushed forward and saw a rough set of bricks

wedged into the dirt. Pine slipped up them and peered out, her gun making arcs in front of her. She took a moment to get her bearings.

She was in a small clearing in the woods. Pine heard a sound to her left.

She glimpsed a figure skirting through the trees, and she ran that way, reaching a path that wended through the woods.

"Straub!"

The figure stopped and turned.

Straub put Jenny down on the ground and squatted down, using her as a shield. The girl was dressed in the mannequin's outfit.

"Let me go," she cried out again.

He put the gun against her head, and Jenny froze.

Straub looked at Pine, who was aiming at him with her Glock.

"Stand down, Agent Pine," said Straub calmly. "I need to get away and you need the little girl. I think we can work something out. I assume you have experience in this sort of thing."

"Pretty recent, actually," she replied grimly.

"I've got another car nearby. You let me go and you have my word that I'll leave the girl safe and sound somewhere and call you with directions to her."

"You want me to take the word of a man who's killed five people?"

"You're wrong there. I didn't do the boy, Britta did."

"Bullshit."

"That little lady has a dark side, Pine, that maybe you missed. I told her how to do it, though." He tapped the back of his neck. "You hit the base of the spine here, it's lights out."

"And where did you learn to do that?"

"Spent some time in the Army. They teach you shit. I never used it against a kid, though."

Pine looked at Jenny. The girl was clearly scared, but she had shown her feistiness.

"Why would Britta want to kill Frankie?"

"She said it was her duty. And she seemed to think she was doing the kid a favor. But don't expect me to explain the woman. So do we have a deal?"

"Not a chance."

With more urgency, Straub said, "Well, that's unfortunate. The way I see it, if you don't let me go, she's dead. If you do let me go, she has a chance. Sounds fair to me."

"You're not leaving here with Jenny."

Straub's features turned ugly.

"Use your brain. I've got nothing to lose. Georgia has the death penalty. I think I already qualified for it."

"What were you going to get out of this?"

"Ten-million-dollar insurance policy on Myron. Britta was going to take care of him."

"She did. But she's also dead."

"Well, too bad, but I've got my own problems."

Sirens could be heard in the distance. "Cavalry's on the way."

"Don't really care," said Straub. "Kill or be killed, it's been sort of my whole life. So the ordinary scare tactics won't cut it."

"You tried to frame Cy Tanner and then Jerry Danvers."

"Well, you didn't arrest Tanner despite all the evidence we planted."

"It was *too* well planted. Including someone watching his house in the Pagani. I guess you were trying to implicate Myron, too."

"That was Britta's idea. I thought it was too many cooks in the kitchen myself, but she was calling the shots."

"Speaking of, the night Jack Lineberry was shot: That was you, wasn't it? But you were aiming at me. Only you weren't counting on the fact that he had let me drive."

He glanced down at his arm. "Got a little scratch from your shooting. But, yeah, you were a problem. And when you didn't take Tanner into custody, we moved on to Plan B."

"Jerry Danvers didn't follow your instructions. And he didn't get blown up, although I almost did. I suppose that was why you wanted me to go out there."

"Two birds with one stone if I was really lucky, and evidence left behind to show Jerry was the killer."

"And the household staff?"

"Gave them the day off. Told them Lineberry had authorized it."

"But as soon as I realized Jerry had never left the hospital, your story fell apart."

"Yeah, well, I had a tight time line because Britta insisted that this little girl be the last victim." Straub pressed the gun tighter against Jenny's head. "And if you won't let me go I guess I have no choice but—"

The bullet hit him directly in the side of the leg, crushing bone and slashing blood vessels. He immediately cried out, dropped his gun, and clutched at his leg.

Pine rushed forward, seized Jenny's hand, and pulled her away after picking up Straub's pistol.

She looked up to see Laredo sprinting toward them carrying a rifle.

Pine handed Jenny off to him and knelt down next to Straub.

"Shit," he screamed, his face contorted. "Help me, I'm bleeding out."

She slipped her belt off and used that as a tourniquet around his upper thigh. The blood flow slowed considerably. She phoned 911 and gave them her location.

Pine put her phone away and looked down at Straub, whose features were still seized up in pain. "It didn't hit your femoral artery."

"How do you know that?" he snarled.

"Because you'd already be dead."

"Just . . . just shoot me. Do it. I'm a dead man anyway. Save everybody the trouble."

"As much as I'd love to, I can't."

"Why the hell not?" he screamed.

"It's not how we do things at the FBI."

The ambulance arrived a few minutes later, and they loaded Straub in. A grim-faced police officer rode in the back with him.

As the vehicle pulled away, Pine looked over at Laredo, who was holding Jenny's hand. The rifle was slung over his shoulder.

"Where'd you get that?"

"Found a park ranger. They use it to scare off or kill dangerous critters. He let me borrow it because I asked nice and flashed my badge."

"That was a big risk taking that shot," she said.

"First in my class at Quantico for marksmanship. And you don't know this, but I did a two-year stint as a sniper with Hostage Rescue. And you're not the only risk taker in the Bureau," he added.

"How'd you get here so fast?"

"Remember, track team in college?"

Pine smiled. "Right. Well, thanks." She squatted down in front of Jenny. "You okay?"

Jenny nodded.

"You're safe now. You ready to go see your granddad? We better go and tell him you're okay. Sound good?"

Jenny nodded and sniffled.

Pine started to pick her up, but Jenny clamped her

hand tighter around Laredo's and looked up at him with wide eyes.

Pine rose and whispered to Laredo, "Maybe you're better with kids than you think."

They slowly walked out of the cemetery and back to the living.

75

"They met at a tech show the Pringles were attending in Vegas," said Pine to Laredo, Blum, and Graham.

They were sitting in the parlor at the Cottage. Jenny had been reunited with her grandfather and the Quarleses. Pine had just returned from interviewing Straub in the hospital.

"Straub and Britta had a fling out there," continued Pine. "That makes sense because there was certainly no love between Britta and her husband. When a position opened up with Jack Lineberry, Britta gave him a heads-up and a recommendation. So he got the gig. Straub's ex-military. Pulled a tour in Afghanistan, then got discharged for drug use. He rehabbed himself, got into private security, and moved up from there."

"You said he killed all those people for money?" said Blum disgustedly.

"Ten million bucks. He had used chloroform on Jenny. He was going to leave her at the base of the statue. Luckily, because we delayed the plan, the chloroform wore off."

“Did he pick the places to leave the body or did Britta?”

“He says he did except for the last one. That way he could plan his ingress and egress.”

“How did he get inside the Drummer Boy museum?” asked Blum.

“He had dated Lily,” replied Pine. “And surreptitiously got an impression of the museum key and the security code from her.”

“And the bizarre clothes?” asked Graham.

“He dressed them up like that to throw us off, make us think it was some serial killer with a Civil War fetish. And the veil and the tux alluded to a husband and wife, the family that Britta was symbolically killing. He told me he picked the grave site of one of the Raiders because he thought it would be funny for a black guy to be left there. I really didn’t get his sense of humor.”

Pine added, “Britta knew the Quarleses and found out about Jenny from them. Straub said when Britta learned Jenny’s mother was a drug user, she thought it was best that Jenny die. She said a bad mother like that didn’t deserve a child. That Jenny would be in a better place. Straub really had to hustle to snatch her, because they always intended to kill the last victim during one of the reenactments and leave the body in the cemetery.”

Graham said, “How come Straub told you all this?”

"He did a deal with the authorities. Talk and they won't pursue the death penalty."

"Why would Britta do these terrible things?" asked Graham.

"Straub said Britta wanted to avenge her kids. She blamed Gillespie for Mary's acting in porn films and getting hooked on drugs. And she blamed Hanna Rebane for being Mary's lover in a bunch of films."

"And Clemmons?" Blum asked. "Why did she have to die?"

"Straub was the new 'man' in Hanna Rebane's life that Clemmons alluded to. That's how he got close to her and then killed her. He was careful never to let anyone, especially Clemmons, see them together. But he eventually got worried that Rebane might have described him to Clemmons or told her some information that could help us track him down. So when we started poking around he decided she had to die." She glanced at Laredo. "And I'm not sure Britta crashing the Pagani was an accident. Straub told me that she had planned on committing suicide when this was all over."

"One seriously disturbed lady," replied Laredo.

"Your real shooting skills saved the day, Eddie. But for that, Jenny would be dead."

"Hey, that's what partners are for."

★

Later, Pine was sitting in her bedroom when Blum knocked on her door.

Blum said, "We have one mystery left to solve."

Pine rose and looked out the window. "No, not one mystery. Several. Including where is Ito Vincenzo. And where is my mother. And, most important, what happened to Mercy. And I'm not sure I'll ever solve them."

"But you do think it possible that Mercy is still alive, don't you?"

Pine came to sit on the bed again. "That's the way I *want* to see it. But Ito told my father that he was responsible for one daughter being dead and the other one badly injured. So . . ."

"Well, if she is alive, there certainly are tools available today that might be of some use."

"Such as?" asked Pine.

"Genealogy sites. You put in your DNA and they do what they do."

Pine waved this off. "I've tried that. It's not that simple in my case because the process they typically use wouldn't necessarily help me find a match with Mercy."

"But it would if the Bureau lends a hand."

"And you think the Bureau would?"

"You just saved another little girl from certain death and solved the murders of multiple people. I would think the Bureau would give you anything you wanted at this point."

"Why do I think you've already checked into this?"

"Will you trust me on this?"

Pine let out a long, troubled breath. "I suppose I'll have to."

76

Two days after Pine had provided the DNA sample and it was compared by the FBI against millions of others on a number of online sites, a match of sorts came back.

Only it had nothing to do with Mercy Pine.

And it would provide the second biggest shock of Pine's life, after losing her sister.

When Pine was told about it, she sat in her room at the Cottage staring at the wall. It was like a theft of her identity that had nothing to do with the cyberworld and everything to do with simple flesh and blood.

Finally, she rose and left her room.

In the foyer she spotted Blum, who had obviously been waiting for Pine to come down.

Blum said, "Would you like me to go with you? I'd be glad to."

Pine shook her head. "I think it needs to be just me."

"Then I'll be right here when you get back."

Outside, she ran into Eddie Laredo, who was packing up his rental.

"Well, I guess I'll see you around, Atlee."

Her mind was a thousand miles from here, but she put a hand on his shoulder. "You saved my butt more than once down here."

"Like I said, that's what partners are for."

"So, things are good between us?"

"They are from my side. I've already called Denise and we're in discussions to give me more time with my sons."

"That would be great. They need their father. Their *real* father."

He looked at her closely. "What about you? Back to Shattered Rock and being the only FBI agent at the Grand Canyon?"

"After I finish up something here."

"Maybe I'll come out to visit you."

"I would like that."

"Just as friends, though," he added with another grin.

"Nothing wrong with that, Eddie."

She gave him a hug and a kiss on the cheek and watched him drive off.

Then Pine climbed into her SUV and headed out, too.

Thankfully, the trip to Americus was mercifully short, because she wasn't sure how much longer she could manage to hold it all together. She felt in some ways that she was walking the last mile to her own execution.

Jerry Danvers was sitting outside of Jack Lineberry's private hospital room. He had been transferred from the ICU two days ago and was expected to be released in another few days.

Danvers looked at her with new respect and said contritely, "I guess you saved my bacon and then some."

"Right," she said absently.

"And who would have believed that about Straub?"

"I need to see Jack. Now."

He looked at her funny. Pine knew she was acting oddly, but she didn't care.

"Okay, you can go on in. He's just finished his lunch. I'm sure he'll be glad to see you."

"I'm not sure about that at all," said Pine.

She went in and closed the door behind her.

Lineberry was sitting up in his bed and looking much stronger.

She approached slowly and sank down into the chair next to the bed, never once taking her gaze off him.

He looked back at her with great trepidation, and sadness. And also with perhaps a bit of relief thrown in. He said, "I can tell by the look on your face that you finally know."

"You're my father," said Pine.

"I am, yes." Tears started to slide down his face as he said this.

Pine had something she wanted to say, and now

was the time to say it. "But you have another daughter out there somewhere. And my mother, the mother of your children, too. Maybe together we can find them."

Lineberry tentatively reached out his hand. "Do you really believe we can?"

Pine's strong fingers closed around his as she said quite firmly, "I don't think we have a choice."

Acknowledgments

To Michelle, Atlee Pine rides again. Thanks for being with me every step of the way.

To Michael Pietsch, for being a great publisher.

To Ben Sevier, Andy Dodds, Elizabeth Kulhanek, Jonathan Valuckas, Brian McLendon, Karen Kosztolnyik, Beth deGuzman, Albert Tang, Bob Castillo, Kristen Lemire, Anthony Goff, Michele McGonigle, Cheryl Smith, Andrew Duncan, Joseph Benincase, Tiffany Sanchez, Morgan Swift, Matthew Ballast, Alison Lazarus, Rachel Hairston, Karen Torres, Christopher Murphy, Ali Cutrone, Tracy Dowd, Martha Bucci, Rena Kornbluh, Jeff Shay, Carla Stockalper, Thomas Louie, Sean Ford, Laura Eisenhard, Mary Urban, Barbara Slavin, Kirsiah McNamara, and everyone at Grand Central Publishing, for doing so much for me.

To Aaron and Arleen Priest, Lucy Childs, Lisa Erbach Vance, Frances Jalet-Miller, John Richmond, and Juliana Nador, for keeping me on the straight and narrow.

To Mitch Hoffman, for doing what you do best!

To Anthony Forbes Watson, Jeremy Trevathan, Trisha Jackson, Alex Saunders, Laura Sherlock, Sara Lloyd, Claire Evans, Sarah Arratoon, Stuart Dwyer, Jonathan Atkins, Anna Bond, Leanne Williams, Natalie Young, Stacey Hamilton, Laura Ricchetti, Charlotte Williams, and Neil Lang at Pan Macmillan, for being a brilliant publisher and such a positive force in my life.

To Praveen Naidoo and the team at Pan Macmillan in Australia, for keeping the Baldacci train going Down Under!

To Caspian Dennis and Sandy Violette, for being amazing, and also for loving wine as much as I do!

To Mark Steven Long, for copyediting.

To auction winners Beth Clemmons (Gloucester-Mathews Humane Society) and Max Wallis (Light of Christ Anglican Church), for supporting such terrific organizations.

And to Kristen White and Michelle Butler, for doing everything else, and it's a lot!

Go back to where it
all began for Atlee Pine

Long Road to Mercy

DAVID
BALDACCI

Read on for an extract from the first book in the series . . .

1

Eeny, meeny, miny, moe.

FBI Special Agent Atlee Pine stared up at the grim facade of the prison complex that housed some of the most dangerous human predators on earth.

She had come to see one of them tonight.

ADX Florence, about a hundred miles south of Denver, was the only supermax prison in the federal system. The supermax component was one of four separate encampments that made up the Federal Correctional Complex located here. In total, more than nine hundred inmates were incarcerated on this parcel of dirt.

From the sky, with the prison lights on, Florence might resemble a set of diamonds on black felt. The men here, guards and inmates, were as hardened as precious stone. It was not a place for the faint-hearted, or the easily intimidated, though the deeply demented were obviously welcome.

The supermax currently held, among others, the Unabomber, the Boston Marathon bomber, 9/11 terrorists, serial killers, an Oklahoma City bombing conspirator, spies, white supremacist leaders, and assorted cartel and mafia bosses. Many of the inmates here would die in federal prison under the official weight of multiple life sentences.

The prison was in the middle of nowhere. No one had ever escaped, but if anyone did, there would be no place to hide. The topography around the prison was flat and open. Not a blade of grass, or a single tree or bush, grew around the complex. The prison was encircled by twelve-foot-high perimeter walls topped with razor wire and interlaced with pressure pads. These spaces were patrolled 24/7 by armed guards and attack dogs. Any prisoner reaching this spot would almost certainly be killed by either fangs or bullets. And few would care about a serial murderer, terrorist, or spy face-planting in the Colorado soil for the final time.

Inside, the cell windows were four inches wide and four feet long, cut in thick concrete, through which only the sky and roof of the facility could be seen. Florence had been designed so that no prisoner could even tell where in the structure he was located. The cells were seven-by-twelve and virtually everything in them, other than each inmate, was made from poured concrete. The showers automatically cut off, the toilets could not be stopped up, the walls were insulated so no inmate could communicate with another, the double steel doors slid open and closed on powered hydraulics, and meals came through a slot in the metal. Outside communication was forbidden except in the visiting room. For unruly prisoners, or in the case of a crisis, there was the Z-Unit, also known as the Black Hole. Its cells were kept completely dark, and restraints were built into each concrete bed.

Solitary confinement was the rule rather than the exception here. The supermax was not designed for prisoners to make new friends.

Atlee Pine's truck had been scoped and searched, and her name and ID checked against the visitors list. After that she was escorted to the front entrance and showed the guards stationed there her FBI special agent credentials. She was thirty-five, and the last twelve years of her life had been spent with a shiny badge riding on her hip. The gold shield was topped by an open-winged eagle, and below that was Justitia, holding her scales and sword. It was fitting, Pine thought, that a female was depicted on the badge of the preeminent law enforcement agency in the world.

She had relinquished her Glock 23 pistol to the guards. Pine had left in her truck the Beretta Nano that normally rode in an ankle holster. This was the only time she could remember voluntarily handing over her weapon. But America's only federal supermax had its own set of rules by which she had to abide if she wanted to get inside, and she very much did.

She was tall; over five eleven in her bare feet. Her height had come from her mother, who was an even six feet. Despite her stature, Pine was hardly lithe or willowy. She would never grace a runway or magazine cover as a stick-thin model. She was solid and muscular, which had come from pumping iron religiously. Her thighs, calves, and glutes were rocks, her shoulders and delts sculpted, her arms ropy with long cords of muscle, and her core was iron. She also had competed in MMA and kickboxing and had learned pretty much every way that a smaller person could take on and subdue a larger one.

All of these skills had been learned and enhanced with one aim in mind: survival, while toiling in what was largely a man's world. And physical strength, and the toughness and confidence that came with it, was a necessity. Her features were angular and came together in a particularly attractive, almost bewitching, manner. She had dark hair that fell to shoulder length and murky blue eyes that gave the impression of great depth.

She had never been to Florence before, and as she was escorted down the hall by two burly guards who hadn't uttered a word to her, the first thing that struck Pine was the almost eerie calm and quiet. As a federal agent, she had visited many prisons before. They were normally a cacophony of noise, screams, catcalls, curses, trash talk, insults and threats, with fingers curled around bars, and menacing looks coming out of the cells' darkness. If you weren't an animal before you went to a max prison, you would be one by the time you got out. Or else, you'd be dead.

It was *Lord of the Flies*.

With steel doors and flush toilets.

Yet here, it was as if she was in a library. Pine was impressed. It was no small feat for a facility housing men who, collectively, had slaughtered thousands of their fellow humans using bombs, guns, knives, poisons, or simply their fists. Or, in the case of the spies, with their treasonous acts.

Catch a tiger by its toe.

Pine had driven over from St. George, Utah, where she used to live and work. In doing so she'd motored across the entire state of Utah and half of Colorado. Her navigation device had told her it would take a little more than eleven hours to traverse the 650 miles. She had done it in under ten, having the benefit of a lead foot, a big-ass engine in her SUV, and a radar detector to get through the inevitable speed traps.

She'd stopped once to use a restroom and to grab something to eat for the road. Other than that, it had been pedal to the floor mat.

She could have flown into Denver and driven down from there, but she had some time off and she wanted to think about what she would do when she got to her destination. And a long drive through vast and empty stretches of America allowed her to do just that.

Having grown up in the East, she'd spent the majority of her professional life in the open plains of the American Southwest. She hoped to spend the rest of it there because she loved the outdoor lifestyle and the wide-open spaces.

After a few years at the Bureau, Pine had had her pick of assignments. This had been the case for only one reason: She was willing to go where no other agent wanted to. Most agents were desperate to be assigned to one of the FBI's fifty-six field offices. Some liked it hot, so they aimed for Miami, Houston, or Phoenix. Some aimed for higher office in the FBI bureaucracy, so they fought to get to New York or DC. Los Angeles was popular for myriad reasons, Boston the same. Yet Pine had no interest in any of those places. She liked the relative isolation of the RA, or resident agency, in the middle of nothing. And so long as she got results and was willing to pull the duty, people left her alone.

And in the wide-open spaces, she was often the only federal law enforcement for hundreds of miles. She liked that, too. Some would call her aloof, a control freak, or antisocial, but she wasn't. She actually got along well with people. Indeed, you couldn't be an effective FBI agent without having strong people skills. But she did like her privacy.

Pine had taken a position at the RA in St. George, Utah. It was a two-person outfit and Pine had been there for two years. When the opportunity arose, she had transferred to a one-agent office in a tiny town called Shattered Rock. It was a recently established RA due west of Tuba City, and about as close to

Grand Canyon National Park as it was possible to be without actually being in the park. There, she enjoyed the support of one secretary, Carol Blum. She was around sixty and had been at the Bureau for decades. Blum claimed former FBI director J. Edgar Hoover as her hero, though he'd died long before she joined up.

Pine didn't know whether to believe the woman or not.

Visiting hours were long since over at Florence, but the Bureau of Prisons had accommodated a request from a fellow fed. It was actually twelve a.m. on the dot, a fitting time, Pine felt, because didn't monsters come out only at the stroke of midnight?

She was escorted into the visiting room and sat on a metal stool on one side of a sheet of thick polycarbonate glass. In lieu of a phone, a round metal conduit built into the glass provided the only means to verbally communicate. On the other side of the glass, the inmate would sit on a similar metal stool bolted into the floor. The seat was uncomfortable; it was meant to be.

If he hollers let him go.

She sat awaiting him, her hands clasped and resting on the flat, laminated surface in front of her. She had pinned her FBI shield to her lapel, because she wanted him to see it. She kept her gaze on the door through which he would be led. He knew she was coming. He had approved her visit, one of the few rights he possessed in here.

Pine tensed slightly when she heard multiple footsteps approaching. The door was buzzed open, and the first person she saw was a beefy guard with no neck and wide shoulders that nearly spanned the door opening. Behind him came another guard, and then a third; both were equally large and imposing.

She briefly wondered if there was a minimum heft requirement for a guard here. There probably should be. Along with a tetanus shot.

She dropped this thought as quickly as she had acquired it, because behind them appeared a shackled Daniel James Tor, all six feet four inches of him. He was followed in by a trio of other guards. They effectively filled the small enclosure. The rule of thumb here, Pine had learned, was that no prisoner was moved from one place to another with fewer than three guards.

Apparently, Tor warranted double that number. She could understand why.

Tor had not a hair on his head. His eyes stared blankly forward as the guards seated him on his stool and locked his chains into a steel ring set into the floor. This was also not typical of the visiting policy here, Pine knew.

But it was obviously typical for fifty-seven-year-old Tor. He had on a white jumpsuit with black rubber-soled shoes with no laces. Black-framed glasses covered his eyes. They were one piece and made of soft rubber with no metal pins at juncture points. The lenses were flimsy plastic. It would be difficult to turn them into a weapon.

In prisons, one had to sweat the small details, because inmates had all day and night to think of ways to harm themselves and others.

She knew Tor's entire body under the jumpsuit was virtually covered in largely self-inked tats. The ones that he hadn't done himself had been inked on by some of his victims, forced into becoming tattoo artists before Tor had dispatched them into the hereafter. It was said that each tat told a story about a victim.

Tor weighed about 280 pounds, and Pine calculated that only about 10 percent of that would qualify as fat. The veins rippled in his forearms and neck. There wasn't much to do in here except work out and sleep, she assumed. And he had been an athlete in high school, a sports star, really, born with a genetically gifted physique. It was unfortunate that the superb body had been paired with a deranged, though brilliant, mind.

The guards, satisfied that Tor was securely restrained, left the way they had come. But Pine could hear them right outside the door. She was sure Tor could as well.

She imagined him somehow breaking through the glass. Could she hold her own against him? It was an intriguing hypothetical. And part of her wanted him to try.

His gaze finally fell upon her and held.

Atlee Pine had stared through the width of glass or in between cell bars at many monsters, a number of whom she had brought to justice.

Yet Daniel James Tor was different. He was perhaps the most sadistic and prolific serial murderer of his, or perhaps any, generation.

He rested his shackled hands on the laminated surface, and tilted his thick neck to the right until a kink popped. Then he resettled his gaze on her after flicking a glance at the badge.

His lips curled momentarily at the symbol for law and order.

"Well?" he asked, his voice low and monotone. "You called this meeting."

The moment, an eternity in the making, had finally come.

Atlee Pine leaned forward, her lips an inch from the thick glass.

"Where's my sister?"

Eeny, meeny, miny, moe.

1

Hal Parker was resolutely closing in on his prey, and he felt his blood pressure amp up with every firm step he placed into the dirt. He could tell he was nearing his target by the frequency and volume of blood that had fallen onto the darkened ground, like dulled rubies scattered in the rich soil. He had obviously wounded rather than killed his quarry.

A carcass delivered was part of the deal if he was to earn his fee. He was heartened by the blood loss. It evidenced the inevitable, especially in an unforgiving climate like this.

He moved slowly and methodically forward. Fall was nearly here, but summer was still hanging on, dragging its heat-flamed and moisture-rich knuckles across the stark tundra. Right now, he felt like an egg in a heated skillet. If it were winter, he would be encased in special clothing, and he would never, under any circumstances, start to run after his prey. If you ran when it was fifty degrees below zero, your lungs would hemorrhage and you'd drown in your own engorged corpuscles.

Yet when it was this hot and humid, dehydration could kill you just as quickly, and you'd never feel it coming until it was too late.

Parker wore a bright tactical headlamp that literally turned night into day, at least on his narrow path. He figured he might be the only living person within many square miles. Clouds scudded across the sky, all bloated with moisture and surrounded by unsettled air. He was hoping the rain would hold off just long enough for him to finish the job.

He looked to his left, where Canada sat not too far away. Over an hour south was the town of Williston, which was the very center of the fracking universe here in North Dakota. But the Bakken shale region was so enormous that the land under Parker's feet collectively held hundreds of millions of barrels of oil along with hundreds of billions of cubic feet of natural gas. Maybe more, he thought, because who the hell could really know the extent of it?

Parker squatted as he assessed his next move.

He gazed ahead, rotating a hundred and eighty degrees on the compass, calculating time and distance based on the size of the blood splotches. He rose and moved forward, picking up his pace slightly. He wore a hydration pack with a large camel bladder and a feed line next to his mouth. His clothing was lightweight, yet sturdy, constructed from self-wicking material. But he was still hot and sweaty at eleven o'clock at night. And each intake of air felt like he was popping habaneros. Mother Nature always had the upper hand over man, he knew, no matter how much fancy equipment man put on.

He wasn't certain how his quarry, a wolf that had already killed two cows from his employer's herd, had even gotten away. He'd had a decent sight line on it from about four hundred yards away. The thing had just been sitting there, still as a deer sensing trouble. His rifle round had entered the upper torso, he was sure of that. It had barely moved with the violent impact, so he was sure it had been a kill shot. But when he'd gotten to that spot, it was gone and the blood trail he was now following had commenced.

He cleared a slight rise in the ground. The area he was in was known as the Great Plains, which was somewhat a misnomer, since the land could be quite hilly. But then the bumpy fringes of the northern Badlands crept up here, like the trickles of river water forming finger coves. But drab buttes and flat grasslands coexisted just fine for the most part. A night fog was sweeping in, eroding his visuals. He frowned, and though he was a veteran at this, he felt his adrenaline spike.

He heard the far-off rumble and then the whistle of a train probably carrying a column of tanker cars loaded with oil and with natural gas, which after being pulled out of the earth was then liquified for transport. The whistle sounded sad and hopeful to him at the same time.

Then another rumble came. This time it was from up in the sky. A storm was racing in, as storms often did around here. He had to pick up the pace.

He gripped his Winchester rifle tightly, ready to raise the night scope to his eye in an instant and to deliver, he hoped, the true kill shot this time. The next moment Parker saw something. Fifty feet and to his left. A shadow, a shade darker than its surroundings. He looked down at the ground, shining his light there. Now he was surprised and then puzzled. The bloody marks distinctly went off to the *right*. How could that be? His quarry hadn't suddenly developed the ability to fly. Yet maybe it had sharply changed direction up ahead, wobbling on weakened legs before collapsing.

He trudged forward, wary of a trap. He drew within fifteen feet of the spot and stopped. He squatted down again, and under the brilliant beam of his tac light, he took a long look around at the vast space in front of him. He even gave a behind-the-back look just in case his quarry had managed to outflank him and was sneaking up from the rear. Parker had fought in the first Gulf War. He had seen the crazy shit that sometimes took place when living things were trying to kill each other. He wondered if this was one of those times.

Still squatting, he crab-walked forward to within ten feet of the spot. Then five.

He felt his gut tighten. He must be seeing things.

He sucked on his water line to increase his hydration. But the thing was still there. It was no mirage. It was . . .

He gingerly rose and carefully treaded the final few feet to the spot and looked down, his powerful light illuminating every detail of the nightmare he had just discovered.

It was a woman. At least he thought it was. Yes, as he leaned closer, he saw the plump breasts. She was naked, but she had also been butchered. Yet there wasn't a drop of blood to mar the pristine ground around her.

The skin covering her face had been cut from the back and then pulled down, coming to rest on the exposed bone of her chin. Her skull had been sawed open and the top part removed and laid to the side of her head. The revealed cavity was empty.

Where the hell was her brain?

And her chest. It had been apparently cut open and then sewn back together.

He glanced at the compact dirt around the body. His brow screwed up when he saw the distinct marks on the ground there. They seemed familiar to him. Next moment he forgot about these marks and slowly sank to his knees as it occurred to him where he had seen such suture patterns on a human chest before.

It was called a Y incision. He had seen it in numerous TV cop shows and movies. It was the proverbial cut-up body on the slab in the morgue, only he wasn't in a morgue. He was in the middle of expansive, unblemished North Dakota without a coroner or TV show in sight.

A postmortem had been performed on this unfortunate woman.

Hal Parker turned to the side and threw up mostly bile.

The soil was no longer pristine as the skies opened up and the rain began to pour down.

2

"North Dakota," murmured Amos Decker.

He was sitting next to Alex Jamison on a small Embraer regional jet. They had taken a jumbo 787 to Denver, where they'd had an hour layover before boarding the far smaller aircraft. It was like going from a stretch limo to a clown car.

Decker, who was six-foot-five and weighed nearly three hundred pounds, had groaned when he'd watched the small jet maneuvering to their gate, and groaned even more when he'd glimpsed the tiny seats inside. He'd had to wedge into his allotted space so tightly that he doubted he would need his lap belt to keep him safe in case of turbulence.

"Ever been there?" asked Jamison. She was in her early thirties, tall, superbly fit, with long brown hair, and pretty enough to be repeatedly stared at by men. A former journalist, she was now an FBI special agent. She and Decker were assigned to a task force at the Bureau.

"No, but we played North Dakota State in football

once while I was at Ohio State. They came to Columbus for the game."

Decker had played college ball for the Buckeyes and then had an abbreviated professional career with the Cleveland Browns before a devastating injury on the field had left him with two conditions: hyperthymesia, or perfect recall, and synesthesia, meaning his sensory pathways had comingled. Now he could forget nothing and saw things such as numbers in certain colors and, far more dramatically, dead bodies in an unsettling shade of electric blue.

"Who won?" asked Jamison.

Decker gave her a heavy-lidded glance. "You trying to be funny?"

"No."

He shifted about a millimeter in his seat. "It used to be called D-I and D-II when I played. Now it's FBS and FCS." When Jamison looked puzzled he added, "Football Bowl Subdivision and Football Championship Subdivision. Ohio State, Alabama, Clemson, Michigan, USC, they're all FBS schools, the top tier, the big boys. Schools like North Dakota State, James Madison, Grambling, Florida A&M, they're FCS schools, or the second tier. Now, North Dakota State has gotten really good as of late. But usually, when they play each other it's a rout for the FBS schools."

"So why schedule them?"

"It's an easy win for the top tier and a big payday for the other squad."

"But it's not a particularly good game to watch?"

"It's always a good game when you win. And if the score is a runaway, the starters get to sit the bench after the third quarter or maybe even the first half. When I was a freshman that's how I got to play. When I was a starter, I appreciated the extra rest a blow-out got me."

"Doesn't make sense to me. One team slaughtering another for money."

"It really only made sense to the school boosters and the NCAA bean counters."

Jamison shook her head and gazed out the window as they descended beneath the dark, thick clouds. "Looks stormy down there."

"It's basically hot with humidity through the roof for the next couple of days, with a bad thunderstorm, falling temps, and wicked wind pretty much guaranteed every evening. But then it won't be long before the blizzard season sets in and this place looks like Antarctica."

"Great," said Jamison sarcastically.

"But look on the bright side."

"What's that?"

"You won't have to do your daily workout for the next couple days. You'll lose two pounds of water just walking to the car. But after that you'll have to fatten up for the winter."

The plane shed more altitude. Working against heavy headwinds and unruly patches of air, the jet felt like it was a pebble skipping across rough water. Jamison gripped her armrests and tried to breathe deeply as her stomach lurched up and down. When the plane's tires finally hit the asphalt and bounced to a landing on the runway, she slowly released her grip and pressed a hand against her belly. A jagged spear of lightning appeared off in the distance.

"Okay, that was fun," she said breathlessly before eyeing Decker, who looked, if anything, sleepy. "That didn't bother you?" she asked.

"What?"

"The turbulence!"

"It wasn't a big deal," he said offhandedly.

"What's your secret then? Because it looked like everyone else on the plane was praying, flight attendants included."

"I survived a crash landing when I was in college. Engine went out on takeoff. Pilot circled back around, dumped some fuel, then the other engine died and he had to go in for an immediate landing. Found out later it was a twin bird strike. We hit hard enough to take out the landing gear and crack the fuselage. Everybody got off before the jet fuel ignited and fire ate the plane. I did lose my duffel of clothes," he added casually.

"My God," said a pale Jamison. "Then I'm surprised you're not more nervous than I am."

"I looked up the odds. They're about a billion to one for my having a second incident in my future. I feel like I'm golden now."

They deplaned, signed the documents for their rental SUV, and headed out from Williston Basin International Airport.

"Wow," said Jamison when they got outside and the wind slammed into them. Even the giant Decker was buffeted. "I don't think I packed the right clothes," she noted miserably. "I should have brought more layers."

"What more do you need than pants and a shirt and a badge and gun?"

"It's different for women, Decker."

Jamison drove while Decker punched the directions into his phone navigation. Then he settled back and watched the road zip by. It was six o'clock in the evening and they were headed right into a gathering storm. Nasty black cumulus clouds reared up ahead of them like a towering serpent about to do some serious business over this patch of the upper Midwest.

"Irene Cramer," said Decker softly as they drove along.

Jamison nodded and her features turned grim. "Found dead in the middle of nowhere by a guy tracking a wolf."

"Most notably she was apparently autopsied," added Decker.

"That's a first, at least for me. How about you?"

"I've seen cut-up bodies, but not like the photos I saw. The crime scene was pretty clean except for the guy's vomit."

"Serial murderer? Is that why we got the call? Bogart didn't really say."

Ross Bogart was the head of their small task force. He was the one who had ordered the pair to North Dakota after the briefest of briefings.

"Maybe."

"Did Ross sound strange when he talked to you?" asked Jamison. "He did to me."

Decker nodded. "He couldn't tell us something that he wanted to tell us."

"How do you know that?"

"He's a straight shooter who has to answer to political types."

"I don't like mysteries at both ends of a case," groused Jamison.

"I don't think this is necessarily a serial murderer."

"Why not?"

"I could find nothing to match it in the databases. I checked before we flew out."

"Could be a new player."

"New players aren't usually this sophisticated."

"He might be trying to make a name for himself," pointed out Jamison.

"They're all trying to make a name for themselves," replied Decker.

"But they don't call the Bureau in for a local murder."

"I think we need to look at the *victim* and not the killer for that reason."

"You believe Irene Cramer was important to the Feds for some reason?"

"And it may also explain Bogart's reticence."

"Regardless, we're clearly looking at a killer with forensic skills."

"That could apply to quite a few people, including people on our side of the field."

"An ME gone bad, maybe?" suggested Jamison.

Decker looked uncertain. "You can probably find a YouTube video of someone cutting up a mannequin. But the report said the cuts were professionally done."

"You think this guy has had . . . what, practice?"

"I don't think anything, at least right now."

"Did you notice the highway here is all concrete?" said Jamison, glancing out the window.

"Asphalt apparently doesn't hold up well in the extreme elements they have up here," noted Decker. "Although I'm not sure how durable the concrete is, either."

"Well, aren't you a wealth of information."

"I can Google stuff just like anybody else."

"How much longer do we have to go?" asked Jamison.

Decker glanced at his phone screen. "Says forty-five minutes, nearly to the Canadian border."

"So I guess that was the closest airport back there."

"I think that was the *only* airport back there."

"This has already been a long, exhausting day."

"And it promises to be a longer night."

"You're going to start the investigation tonight?" she said, a little incredulously.

Decker gave her a stern look. "Never hurts to hit the ground running, Alex. Particularly when someone is dead who shouldn't be."

3

"What are those?" asked Jamison as they neared their destination.

She indicated fiery gold plumes that winked in the darkness like ghoulish holiday lights as they zipped past.

"Gas flares," said Decker. "Coming off the oil wells. Natural gas is found with oil. They drill for both up here. But they sometimes vent the gas off and ignite it at the end of the oil well head. I guess it costs too much to do anything else with it in certain situations and they don't necessarily have the infrastructure to pipe it out of here."

Jamison looked stunned. "Do you know how much gas we're talking about?"

"One stat I read said each month the gas they burn off could heat four million homes."

"Four million homes, are you serious?"

"It's what I read."

"But isn't that bad for the environment? I mean, they're burning pure methane, right?"

"I don't know about that. But it probably is bad."

"All those flames are eerie. I'm conjuring images of zombies marching with torches."

"Better get used to them. They're everywhere, apparently."

And as they drove along, they did indeed appear to be everywhere. The landscape was like an enormous sheet cake with hundreds of candles.

They passed by large neighborhoods of trailer homes, along with paved streets, road signs, and playgrounds. Vehicles, most of them jacked-up, mud-stained pickup trucks or stout SUVs, were parked under metal carports in front of the trailers.

They also drove past large parcels of land on which sat the flame-tipped oil and gas wells along with metal containers and equipment with imposing security fences around them. Hard-hatted men in flame-resistant orange vests drove or rushed around performing tasks. From a distance, they looked like giant ants on a crucial mission.

"This is a fracking town," said Decker. "Only reason there still is a town. Thousands of workers have migrated to this part of North Dakota to suck up the shale oil and gas found in the area. 'Bakken' shale rock, to be more specific. I read there's about a hundred years of the fossil fuel in the ground here."

"Okay, but haven't they heard of climate change?"

"Hey, it's a job."

"Yeah, a job today, no planet to live on tomorrow."

"Preaching to the choir. But when you're trying to

put food on the table today? And people can make six-figure salaries here working the energy fields? They've had booms and busts before, but they seem to have things in better shape now."

"Google again?"

He shrugged. "I'm a curious guy. Plus both my brothers-in-law work in the oil and gas fields. I guess I picked some stuff up because of that."

They passed a fifteen-gas-pump truck stop that had a restaurant attached and also showers, a Laundromat, and a store that multiple signs said sold hot pizzas, propane, diesel exhaust fluid, truck driving logs, fans, and antifreeze, among many other listed items. On one sign were enormous photos of alluring waitresses in short shorts and low-cut tops. Another sign proclaimed the facility had the best adult entertainment DVDs in the entire state of North Dakota. The parking lot was packed with semis of every size, color, and style, with emphasis on chrome fittings, spike wheel caps, and spray-painted murals on the cabs. They ranged from dragons and firearms to American flags and busty, nude women.

"Well, I guess we know what's popular up here," said Jamison.

"It's not just up here where that stuff is popular," replied Decker drily.

They next passed RV parks that were packed and a shopping mall that looked freshly risen from the dirt. The mall had a BBQ restaurant with a sign promising the best southern pulled pork around; then there was a Subway, a China Express, a twenty-four-hour gym, a bar and grill, and even a sushi bar. There was an electronic marquee mounted on one wall that set forth the current prices for oil and natural gas. Next to the mall was a large brick church. On the front of its outdoor sign someone had arranged black letters to read, GOD CREATED THE HEAVENS AND THE EARTH AND THE OIL AND THE GAS. SHARE THE WEALTH. DONATE TO GOD. WE DO VENMO. BIBLE STUDY CLASS EVERY NIGHT AT 7.

Jamison glanced in the rearview mirror. "There's a column of semis and dump trucks right on my butt, and they have been for the last half hour." She glanced at oncoming traffic. "And an army of them heading the other way. And the whole place smells of diesel fuel."

"They're bringing in equipment and supplies, including the chemicals they inject into the ground. Apparently it goes on 24/7."

"And the trucks heading the other way?"

"Taking the oil and gas out, I guess." He pointed ahead. "We have to get off this road soon. They built a loop around the town so the trucks wouldn't have to drive through downtown with their loads."

Jamison took the next exit, and they shortly saw a cluster of lights in the distance. "I take it that's the town we're headed to."

"Yep. London, North Dakota."

"I wonder how it got that name," said Jamison.

"Maybe some guy from England came here and planted a flag. Right in the middle of a sea of oil and gas. Population's around fifteen thousand, and over half of them work in the oil fields and the other half service them. And that's about triple what it was just three years ago. And it'll triple again in half that time if things keep going as they are."

"Boy, you really did read up on this," commented Jamison.

"I like to know what I'm getting into."

She looked at him curiously. "And what do you think that is, apart from a murder investigation?"

"This is the Wild West, Alex. It's like the California Gold Rush of 1849, only on steroids."

"So what exactly are you saying?"

"That the ordinary rules of civilization don't necessarily apply up here."

They drove down the main street that was bustling with people despite the coming storm, and reached a dead end when the first drops of chilly rain began to fall.

"Directions, please."

"Next left," said Decker.

They pulled to a stop in front of what turned out to be a funeral home.

Now Decker shot Jamison a curious glance.

"North Dakota is a coroner state, not a medical examiner state. The local guy here also runs this funeral home, crematorium, and mortuary. Full service."

"You read up on it?" he asked.

She smiled impishly. "I'm a curious *gal*."

"Is he at least trained in forensics?"

Jamison shrugged. "We can only hope."

"Boy, this case is starting off with a bang."

They barely beat the sheets of driving rain as they sprinted for the front door to see a dead person.

4

They introduced themselves to Walt Southern, the coroner and owner of the funeral home. He was medium height and in his midforties with thinning sandy-colored hair and a runner's lean physique. He wore tortoise-shell glasses, his dark slacks were cuffed and pleated, and his sparkling white shirt seemed to glow under the recessed ceiling lights.

He looked at them in surprise. "But why is the FBI interested in this case?"

"Wait, didn't you know we were coming?" asked Jamison.

"No, nobody told me."

"Well we're here and we've been assigned to investigate this murder. We've read your post report. Now we need to see the body."

"Now hold on. I can't let you folks do that without checking with the detective on the case."

Decker said, "Then call him. Now."

"He might not be in."

"You won't know till you try."

Southern moved off to a corner of the room, took

out his cell phone, and made a call. He spoke with someone and then rejoined Decker and Jamison, not looking thrilled.

"Okay, I guess you Feds always get your way."

"You'd be surprised," said Decker.

"Well, let's get to it. I've still got a body to prepare for a viewing tomorrow, and the family was real particular on her clothing and makeup."

"Do you bury people here during the winter?" asked Decker.

"We prefer not to. Have to dig through the snow, and then the ground is iron hard. Hassle even with a backhoe. And who wants to stand outside saying good-bye to a dearly departed when it's sixty below? Funny how quickly tears dry and people beat a retreat when their fingers, toes, and ears are getting frostbite. But most people these days opt for the quick-fried route anyway over a plot of dirt."

"'Quick-fried'?" asked Jamison.

"Cremation." He chuckled. "I mean, doesn't that mean they're opting for Hell in a way?"

"Can we see the body?" said Decker with a frown.

Southern led them down a short hall, and they passed through into a small utilitarian room smelling strongly of antiseptic, formaldehyde, and decomposing flesh.

In the middle of the room was a metal gurney. The bulge under the sheet was what they had come for.

Hopefully, the body would tell them a story about who had killed its owner.

Jamison glanced at Decker, who was already seeing the room in electric blue. It was a testament to how many dead bodies he saw that this no longer bothered him. Well, almost.

"This is the first time I've done a postmortem on a victim who'd already been autopsied," noted Southern.

"You've been trained to do this, I assume?" asked Decker bluntly.

"I'm properly credentialed," replied Southern, who seemed to take no offense at the question. "Just because it's not my main business doesn't mean I don't take pride in it."

"That's good to know," said Decker curtly.

Southern lifted the sheet off the corpse, and they all three stared down at what was left of Irene Cramer.

"Cause, manner, and time of death?" asked Jamison.

"The cause and manner are pretty straightforward." He pointed to a wound in the middle of the chest, appearing a few inches above the bottom intersection of the Y incision. "Long, sharp, serrated knife penetrated here and bisected the heart. The manner was homicide, of course."

"Killer was pretty accurate with the knife strike," noted Jamison as she leaned in for a closer look. "Clean and efficient. Only one stab did the deal."

"My thinking, too."

"So, unemotional. No savagery or lack of control," opined Decker. "Killer might not have known the victim. Or at least had no personal relationship with her."

"Maybe not," said Southern.

"And the time of death?" asked Decker.

"Okay, there we get into the speculation zone," conceded Southern. "Based on what I found out, she's been dead maybe about a week to ten days."

Decker did not look pleased by this. "That's a pretty big range. You can't narrow it down more than that?"

"Afraid not," said Southern, looking unhappy. "If this comes down to whether an alibi gets someone off or not, well, my report's not going to be a bit of help on that. I'm sorry."

"Insect infestation?" asked Jamison.

"A lot. That allowed me to gauge the week or so. After that, it gets dicey. At least for me. Again, I know what I'm doing, but this isn't exactly the FBI lab here."

"Had she been lying out there long, then?" asked Jamison.

"That's both hard and simple."

"Come again?" said Jamison.

"If she'd been out there too long, the animals would have gotten to her. They hadn't."

"That's the simple part, so what's the hard?" asked

Decker. "The insect infestation doesn't reconcile with that?"

"Bingo. Lots of bugs, but no animal bite marks. And another thing, the lividity was fixed. Shows that after death she was in a prone position."

"The report I read says she was found *supine*," noted Decker.

"Right, but you can see that the lividity discoloration does not jibe with that. Blood won't collect around parts of the body that are in contact with the ground. But once lividity is fixed, meaning when the hearts stops beating and the large red blood cells sink via gravity into the interstitial tissues, they don't move again. The discoloration stays where it was."

"So she was obviously killed and laid on her face. But then the body was at some point turned on its back because that's how she was found," said Jamison.

"Right. *After* lividity was fixed."

"Bleed-out would have been minimal, since the heart would have stopped shortly after the knife strike," said Decker. "But there would have been some, and none was found at the crime scene. That means she was killed elsewhere and placed there, which would also explain the lividity discrepancy."

Southern nodded. "But with such major insect infestation you would expect animal intrusion as well. I mean, if she'd been lying outside all this time, the critters we have around here would have gnawed her to bone in far less than a week, which is the bare minimum I put her TOD at." He paused and added matter-of-factly, "Other than that she was in excellent condition. Very healthy. Heart, lungs, other organs, shipshape."

"Yeah, the woman's in great shape, except she's dead," said Decker grimly.

"How much skill are we talking about with the killer doing his own postmortem?" asked Jamison.

"The incisions were first-rate. I'd say the person had some medical training. And he, if it was a he, knew the forensic protocols. What was the source of that knowledge and training, I couldn't venture to say."

Decker pointed to the Y incision. "How about the tools he used? Regular knife or medical grade?"

"I'd say he had some hospital scalpels *and* a Stryker saw or something like it to cut open the skull. And the thread he used to suture the Y incision is surgical grade."

Decker looked the body over and had the coroner help him turn the woman.

"No tats or distinguishing marks," noted Decker.

"No liver spots or sun damage. She was too young for age spots, but her skin was not tanned, either. She wasn't out in the sun much."

They turned her back over and Decker ran his gaze over her once more.

How many bodies had he stared at in precisely these circumstances? The answer was easy. *Too damn many.* But if he didn't want to look at bodies, he'd have to change careers.

"Anything of interest in her system?" asked Jamison.

"Almost nothing in her stomach, so she hadn't eaten recently. No obvious signs of drug use. No needle marks, that sort of thing. Tox reports haven't come back yet."

"Anything else out of the ordinary?" asked Decker.

"I think her having a postmortem done on her before she got to me is enough out of the ordinary for any case." Southern tacked on a grin.

"So your answer is no?" persisted Decker.

The smile fell away. "Right, my answer is no."

"Is she from around here? Who made the ID?"

Southern placed his arms over his chest. "Once I put her face back on somebody from the police department recognized her."

The door opened at that moment and a man around Jamison's age walked in. He wore jeans, scuffed tasseled loafers, a checkered shirt, and a navy blue sport coat. He was about six feet tall, lean and wiry with a knot of an Adam's apple and a classic lantern jaw. His hair was dark brown and thick, and a cowlick stuck up in the back like a periscope.

He looked first at Decker and then at Jamison. "Lieutenant Joe Kelly with the London Police Department," he said by way of introduction.

"He's the one I called," said Southern.

Kelly nodded. "I'm with the Detective Division. Sounds impressive until you understand I'm the only one."

"The only one working *homicide*, you mean?" said Decker.

"Homicide, burglary, armed robbery, domestic abuse, human trafficking, drugs, and I forget the others."

"Quite the one-man show," remarked a wide-eyed Jamison.

"It's not by choice. It's by budget dollars. We doubled the size of the force after the last oil bust went boom again, but it hasn't caught up to detective level yet. Just uniformed bodies on the streets and in the police cruisers. They'll get around to promoting a uniform to detective about the time the next bust comes along and we all get fired." He stared up at Decker. "They grow all of them as big as you at the FBI?"

"Yeah, sure. But the other guys wear shiny armor. I like my denim."

Kelly took a moment to show them his credentials, and they reciprocated. Then Kelly glanced at Southern. "Sorry I didn't come straight over, Walt. Little bit of trouble at the OK Corral. Was driving by when it happened and heard the ruckus from outside."

"Another fight?"

"Another something. Stupid name for a bar anyway. Too much testosterone, money, and liquor. I'm not a fan of that combo."

"Walt said someone at the department recognized the victim once she was put back together," said Decker.

"That someone would be me," replied Kelly.

Decker hiked an eyebrow. "How's that?"

"I left out one of the other things I'm responsible for here in London. Prostitution."

"So Cramer was a hooker?" said Decker.

Surprisingly, Kelly shrugged. "I don't know for sure."

"Why not?" asked Jamison. "Seems to be pretty easy to tell whether someone is or isn't."

"You'd think. Now, the term 'streetwalker' is pretty outdated these days, but up here, we still have them. The guys drive by in certain sections of town and the ladies hook up with them right then and there. With that said, a lot of the arrangements are made online so as to avoid doing any direct soliciting in public."

"So was Cramer arranging things online?" asked Decker.

"I'm on the computer all the time looking for sites that offer this stuff. I know where to look, at least for the sorts of things that go on here. I found one site advertising 'consulting services' for men in the oil and gas field here in London. Even though the site took pains to make it look somewhat legit, because these folks know cops are looking, there was one picture on that site that looked really familiar to me. I mean, don't get me wrong, she looked really different, makeup, hair, clothing, but I recognized Cramer. I'd seen her around town," he added hastily. "So at the very least, it seemed that she was in the 'escort' business in some way. She called herself Mindy on the site, for what that's worth."

"So it wasn't a shock when you found out she was dead?" said Jamison. "I mean, prostitution is a high-risk occupation."

"Well, it *was* surprising, actually, because murders are rare, at least around here, even for prostitutes. And it *was* a shock *how* she was found."

"I can see that," replied Decker evenly, watching Kelly closely.

"But what I don't really get is why you folks were even called in for this. After Walt called me I went to talk to my chief. It was only then that I found out the autopsy and police reports had been sent to DC after a request came in from the Feds. I mean, it's a weird-ass murder, sure, but there are lots of weird-ass murders, and the locals handle them by and large."

Decker said, "Why do *you* think we were called in? You must have a theory."

"Why should I have a theory?"

"You strike me as the type."

In answer Kelly pointed to the table, and the body on it. "She's got some connection to something that has you Feds interested. I just don't know what that is, but I'd sure like to."

"Wouldn't we all," muttered Decker.

OUT NOW

One Good Deed

Murder and family secrets, a touch of romance and deeply felt revenge – with the twist of all twists – make up the ingredients of this gripping page-turner for all those who love mystery, crime, Raymond Chandler and Agatha Christie from one of the world's favourite thriller writers, David Baldacci.